T0365035

The Making *of a* Master

Ted Scott

BALBOA.PRESS
A DIVISION OF HAY HOUSE

Balboa Press books may be ordered through booksellers or by contacting:

Balboa Press
A Division of Hay House
1663 Liberty Drive
Bloomington, IN 47403
www.balboapress.com.au
AU TFN: 1 800 844 925 (Toll Free inside Australia)
AU Local: 0283 107 086 (+61 2 8310 7086 from outside Australia)

Print information available on the last page.

ISBN: 978-1-5043-2258-4 (sc)
ISBN: 978-1-5043-2274-4 (e)

Balboa Press rev. date: 09/29/2020

THE LITTLE BOY ran exuberantly across the field. His mother, laughing, struggled to keep up. It was so exhilarating for both of them. Finally, exhausted, he stopped. He flopped down on the soft grass and pressed his face to the earth.

"Whatever are you doing?" she asked.

He turned his head toward her and smiled. "I am thanking the gods for being so kind to me."

His mother smiled at the act of gratitude, and the joy in his face was soon mirrored in hers. "You are a good boy, Qiang," she said.

Like any mother, she dreamed of what her son might become. This is that story.

IT WAS LATE afternoon. A little smoke seeped from the squat chimney on the roof of the slab hut. It signaled that cooking was underway in the sparse abode of the peasant family who lived there.

The man of the family, Chao, was still laboring in the field. His sustenance and that of his small family was drawn from a little rice paddy adjacent to the hut. His wife, Nuan, was preparing a simple meal for the evening. She merely had to look out from the aperture in the wall of her meager kitchen to see her husband tending to his crop. The opening was sealed by a wooden shutter that she raised when the weather was fair. And today, the weather was mild, the sun was shining, and it was a relief to open her kitchen to elements that were so benign.

Her son played happily on the floor at her feet. He was such a joy to her. What a fortunate mother she was to have been blessed with a child of such equanimity. And now, she was with child again. Soon, her son, Qiang, would have a sibling. She fervently hoped that the next child would be as placid and as loving as Qiang.

IN DUE COURSE, the baby arrived. Nuan was attended by the local midwife. The birth was not particularly difficult, and Nuan was elated that the baby was a girl.

Unfortunately, Chao was not so impressed. "When I am old and can't work the fields, what use is a girl?" he asked his wife. In disappointment, he stomped out of the house, slamming the door behind him, and went to the local inn to carouse with his friends.

When Qiang was allowed to see his mother, he raced in and embraced her. Nuan was overjoyed to see him and was gratified by his loving response. Then, Qiang asked if he might see the new baby. Nuan carefully unwrapped the infant from her swaddling clothes so her face was exposed.

Qiang was ecstatic. "Oh, Mama, how beautiful she is!" he exclaimed. He kissed her wide, bright face and implored, "Might I hold her?"

Nuan said, "You must be gentle. Here—come up alongside me in my bed, and I will help you hold her."

The young boy sprang upon the bed and, with his mother's assistance, held the precious little bundle. Oh, how his face beamed, and oh, how his heart surged with love for this little creature, so beautiful and so vulnerable.

"What is she called?" the little boy asked.

"She will be called Lan because she is our gorgeous little orchid."

QIANG HAD GROWN a little older now. It was time for him to attend the village school. His father, Chao, was not greatly in favor of this. His ambition for Qiang was to take over the family farm, and as far as he was concerned, the sooner Qiang got to know the essential tasks of farming, the better.

But Nuan argued that Qiang was still too young and, in many ways, too small to be of great assistance in the fields. Chao reluctantly agreed. And so it was that Qiang set off every morning to attend school in the village.

On the first day, Nuan went with Qiang to show him the way. But the school wasn't far, and the track was direct. Therefore, Qiang was soon allowed to make his own way to school.

Qiang rather enjoyed school. He was an ardent learner and an earnest student.

On his way to school, he had to walk through the farming community, passing by huts and fields that were much like those of his own family. But close to the school, his path took him by a large tree. On his first unaccompanied trip, he stood by the tree, overwhelmed by its size and beauty. He did not know what sort of tree it was. It was like no other tree he had seen before. The trees in the fields near the family home were much less imposing than this mighty giant.

In the days that followed, it became Qiang's practice to stand before the tree for a little while and bask in the aura of its splendor and its grandeur before moving on. He wondered at its age and how many birds might have nested in its vast canopy. A few days after he first was allowed to go unaccompanied to school, he noticed a man sitting at the base of the tree. Qiang looked at him closely. He was an elderly man, dressed in saffron robes. He sat upright, close to the tree's bulky trunk, with his legs crossed and his eyes closed. Qiang wondered, momentarily, who he might be and what he was doing, but he shrugged his shoulders and hurried off to school.

Every day, he stopped by the tree. Its magnificence was somehow inspiring, but he could not avoid noticing the man at the base of the tree. He seemed always to be there. The man was invariably dressed in his saffron robes and sitting cross-legged on the ground. Sometimes, like the first day Qiang had noticed him, the man had his eyes closed, but at other times, he looked straight ahead, without blinking. His face was calm, and although his back was erect, he seemed very relaxed.

Then one day, Qiang advanced toward the man sitting at the base of the tree. Respectfully, he said, "Sir, I have noticed for some time that you sit here, day in and day out, at the base of this tree. Tell me—what is your purpose?"

The man smiled but did not move. "Well, young sir, I have been waiting for you."

"But I don't know you," said the boy.

"And I don't know you," responded the man, "but I knew one day you would come."

The boy was intrigued by this response. "How could that be so, sir? If you don't know me, you couldn't have possibly known you would meet me."

"You probably won't understand, little man, but I know that when my mind is in order, right things happen to me. I have been sitting here meditating these many days, preparing my mind. Now that it is in order, you have appeared, and so I know it must have been you for whom I was waiting."

"What is this 'meditating' you talk about?"

"It is a way of quieting our minds. Our minds are multilayered. On the surface, there is a flurry of activity—thoughts, sensations, and various mental constructs. This is all that most people experience of their minds. But underneath, there is a great ocean that is peaceful and beyond the reach of the storms of the world. If we can tap into the resources of that great ocean, the distractions of the world will become trifles, and our sense of well-being will grow beyond anything that is in the least susceptible to worldly intrusions. It enables the pure light of our being to shine into our lives."

"Sir, I am not sure that I understand what you are saying, but it sounds something remarkable." Qiang paused a moment and looked intently at the man before continuing. "But in your eyes, I can see a great serenity." When he looked into his father's eyes, he only seemed to see fear and pain. After a short pause he enquired, "If that is the outcome of this endeavor, might I also learn meditating?"

"Indeed, indeed! It is the very reason I have come. Here—sit beside me. You are young and supple, so you should have no problem assuming the lotus position."

Then the man began instructing Qiang in the special breathing techniques and the various processes of stilling the mind. After fifteen minutes or so he said, "That is enough for today. Come again tomorrow, and we will do a little more."

Qiang thus assumed a daily routine, learning meditation from the adept. As he progressed, his lessons got longer. Finally, after six months or so, he would sit and meditate with his teacher for almost an hour.

One afternoon, his teacher said, "You are now quite adept at meditation. Therefore, it is time to teach you the mantra of the adepts."

"What is a mantra?"

"It is a device to aid your concentration. This is a very special mantra, taught to specially selected meditation pupils. It originates from the masters who originally brought the practice to our country from the West. It is recited in an ancient language, which is now unfamiliar to all but a select few. Let me teach it to you."

His teacher recited the mantra. It was short, a mere eight words, and although the words were unknown to Qiang, it sounded beautiful—melodious, in fact.

"That sounds lovely!" the boy exclaimed. "But what does it mean?"

"Well, to begin with, each word, in turn, is for a breath—first an in-breath and then an out-breath. So it covers a cycle of four completed inhalations and exhalations, and then it is continually repeated. Once you have learned the words, you can either physically speak them slowly, or you can merely say them in your mind. We could translate the meaning thus:

Bring love,
And peace,
And hope,
And joy.

It is a special privilege to learn this mantra, and it should not be divulged to another, unless you are sure they will be devoted to the practice and display loving kindness. This special mantra is called the An Cheng mantra, which means 'tranquil journey.' Now, let us practice it."

"Oh, indeed I will, sir. It is so lovely. But how can you be sure I will be devoted to loving kindness and faithfully maintain my practice?"

His teacher merely laughed. "Well, little master, I knew that before you were even born! But no more talking; let us learn the lesson."

Qiang shook his head at this enigmatic response but, knowing he would get no further, concentrated on learning his lesson.

NUAN NOTICED THAT her son often was tardy in returning home from school. Chao complained that the boy was not doing his fair share of work in the fields. He threatened that he would withdraw the boy from school so that he might be of more assistance to his father. Nuan knew that Qiang liked school. He was doing well with most of the school subjects, but he was showing a particular skill at calligraphy and often proudly brought home samples of his work to show his mother. She decided she needed to find out the cause of his delay in coming home, as she was concerned that the boy might have to face his father's wrath.

Nuan gathered up Lan in her arms and trudged off toward the village school. Before long, she found herself at the tree, where Qiang and the man sat together, meditating. She was surprised and somewhat concerned by the sight.

"Qiang, whatever are you doing?" she called.

The man stood up and said quietly to the boy, "Takygulpa, your mother is here."

The boy opened his eyes, stood up, and smiled at his mother.

Again, Nuan asked in a concerned voice, "What are you doing, son?"

"This gentleman is teaching me to meditate."

She shook her head. "Sir, what nonsense is this? And why did you call my son Takygulpa?"

The man replied, "Madam, meditation is not nonsense; it prepares the mind. True well-being comes only from a well-prepared mind. Your son is a good learner. And why did I call him Takygulpa? Well, in my tradition, that name means 'still, deep waters.' This is the nature of his mind. There are not many like him. One day, he will be known as Takygulpa Rinpoche, acknowledging his skills as a master and a sage."

Nuan glared at him. "Don't fill his mind with such nonsense. He will be full of himself."

"On the contrary, madam - I haven't been filling his mind at all. I have been emptying it. And have no fear about him being full of himself. This remarkable boy has no problem with his ego whatsoever, and I doubt if he ever will. But come now, Takygulpa; go to your mother. This phase of your training is complete."

The boy turned to him. "But sir, I have found your instruction so beneficial, and I wish to know more."

"You have already accomplished much. Develop the skills we have worked on. When your mind is ready for further instruction another teacher will come."

Qiang looked somewhat disappointed by this response. Finally, he looked up at his teacher and said, "I will try to do as you have bade me. But could you tell me who you are? In these months of instruction, for which I am eternally grateful, you never told me your name."

"My name is not so important as your instruction, little master. But if you must know, I am called Chogken Rinpoche."

AFTER THIS, QIANG went promptly home from school in the afternoons and helped his father. He was happy enough, working in the field. There was a certain gratification about being useful and productive, and although not a big lad, Qiang was wiry and imbued with great stamina.

Much to his father's consternation, however, Qiang continued to meditate. When he had any spare time, he would find somewhere quiet and perform his practice. The boy often used the An Cheng mantra that he had been taught, but rather than repeating it audibly, he went over it in his mind, synchronizing his breathing with the melodious words. He would awake earlier than the others in the household and spend a little time meditating before the others arose. His father grumbled about Qiang wasting his time when he could be doing something "more useful." His mother, however, defended him, arguing that the boy did all that was required of him in the way of chores and helping his father in the fields. Surely, she argued, he was entitled to a little time of his own. Chao decided not to press the issue.

The weather was growing colder now. Qiang and Chao harvested the rice and winnowed it. They sold a little to buy other essentials. Then they stored as much as they could, in anticipation of the winter, along with a few root vegetables they'd grown in a little garden near the hut.

Now that the crop had been harvested, there was little work required, except to tend to the few farm animals they had and repair the farm implements. In the afternoons, Chao would take Qiang into the forest, where they would trap a hare or game bird or catch a fish from the stream. Sometimes, they would gather field mushrooms or wild berries.

Chao was a rather taciturn man, and so he spoke little to his son, but he often emphasized it was a man's duty to provide for his household. Qiang enjoyed these foraging expeditions and learned a lot from his father, who had a good knowledge of the natural environment. Consequently, they were able to regularly supplement their meager supplies with their catch and harvest from the nearby forest and streams. As winter neared, they also gathered firewood, sufficient to cook and warm the little hut through the cold, dark months of winter.

But then the snows came. They seldom ventured outside at all, except to feed the few animals in the shed at the rear of the hut. Nuan patched and sewed to maintain their well-worn clothes. Chao sharpened and repaired the tools he used in the fields.

Over the intervening few years since Lan's birth, Chao's feelings toward his little daughter had softened, and he took pleasure in fashioning a few handmade toys for her. Qiang admired his father's handiwork, and his father took the time to teach him how to make such toys.

The small hut essentially comprised three rooms. There was a main living area, where there was a table and chairs and a fireplace. Adjoining this were two small rooms. The parents slept in one room and the two children in the other.

It was now extremely cold, colder than Nuan and Chao had ever experienced since they had come to the hut, shortly after their marriage. During the day, they huddled as close as they could to the small fireplace. They warmed themselves with a little tea and boiled rice. At night, once the fire had subsided, they went immediately to bed and sought what warmth they could by donning warm clothes and placing their threadbare blankets over their bodies.

One such night, Qiang awoke to the sound of his little sister whimpering and shivering from the cold. He so loved his little Lan that he could not bear to see her suffer. He immediately took the blanket from his own bed and covered her with it. He sat alongside her for a while, with his arm across her delicate little body. She seemed warmer now and very soon was back to sleep.

At first, he did not know what to do. It was hardly worth going back to bed without a blanket to cover himself. Finally, he sat down on a little mat and began meditating. How long he was there, he could not tell—once his mind was still, there was little sense of the passing of time.

Sometime later, because it had become so cold, Nuan got up to check on her children. She lit a small oil lamp she had left beside her bed. Holding the lamp in front of her, she shuffled into the adjoining bedroom and was astounded to see Qiang sitting cross-legged on the floor. The light of the lamp brought him back to awareness of the sensate world. He opened his eyes and looked up, with a loving smile, at his mother.

"Qiang," she said quietly, not wanting to wake Lan, "whatever are you doing?"

"Just meditating, Mother."

"But where is your blanket? You must be so cold!"

"I heard Lan whimpering from the cold, Mother, so I put my blanket over her. Her discomfort hurts me more than the cold could."

"But you must be so cold!"

"Well, actually, Mother, I am not. When I meditated, I went to a beautiful place where it is still summer, and after a time, the warmth of my mind seemed to seep into my body, and I am now quite comfortable. Is Lan still asleep?"

Nuan's eyes filled with tears at the unselfishness of her son and his concern for his sister. She stumbled forward and hugged him. But then she stood back. "Why, son, you are quite warm. How can that be, on such a cold night, with you in such meager attire and no blanket?"

"I cannot tell you exactly how it happens, Mother, but my mind has made me warm."

"Takygulpa," she whispered to herself.

"What was that, Mother?"

"Nothing, son. Here—climb back into bed. I have an old robe here somewhere I can throw over you. You are a good brother."

Qiang smiled. "No, Mother. How lucky I am to have such a beautiful little sister and a mother who is so concerned for me that she would get out of bed to check on my welfare on such a terribly cold night!"

To their great relief, there were few cold nights left in the winter. The sun now appeared with a little more warmth in it. The days got longer, and soon, Chao and Qiang were out in the fields, preparing the soil for the next crop.

For some reason, probably her own inability to explain it, Nuan never told Chao of the night she had found Qiang uncovered in the winter's cold but seemingly warm and comfortable.

Qiang continued his schooling. He was a good student and performed well across the curriculum, but his special talent was in calligraphy.

THE NEXT YEAR was a good one for the family. The elements were kind, and, as a result, the harvest was bountiful.

Qiang continued his studies at school but still found time to contribute to the work in the fields. His greatest delight was to come in from the fields and play with his little sister, Lan. She always ran to him when he came home. He, in turn, always had something for her, however small. One day, it would be the mottled feather from a grouse; the next, it would be a couple of sweet berries he had found, or perhaps it would be a snail shell or a shining chrysalis aspiring to be a butterfly.

Nuan would watch and marvel at the little boy's love for his infant sister. How content she was that summer. The larder was always full, the children seemed happy, and even poor Chao, who always felt so pressed to provide for his family, felt comfortable that he had managed well in this season of plenitude.

On long summer evenings, the children would go out to play, and Nuan and Chao would sit on a bench by the lychee tree. They would eat a few fruits together and occasionally have a sip of the sweet, golden wine that Chao made from fermenting the fruit, which he called *huáng jiǔ*. The couple's contentment as they rested, enjoying a little quiet time together and watching the children play happily, was complete.

BUT UNFORTUNATELY, THAT wasn't to last.

For three years in a row, the rains didn't come.

The rice crop was much smaller than before. The little garden beyond the house provided little additional sustenance.

The family struggled. Nuan was philosophical about their situation and was positive about the future, but Chao was greatly distressed. He felt so responsible for the welfare of his little family that he quickly came to the conclusion that he was, somehow, personally deficient.

Qiang was now ten years old. He obviously was very intelligent, and he was very curious. In his desire to learn, he continually asked questions, and despite his age, many of those around him found this challenging. His teachers found his directness and intelligence quite testing even though he was always polite and deferential. His queries continually exasperated his father. But Nuan, the ever-loving mother, tried her best to meet the demands of his growing intellect. But underneath it all, she knew that she did not have the capacity, the experience, or the education to meet the intellectual needs of her son.

At school, Qiang's precocious talents were becoming evident. While he far excelled his peer group in almost every way, his most outstanding talent was his calligraphy. His teacher readily admitted that he had nothing left to teach the child and that, in most respects, the boy's work now outshone his mentor's.

It was early autumn. The harvest had again been disappointing. There would not be surplus rice to trade for other things. Most worrying for Chao was that he had to pay tax to the emperor, and though the tax was not huge, he could see no way of finding the wherewithal to pay his dues. The emperor's tax collectors called by each year in the late autumn and Chao was beside himself with worry. In their society, the ownership of all land was ultimately vested in the emperor. Failure to pay the prescribed taxes could mean eviction.

Then one day, a man appeared at their doorstep. He knocked on the front door and waited patiently for a response. He was a tall man of advanced years. He was dressed in a saffron robe, and his demeanor was serene and dignified.

Chao answered the door and was a little taken aback by the appearance of this stranger. He fervently hoped he was not a tax collector. Rather abruptly, he asked, "What do you want?"

Visitors to their household were rare and normally were only their near neighbors, coming to give them a couple of eggs or wanting to borrow a hoe.

Intrigued, Nuan had followed her husband to the door.

"Sir," said the stranger, "I am in need of a calligrapher. I have heard there is someone in this household called Takygulpa who is an accomplished calligrapher."

"I am sorry, my friend," responded Chao, now relieved that the visitor was not a tax collector, "but there is no one here of that name."

As Chao began to close the door, Nuan called urgently, "Wait.Wait! Who did you say you were looking for?"

"I was given to believe that a young man lived here who is a skilled calligrapher. My informant said that he has been called Takygulpa."

Nuan nodded. "That is our son. He is named Qiang, but there was a teacher once who referred to him as Takygulpa."

Chao raised his eyebrows at this assertion and, somewhat bewildered, allowed his wife to continue.

"What do you want of him?" Nuan asked.

"I would have him work for me. A wealthy official from the court of the emperor is seeking to have a calligrapher copy a number of important books from the emperor's library for his own use. He is happy to pay well for someone competent to do the work."

"But how did you hear of my son," asked Chao, "and why do you call him by that strange name?"

"I heard of your son from the teacher your wife mentioned. That teacher is a Buddhist master and a colleague of mine. He was called

Takygulpa by that master because, in our tradition, that name means 'still deep waters,' which is a reflection of the quality of his mind. To be given that title is a measure of high esteem."

Chao shook his head in disbelief, but he soon recollected the man's proposal and asked, "You said that my son would be paid well for his work. What do you mean by that?"

"He will be paid by the page for all the work he transcribes."

Chao asked his visitor to detail such payments. He was bewildered by the amount he offered. "But that is far more than I could earn laboring on my farm and selling my rice."

"This is very important work, and your son must be properly recompensed."

Nuan broke in. "But we don't have parchment, ink, and brushes for Qiang to do this work."

"No matter," said the man. "If you agree to our terms, we will provide all the materials necessary."

Chao looked inquiringly at his wife. This seemed beyond the simple farmer's comprehension.

"It is indeed a generous offer," she mused, "and would certainly ensure that we could pay our taxes. Husband, let us ask the boy."

Chao merely shrugged his shoulders.

"Qiang! Qiang!" called Nuan.

The boy had been just outside playing with his little sister. On hearing his mother's call, he came running. He stopped abruptly on entering the room when he saw the stranger standing there.

"Yes, Mother?" he quietly inquired.

"Son, this man has come to ask if you would use your skills at calligraphy to copy some of the books from the emperor's library. He is prepared to pay us well for your work."

The boy was well aware of the family's perilous situation, as his parents talked about it often. He thought a moment and then said, "Mother, I would be happy to be able to make a contribution to our household, but might I ask the gentleman some questions?"

Chao scowled. "Don't be impertinent, boy. It is not your place to question this man."

The visitor merely smiled. "Oh, but you are wrong, sir. Let your son ask his questions. I find no offense in the questions of the little master."

The farmer was decidedly uncomfortable about all this. Qiang turned to him and quietly asked, "May I, Father?"

Chao reluctantly nodded.

In deference, the boy said, "Thank you, Father." He then turned to the visitor. "Sir, what are these books that you require me to transcribe?"

"Well, young man, they are books of wisdom from the Buddhist tradition."

"How am I to copy them if I can't understand them? My calligraphy has to be more than a literal translation. I can only transcribe well that which I understand and can appreciate. The characters that my brush paints onto the parchment only have integrity when they can be rendered into script with empathy."

Chao and Nuan were surprised by the boy's question. He sounded so serious and like an adult, in a way they had never before witnessed.

"I have been assigned the task of explaining these works to you. It is important that you come to understand these books of wisdom. That is as important—or perhaps, more important—than how well your calligraphy renders the transcription. I will be your teacher to help you master these scriptures so you can faithfully render their transcription."

Qiang gazed into the man's eyes and saw the same tranquility and equanimity of the teacher who had taught him to meditate. He smiled. "Thank you, sir. I am ready for this new learning and pray my humble skills with the brush may satisfy my benefactor."

Nuan clapped her hands. "It is settled then. Qiang will work at your task under the conditions you have offered."

The man turned to Chao, who merely nodded his agreement.

"Excellent! I will bring the requisite materials to you in the next day or so, and we will make a start."

He made as though to depart, but Nuan put her hand on his shoulder, gently restraining him. "Wait, sir! Can you tell me how you are called?"

"In my community, I am called Chagsarka Rinpoche."

"Thank you. And thank you also for giving us this opportunity."

The man smiled. "Madam, I had no choice in the matter. This is my destiny. But it is a pleasant task, and I am sure I will enjoy working with the little master."

Nuan remembered the parting words to Qiang from his first teacher: "When your mind is ready for further instruction, another teacher will come." She was sure she had just met the boy's next teacher.

TWO DAYS LATER, Chagsarka Rinpoche returned, accompanied by a strong young man pulling a laden handcart. Its contents included a large amount of Xuan paper inside a wooden chest, bottles of ink, and boxes of assorted-sized brushes. Upside down on the lid of the chest was a small table. Nestled inside its wooden legs was a chair.

On hearing the clatter of the handcart's wheels on the rough path to the house, Qiang ran to the front door. Seeing the two approaching the house, he called to his mother and father. They soon joined him. By this time, the young man had drawn the handcart right up to their front door.

Chagsarka Rinpoche stepped forward and bowed. "Greetings," he said. "Here are your supplies. Where can we deposit them? You must keep them somewhere safe because they are quite valuable. The paper needs to be kept somewhere dry. To help preserve it, I have packed it inside the chest." So saying, he opened the lid of the chest, drew out a piece, and put it in Qiang's hands. "Here pupil, is what you will be working with."

The boy's eyes opened wide in amazement. He caressed the substance gently with careful hands. He turned to his mother and offered it to her. "Oh, Mother, feel how soft it is! I have never had material like this to work with. I must be particularly careful that I make no mistakes and ruin it."

His teacher chuckled. "Our benefactor will only accept the finest, and that is what he has provided for you to work with."

They unloaded the handcart and brought its contents into the small cottage. After a debate about where everything should be stored, it was agreed that they would set up the little table in the main living area, not too far from the fireplace, where it was likely to be drier and warmer, so that the paper might not deteriorate. Accordingly, the chest full of the Xuan paper was stored neatly under the little table. The boxes of ink and brushes were deposited to the left of the table, within easy reach.

Chagsarka Rinpoche beckoned to the boy to sit at the table. Qiang duly did so. The chair and the table provided matched the boy's physique.

"That should be good for your calligraphy, young master."

The boy nodded, overwhelmed by the resources with which he had been provided.

"In two days, I will come to you with the first manuscript, and then we can begin our work."

Thus saying, his new teacher and the strong young man who had pulled the handcart bade their farewells and left.

Chao and Nuan stood for a while, admiring the materials that had been provided for their son. Qiang fingered the paper, admired the brushes, and examined the ink.

"Mother, Father, these things with which I have been provided are magnificent. They are far better than what I used at school."

Chao didn't know what to say. Nuan merely patted her boy on the head and said, "You have been provided with superb resources. It is important that you work hard so as not to disappoint your benefactor."

"I will do my best, Mother."

TRUE TO HIS word, the teacher arrived early in the morning, two days later, with a large manuscript. After being let into the house, he deposited the work on the table he had provided for the boy.

Qiang was overwhelmed. He had never seen a document so large.

"What is this huge tome?" he asked. "Surely you don't expect me to copy all of this?"

The master laughed. "This is a sacred Buddhist text called the Tripitaka. And no, you don't have to transcribe the entire manuscript. Your benefactor has given me a list of his favorite passages, which he would have you copy."

"Why is it sacred?"

"It contains the principal teachings of the Buddha. In essence, it shows the way to Nirvana."

"Who is this Buddha? Was he a god?"

"No, he was not a god. He was an enlightened man. He resolved to find a way to relieve the world of suffering. This book outlines his method and his philosophy, which shows the way for others to reach this attainment."

"And this Nirvana you speak of—is it a physical place that he found?"

The master smiled. "No, it is not a place but a state of mind. The Buddha showed us that we can overcome suffering and be more effective human beings if we train our minds. You already have had some instructions on this process. As we learn the thinking of the Buddha, you will find other ways and a whole philosophy that will make you aware of how the universe works and how to assist other sentient beings."

"Why is the manuscript so large? Are his teachings so complex?"

"The basic concepts are really quite simple. When you are ready, I will teach them to you. The manuscript is large because it tries to address many issues. There are three sections. First, there is the Vinaya Pitaka. This deals with how monks and nuns should behave. Second, there is the Sutta Pitaka, which outlines the thoughts of the Buddha and some of his disciples. And finally, there is the Abhidamma Pitaka, which outlines the psychology of Buddhism and its philosophy. Our benefactor has asked that we concentrate on the latter two sections. And of course, you will benefit most from these."

"Was this all written by the Buddha himself?"

"No. After the Buddha died, his disciples all assembled in a grand council. They were led by Mahakashypa, the Buddha's successor. They systematically recounted all the Buddha's teachings that they could recollect. They committed these teachings to memory, and initially, they were communicated orally. It was centuries later before they were written down for posterity."

"When will we start our transcription?"

"As soon as possible because it will be a long job. Even though we will concentrate on various selections from this work and not transcribe it in its entirety, it still will take you a long while to do the work that is required. I have some business to attend to at the emperor's court tomorrow, but on the day following, I will come again. Then we can commence."

Even though the task seemed daunting, Qiang was excited by the prospect of becoming familiar with this historic and important document. He was eager to begin.

ON THE APPOINTED day, the teacher duly arrived. Nuan let him inside, and he sat on a stool alongside the table he had acquired for Qiang.

The boy was both anxious and elated. At last, he could use his talents and transcribe this historical and seemingly important spiritual tome. He was concerned that he should not disappoint his benefactor. His teacher opened the manuscript to expose the first passage that they would transcribe.

"What is this I am to write about, Master?" he asked politely.

Chagsarka Rinpoche looked at the boy and smiled. "I can understand your impatience, but we cannot begin yet."

"Why not?"

"Because you are not ready."

The boy was surprised. "But Master, I am ready. I have taken out the paper and prepared the inks and the brushes."

"Hah," said his teacher. "Those are trivial things. Those are not the important things to do to prepare to do work of this magnitude."

"But I am trained in calligraphy, as my teachers will attest, and all I need are the materials to meet the needs of your client."

"Well, your teachers may have honed your manual skills to do this work, but this is only half the training you need."

"I do not understand! What else could I possibly need?"

"The most important prerequisite—a trained mind."

Qiang looked puzzled.

The man laughed. "It is all right. You have made a beginning. You know the basic techniques of meditation that your previous teacher taught you. Now you must learn more specific techniques to cultivate what we have traditionally called mindfulness."

"What is this mindfulness?"

"It is the ability of your mind to be totally aware and focused. In essence, a well-trained mind is aware of everything within its purview but can concentrate on a single object, action, or activity to the exclusion of all else. In the untrained mind, attention shifts from object to object, and distraction is prevalent. Paradoxically, even though its attention continually flits around, the untrained mind is less aware of background and surrounds. The master, having attained mindfulness, is aware of everything but is able to keep it from distracting him, unless there is some imperative, like physical danger."

"How am I to attain mindfulness?" asked the boy.

"I will give you exercises that will enhance your skills in this important area, but this will take some time. It is like building up a muscle in your body for physical activity, like wrestling, archery, or lifting. You will improve gradually, over a long time. When you master mindfulness, you will be able to enter into a state called meditative quiescence, in which the senses are entirely withdrawn. The attention is totally focused into the domain of a purely mental experience, so that you no longer even have a sense of having a body. The mind is utterly still, with no thoughts arising, and it is imbued with an exceptional degree of attentional clarity. You also will see, at the beginning, that it is quite difficult. Don't be discouraged. You have the strength of character to do this. That is why you have been selected. Come; let us begin. First, I would ask you to close your eyes."

Qiang did as he was bidden.

"Good! Now imagine you are outside in the garden. I noticed as I came in today that there are flowering plants in your garden. Are you familiar with them?"

Qiang nodded.

"I want you to picture one of those flowers in your mind. Examine it very thoroughly. Look at it from each side, above and below. Try to see every individual petal, noticing their colors and their texture. Notice the stamens and how they contrast with the petals. After a time, your attention is bound to wander. Gently bring it back to the flower. To keep your attention sharp look for something extra each time you picture the flower, something unique or interesting."

The master led the boy through this exercise, and after about half an hour, he asked him to stop.

"That was difficult," said Qiang. "It seemed as if I could only hold my attention on the flower for a minute or two."

His teacher smiled. "That is acceptable to begin with. You will get better. Now, let us go to the Tripitaka."

He selected the passage where he wanted the boy to start his transcription. He explained it thoroughly. He was pleased with the boy's curiosity and insightful questions.

Then, finally, he said, "You seem to have a good grasp of the content. Now it is time to use your brushes and ink. But as you work, I want you to practice your mindfulness. As you draw every character, concentrate on each stroke. Make each character embody the meaning that the work has for you. I will return tomorrow morning to check on your progress."

THUS BEGAN A daily ritual for Qiang. Each morning, he would help his father for an hour or two. Then, his teacher would arrive. Chagsarka Rinpoche would give the boy exercises to extend his mindfulness. Then, there would be some tuition in the Tripitaka, and then the boy would spend the afternoon transcribing the selected passage.

Over time, Qiang's mindfulness grew, and he could focus his attention for long periods. Because of this and the ongoing practice, his calligraphy improved even further. Chagsarka Rinpoche displayed Qiang's work at the emperor's court among the courtiers. It attracted great admiration, and his reputation spread.

The fee paid by his benefactor added to the household income so that now the family was quite comfortable. In recognition of the boy's contribution, Chao hired a carpenter, and they added another small room to the cottage, which Qiang moved into. There, he was better able to store his writing materials. There was less chance also that the comings and goings of the other household members might spoil his work.

The income garnered from the boy's work was also such that they were able to put aside enough for the tax collector.

When they ate in the evenings, his mother would ask what he had learned that day. Qiang would summarize the passage that they had studied. His mother and sister, Lan, showed great interest in the Buddhist teachings. They often would stay at the dinner table a while, mulling over the meaning of it all. Chao, on the other hand, would go outside and smoke his pipe in the coolness of the evening.

These were happy times.

For four years, the boy labored, and his output was prodigious. After finishing the selected passages from the Tripitaka, his teacher introduced Qiang to a number of other famous sutras. After this period of instruction, Qiang was familiar with a huge body of Buddhist teachings. Because of his laborious transcription and his keen attention, enhanced by his growing mindfulness, many of the teachings remained vividly imprinted in his young mind.

Then one day, Chagsarka Rinpoche came to the house, and Qiang sat down cross-legged on his little mat, awaiting his teacher's instructions.

"No, no," he said to the boy, "I am afraid my lessons are now completed, little master."

"But sir, there is still so much to learn."

"From now on, you must guide your own learning. This is not beyond you now. I have provided you with a very good foundation."

"But what resources do I have?"

Chagsarka Rinpoche laughed. He reached down and patted the youth on the top of his head. "Why, you have this. And there are three other resources that will compel your further learning."

"And what are they?"

"First, there is your experience. Life is the greatest teacher of all." His teacher paused and frowned a little before continuing. "Second, you have been given access to special meditation training, including the An Cheng mantra. Do you still practice that?"

"Indeed, I do, sir, and I still derive great pleasure from it."

"And third, another teacher will come. He will be hard to recognize, but he will teach you difficult lessons nevertheless. But now, I must go."

The youth knelt at his master's feet. "I know I cannot persuade you otherwise, but I wish you could stay. If you must go, let me express my great gratitude for all you have taught me. It has been a marvelous experience. And Master, how might I recognize my next teacher?"

The teacher seemed moved by these words. "It is I who am grateful, little master. Not many men are given the opportunity of shaping the path for a great sage—and that is what you are destined to become. I cannot give you any advice about how to recognize your next teacher, except to tell you that he will be the one you least suspect!"

"Sir, there is still a large store of paper, brushes, and ink. I will pack them up and hold them till you can get someone to collect them."

The man smiled. "Don't bother, young man. They are yours. I want you to keep working on your calligraphy. It will prove useful again for you one day." He then turned on his heel and, without a backward glance, marched out the door and down the path toward the city.

THE HOUSEHOLD WAS poorer now, having lost Qiang's regular income. But that was partly compensated by the fact that he had more time to spend in the fields, enabling Chao to sow more rice and raise a few more chickens and goats.

Qiang had developed into a strong but rangy youth. Continuous work in the fields had toughened him and strengthened him. Chao was growing older and soon found that the boy was his equal in carrying out the farm work. He smiled contentedly at this. Wasn't this the way it was meant to be? Wasn't this the reason men wanted sons—to help and support them in their later years?

The boy was happy enough working in the fields. Although the work was rather monotonous, and he hardly spoke to anyone during the day, it offered him an opportunity to continue to train his mind. Each routine became a meditation for him—hoeing the field, threshing the rice, milking the goats. He mulled over the material that Chagsarka Rinpoche had given him to transcribe. He had memorized large tracts of it, and he went over and over his favorite passages, drawing out all the nuances of meaning.

When his work outside was completed each day, he would retire to the cottage and practice his calligraphy by writing out his favorite passages. His sister, Lan, often sat with him, silently admiring his work. Lan, like most peasant girls, had never been to school. When Qiang finished a piece, she would ask him what he had written, and he would patiently explain it to her.

Then one day, he said to her, "Perhaps I should teach you to read, little sister, and then you could read my work for yourself."

She clapped her hands and embraced him. "Oh, brother, I would like that so much!"

Then in the evenings, as he worked with his little sister alongside him, he would explain what each character signified and how, collectively, they formed sentences. As the months went by, Lan, who was obviously also very intelligent, learned to read. How Nuan's heart swelled with pride as she watched her children together—Qiang improving his adeptness at calligraphy and Lan learning to read.

One evening, when Nuan had called the family to supper, Qiang spoke deferentially to Chao. "Father, before we eat, might I beg your indulgence to take a moment to show you something?"

Chao, being in a good mood because his crops were prospering, was intrigued by this request, and he nodded his assent. Nuan was also curious to know what her son was up to.

Qiang called, "Lan, you can come in now."

The girl duly appeared, holding a sheet of the soft paper.

"Show Father and Mama what you have," he said.

The girl turned the paper around so they could see that it was full of writing, comprising the most beautiful characters formed by artful and ornate brush strokes.

"Now read to them what it says."

Lan read from the paper. "The Buddha taught that there were four Noble Truths. This is the first of the four Noble Truths. To live means to suffer, because human nature is not perfect, and neither is the world we live in. During our lifetimes, we inevitably have to endure physical suffering, such as pain, sickness, injury, weariness, old age, and, eventually, death. We also have to endure psychological suffering, like sadness, fear, frustration, and disappointment, although there are different degrees of suffering, and there are also positive experiences in life. Life, in its totality, is imperfect and incomplete because our world is subject to impermanence. This means we are never able to keep permanently what we strive for, and just as happy moments pass by, we ourselves and our loved ones will pass away one day too."

Lan put the paper down and looked expectantly at her parents.

Nuan immediately clapped her hands. "Well done, my little orchid. What do you think, husband?" She glanced sideways at Chao.

He shook his head. Lan was concerned that this was a sign of disapproval, but it was merely an indication of his amazement.

After a moment or two he finally found voice. "I don't understand what you have read, and I am not sure that I know what benefit this new skill will bring you, but I am surprised and pleased at your achievement! Well done, daughter! Now, let us eat."

They all knew Chao was never effusive with his compliments, and considering his taciturn temperament, this was fulsome praise indeed! Nuan was particularly pleased. Despite Chao's initial protestations after Lan's birth, Nuan knew her husband, in his own way, loved their daughter well.

Nuan smiled indulgently at her two offspring. Lan rolled up her piece of paper and returned it to Qiang's workroom and then sat down to enjoy the frugal meal. Her father's approval left her with a quiet satisfaction that even partaking of her mother's cooking could not match.

After dinner, Chao retired outside to smoke his pipe. The other three stayed at the table a little longer and discussed the four Noble Truths and their meaning.

THE MONTHS PASSED, and Qiang and Lan sat together for a while each evening—he writing and she reading the words as he formed them. Qiang would give Lan a commentary on the particular passage he was working on, recalling the lessons of his teacher.

One evening, when they had finished for the evening, Lan asked Qiang, "Brother, might I be permitted to use your brush?"

The youth was surprised at this request. "Why, little sister? I have taught you reasonably to read, but I am not sure I can teach you to write as well."

Lan laughed. "That is not why I want your brush."

"Then why, Lan?"

"I want to paint. Could I just try for a little while, on some of the material you have discarded?"

"Well, you can try. I don't know anything about painting, but I have heard that painters use different brushes than calligraphers."

"I am sure I can make do with your brushes."

Surprisingly, although she'd had no tuition, the girl had a talent for painting. Her initial attempts were somewhat awkward and lacked style and fluency, but they were relatively accurate portrayals of simple things, like a clump of bamboo, a small bird, or a flower.

Qiang was surprised. "Why, Lan, you can paint!"

She smiled. "Well, just a little, brother, but with some practice, I will improve."

So, in the evenings, the two worked together, reading, writing, and painting. As the months went by, Lan gradually developed a unique style, such that she could depict whatever she wanted in a few, spare, well-fashioned strokes. By then, however, they had run out of material on which to paint. She had used up all the discarded paper, working on both sides to perfect her technique.

Then, Qiang had an idea. "Lan, will you illustrate my works? You could paint something on each page to help represent the essence of what I am trying to communicate. I will leave a little area for you to illustrate the piece."

"Oh, how wonderful! That is a marvelous idea." She went to her brother and hugged him.

Now, as Qiang finished transcribing each passage, he sat with Lan, and they read it together. Then, they agreed on how it might be illustrated. Over the next few months, they put together quite a body of work in this fashion.

One evening, Qiang went to his father again and asked, "Before we eat this evening, might I beg your leave to show you and Mother something?"

Chao scowled a little, but then, remembering the last time his son had made such a request, he nodded. "I suppose, if you must."

Qiang then called out, "Mother, would you come here? There is something that Lan and I would show you."

Intrigued, Nuan, who had been just outside picking some herbs for use in their dinner, walked into the room.

Qiang called, "We are ready, Lan."

At this confirmation, Lan came from Qiang's study holding several sheets of paper.

"Well, what have you this time, my girl," asked Chao. "Are you going to read for us again?"

Qiang intervened. "No, Father, she is not going to read. I have just finished transcribing a famous sutra, and Lan has illustrated it for me. Show them, Lan."

Lan took the first sheet and displayed it to her parents. On the top was an exquisitely fashioned little bird. On the left border, there was some bamboo. At the bottom, there were a few flowers. Each painting was deliciously evocative yet quite sparse. The brush strokes were indeed few, but the objects painted were clear and distinct and beautiful, despite the thrift of their architecture.

Nuan, in her characteristic way, was thrilled and clapped her hands in admiration. Chao was speechless. Then he sought confirmation. "Did you say, Qiang, that Lan painted these pictures?"

"Yes indeed, Father."

"Well, again, I can't think of what possible use such a skill is, but"—he turned to his daughter and smiled—"they are indeed beautiful."

Lan blushed and then demurely glanced at her feet. "Thank you, Father."

Qiang then showed their parents the rest of the collection, which was met with great admiration and approval. Lan was so happy! She had always treasured her mother's unconditional love, but she never expected to gain such approval from her father.

After a few minutes of indulgence, Chao cleared his throat. "Thank you, Lan, for sharing your work with us. But that is enough now. Let us eat."

Lan could hardly eat; she was so excited and so gratified by her father's praise.

HARDSHIP STRUCK AGAIN. The drought returned, and the family struggled to make a living from the farm and the farm animals.

At first, they had enough to eat but had little surplus to trade or sell. Chao's skill as a hunter and forager served them well, and he often augmented their sparse rations with a hare or a fish or some wild mushrooms or berries. As the drought wore on, however, even the animals and birds were becoming less plentiful, and the streams where he had habitually fished began to dry up.

The family's fortunes plummeted. Mere existence became a struggle. It was hard enough to find sufficient sustenance for the little family, let alone have surplus to trade.

One day, Qiang said to his mother, "Mother, I have a huge stock of manuscripts that I have transcribed and that Lan has illustrated. Is it not possible that we might sell some of these to augment the family income?"

"Oh, son, I do not know how we could do that. The people around us are poor and not inclined to make such purchases. I can only think that we could sell such artefacts at the emperor's court, where there are people who have money to dispose of."

"Then let me go there, and I will try to sell some of our work."

"No, you can't do that. Your father needs you in the fields."

"But Mother, the fields are drying out. It is no use cultivating and planting when the plants have no moisture to nourish them. We have carted water from the stream to keep a few plants alive, but it is a hopeless task. Until it rains, my work in the fields is largely futile. Let me take some pieces from our collected works to the court and see if they can be sold."

Nuan thought for a while. "I suppose it might be worth a try. Let me talk to your father."

IT WAS EARLY summer. Qiang walked briskly down the track toward the city. The parched fields that bordered the path were a somber reminder of the acuteness of the drought.

The youth had never before been to the city, and so as he walked, he was beset with conflicting emotions. He was excited at the prospect of going there and discovering for himself what city life was like, but his excitement was tempered with trepidation. What if he could not find the emperor's court? And even if he did, what if no one would purchase his wares?

His father had reluctantly agreed to the enterprise, but Qiang sensed that his father interpreted the need for it as somehow a recognition of his inability to provide for his family. Qiang felt sorry for his father. He worked hard and did what he could to support his wife and children, but he seemed to take their misfortune so personally. But even more than that, Qiang felt sorry that his father's mind seemed so troubled, while the two teachers whom Qiang had been fortunate enough to have seemed so untouched by the world. They had such a depth that whatever occurred in their day-to-day lives appeared to touch them very little. He wished his father could share their equanimity. He was pleased that his mother, Nuan, always seemed to preserve her optimism. She could always find something to smile about, even when their circumstances seemed dire.

He clutched his little bundle of manuscripts under his arm and walked resolutely toward the city. In a little sack strapped to his back, he carried a little water and a piece of cheese, made from the sparse milk of their goats, who now were struggling without adequate feed.

He and Lan had reviewed their work the night before and carefully selected what were, in their opinion, the ten best works. He wished his little sister could have come with him, but he knew his parents would not have allowed it. He loved Lan so dearly, and he had come to admire her work. It would not have occurred to him to try to pass off her work as his. This was a truly joint endeavor, and in his mind, Lan's beautiful little illustrations were just as valuable as his calligraphy.

He felt a great need to sell some of their manuscripts to ease his father's burden and to provide for his caring mother and the little sister he loved so much. Yet strangely, despite the desperateness of their situation, he still felt at ease. Intuitively, he understood that even though things seemed difficult, underneath, at some fundamental level beyond his consciousness, all was well.

QIANG SAT CROSS-LEGGED on the pavement. It had been easy to find the emperor's court. He had gotten directions from a couple of people when he reached the city, and now, he was sitting near the entrance to the court. He had laid out a couple of the best pieces on the paved area in front of him, and he hoped someone would take some interest in the work that he and his sister had lovingly created.

He watched intently as the seemingly endless procession of people passed by. Hardly anyone gave him a glance as they rushed to and from the emperor's court. After two hours, he took a little sip of water and had a bite of the cheese. He was beginning to be concerned that nobody would show interest.

After a time, he remembered his first teacher, who had taught him the basics of meditation.

He recalled him saying, "I know when my mind is in order, right things happen to me. I have been sitting here meditating these many days, preparing my mind."

Then Qiang began to meditate.

"WHAT HAVE YOU here, young man?"

An elderly gentleman in white robes was kneeling down, examining the manuscripts. He had a round face, a bald head, and a most benign smile.

"My, this is exquisite calligraphy—and such lovely little illustrations. Are these your works?"

"Oh no, sir, not entirely. I just do the calligraphy. My wonderful sister embellishes it with her beautiful paintings."

"And this is one of my favorite works—the Diamond Sutra. How did you come to know about this?"

"I indeed was blessed to have a master who instructed me in many of the sacred texts of Buddhism."

The elderly man raised his eyebrows. "You seem so young to have had a master to instruct you thus."

"Oh, sir, I have been so fortunate!"

"Then what are you doing here?"

"Well, sir, in recent times, things have become difficult for my family. My father is a farmer, and the drought has meant that we have had little produce to consume or sell. I was hoping that I might sell some of the work that my sister and I did to augment the family income."

"They are indeed exquisite. I would be happy to purchase some of these." The elderly man examined the entire bundle of manuscripts. He chose three. Two of the pieces were transcriptions of the sutras, but the other was a quote from one of the ancient sages.

"I would be pleased if I could purchase these," he said.

He offered a considerable amount, which Qiang immediately accepted.

"You are more than generous, sir."

The elderly man shook his head. "No, young man, this work of yours and your sister is worth every penny. I only hope these sales help your family through these trying times."

Qiang bundled up the selected pieces, wrapped them in some parchment, and tied the whole with a little ribbon. "I trust, sir, these few works will provide you with some joy and insights."

The elderly man gave Qiang the agreed-upon number of gold pieces. "I am sure that this is a bargain that I will never regret, young man." He started to walk off along the pavement toward the town center when Qiang spoke again.

"Can I ask you, sir, seeing as you have been so beneficent, what you are called?"

The purchaser of the works merely laughed. "What does it matter?"

Qiang, struggling to understand, shook his head.

"It is enough that you and I have met," the man said. "There is benefit for each of us in this encounter. And I suspect there will be more to take from this encounter one day. But if it is important to you, my name is Fung Tszu."

Soon after, as the sun was now low in the sky, Qiang gathered up his things and began the long march home. When he arrived, both his mother and father were astounded by the amount he had been paid, but Qiang was realistic. "I will go again and again to the court, if it helps our household economy, but I warn you—I might not be able to attract such a benefactor again so quickly."

QIANG CONTINUED TO go to the court each day. Although many courtiers passed by, only a few stopped to look at the work. Mostly, they just admired the skills of Qiang and his sister but then moved on. The old man who had bought the pieces from Qiang previously stopped to chat a couple of times. His kindness and interest helped Qiang's resolve to continue to sell his wares.

One day, as he was gently meditating, he became aware of an approaching figure. He looked up to see a rather austere-looking man approaching. He was tall and rangy, his long limbs cloaked by a dark robe. His face was gaunt and long, made even more chilling by somber eyes set well back in his face. When he reached Qiang, he paused and looked at the work displayed on the pavement. The parchment he had spread out contained a quote from an ancient Buddhist sage from a faraway country to the east.

Qiang's parchment had these words written on it:

> To study the way is to study the self.
> To study the self is to forget the self.
> To forget the self is to be enlightened by all things.
> To be enlightened by all things is to forget the barrier between self and other.

The man laughed derisively. "How would a peasant boy know the words of a master? And what causes you to lay his sacred word on the ground like so much dirt?"

Qiang was nonplussed by this response and hardly knew how he should reply. He did not immediately respond. He took a few breaths to quiet his mind. Finally, he responded. "Sir, I am only trying to sell these manuscripts to help my starving family. We are a farming family, and the drought has meant that our crops have failed, and we have little income or sustenance."

The man looked steely-eyed at the unfortunate Qiang. "Your pathetic bleating has no impact on me. The only opportunity you have to impress me is to demonstrate that you know the import of what you have written."

The lad relaxed a little now because he was confident that he knew the meaning of the sage's quotation. "I believe, sir, that the author—the venerable Dogen Zenji—was trying to prove how the ego perverts our relationships with others and our opportunity to relate productively with the world. Those who understand know that we all are one, but if the ego is allowed to sully our view of the world, then we are doomed to a life of dissatisfaction and separation."

The austere man scowled at Qiang. He seemed a little surprised at the maturity of the boy's response. He was silent for a moment but then said, "You have tried to explain too much at once. A sage needs to be more careful in his interpretation. Each word is full of meaning; each sentence is a treasure. A man of wisdom must unlock that treasure. Let me make a compact with you. I will come here for four days, and I will ask you to explain each line of the sage's work. If I am satisfied that you truly understand, I will purchase this manuscript from you."

Qiang pondered for a moment but soon responded. "I will try to meet your demands. When shall I see you again?"

The man scowled down at the lad and said curtly, "I will be here tomorrow in the midafternoon."

IT WAS A long walk home. Qiang normally hurried home, keen to be back to answer his mother's and little sister's questions. But today, he walked slowly. His mind was full of the first line of Dogen Zenji's quotation, which resonated in his mind.

To study the way is to study the self.

Qiang took "the way" to mean the universal principles that governed all things. The "self" was a projection of the insecurity of the individual but part of the universe and strangely entangled in it. And in that sense, to study the way must mean also studying the self.

But the self, in some ways, stood between the universe and what is observing the universe. Qiang's masters had called this faculty that does the observing the "witness." The self was, therefore, like a lens through which the witness perceived the universe. In this respect, even though the individual was not aware of it, the way could never be perceived without the medium of the self. And the masters had warned that as a result of the mediating influence of the self, no two persons saw the world similarly. And indeed, the only way that an individual might perceive the world properly was to put aside the distorting lens of self. Hence, to see the world properly, one needed to know enough about the self to learn how to put it aside.

And didn't the Buddha, when announcing the Noble Eightfold Path, begin with the notion of 'right view'? The Eightfold Path described the way to the end of suffering. Right view was the beginning and the end of the path. It simply meant to see and understand things as they really are.

"Right view enables us to grasp the impermanent and imperfect nature of worldly objects and ideas," Qiang thought. It leads us to the understanding of the true nature of all things.

Qiang's mind coursed back and forth over this difficult terrain. Two hours later, when he reached the comfort of the family abode, he was still contemplating the complexity of this one pregnant line in the sage's quotation.

The young lad came through the door obviously distracted.

The ever-perceptive Nuan asked, "Son, are you all right? How did things go today?"

He smiled at his mother. "I am fine, Mother. As for today, I have encountered a man who has given me a test before he will buy."

Nuan wrinkled her brow in consternation. "That seems a strange thing to do."

"Never mind, Mother. I am enjoying the stimulus of the intellectual exercise. I might not satisfy the man, but I already have learned a lot by contemplating the exercise."

THE NEXT DAY, Qiang waited patiently on the pavement, close to the emperor's court. Courtiers came and went, but none stopped to look at the young man's work. This was of little concern to Qiang. He meditated for a long while, and, surprisingly, when he thought his mind was in order, he noticed a shadow on the pavement and looked up to see the gaunt figure of the austere man.

The man scowled. "I did not expect to see you here today."

"Why ever not?" queried Qiang.

"I have set you a difficult task, and I didn't think you would be up to it."

"Oh sir, I am not the most intelligent person, but I must confess that I am stimulated by an intellectual challenge. I enjoyed contemplating on that first line of the sage's statement. He is indeed wise, and I was not aware of the depth of his wisdom until you set me the challenge."

The austere man frowned. "What makes you believe you have plumbed the depths of the sage's wisdom? It is not normally the province of ill-educated youths."

Qiang smiled benignly. "That is possibly so, sir, but I have had some instruction from masters of considerable wisdom. I do not propose that I have such wisdom on my own account, but I have had my eyes opened more than most."

"Let us not waste our time in such self-indulgence. Explain to me the first line of the sage's work."

Qiang related the conclusions he had reached while on his walk home the previous day.

Before he could finish, the man snarled, "Enough! That is a fair interpretation of the work, but I cannot believe you came to this conclusion by yourself."

"No, sir, I did not. I relied somewhat on the instructions that I have had from my mentors, as I have mentioned. I do not wish to portray myself as someone who has extraordinary wisdom. I am just the beneficiary of teachings from those who are far wiser than I am."

"That will do! You do not have to put on the face of humility. Come again tomorrow, and tell me what the second line of the sage's writing means."

And with that, the austere man marched off sullenly, into the distance.

Qiang was rather nonplussed by this response. But being pragmatic about the adventure, he then turned his mind to the next line:

"To study the self is to forget the self."

AS QIANG WALKED home, his mind was full of just one thing: "To study the self is to forget the self." When we are engaged in intensely studying something, it is natural that we should forget the self. But how could we forget the self if that is the object of our study?

Then, it occurred to him that if the self is the object of the study, then it cannot also be the subject. It is seen as something separate and removed, not something with which to identify, but something whose innate characteristics were sought.

He remembered the words of his master: "Can the eye see itself?"

Well, of course not, but the eye can see other eyes. The self, then, can understand and observe other selves. But in this process, it cannot knowingly look at itself and be both subject and object at once. So, in practical terms, to study the self is to forget the self. The self is put aside and logically can't be invoked while it is studying the phenomenon of self.

Qiang went over and over these thoughts as he made his way home, and by the time he arrived, he was satisfied that he had uncovered the rationale behind this enigmatic statement.

When he finally appeared at the door of the humble cottage, Nuan asked, "How did it go today, son?"

"Well, Mother, I haven't sold anything yet, but I must say, I gained something in terms of understanding."

Nuan shook her head in perplexity but didn't comment further.

QIANG SAT ON the pavement outside the emperor's court, meditating on the line he had been set to study. He initially had thought that the undertaking would be boring, but he was surprised to see that it was not so. The depth of the content in the sage's words gave plenty of scope for contemplation and intellectual challenge.

As on the previous day, Qiang became aware of a presence before the austere man's shadow fell on him, and he looked up.

Without any pleasantries and with the perpetual scowl on his face, the man demanded, "Well, boy, what have you to say for yourself?"

Undeterred, Qiang set about elaborating on his thoughts—that because the self could not be both subject and object at the same time, it was necessary to put the identification with self aside, if one was to truly study the self. He was about to call on some quotes from various sages when the man halted him.

"Enough! Don't waste my time. Your understanding is sufficient. Come again tomorrow with your interpretation of the third line."

Qiang said, "As you wish, sir."

The man turned on his heel before Qiang finished speaking and strode into the distance.

"To forget the self is to be enlightened by all things." The young man wrinkled his brow as he contemplated the line.

He had walked for some time and was now clear of the city and into the countryside. The fields were brown and dry and barren. There must be many like him and his family, he thought, who were struggling to survive in the drought.

He smiled, despite the desolation around him, because he loved these words from the sage. They made perfect sense to him. When the self is dominant in our thoughts, we strive to protect it. As a result, there are things we can't afford to know because they threaten our sense of self. Therefore, in many ways, putting aside self removes the obstacles to learning. Every fact can be evaluated objectively because the self is no longer under threat.

He went over and over these thoughts, exploring every nuance and testing every argument.

When he arrived home, Nuan asked, "How did it go today?"

"It went well, Mother. I seem to have satisfied my inquisitor. But more than that, I enjoyed the exercise and learned a lot along the way."

Nuan smiled indulgently at her son. He always seemed to be happy. His equanimity was contagious. She loved him so much and would indulge him as well as she could, but she always felt that he gave her far more in return, even sometimes when she couldn't understand at an intellectual level.

ON THE THIRD day, Qiang went again to the emperor's court. He felt quite sure that he had emptied the third line of its wisdom and could express it in a convincing way.

As usual, he took up the lotus position and meditated on the pavement. Surprisingly, he again sensed the austere man's approach when he was quite a long way off. He looked up and greeted him.

The man maintained an indifferent attitude and asked rather brusquely, "Well, what have you made of the third line?"

"To tell the truth, sir, I am greatly taken by it. It resonates strongly with me."

"Don't waste my time with platitudes, boy. What does it mean?"

Qiang patiently explained the conclusion he had reached on how the self, in its defensiveness, prevented learning.

As on the previous occasions, before he could complete his explanations, the man cried, "Enough. You seem to have some rudimentary understanding of the text. That will do. Come again tomorrow and explain the last line to me."

The lad reflected on the last line: "To be enlightened by all things is to forget the barrier between self and other." As he walked home, he mused over these words.

To be enlightened by all things surely implied that he must be receptive to all knowledge. If each person in the world could be receptive to all knowledge, then they would each have a shared understanding of the universe.

But as he had come to realize, it was the concept of self that prevented an objective understanding of the universe. And more than that, it was the concept of self that tended to make people think they were somehow special and better than or different from others. Once this divisive notion is put aside, it is evident that we are all indeed one. Once the parochial notions of self are put aside, we are left with the realization that the essential component of our humanity is our consciousness, and surely that is the same platform of identity that all of us share.

ON THE FOURTH day, surprisingly, the austere man was waiting for Qiang. Qiang had come to the court precinct and was about to sit down on the pavement, as he usually did, but the man was waiting, just along the footpath. Strangely, he seemed to have a rolled-up manuscript of his own tucked under his arm.

Once he saw Qiang, he strode steadfastly to him and demanded, "And what about the fourth line? Do you understand that?"

"I think so, sir," said Qiang humbly and began his explanation.

As on the previous days, before Qiang could complete his explanation, the austere man snarled, "That is enough. Here is your fee." And so saying, he gave Qiang a generous amount of money and took the manuscript that Qiang had laid out. "It is beyond me to understand how a wretched farmer's son could understand the words of a sage. But this was my contract with you, and I am obliged to honor it. If you, little cur, are somehow destined for greatness and because you have a modicum of understanding of sacred writings, I will leave you something to help you on your way."

And so saying, he threw the document he held onto the ground and marched off into the city.

Qiang picked up the document, unwrapped it, and rolled it out. It was titled "The Sutra of the Rising Moon." It was a short piece, and before he trudged back to his home, he took a few minutes to read it.

The Sutra of the Rising Moon

THE MOON RISES *inexorably, and no man can stop it.*

The moon plays its proper role in the heavens, and the heavens are always in order.

When it is the season to rain, rain comes, whether a man wishes for it or not.

Summer and winter come and go, sometimes hotter and sometimes colder, and a man puts on a coat or takes one off, but the trees cope unclothed, and the rocks are unmoved.

The way of things is in accordance with the purposes of heaven. The universe bestows on us gifts. The unaware interpret these gifts as hurtful or benign. Those who are aware interpret each gift as an opportunity to learn. The universe is neither beneficent nor malevolent; it is educative.

As much as a man might seem discomfited by what happens, whether or not it seems so to he who knows, "All is well."

The nations of the earth are populated with hordes of people, with each individual trying to assert how he is different and special. But the sage knows this is an error. Each may believe he has some special purpose, but no man can subordinate the purpose of heaven. When we cling to our certainties, likes and dislikes, deeming them essential to our sense of self, we become alienated from the way.

The clouds in the sky are full of raindrops that, when the heavens are ready, will fall to the ground as precipitation. They have no false pride and do not assert their specialness or difference.

The mighty sun shines indiscriminately on the whole earth. Each sunbeam seeks out a spot to bless with its warmth and light. But each ray does not suppose that it is better, stronger, brighter, and warmer than its neighbor.

Each raindrop understands that it is the emanation of the generosity of the cloud.

Each sunbeam knows it is an expression of joy, just like its fellows, of the sun.

Every man also is an emanation of the heavens—not special except in his imagination. But each man is imbued with consciousness and, as a result, has a self that strives to convince him of his uniqueness and specialness and thus creates the separation between one and another that only exists through the selfish perception of uniqueness.

When a person masters the perception of "right view," it is obvious that "all is one." There is no separation between one man and another.

When that realization is obtained, everything is as it should be. The moon rises when it chooses to rise, as ordained by heaven. The rains come as they should come, by the ordination of heaven. And men live their lives in the perfection that is ordained by heaven. And despite evidence to the contrary, the wise man knows that all is well. And having put aside his need for a sense of separateness, he also knows that all is one.

QIANG WAS NATURALLY perplexed by this turn of events. The austere man had been somewhat belligerent. Yet he had paid generously for the work Qiang had created with his little sister. And now, he had bestowed on Qiang this short sutra. Qiang read it over some three or four times. While he thought it was lovely, it seemed to contain no additional insights. Perhaps, Qiang reasoned, this was his own ego getting in the way.

Pleased with the day's outcome, he returned home with a light heart.

When Qiang showed his mother the fee he had earned, Nuan was especially delighted. "Why, this is enough to sustain us for many months, perhaps until the rains come."

He showed the sutra to the family, and after dinner, when his father went outside to smoke his pipe, Qiang read it to his mother and sister. They enjoyed it, and the three discussed its meaning until it was time to retire.

THE NEXT DAY, Qiang took his wares back to the court.

To his surprise, there was little traffic along the pavement where he habitually took up his position.

A young peasant came walking by.

Qiang hailed him. “Good morning, my fellow. Can you tell me why there are so few people here today?”

The lad laughed. “Don’t you know? Every year at midsummer, the emperor takes his court up to his retreat in the mountains, where the weather is cooler. They will stay there now until autumn.”

A little surprised at this development but still maintaining his equanimity, Qiang thanked the young fellow, packed up his goods, and returned home.

THE SUMMER WAS hot. There were no rains of any consequence, and the fields were so parched that when the heat storms generated their incessant winds, the soil was blown into the air in clouds.

Still, the little family was able to sustain itself on the payments Qiang had received at the emperor's court for the artwork he and his little sister had created.

Others around were not so fortunate. One day, their neighbors came to tell them that they were moving to another province. These were their closest neighbors, with whom they had shared produce and implements. The little family consisted of a couple and three children. When they came to say goodbye, the children looked emaciated. But the family still was generous. They left a few skinny chickens and a very gaunt goat.

"We are not able to pay the emperor's taxes. And we cannot take the animals with us," the husband explained. "We would be glad for you to have them."

Chao thanked him and wished the farmer and his family good fortune on their relocation. While he was sad to see them go because they had been good neighbors, something in him seemed to want to go with them. He felt desolate, living off his son's earnings and now the charity of a few friends. He felt the pain of not believing he could provide properly for his family any longer.

EVEN THE BENEFICENCE of the emperor's court could not sustain them forever. There were no more acquisitions from the courtiers. The months went by, and they just brought more misery.

The land remained parched and could not provide the little family with any sustenance of consequence. Even more than that, the little hoard of money they had stored from Qiang's sale of manuscripts continued to dwindle. And what was left of it was of little use anyhow. In this parched land, there was no longer produce to buy. They began to pay inordinate amounts for a few eggs here or a squash there.

Chao was beside himself, as he saw his family was also beginning to starve.

ONE DAY, CHAO was assaulted with the final insult.

There came a knocking at the door.

Who could it be? They no longer had any neighbors. And it was very unusual for friends or acquaintances to drop by in these difficult times.

Chao went to the door and found two men—one tall and gaunt, the other swarthy and heavyset.

"What do you want?" Chao asked rather abruptly, his manner reflecting an inner sense of foreboding.

The tall fellow stepped forward. "We are the emperor's tax collectors. We have come for your taxes."

Chao's heart sank. "How do I know you are not imposters?"

"We can show you our credentials," said the swarthy fellow, pulling out a sheet of parchment.

Although Chao couldn't read, he could recognize the emperor's seal at the bottom. It was similar to documents tax collectors had produced previously, and he had no doubt of its authenticity. Seeking to buy a little time, he responded, "I cannot read. How do you expect me to make sense of that?"

"That is strange," the tall man retorted. "We have heard from one of the emperor's courtiers that a famous calligrapher resides here."

Chao shook his head. "Well, I cannot read, let alone write script."

"Then who is the calligrapher? You are not implying that the courtier was lying."

The farmer was now trapped. He did not want to admit that he did not have the wherewithal to pay his taxes, but he knew if he intimated that the emperor's courtier was lying, there might be dire consequences as well. He scowled and then said, "My son is the calligrapher."

"Call him here to examine our documents."

Against his better judgment, Chao called, "Qiang! Come here, please, son. Your father needs you."

Qiang came running to his father's call but stopped short when he saw the two strange men. He slowly approached with some consternation because he could see the concern in his father's face.

"These two fellows purport to be the emperor's tax collectors. They have a document that they maintain establishes their credentials. Will you examine it for me, please?"

The swarthy fellow held out the manuscript, and Qiang took it from him. His eyes scanned the text. It only took a few moments.

"Father, this document seems to delegate to the holder the authority to collect the emperor's taxes. It also gives them broad powers to effect the collection of the taxes. It stipulates that once demanded, the landholder has thirty days to raise the required amount or face eviction."

The tall fellow put his hand on Qiang's shoulder, although the lad tried to shy away. He smiled in a belligerent and arrogant way. "You have done well in interpreting the emperor's command." He then turned to Chao. He told him the amount of tax that was due. "Now, as the boy said, you have thirty days to pay for your privilege of using the emperor's land or else you must leave."

"We don't have the taxes," Chao admitted. "Doesn't the emperor know that we have been besieged by a great drought? Our crops have continually failed, and as a result, we have struggled to feed ourselves, let alone sell any produce."

The tall fellow turned to the swarthy man. "We seem to have heard this story before. Do you think these people are conspiring to deprive the emperor of his rightful dues?"

The other man laughed. "It would seem so. Maybe if we got rid of this lot and found some who could properly tend the emperor's land, the emperor would be better off."

Qiang could see the ire rising up in his father. This was the greatest insult they could inflict on the peasant who prided himself on being a competent farmer. It was evident that these men had no idea about tending the land. He also sensed that they were consciously goading his father, perhaps hoping for an inappropriate response to enable them to use their unequal power to shame and denigrate this simple but well-meaning man. He was afraid that Chao might respond in anger and do something he might regret.

Before his father could speak, Qiang turned to him and said, "Sir, unfortunately, we must obey the emperor's command. We cannot now pay the taxes, but let us beg these fellows to allow the thirty day's grace the emperor has made available."

Poor Chao now was now almost in tears at the thought of being evicted from his farm. His heart was beset with a smoldering rage at the insults of the tax collectors. He hardly knew how to respond but nodded his assent to Qiang's suggestion.

The boy then turned to his father's tormentors. "Come back in thirty days, and we will see what we can do to raise the taxes for the emperor. Also, when you go back to the emperor, remind him that I have some skills that his courtiers seem to believe are valuable. If I was able to perform such work to relieve my father of the tax burden, I would be happy to do so."

The two men laughed. Qiang could not determine whether their mirth was directed at the ignominy they had constructed for his father or the impertinence that he had showed in offering his services to pay off the debt of the taxes.

THE LITTLE FAMILY sat around the small table where they normally ate together. Chao was obviously devastated. "We have no way to raise the taxes," he finally said.

Nuan, even though she was brave and stoic, could not suppress a few tears running down her face. "What are we to do?" she asked.

Chao sat silently for a long time. Then he said, "We must leave this place. If we must go, let us go with dignity. I won't have those ruffians coming back and evicting us. That would be too much to bear."

"But where can we go?" asked the ever-practical Nuan.

"There is only one place to go. We will go to my brother in Chuang-Ho province and stay with him until we can sort something out. I have no doubt he will help us. He has a bigger farm than we do, and he lives close to the river Tchi-Tsu, which never runs dry. In return for his hospitality, Qiang and I can help him farm his land until we can find something else."

"It will be a long trek, husband. Chuang-Ho province is many days' march from here."

Chao sighed. "I know that, wife. It is probably a ten- or twelve-day walk, and the journey may be arduous, but I know of nothing else to do."

Qiang was always the optimist and wanted to assuage his father's pain. "We can manage the journey, Father. You and Mama are strong and resilient, and I will help Lan."

Chao was never one to show his emotions, but he bit his lip and said, "I have failed you all." He got up and walked outside.

Neither his wife nor his children dared follow because they knew he would be weeping, and he would find it an insult to his dignity to be so observed.

IT WAS QUITE early in the morning when they set off. The worst of summer was now over.

Chao pushed a large handcart; Qiang, a slightly smaller one. They took with them only clothes, bedding, gardening implements with which to help Chao's brother in tending the farm, a few basic cooking utensils, and all the remaining food they had in the household. However, at Nuan's insistence, included in Qiang's load was his bundle of manuscripts, wrapped in oilskin and canvas to keep them from the elements. Nuan and Lan both carried water in goat-skin containers strapped over their shoulders.

Chao, with Nuan striding beside him, led the way. Qiang and Lan followed.

This was a great adventure for the children who (except for Qiang's forays into the city to sell his manuscripts) had never ventured beyond the local village, the school, and the neighboring farms. Despite the weight of the current circumstances, they were in good spirits. Qiang was now strong and physically robust. He had no trouble keeping up with his father. Every now and then, when Lan tired a little, he would allow her to sit on the front of his cart to give her a rest.

On the first day, they made good progress. The terrain was largely flat and the path even and smooth so that pushing the handcarts was not unduly arduous. They stopped for a while in the middle of the day and rested under a large shade tree. They drank a little water and ate a sparse meal from the provisions they carried. Chao and Nuan lay down on the bare ground under the tree and napped for perhaps a half an hour, while Qiang and Lan talked quietly.

Then, after his short repose, Chao arose and stirred his wife and made ready to begin their trek again.

On the track, they passed an occasional peasant going the other way. Sometimes, the peasant would stop and ask about the little family and why they were traveling as they were. Chao would have none of this and urged the other members of the family to continue without responding to the questions of their fellow travelers.

It was late afternoon. Qiang was walking alongside his father. Lan was perched precariously on the front of his handcart. The boy could see that his father was tired.

"Father, we will need to stop soon. Where will we spend the night?"

"I have not been this way for some time, Qiang, but as I remember, we should soon come upon a little stream with shady trees on its banks. There, we shall make our camp for the night."

In due course, the group saw a tree-lined watercourse ahead. They were heartened by the sight, for it had been an arduous day, and all were looking forward to rest. With some consternation, when they arrived at what Chao had remembered as a little stream, they were confronted with a dry riverbed. Chao had not reckoned on the impacts of the prolonged drought.

The poor man was dismayed by this outcome. "We have little water left in our skins. We will need to refill them to make the next leg of our journey."

It was late afternoon now, with perhaps an hour of daylight left.

Qiang spoke up. "Mother, is there enough water to make dinner."

Nuan examined the skins and nodded her head.

"Father," Qiang said, "let us empty the remaining water into the cooking pots. Mother can start dinner, and I will look for water."

"But where will you look?" his father asked.

"I will take the skins with me and walk down the creek bed. There is likely to be a rock pool somewhere where some water remains or perhaps somewhere where the sand is still moist, where digging a hole might uncover a little water."

"I should come with you."

"No, Father. It would not be prudent for us to leave my mother and my sister alone in such a place. If you will help them unload the necessary equipment for tonight's stay and help fashion a cooking fire, I will try to find some water."

While Chao could see the sense in this, it rankled him that he must rely on his son to remedy the situation. The poor man was affronted that he had gotten his little family into such a dilemma and had to rely on someone else to resolve their dilemma.

Finally, he agreed, and Qiang headed off in search of water.

Once he was out of sight of the others, he sat for a while in the lotus position and meditated. It was a mindfulness technique he utilized. He knew that his awareness was now crucial to this endeavor, and taking fifteen minutes to meditate and heighten the acuity of his senses seemed a worthwhile investment.

When he arose from his meditation, he felt relaxed and strangely confident that he would succeed. He walked slowly down the creek bed. In these reaches, the creek bed was rocky and uneven.

After walking twenty minutes or so, he heard the sound of small finches. He knew that the birds often came to drink in the evenings. As he approached the source of the sound, there was a great flutter, and a flock of small finches scattered into the fading light. He scanned the creek bed but could see no sign of water. He sat upon a rock in the middle of the dry creek bed and tried to gather his thoughts together.

He looked right and left but to no avail. There was no sign of water. He was about to move on when he noticed that his feet felt cool—no, it was more than that; they were damp! He knelt down and was elated to see that there was a small pool of water under the rock on which he had been sitting. It was only a small puddle, but as he explored its dimensions, he could feel the rock behind was dripping. The water table above this rock dam was supplying a little trickle of water continuously into the rock pool. The pool, in turn, was sheltered from the sun by the overhanging rock precipice on which he had been sitting. He placed one of the water skins into the little pool, and after ten minutes or so, it was three-quarters full. The pool was not deep enough to extract more water. He picked up the container, slung it over his back, and proceeded farther downstream. He knew this was not enough water to sustain the four of them for another day.

The light was fading now, and Qiang was beginning to be concerned that he would not find enough water for tomorrow's journey. Finally, the rocky floor of the creek bed gave way to gravel and then sand. He walked for some time, peering in the gloom to find a sign of water but to no avail. Finally, he stopped. There seemed little point in going on because he could not see enough to find signs of water.

He sat down on the sand and quieted his thinking. He focused on his breathing. Voicelessly, he repeated in his mind the An Cheng mantra.

But then, when his mind was stilled, a soft sound entered his awareness. He focused all his intense attention on the sound. It was intermittent, and when it came again, he had to strain his senses even to detect it. There was no doubt that there was a sound, but not wanting to strain himself in determining what it might be, he again stilled his mind and focused only on where the sound was coming from.

It seemed a long way off. After a while, he became convinced that the sound was emanating from farther downstream and to his left. He arose from his lotus position and moved toward it. In the dim light, he could see a high, rocky cliff, hovering above the sandy creek bed. After he had walked fifty meters or so, he again sat down and listened intently.

The sound was louder now. It sounded like *splot*, and then, about thirty seconds later, there was another *splot*. He smiled. It was the sound of drops of water falling from somewhere in the cliff face, onto the rocks below.

He walked to the base of the cliff. He bent down and felt the sand at his feet. It was moist! Using his hands, he excavated a sizeable hole, and—to his great relief—at the bottom of the hole was a little pool of water.

After half an hour or so, by enlarging the hole and waiting for it to replenish itself with water, he was able to fill both skins.

Somewhat exhausted, he wended his way back to the little camp where his family was waiting. It was quite dark by the time he got there. He was able to find the camp easily enough in the dark because the embers of the cooking fire still glowed a little in evening gloom.

He walked toward the camp and, so as not to alarm anybody, he called out, "Father, Mother, it is me, Qiang. I am back."

Lan rushed forward to greet him. "Oh, brother, I have worried so much about you! It is good to see you return." She hugged him tightly. Then she looked at his load. "My goodness, you have filled our skins! We will not go thirsty tomorrow. Oh, how wonderful you are!"

Qiang smiled. "Ah, little sister, I tried as best I could to ensure that you and my family would not suffer from lack of water."

Nuan came forward and embraced him also. "I have saved some food for you. You must be hungry."

"Thank you, Mother."

Finally, Chao said, "You have done well, my son."

Qiang could see that his father's compliment came at the expense of reinforcing his own sense of inadequacy. "You would have done just as well, Father, but you have been here protecting our loving mother and my precious little sister. That is a very important duty, and I thank you for that."

Qiang's praise of his father seemed to temporarily assuage Chao's feeling of inadequacy.

Qiang ate his dinner that his mother had saved for him. The evening was mild, and the prospects for the morrow seemed promising enough. Still, Qiang went to bed with an ominous sense of foreboding.

ON THE MORROW they packed their frugal possessions into the handcarts and set off again. They were in good spirits, and consequently, they made good time, putting many kilometers behind them before they stopped to rest and eat a little.

The morning had been fine and cool, and walking had been pleasant enough. But after their short sojourn, as they arose to continue their journey, Chao stopped abruptly.

"What is it, husband?" asked Nuan quietly.

Chao was silent for a moment before responding. "Look at the sky."

Ahead, in the direction of their journey, was a huge bank of black clouds tinged with green. It was the most foreboding sky Qiang had ever seen.

"There will be much rain up ahead," murmured Nuan.

"And probably hail or snow!" Chao said.

Lan looked imploringly at her father. "What are we to do?"

"We can't turn back now. We must press on. Find your weatherproof cloaks, and keep them at hand. We will go as far as we can before the rains come, and then we will seek shelter."

They walked for some time. The light got gloomier as the storm front approached. Finally, Chao stopped to take stock. Turning around, he noticed that Qiang was no longer with them. He frowned but then saw the lad farther down the track, jogging to catch up.

"What were you doing, boy?" Chao demanded.

"I was afraid it might be wet and cold this evening, Father, so I took the precaution of collecting a little firewood, in case we find a little shelter."

His father nodded. "Yes, I suppose that might be useful."

On they walked. The track now led them into a valley. To begin with, it was flanked by low hills, but as they progressed, the ramparts on either side grew steeper and higher. The wind started to pick up. It buffeted them and chilled them with its icy gusts. They put their cloaks on and, gritting their teeth, walked into the approaching storm.

A few spots of rain began to fall. Despite the rising stormaround them, Qiang practiced his walking meditation.

His senses were acutely aware. He felt the icy spots of moisture on his face. He was strangely exhilarated by the embrace of the chill wind. Despite the anxiety of his family members, he was calm and assured. He was sure that they would find shelter.

Chao pushed doggedly forward. He seemed to know nothing else to do but confront the storm. Resolutely, Nuan and Lan followed.

Suddenly, there was a tremendous boom and a blinding light, as lightning struck a tree on the top of a cliff on their left. They briefly stopped. Lan began to whimper in fear. Qiang put his arm around her to comfort her. He looked at the cliff where the lightning had struck. It was perhaps a hundred meters away. He smiled.

"Father, Father! Look! There is somewhere we might seek shelter." He pointed at the base of the cliff. There was a rock ledge that protruded four or five meters beyond the base.

Chao turned to examine his son's discovery. "It is not much," he said, "but I suppose it will have to do."

They scrambled over to the cliff. They made their way to the shelter that the projecting rock ledge provided. It was immediately obvious that others had sheltered there in the past. There were the remains of campfires and other detritus strewn about to attest to the fact that there had been other travelers who had benefited from the shelter of the rock overhang.

They had barely ensconced themselves in the security of the shelter when the heavens opened. First, there was hail. It was so intense that it stripped the leaves off the nearby trees and piled up on the ground in a grimy white blanket. The hail lasted perhaps twenty minutes. The little family huddled together for warmth as the hailstorm spent itself.

When the hail ceased, the valley was almost in darkness, even though it was only afternoon.

Qiang said, "Let us make a fire while there is still light."

Chao, seemingly wanting to demonstrate his usefulness, said, "I will do that."

"Thank you, Father. While the hail has stopped, I will gather a little more fuel, if I can. I feel we may be here a while."

"Very well," said Chao.

When Qiang returned, he had an armful of firewood.

Chao had a nice little fire burning, and the family was huddled about it.

"Here is some more firewood, Father. Some of it is a little damp, but I am sure it will burn."

Chao seemed genuinely pleased. "Thank you, son. That should keep our fire burning through the night, should we need it."

Nuan then set about preparing a little meal for the travelers.

Soon after however, the downpour commenced.

It rained harder than Qiang had ever experienced. He was amazed by the fact that within a half hour, a little waterfall began to pour over the rock ledge at the entrance to their refuge. The rain was so heavy and the light now so dim that he could barely see ten meters beyond their shelter.

The wind outside was ferocious. However, their shelter seemed to be largely in the lee of the prevailing wind. Sometimes, a swirl of wind would deposit a few drops of rain on them, but by and large, they remained dry, despite the torrential rain.

Thus, they spent a fitful but reasonably dry night. While it was not discussed, there was some concern about what the morrow might bring. While Qiang had concerns for his family and how they might progress, his mind was disciplined enough to understand the futility of worrying about it all, and he slept soundly till morning.

The others were still asleep when he awoke. There were still some embers glowing from their little campfire. He carefully renewed the fire, adding a little more fuel and blowing on it until there were again a few flickering flames.

It was still raining heavily, having done so all night.

He commenced his meditation practice.

ONE BY ONE, the other three awoke. They were dismayed to see the rain continuing.

They ate a sparse breakfast. Nuan made tea, and they sat and sipped tea while watching the deluge outside. Their little refuge had remained dry, and although they were comfortable enough, Chao was anxious to resume their journey.

"We must set off soon," he said, "or our provisions will not last." He hung his head and sighed.

"What is it, husband?" asked Nuan.

"The gods have abandoned us," he said through gritted teeth. "For so long, we have had drought, and that drought, in the end, forced us off our land. And now, no sooner are we gone than the rains have come. If we had stayed, I would now be able to plant crops again and to earn a reasonable livelihood. But now I have destined us all for poverty and hardship."

Lan began to weep quietly. Qiang could see that her concern was not only for the welfare of the little family but for the state of mind of her father, who was prone to lapse into self-incrimination.

Qiang said firmly, "We had no choice, Father. We could not have paid our taxes, and we would have been dispossessed if we had stayed. And we have no idea whether this rain has fallen on our little farm. Come; if we stick together, we can deal with whatever comes."

Nuan looked admiringly at her son and concurred. "The boy is right. This is not your fault. We will make out."

Chao merely shook his head. He moved away from the others and sat on a rock at the edge of their little refuge, placing his head between his hands.

Nuan sighed. She had become used to Chao's self-denigration and pessimism. She knew that nothing she could say or do would cheer him up.

By midmorning, the rain had eased. Even though it still drizzled, Chao stood and said, "Come; we must be gone. Put your cloaks back on and reload the handcarts. We must strike out again."

The little family dutifully followed his instructions, and within five minutes, they were trudging back to the track. The track was now muddy and slippery. Some of the streamlets were still flowing, engorged by the night's downpour. Here and there, they spilled over the track, and the little party had to cross them. Because the water still ran strongly and the ground underfoot was uncertain, their progress was slow.

The track meandered up the valley of a stream, and after some hours of travel, they had progressed into higher territory, where the streams were smaller and the going a little easier.

By midafternoon, they had reached the crest of the hill and were surprised to find that the track now joined a rather wide roadway. The roadway was paved in parts and showed signs of much wear. This was obviously a major thoroughfare.

The rain had completely stopped now, and they packed away their cloaks. The firmer going made it easier to push the handcarts, and the paving and gravel of the road surface meant there was less mud to contend with.

They were now on a major trade route, and it wasn't long before they began to encounter other travelers. The first group they came across comprised three men leading three packhorses. The horses were laden with produce. They were obviously merchants.

As they approached, Chao raised his hand in acknowledgment and awaited the leading merchant to arrive.

As the man approached, Chao called out, "Good day, sir! How go you?"

The man smiled and replied, "Good day to you as well. How go I? I go wet! We have experienced a great deluge, and the road has been made difficult because there are places where water is across the road, places where landslides have partly blocked our passage, and places where the deluge has resulted in mud being deposited on the road, which has made it difficult to traverse. And I fear it may get worse because I believe there is likely to be more rain. Where are you heading?"

"We journey to my brother's farm in Quang Ho province."

The merchant frowned. "Then take good care because the River Tchi-Tsu is in high flood. I cannot remember it so high, and I have traveled this way for almost forty years."

Chao was a little dismayed. "Thank you for your warning," he responded. "We will just have to deal with that as best we can."

The merchant smiled and moved on. He called back over his shoulder, "Good luck!"

The merchant's companions and their packhorses went by, and Chao exchanged pleasantries with them, but his mind was elsewhere.

CHAO AND HIS family trudged off into the afternoon. The wagons plying the road had formed ruts in the mud, making it difficult to push the handcarts. Chao seemed to grow more disconsolate as the day wore to its close. As evening drew, near both Chao and Qiang were exhausted. Qiang still insisted that his little sister climb up on his cart where the road was particularly muddy. She smiled her gratitude and encouraged him. Indeed, enigmatically, he seemed to find his burden lighter when she was part of his load. Despite the discomfiture, they laughed and joked.

Nuan's heart swelled to see the love of the two siblings for each other, but when she turned to look at her husband, her heart sank. She knew he was suffering silently. The blackness in his mind was mirrored in his visage. She had seen this depression well up in him on many occasions, but she knew that his state of mind, for whatever reason, was worse than she had ever experienced it. She did not know what to do.

Chao was a good person. He had worked so hard to sustain them on their little farm. He took pride in his ability to care for his family. But that had now been taken from him. That was what he thought defined him most—that he was an able provider for his family. That was the ethic his father had drummed into him, that a man must take responsibility for his family. A good man provided well for his wife and his offspring. If only the weather had been kinder, he could have done that.

As Nuan walked alongside him, she put her arm on his back to try to console him. He was so self-obsessed that he didn't even notice.

In the late afternoon, they came to a place where there was a huge pavilion. It was one of the way stations that the emperor maintained so that he and his entourage could get from the summer palace to the winter palace in some comfort. There was a little community around about, whose job it was to prepare the pavilion for the emperor when he came that way. The emperor supported the little community so that on the two occasions he came that way every year, he could be accommodated in comfort. Whether at his instruction or at the whim of those charged with its upkeep, it had been opened up to accommodate the pilgrims passing that way and who had to endure the privations imposed on them by the bad weather.

Gratefully, Chao and his little family took refuge there and prepared to spend the night. Chao knew that the next morning would take them across the Tchi-Tsu River, and they should soon be at his brother's farm.

THERE WERE PERHAPS fifty or sixty travelers sheltering in the emperor's pavilion.

They chatted quietly as they settled in for the night. The keepers of the pavilion had started a fire in a huge fireplace, which was also a cooking fire. There were oil lamps hung strategically around the perimeter of the shelter, the light of which seemed to brighten as the gloom of the outside increased.

Nuan queued up with the other women to take her place at the fireplace to prepare the family's evening meal.

Chao sat and talked to a couple of the fellow travelers. His depressive state of mind seemed to have temporarily left him. He was relieved that his small family had come to this place and did not have to search for shelter this evening after their arduous day's traveling.

Qiang and Lan sat quietly talking. The youth had wrapped his cloak around his little sister, who had begun to feel the chill of the approaching evening.

Lan said, "Brother, I am afraid. I do not know what is to become of us. Our father seems so distraught. The way to our uncle's farm seems so arduous, what with the rain, the mud, and the difficulty in traveling. We do not have many provisions. If we are unduly delayed, we might surely starve.

Qiang smiled reassuringly at his little sister. "Do not concern yourself. All is well."

"I know you mean well, brother, but how can you say that when we are in such a perilous situation? And what about our poor father, who seems so distressed?"

"Well, unfortunately, Father does not know who he is."

"What a strange thing to say. He is Chao, husband of Nuan, father of Qiang and Lan. He is a farmer and provider for us all."

"Unfortunately, that is what he believes."

"Why do you say 'unfortunately'? That is who I believe he is as well."

"Well, in a very superficial sense, you are indeed correct. But I ask you, if his name was different, would he still be the same person?"

"Of course!"

"If he had never married and had no children, would he still be the same person?"

Lan mused over this question. "Well, I suppose he would be."

"And what if he had never been a farmer but perhaps a blacksmith?"

"Well, no! I suspect it would have made no difference to his sense of self."

"There you are, little sister. That is not how he perceives himself at all! Our father has invested so much of himself into being a farmer and a provider for us that now that he cannot be those things, through no fault of his own, he feels his sense of who he is has diminished, and consequently, he suffers. This is a wrong notion, and I feel powerless to convince him otherwise because he has taken such pride in his abilities as a farmer and provider."

Soon after, Nuan came back with their food, having at last gained her turn at the fireplace. "Lan, go fetch your father that we might eat."

Dutifully, Lan went to find her father and led him back to the little family.

QIANG HAD NOTICED that among the travelers were a few merchants. They seemed reasonably wealthy. While his family chatted quietly under the pavilion, he uncovered his roll of manuscripts from his handcart. He separated a few of the manuscripts that he and Lan had manufactured and went to show them to the travelers.

He was surprised to find that there were a few willing buyers. While not paying the generous amounts that his benefactors at the emperor's court had offered, the returns were still ample.

With the money thus acquired, he was able to purchase a cache of food from his fellow travelers, some of which carried such produce to market, sufficient to sustain the family for many days.

When he returned to his family, they were all asleep, except for his mother.

"Qiang, whatever have you been doing?" she asked.

The lad said nothing but showed her the produce he had bought with the proceeds of his sales.

She hugged him. "I do not know what has given you such talents, but you are indeed a special son."

Qiang shook his head. "I am not special, Mother. If I am able to contribute something useful to this difficult world, it is only because of you and my father and the fortunate circumstances I have been privileged to experience."

Nuan kissed him. "Whatever you believe, I believe that the gods have truly blessed me with a son such as you."

EARLY IN THE morning, Qiang woke first, as usual, and engaged himself in his meditation practice. When they had all awoken, they ate a little food left over from the previous night. Chao declined to eat at all and seemed surly and distracted.

Nuan showed her husband the provisions that Qiang had been able to acquire the night before. He was temporarily relieved that their condition was not as perilous as he had previously believed, but before long, the realization that his son had saved them from starvation began to weigh heavily on his mind. Again, he was reminded of his own shortcomings. Surely it was a father's responsibility to provide for a family, not a son's!

Before most of the others who had taken shelter in the pavilion had risen, the little family again resumed their journey.

Qiang tried to cheer his father. "It won't be long now before we are at your brother's place."

Chao merely frowned. He did not know how they would be greeted. He had not seen his brother for many years, but he knew that his brother had a wife, and surely, by now, they would have children. What if his brother thought their arrival was an imposition? In these parts, family was indeed important. But what if the arrival of Chao's family threatened the ability of his brother to care for his own family? Then he would be devastated that not only had he been not only able to provide for his own family but that he had risked the welfare of his brother's family.

The day was clear and fine. Despite the brightness of the day, the little troop progressed with a cloud of darkness over them, emanating from Chao's depression. The going was easier now. The sun had dried the mud, and their feet and the handcarts traversed the terrain with little impediment.

Sometimes, where the mud had been deep, the wheels of the handcarts broke through the firmer surface that the sun-dried crust afforded and were impeded by falling through the crust and having to contend with slush underneath. Fortunately, this was infrequent and short-lived in its impact.

After walking for an hour or so, they came to the river. They trudged along the well-trod path on the south bank of the Tchi-Tsu. The river was high from the recent rains, and it surged with a brown muddy torrent, barely contained by its banks.

At midmorning, they sat beneath a large tree that overhung the path and had a little water. Chao's obvious surliness quelled any inclination for bright conversation. Qiang and Lan sat by themselves, a little removed from their parents, and talked quietly.

After perhaps a half hour's rest, they resumed their journey. The path was busy enough, with other travelers coming and going. Chao led the way, with Nuan trailing close behind. Qiang and Lan lagged a little in the rear. They continued to chat, and occasionally, when Lan tired, Qiang, as usual, would let her sit up on the front of the handcart.

Behind them on the track, going in the same direction, was a solitary horseman. He sat erect, attired in black robes, on the back of a sturdy dark horse. His haughty bearing and noble demeanor was such that the occasional travelers he passed moved quickly to make way for him. His austere dress and aloof manner was enough to dissuade them from conversation.

THE SUN BEAT down from the clear blue sky. The bright light illuminated the landscape and seemed to cheer the travelers. Those they passed gave cheery greetings and smiled at the little family. But neither the weather nor the cheery disposition of the passing travelers could break Chao's somber mood.

He barely noticed the passersby. His mind was in turmoil, full of self-recrimination. Perhaps if he had been a better farmer, perhaps done a little better during the drought, they might have had the wherewithal to pay the emperor's taxes. Maybe there were other crops he could have planted. Perhaps there were cultivation techniques that might have used less water. He replayed these issues in his mind over and over again, which just reinforced his own self-criticism.

Chao was essentially a good man who had strived hard to do what he thought was best. His greatest pride was having cajoled a meager living from a hostile land and caring for his family. Against these measures, he now seemed to be an abject failure. These aspirations, that essentially defined his sense of self, were dashed.

How ironic it seemed that he had endured all the searing years of drought, only to end up alongside a river that was bursting its banks. How he had yearned for a little moisture in his soil to nurture his crops. Now, they had had to overcome mud and water to progress. It seemed as though Nature mocked their puny efforts to escape to a viable future.

There, on their left, was a huge torrent that seemed to laugh at Chao's failure as a farmer—he had struggled to cart a few buckets full of water to sustain a half-dozen plants. The flooded river was tearing trees off its banks in its wild desire. The very elements that he had depended on and were so ungenerous were now so profligate as to taunt him. The lack of water had destroyed his efforts at farming. Its huge abundance was now obstructing his desire to start a new life,

The path wended its way along the riverbank. Whereas in more normal times, the river bed would have been ten meters or more below the riverside path, now, engorged by the floodwaters, the water's level had risen to less than four meters from their feet as they trudged along the path.

Chao stoically led the way, pushing his handcart. He was closely followed by Nuan and Lan. Qiang brought up the rear, pushing the second handcart. When they had set off in the morning, they had distributed their load between the two handcarts. Chao resolutely insisted that the cooking equipment and the farm implements, which were the heavier objects, should be stowed in his cart. Qiang's cart contained some bedding, clothing, the cache of food he had purchased the night before, and, of course, his precious manuscripts.

By noon, Qiang could see his father was tiring. At his insistence they exchanged loads. His father was initially reluctant to do so because this was just confirmation of his inadequacy. But the young man was persuasive and assured Chao that he had made a sufficient contribution by just wheeling his cart thus far. Qiang soon noticed that his father's load had indeed been more than his. But he was young, optimistic, and very resilient.

He knew that pushing the heavy load would not unduly tax his body if his mind was in accord with the universe. From his masters, he had learned many meditative techniques, one of which was walking meditation. He began this practice, and soon the load of the handcart left his consciousness, to be replaced with mindfulness. This, in turn, connected him with the environment around him. He soon heard bird songs, noticed the trees, and appreciated the foliage of the ferns along the way. Even the different textures of the mud and how it had been sculpted by the run-off from the rain interested him.

Finally, in midafternoon, they came to a bend in the river. They approached the point that the bend had projected out into the torrent. From its prominence, they could see a bridge up ahead.

Chao sighed. "At last," he murmured to himself. His memory of the journey to his brother's farm suggested they were now but a day or two away.

Beneath them, the muddy torrent clawed at the vegetation on the river's banks and eroded the soil. Suddenly, without warning, part of the bank washed away into the torrent, taking part of the path with it. The major slip occurred where Nuan and Lan had been walking together, just behind Chao.

Nuan pressed herself against the bank on the slender remnants of the path that still remained. Lan, however, slid with the yielding earth into the river. Alerted by his wife's and daughter's screams Chao turned but had little chance to act before Lan plunged into the river. Fortunately, she was able to grab a sapling on the riverbank, just at the water's edge. Qiang could see her struggling to maintain her hold as the fierce torrent gripped her body and tried to take her with it. Two little forlorn arms were wrapped around the trunk of the small tree as she struggled to hang on and keep her head above the water.

Qiang could see that the girl did not have the strength to long prevail against the river's torrent. Then the path under him began to fall away as well. He abandoned his handcart, slid down the muddy bank, and grasped his little sister. He crooked a strong, long arm around the sapling and held her close to him with his other arm. But he was also immersed in the torrent, with his head and shoulders struggling to rise above it.

On the path above, the instability of the earth was such that Qiang's handcart toppled down the bank as well, fortunately missing the lad and his sister. The cart and its contents were lost in the torrent.

The force of the raging water threatened to wrench Qiang from the little tree. Strangely, he was not afraid. Neither he nor any members of his family could swim, but Qiang knew that even the strongest swimmer would not survive in this great maelstrom attempting to pry him and his little sister from their precarious hold.

He held his sister close. She was terrified, and she sobbed in her despair.

"Do not be afraid, Lan. All is well," he said.

She could hardly believe his words, but as she looked up into Qiang's serene face, her tension was temporarily abated. The force of the water tested the strength of his arm crooked around the sapling. He closed his eyes and tried to draw on the strength of his mind that he had cultivated for so long with his meditation and mindfulness practice.

He could feel the warmth of his little sister's body close to him. How precious she was to him. Then, gradually, his mind overcame the exigencies of this difficult environment. The sapling that he had his arm around seemed to reassure him that it was strong enough to sustain the force of the torrent. In his mind, his arm had grown into the little tree and merged with it. He could feel the strength of the tree's roots, probing into the soil. He immersed himself into the conjunction of tree and earth. He knew now that he could resist the forces of the torrent. Even in this perilous situation, he was able to pause, take few breaths, and still his mind.

Then he called out, "Father, find a rope to let down to us. I need to have you extract Lan from this torrent."

Chao and Nuan were beside themselves with fear. Here were their two children, immersed in the water. The strength of the current was huge. They could see it washing away the bank and undermining the trees along its course. Their hearts were filled with terror. But there was some rope. They had strapped their valued possessions into the handcart with a crisscrossing of rope ties to prevent their precious load from being displaced.

At once, Chao began untying the ropes. After a few minutes he had speedily joined three or four pieces into a longer length of rope and cast it down the river bank. In his haste to rescue Lan and Qiang, he had acted quickly, but he was dismayed by the result. There was not quite enough rope to reach their children ensconced in the extreme force of the water. He quickly pulled the conjoined pieces of rope up to the top of the bank. Then, he noticed there was still a tie across the handcart that he had overlooked. Quickly, he untied it and plaited it on to the other rope segments. He threw it down the riverbank and, to his great relief, was able to place the extended rope next to his son.

Qiang held firmly to the little sapling. "Lan," he said, "you must now hold on to me very tightly because I have to let go of my grip on you to get the rope around you so that you can be raised from the river's clutches."

Lan was terrified, but her brother spoke with great confidence and great authority. He took the end of the rope and passed it around her at the top of her chest and under her armpits. Working with his free hand, he wrapped the rope around itself behind her back. He forced an opening and managed to thread the rope through it.

"Hold tight," he said. Then, with a superhuman effort, he got his torso over her shoulder, took the end of the rope in his teeth, and pulled it tight. He would have liked to have knotted it again, but there was insufficient length. He decided to test the knot.

"Be brave now, Lan. I am going to get Father to take your weight. But I won't let you go until I can be sure that the knot will hold."

Lan nodded.

Qiang then shouted up to Chao, "Father, take up the tension gradually. I want to make sure that I have secured Lan well enough."

The anxious man slowly pulled up the slack in the rope. Lan gritted her teeth as the rope started to bite into her chest. Qiang could see the knot tightening and was confident it would hold.

Finally, he let the girl go and shouted up, "Haul her up now, Father."

Nuan joined Chao in hauling their daughter out of the muddy torrent. She was able to spin around and used her legs to keep her body off the bank, which made the lifting easier. In a moment or so, she lay gasping on the path, alongside her father and mother.

Nuan asked anxiously, "Lan, are you all right?"

"Yes," she said, managing a weak smile, "thanks to my brother's courage."

The effort had exhausted Nuan and Chao. But now they needed to retrieve their son as well.

Nuan crawled across the path to the edge. She stuck her head over to check on her son. What she saw surprised her. The broad face of Qiang was beaming up at her.

"My sister is safe?" he asked.

Nuan nodded.

"The gods have truly blessed us. I am so pleased."

Chao joined his wife at the path's edge. Qiang could see from the strained look on their faces that the ordeal had exhausted them.

"Qiang, I need to get the rope down to you now," said Chao.

"Take your time, Father. I am in no imminent danger. Rest a little while first."

The lad's extraordinary sense of equanimity in the face of such danger was an enigma to his concerned parents. Chao took a few deep breaths. He looked at his wife and daughter. "Can you both help me lift him to safety? He is bigger than Lan, and it will take the strength of all of us to hoist him up."

Lan nodded. "I will do my best, Father. I owe my life to him. But I can't understand why he shows no fear."

Chao shook his head in consternation but then turned to Nuan.

Before he could speak, Nuan nodded. "We have to save him. He is a son worthy of the respect of emperors and the beneficence of the gods. Let us do our best."

Chao, always sensible, said, "I am the largest of us. I will tie the rope around my waist. I weigh more than him, and it is therefore unlikely that he will pull me into the river. Nuan, come behind me, and wrap your arms around me. Lan, I am not sure what help you can give, but if you were to stand alongside me and help me pull, that might be useful."

And so, it was agreed. They readied themselves, and then Chao threw the end of the rope back down to Qiang. Again, it was difficult because the lad, forced to hold firm to the sapling, could only use one arm to get the rope around himself. After a few false starts, he was able to get the rope around his chest and tie a knot.

"Father," he called up, "can you place some tension on the rope so that again I can test the knot?"

Chao duly lay back, using his body weight to tighten the knot.

A few moments later, Qiang shouted, "That is fine, Father. I think the knot will hold. Can you try and lift me up now?"

The three above strained at their task. At first, it was quite difficult. But once they had taken up enough rope, with Chao backing away to keep up the strain, Qiang was free of the water and was able to use his legs. This was helpful in two ways. First, they did not have to drag him up the muddy face of the riverbank, and second, he was also often able to get some purchase on the bank, which relieved the load on those above.

In a moment or two, Qiang was hauled over the edge of the bank and lay gasping on the firm surface of the path. Even in his exhaustion, he smiled up at the exhausted members of his family. "Thank you all," he said. "How wonderful to be back with you again."

Lan lay down next to her brother, hugged him, and cried.

He put his arms around her. "Shush," he said. "All is well."

Nuan smiled, relieved to see her two children safe again. But when she turned to Chao, she could see he was distressed. "Husband, whatever is the matter?"

"Ah, Nuan, the other handcart is now gone. I at least could have gone to my brother's farm and had tools and utensils to help him work the land, but now I have nothing. I will seek his benevolence but have nothing to offer but my bare hands."

She put her arm around him. "Be thankful we still have our children. We will do our best to earn our place with your brother. It will work out."

"I can only hope so," he muttered. But in his mind, again he felt that he had failed them all.

They sat on the path for a little time, gathering their breath, but soon, Chao arose and said, "We must be gone. We have lost our cooking equipment into the river. The food we have will keep us for a little while, but some of it will be of little use now that we can't cook. This is sufficient reason to complete our journey with more urgency."

In deference, the other three arose and readied themselves to go forward.

Lan and Qiang were both wet and muddy from their misadventure, but the weather was mild, and this was no cause for great discomfiture.

Now, as they progressed, they could see the bridge again every now and then through gaps in the trees.

The bridge was an impressive structure. It was a suspension bridge. The only previous such bridges Qiang had encountered spanned small streams, and the bridge floor was suspended from thick ropes that were anchored high on either side of the stream. This bridge seemed to be different, but they were as yet too far removed to see its detail.

THE RIVER BENT a little more to the south now, as did the path, and the bridge was again obscured from view. The trauma of the fall into the river, combined with the effort of walking all day and sometimes having to battle the mud, had wearied the little band. They came to a place where a grassy flat adjoined the riverbank. It was shielded on its southern edge by a rock rampart. A little stream gushed out of a fissure in the rock and made its way over a gravelly bottom to drop into the river. The path led to a little wooden bridge that spanned the stream where it narrowed through a rocky channel about two meters wide.

The sky was clear, and the sun was largely on their backs now. It lit up the grass and brightened their spirits a little. Chao brought the family to a halt.

"Let us rest here for the night. We can wash the mud off ourselves in the stream."

They duly did this, and Lan and Qiang decided they would change their clothes. Qiang took the ropes and the canvas cover off the handcart to find some clothes. He gave a small whoop of glee.

"What is it, son?" Nuan asked.

"Mother, when I acquired our food last night, I forgot that when I stowed it away, I put the rice into the cooking pot and some dried pork in a bowl and some tea in another bowl and then stowed them in the cart. So we are not entirely without the means to cook a meal."

"Oh, that is indeed good news. We can at least have a warm meal tonight to sustain us on our journey tomorrow."

Lan and Qiang duly changed their clothes and then washed their dirty clothes in the stream, wrung them out as best they could, beat them on the rocks alongside the stream in the traditional way, and hung them over a low branch to dry.

Meanwhile, Chao gathered a little fuel and made a fire.

As the sun set, Nuan had made a little meal of rice and pork. They patiently took their turns eating, using the two bowls and their fingers. Nuan insisted, as custom demanded, that if they were to take turns to eat, then Chao and Qiang must eat first. Then they made a little tea, and again, sharing the bowls, each drank a portion.

After the drama and the exertion of the day, it was restful sitting in the waning light around the cooking fire. Nuan, Lan, and Qiang had a congenial conversation. Chao said very little. Soon, he bade them good night and lay on his bed, leaving the others to continue their discussion.

After a time, the others went to their respective beds—a piece of canvas laid out on the ground with a thin blanket to cover them. Soon, they were asleep. But Chao could not sleep. He tossed and turned and ruminated about meeting his brother and how his brother might react at the prospect of four more mouths to feed.

THE MAN IN black dismounted from his horse. He had come to that part of the path where the slip had occurred that took Lan precipitously down into the torrent. He frowned. He hoped that his quarry had passed by without misadventure. He led his sturdy black horse carefully past the slip, compelled, by its incursion onto the pathway, to keep close to the right edge of the track. The sure-footed horse negotiated the hazard without mishap. The man remounted and resumed his pursuit, but superimposed on the steely look of his visage, there was now a sense of concern.

IN THE MORNING, Qiang awoke early. He had a strange sense of foreboding. He was concerned about his father. Chao's state of mind seemed to have deteriorated.

He knew, however, that his best response to these concerns was just to prepare his own mind as well as he could. Accordingly, he arose and walked over to the grassy flat. In the middle of the lush green area was a tallow tree. Qiang sat down on the ample grass, assumed his half-lotus position, and began his meditation.

When done, he went back to the campsite and packed those things the family no longer required for the morning into the handcart. He was gratified that his precious manuscripts, wrapped in their waterproof oilskin cover, fortunately had been stored in the leading handcart and not the one that was lost in the river.

He resuscitated the evening's cooking fire by gathering a little kindling. He placed the kindling on the embers left from the previous night and blew across them. Soon, the fire was rejuvenated, and he added a few twigs and small branches that would continue to sustain it. He took the cooking pot, went to the stream, and filled it with water. It wasn't long before it was bubbling gently over the heat of the fire.

One by one, the others stirred, and as they arose, Qiang gave them each a bowl of tea, rotating the two small bowls among them, as required. After their morning ablutions and a bite or two to eat, they packed their remaining belongings into the handcart. Their campsite lay in the shadow of the rocky escarpment, and the morning was still reasonably cool. Before long, they resumed their journey.

The river and, consequently, the path moved more to the north now, and before long, they rounded a bend. The bridge was evident again, but now it was only a few hundred meters away. Qiang could see what was different about this bridge from the other suspension bridges he had encountered. The bridges he was familiar with had the decking suspended from thick ropes that spanned the stream. Now that they were closer, he could see that this bridge relied on chains with seemingly forged links of steel, which traversed the river's bed, and the bridge decking was suspended from the chains.

Very soon, they arrived at the bridge. It was substantial enough, but it was suspended high above the river, perhaps fifteen meters or so. They stopped at the approach to the bridge. The river was reasonably narrow here, a mere forty meters wide. No doubt this was why the bridge site had been chosen. It rushed through a rocky chasm that constrained its width but, as a result, accelerated the current. Under the bridge, the river ran in a wild, turbulent torrent.

Nuan and Lan appeared afraid. They had watched as a couple of travelers coming from the other side crossed the bridge. The suspension bridge swayed as they traversed the river below, and to the young woman and her mother, making the crossing seemed a dangerous and threatening undertaking.

Qiang sized up the situation. "Father, allow me to escort my mother and sister across the bridge, one at a time. You can stand guard over our possessions. After I have taken the women across, I will come back to help you take our chattel over to the other side."

Chao was in a surly mood. He frowned and contemplated Qiang's words for a moment. Then, he merely nodded his head in agreement.

First, Qiang led his mother over the bridge. "Just hang on to me, Mother, and don't look down. We will be across in a moment."

Nuan clung tightly to her son. Qiang smiled when he saw that she actually had her eyes closed, but soon enough, they came to the other side.

He then went back and attempted to take Lan across.

"Oh, brother," she said, "I am so afraid. I don't think I can walk over the bridge."

"Then you won't have to," responded Qiang. So saying, he gathered her up in his arms and marched across the bridge. She gave a little squeal, but whether it was from fear or mirth, he could not tell. Soon, they had made the crossing, and he placed her on a rock wall, alongside her mother. He looked at them both. "You are both across. Now I must go back and help Father."

As he turned, he could see his father edging his way tentatively onto the bridge.

"Wait, Father! What are you doing?" Qiang shouted.

By this time, Chao was near the center of the bridge. He looked plaintively at this little family. "It is no use," he said. "I can't go on." He then stepped over the chain from which the bridge deck was suspended.

"No, no!" shouted Qiang, and he sprinted over the bridge to his father.

But it was to no avail. Chao launched himself from the deck on the outside of the chain into the torrent.

Nuan and Lan screamed in horror and disbelief.

Qiang was beside himself. He rushed to the point where his father had cast himself into the torrent. He made as if to climb over the chain, but then, to everyone's dismay, a horse with its rider came hurtling across the unstable bridge.

The rider was the fellow dressed in black, who had been following them for some time. He leaped off the horse and grasped Qiang. "Let it be, boy. It is done. There is nothing you or anyone else can do to save him."

By this time, Chao was fifty meters downstream. Occasionally, they could see his head bobbing above the torrent and his arms flailing ineffectually. But in a moment or so, it was over.

Qiang fell to the deck of the bridge and sobbed.

The rider pressed his hands on the boy's back. "It is done, I said. Do not indulge in guilt. There was nothing you could do. It is over. The best thing you can do is comfort your family. Here—lead my horse across the bridge to your family. I will retrieve the handcart that was lodged on the other side of the bridge." He paused a moment, and his eyes softened somewhat. "It is natural that you should experience grief for the loss of a parent, but don't dwell on it. It shall pass. And although you can't see it now through all your pain, you need to accept that all is well."

The lad could see that the man was right, at least in part. As heart-wrenching as it might be, his father had been swallowed up in the torrent, beyond the compass of any mortal to rescue. With tears streaming down his face, he walked slowly back across the bridge, leading the sturdy black horse toward his mother and sister, who stood on the bank, embracing each other and wailing inconsolably.

His mind was as turbulent as the waters that surged under the bridge. Despite the wisdom of the man's words—words that he had used many times himself—he found it impossible to accept that "all is well."

QIANG'S HEAD WAS spinning and his heart was hurting as a result of his father's action. His mind resonated with the words of the man who rode the horse.

"It is done," he had said. "Don't feel guilt."

It was so surreal. He now had disassociated himself from his pain. He paid attention to his breathing. He became aware of his steps as he crossed the bridge. He heard quite clearly the distressing sounds of his mother and sister, but they were just sounds. Although their cries were filled with anguish, and he felt desperately for them, his mind had withdrawn from the emotion to somewhere remote, and soon his mind gained clarity and equanimity again.

This was the worst moment of his life. He had wept with anguish to see his father washed away in the torrent. How could life go on now?

The man's admonition echoed in Qiang's mind. "It is done."

And truly, it was done. He had lost his father. There was nothing now that he could do to change that. He knew from his previous instruction that it was unwise to have his sense of well-being attached to anything peripheral, transient, and unsubstantial. Surely attachment to our parents is a natural human quality, he thought. To lose one's father and to see him die before your eyes is a heart-wrenching experience.

Qiang had loved his father. Of course, he was aware of Chao's shortcomings, but he admired his dedication and his tenacity. He had worked so hard to care for his little family, but in the end, Chao could not meet these expectations of himself, and that was his undoing. He was basically a good man who had devoted his life to the welfare of his family.

When Qiang came to the end of the bridge, he tethered the horse. He gathered his thoughts before going to console his mother and sister.

He knew that life now would be very different. In his society, men led the household. Without his father, that role would now fall to him. Despite his great regard for both his mother and his sister and their own good sense and intelligence, because of cultural imperatives, it was inevitable that they would turn to him for guidance. This imposed on him a huge responsibility. He now needed to be the emotional anchor in their lives. He must be a role model for them. He could not afford to be self-indulgent. He looked away for a moment to compose himself, wiped the tears from his eyes, and then went to his mother and sister.

He gently placed his arms around them. He made no attempt to speak. Indeed, he was not sure that he could do so without sobbing again. But under his strong, warm embrace, Nuan and Lan finally stopped crying and wailing. For a minute or two, the three just embraced each other silently.

After a time, Nuan looked imploringly at her son and said, "Why? Why would Chao take his own life? Did he not know that I loved him? Did he not know that though we have suffered, I apportioned no blame to him? Did he not know that although things went bad for us, I knew he did as well as he could?" Then she fell, sobbing, into her son's strong arms. It was an excruciating experience for Qiang. He could not think for a moment. He merely reiterated the words of the austere man. "It is done, Mother. There is nothing now that we can do to make it otherwise."

Nuan sobbed uncontrollably. Qiang gathered his thoughts. He breathed deeply. He tried to enter into a meditative state. Finally, he said, "My father was a good man. At all times, he tried to do what he thought was best for our family. If there was a fault, it was that he was too good. He tried to do things for our benefit that were beyond his capacity. There is no shame in that. I will remember him and respect him for all the days of my life. We are sad now for his passing, but we should not be. We should be grateful that we had such a man to care for us. He was wrong to believe that he was responsible for our poor fortune, and we shall not remember him in this way. We will remember him as one who strove, with his best endeavors, to provide for us. But he is gone, Mother. It is time now to fashion a life without him."

THE MAN IN black approached with the handcart. Although he looked gaunt, Qiang could see strength in his upright bearing and his sinewy arms and square shoulders. He pushed the cart up to the three. "Here are your things. You don't seem to have much here."

"No, sir," replied Qiang. "We lost quite a few of our possessions back along the track. There was a land slip that took our other handcart into the river."

"My son almost lost his life, saving my daughter from the torrent," said Nuan, her voice still trembling with emotion. Her sorrow could not hide her pride.

"Mother," said Qiang, looking at the man and then turning to Nuan, "I know this man. He is the one who bought the manuscript with the words of the venerable Dogen Zenji from me at the emperor's court."

Nuan eyes opened a little in surprise. "We thank you for your generosity, sir."

"Don't thank me, madam. I have other plans for this fellow. Where are you headed?"

Qiang was surprised at this statement but answered the query attached to it. "Sir, we are headed to my uncle's farm."

"And who might your uncle be?"

Qiang related his uncle's name.

The man raised his eyebrows. "Then you have wasted your time."

"What do you mean?" asked Nuan anxiously.

"That fellow left years ago. Why, it likely would be ten years since he worked that farm."

Nuan raised her hand to her mouth. "Oh, no!" she exclaimed. "I have lost my husband, and now we have nowhere to go." She sobbed a little, and Lan tried to comfort her. Then she looked up at the man. "But, sir, who are you that I should trust your word in these matters?"

The steely countenance of the austere man did not flinch at the implied slight. "Madam, my family name is Ruan Xiu. I am the provincial governor of Fang Sho province. Once you crossed the river, you entered the territory that is under my jurisdiction."

Qiang raised his eyebrows. "Sir, you say that your family name is Ruan Xiu. Do you go by other names?"

The man laughed. "Indeed, I do."

"Then pray tell us what are they."

"You are not ready to know my other names, young man."

Nuan was not done. "It defies belief that if you are the exalted regional governor that you would ride by yourself with no retinue. How do we know that you are not a charlatan or a thief?"

He looked into Nuan's face, the broad lovely face of the protective mother and bereaved widow. He hesitated a moment and then responded. "Well, madam, you have no way of knowing. It probably won't help to tell you that I am not afraid to travel alone. I am well equipped to look after myself. And indeed, once I am here in my own territory, in Fang Sho, I am quite confident that no evil will be done to me, and no evil will be done to you. Of course, you can only take my word for this, and I have no convincing proof immediately at hand."

Qiang looked at Nuan. "Mother, I believe him. He was, after all, at the emperor's court." Then Qiang turned to the governor. "And sir, what did you mean when you said you had other plans for me?"

"Well, young man, from our previous encounter, I knew you were much more than a farmer's son. You demonstrated some rare qualities that should not be wasted. Some of my colleagues have confirmed these qualities as well. The tax collectors reported to the court that your family had abandoned your farm. I was keen to find you so that you were not lost to us. It was not hard to follow your trail, once I made up my mind to find you."

Qiang was bewildered by all this. "Who are these colleagues who have told you about me?"

The man assumed a supercilious visage and laughed haughtily, "Never mind who they are; they are just colleagues whose opinions

I trust." He looked at Nuan, in particular. "Now, what do you wish to do?"

Nuan looked at her children. Her concern was reflected in her face. She turned to face the man. "In truth, sir, I do not know. It seems all our options are gone. We cannot go back. We have been dispossessed of the farm. Yet we cannot go forward because my husband's brother is no longer here to give us succor."

Qiang put his arm around her and took his little sister's hand. "Do not fear, Mother. We will find a way. Despite the fact that we have had a terrible experience today, we still have each other. Do you remember the man who taught me to meditate? He used to sit at the base of the large tree on my way to school."

Nuan nodded.

"He taught me that despite what might happen in the material world, 'all is well.' The problems only exist in our minds. It is natural that we should feel sadness for the loss of a father and a husband who tried his best. But he is gone now, and our ongoing well-being does not require him. I mean no disrespect, for I saw how hard he tried to make a living for us. But we must now put that behind us."

The austere man raised his eyebrows at this utterance and nodded his approval. Nuan, Lan, and Qiang, however, did not see this response. They were engaged in the dilemma of their own circumstances and what to do about it.

"Qiang, I know I will miss your father terribly. How can I be happy without him?"

"We will all miss him, Mother, and that is natural. But I am sure we can still learn to be happy without him."

"Oh, brother," murmured Lan, "can you be so heartless?"

"Ah, little sister, holding on to the image of our father as the only way to happiness is fraught with problems. If we believe that the only way that we could be happy is to have him with us, we will soon be bound by blame and guilt. If we needed him so much, how long will it be before we say how heartless he was to take his own life, with no concern for us? Or perhaps we will ask, what did we do to drive him to his death? Let us be satisfied that he did the best he could. He wasn't heartless. He just expected more of himself than was humanly possible.

And we are not to blame. We loved him as best we could, and we will retain a proud memory of him in our hearts, as a husband and father who strove manfully to care for his family.

"And more than that, if we believe that the only way that we could be happy is to have him with us, then we have doomed the rest of our lives to despair. I don't want that, nor do I want it for you and our mother. And it is quite possible we would have lost him anyhow to disease, misadventure, or, eventually, old age. It is not wise to peg our sense of well-being on such ephemeral things. Let us grieve for him. And let us mourn. But let us also be confident that this shall pass, and while we may miss him, it is possible for us to be happy again without him.

Nuan and Lan both sobbed a little, and Qiang embraced them both. The austere man turned his head and walked a few paces away so as not to disturb their grief and mourning. He led his horse off the path and, holding its halter, sat down on a flat boulder while the little family came to grips with their loss.

NUAN, LAN, AND Qiang huddled together for some time. Nuan and Lan wept, and Qiang tried his best to console them.

Finally, Nuan, ever practical, stopped and looked at her children. "Stop, now. This will never do. We have to make a decision on what we should do now. It seems we have no options left. We cannot return because we have no farm to return to. We can't go to your father's brother's farm, as it seems he is no longer there."

Qiang released the others from his embrace. "We are at a loss, Mother, because we don't know anything about this district. I wonder if there is anywhere I might be able to find work to keep you both?"

Lan was a little indignant at this suggestion. "I am not so useless, brother, that I could not be put to work as well."

Qiang smiled at his courageous little sister. "You are indeed capable, little orchid, but our first task is to source what opportunities there might be."

Nuan nodded her head. "You are right, son, but how might we do this?"

"Well, I suggest we might start by asking the governor."

He turned to Ruan Xiu. The man had been observing the little family, waiting until they might temporarily cease their mourning, such that he might have an opportunity to talk with them.

"Sir," Qiang said, "would you join us so we can seek some counsel?"

"I would be happy to try to help," Ruan Xiu responded. "What is it that you would know?"

"In light of our circumstances, we feel we can neither go forward nor back. If it is possible, I would like to seek employment." Then he glanced at Lan. "And perhaps my little sister as well, somewhere nearby."

The austere man laughed.

Qiang raised his eyebrows at this. "Tell me, sir, what is it that you find amusing?"

"You don't understand, boy. You are now on my estate, and the only employer is me! You would need to walk for many days again to find someone else who might pay for your labor. Even the farm that your uncle once worked is now mine. Do you wish to work for me? I will offer you employment, but don't take my offer lightly, for I have high expectations of you."

Qiang looked puzzled. "But sir, what could you possibly expect of me?"

"If you work for me, Takygulpa, I will test you in every way. This won't be easy for you."

Again, Qiang and Nuan were intrigued that Ruan Xiu called him by the name his previous teachers had bestowed on him.

Before Qiang could respond, the governor continued. "But if you come to work with me, I will make this promise to you. Your mother will never want for anything, and your sister will be found appropriate employment."

Qiang seemed a little perplexed, but he quickly responded, "Your offer, on the face of it, seems generous. Let us be alone a while to consider it."

"Certainly," the man responded, "but let me reiterate that while I will provide for your sister and mother generously, it will not be easy for you." So saying, Ruan Xiu moved away, out of earshot, and resumed sitting on the rock.

NUAN AND LAN seemed agitated by what Ruan Xiu had said.

Nuan blurted out, "Son, I don't want you to go with this man. I am afraid for you."

Lan nodded her agreement. "He said it will be difficult for you."

Qiang shook his head. "If I don't go, it will be even more difficult. How can I care for both of you without income? If you are both secure and provisioned for, then I can bear whatever he does with me."

"I do not trust him," Nuan said.

"Strangely, Mother, while he seems harsh and difficult, I believe he means no ill to me. I can bear a life of deprivation and hardship, provided I know you will be cared for. I am inclined to accept his offer. I do not see an alternative."

Lan frowned, but then she nodded. "I believe he is right, Mother. We have no other option."

Tears ran down the old lady's face. "I, who have just lost a husband, have no desire to see my son harmed. But perhaps you are right, and there is no other option. In our tradition, with your father gone, you must now speak for the household."

Qiang comforted his mother. "I will be all right, Mother, if I can be assured that your welfare is secure. I am, I think, reasonably resilient, and I am not reluctant to be tested if it leads to learning."

The young man beckoned to Ruan Xiu.

As Ruan Xiu drew closer, he inquired, "What is your decision?"

"Sir, my decision depends what assurance you can give me that you will properly care for my mother and sister."

The man directed a steely look at Qiang. "I have given you my word as an imperial governor. Surely that should be enough."

Qiang stood his ground. "That may well be the case, sir, but I hardly know you, and I cannot guarantee you are who you say you are."

Ruan Xiu glared at Qiang. "That is impertinent, boy."

"I know it may seem so, sir, but you see, I would be entrusting you not only with my life, but, more importantly, with the lives of my mother and sister. They mean more than anything to me. If I am to risk my life with you, I need certainty about their welfare."

The steely face softened somewhat. "All right. I will give you this undertaking. When we arrive at my palace, I will write up a deed, setting out my obligations to your mother and sister, and affix my seal upon it."

Qiang knew that no court official would contemplate breaking an undertaking so sealed. It would incur the wrath of the emperor himself.

"I will not require you to enter into my service until this undertaking is met."

Qiang nodded. "Thank you, sir. I could ask for no more. Under these conditions, I will agree to your proposal."

The austere man nodded. "You have chosen well. This will not be easy for you, but it is necessary if we are to make something of you."

Despite the man's continuing enigmatic statements Qiang did not question him, except to inquire, "Sir, how far is it to your palace?"

"Less than two days' walk."

Qiang turned to ready the family for the trek.

RUAN XIU LED the little party down the track. The path meandered by the riverbank, and even when the river was not in sight, the roar of the torrent was audible. The governor rode in front on his sturdy black steed. In deference to the walkers, he walked the horse slowly, but even so, he would sometimes get a little ahead and then wait for them to catch up.

It was a somber party because as they walked, Nuan, Lan, and Qiang bore with them the memories of Chao. Qiang was lost in a reverie, reliving his memories of his father. But to Nuan and Lan, the memory of Chao's death was still a burden, and each, in turn, wondered at her own culpability in his suicide. Nuan did not talk at all, but Qiang and Lan spoke occasionally, in hushed whispers, of their most precious memories of their father. Nuan was quietly stoic, but Lan openly wept as she walked.

They were walking up the river valley, and as they went toward its headwaters, the river grew a little narrower. When they could see it, it appeared now that there were more rapids and cataracts, and the current was swift.

By midafternoon, they came to a fork in the path. Ruan Xiu waited for the walkers to catch up. He pointed to the path on his left. "This is the way we must go now." He looked down and, with some concern on his face, addressed Nuan. "Madam, you seem to be tiring a little." He dismounted from his horse. "Here—sit up here and let my horse, Xun, carry you."

Nuan was taken aback by this offer. "I am happy to walk, Governor. My legs may be old, but they are still sturdy."

"I can see that is true, madam, but a matriarch such as yourself should be accorded some privileges."

"But sir, I have never ridden on a horse, and surely I would fall off, which might cause me greater discomfort than aching legs!"

The man laughed. "My horse is called Xun, which, in the dialect of these parts, means *swift.* But he is an intelligent fellow, and when carrying a precious burden, he is quite careful and gentle. Hold softly onto the reins. They will help steady you."

So saying, he hoisted the surprised peasant woman up onto his horse. He took the horse by the halter and led it slowly down the path.

Qiang and Lan were a little dismayed by this turn of events but appreciated the man's concern.

"Ho, Mother, you will see more of the world up there!" Lan said with a laugh. "Don't gallop off too far in front, or we might lose you!"

Within minutes, the woman was comfortable and stroked the horse's neck soothingly. She had always had an affinity for animals. She smiled, for her family's sake.

Despite his gruff manner, this man might have some human concerns. For Qiang's sake, Nuan hoped so.

THE PATH TOOK the travelers farther into the forested slopes of a high plateau. The going was largely uphill now, and Qiang was glad that Ruan Xiu had removed the burden of walking from his mother.

As the forest thickened, the trees began to form a canopy across the path, thus shielding it from the sun. They walked largely in shadow now, occasionally interspersed with a little dappled sunlight where the canopy was thinner. The increasing altitude, combined with the absence of the sun's warming rays, resulted in a chill. Qiang knew that they were likely in for a cold night.

Late in the afternoon, he strode past Lan and went to talk to the austere man.

Ruan Xiu seemed to sense his approach and turned to face him. "What troubles you?" he asked.

"Sir, I am concerned for my sister and, more particularly, my mother. It is getting cold, and we need to find somewhere to spend the night. We don't have much bedding or clothing to ward off the cold. Therefore, it is essential that we find somewhere sheltered and out of the weather to sleep tonight."

"Do you think I am unaware of that?" the man responded curtly. "Don't take me for a fool, boy!"

Nuan had overheard the exchange. "Don't be concerned on my behalf, son. I will make do."

Ruan Xiu had resumed leading the horse. He strode purposefully on along the path.

Qiang sensed it would not be to any avail to pursue the matter further. Qiang dropped back and resumed walking with Lan. Because of her exhaustion, she did not have the energy to query him about his discussion with the governor.

On they marched, and the light became quite gloomy, so much so that the walkers had to watch carefully so as not to trip over the occasional branch that had fallen on the track. Qiang could now barely distinguish his mother's tiny form on the horse's back, even though she was barely forty meters ahead. He and Lan walked steadfastly on, wearied by the long climb uphill and becoming chilled in the still evening air.

They were unaware that the man and his horse with their mother on it had left the track until they heard a loud call from their right.

"Stop! This is where we will spend the night!"

They stumbled through the gloom to find the man unloading their mother from the horse in front of what appeared to be a wooden hut. He tethered the horse to a post in front of the building. He unstrapped a roll that was attached to the rear of his saddle. He went inside, carrying the roll, and fumbled around for a moment or two. To their surprise, he returned with an oil lamp, showing the way in the deepening gloom. "Bring inside what you need for the night," he commanded.

Qiang and Lan dutifully unloaded the handcart with the appropriate items of bedding and clothing. While they did this, Ruan Xiu helped Nuan inside and made her comfortable on a long bench seat aside a rough-hewn table.

When Qiang and Lan entered, they were surprised to see that there was a fireplace in the hut and a neatly stacked pile of firewood, cut to length, alongside it.

The austere man looked at the young man a moment and then said, "Qiang, take this bucket, go to the well at the rear, and draw some water. Put a bucketful in the trough near where I tethered Xun; then bring a bucketful back in here. We can use a little for cooking, and then we might have enough to wash in."

Qiang was perplexed because this was the first time the governor had called him by his given name.

Then the man turned to Lan. "And, little sister, are you able to cook us a little rice? I have some dried pork and a few herbs as well, if you can use them. The clay jar to the left of the fireplace contains rice."

On hearing this, Nuan protested, "Oh no, sir, let me cook for us. It is my duty to prepare food for the household."

But the man would have none of it. "No, madam. I want you to sit there and rest. These able-bodied children of yours will provide for us."

Lan smiled. "He is right, Mother. You have taught me to cook well enough. I know my meal won't be as delicious as yours would have been, but it will suffice. Rest your legs."

"Do you have cooking equipment?" he asked.

Lan nodded. "I will retrieve the necessary items from the handcart."

The young woman went off to find the requisite cooking pot, utensils, and ingredients to prepare the meal.

For a time, all were busy with their chores, preparing the meal, drawing the water, preparing the bedding, and making preparations for the night. As they did so, the evening grew quite chill. The man unwrapped the roll that he had carried on the back of the horse. In it was a blanket, which he draped over Nuan's old shoulders.

Soon enough, Lan had prepared the meal, and they ate it with relish. Nuan was quietly pleased with her daughter's efforts.

When they finished, they sat a little while in the pale light of the oil lamp, drinking tea.

Qiang asked, "Sir, how is it that when we came to this place, there was already firewood gathered and a jar of rice by the fireplace?"

"I care for my people, boy. Many of them have to travel for trade and other reasons. As a result, in my province, I maintain many such way stations, which I pay local people to maintain with firewood and modest provisions."

Qiang shook his head in wonderment. "You are very generous, sir, and we thank you for your generosity. It has made us comfortable in a night that otherwise might not have been so."

"I am pleased to take care of the comfort of your mother and sister. But that is not what I have in mind for you. For you, there are lessons to be learned."

Nuan frowned and was about to speak, but Qiang intervened. "I am gratified, sir, that you will care for my mother and my sister. If I know that their welfare is secure, I will not resile from any tests you might care to set for me."

Ruan Xiu laughed ruefully. "We will see! We will see! We must now get some rest, for tomorrow we will finish our journey. Now, madam," he said, turning to Nuan, "we must make you comfortable for the night." So saying, he withdrew from his bedroll a thin, down-filled palliasse, which he laid on the floor in front of the fireplace. "Come," he said to Nuan, "you will sleep here." He turned to Lan. "And you, young lady—what bedding have you got?"

"Well, sir, we lost most of what we had when our handcart plunged into the river, but there is still a blanket or two, even though they are very thin."

"Then they will have to suffice. Take them and put them on the floor here, in front of your mother."

"But no, sir, I cannot do that, for there will be nothing to warm my brother." She began to weep. "I do not know what you expect of Qiang, but I cannot see him freeze. Why, only this morning, he plunged into the river to save me. Let me share my blanket with him."

Nuan's mind cast back to the time when Qiang was young, and he had given his blanket to his sister when she was whimpering from the cold. She remembered how he had stoically sat through the cold night with no blanket and how surprised she was, when she tried to cover him, by how warm his little body was. She smiled and turned to comfort Lan. "Take the blankets, daughter. I suspect you will have more need of them than Qiang."

Lan reluctantly obeyed. While it hurt her to deprive Qiang, she could no more disobey her mother than fly to the moon.

Qiang smiled reassuringly at his sister. "Mother is right, Lan. Make yourself as comfortable as possible. Do not be afraid. I have a warm place to go to."

Ruan Xiu raised his eyebrows at this statement but said nothing. He helped Lan with her blankets and then added a little wood to the fire.

Qiang had wrapped himself in his cloak. He removed himself to a corner of the room and sat cross-legged on the floor. His eyes were closed, and his breathing was regular and slow.

Ruan Xiu had a thickly padded coat that reached almost to the floor. He lay down on the floor directly across from Qiang, wrapped a single blanket around himself, and, seeing that the other three had settled, blew out the oil lamp.

The warmth from the fireplace provided comfort to Nuan and, to a lesser extent, Lan, and soon they were both asleep. But the warmth had well and truly exhausted itself before it could reach the far corners of the room, where Ruan Xiu and Qiang had positioned themselves.

THE GOVERNOR AWOKE in the early hours of the morning. The fire had burned down, and now there were just a couple of pale embers glowing in the dark. It was bitterly cold. The old lady seemed comfortable enough, but Lan, though asleep, seemed restless. He suspected that with the sparse protection of her thin blankets, she was feeling the cold. He arose and, treading carefully so as not to wake up the two women, added a little more fuel to the fire and stirred the embers with a poker until a small flame appeared. Satisfied that the fire would rekindle, he retired to his corner.

The light of the flame enabled him to observe the room a little clearer. To his surprise, Qiang still sat cross-legged in his meditation posture, his back straight and his eyes seemingly closed. He shook his head incredulously before seeking the warmth of his blanket and going back to sleep.

RUAN XIU AWOKE slowly. He lay on the floor with his eyes closed. As sleep receded, he became aware of a few sounds. First, there was birdsong. Because of this, he deduced it was morning. There also was the sound of people talking quietly. Without opening his eyes, he knew from their voices it was Lan and Qiang, murmuring to each other. He was glad the cold night had passed; even with the protection of his blanket and coat, his bones ached. He could feel a little more warmth now and wondered why because it was still quite early. It was hard to tell if the sun had risen because the door was closed, as was the shutter over the aperture that served as a window. But his keen senses told him that the fire had been rekindled. He could hear crackling from the burning wood and smelled smoke.

"Oh, brother, I am so sorry that I could not lend you a blanket. The governor seemed not to want you to sleep in comfort, and I was so surprised that Mother also was prepared to leave you at the mercy of the elements. And it was such a cold night! I could only sleep fitfully, and it is indeed a great relief to be sitting again in front of the fire and drinking tea with you. I cannot understand how you seem so relaxed and comfortable. You must have spent a dreadful night. I would not be surprised if you did not sleep at all."

Ruan Xiu lay motionless. He too was interested in the source of Qiang's stoicism. He determined not to interrupt this conversation until he had found some answers.

Qiang laughed quietly. "Oh, little sister, how I love you! You are always concerned about my well-being! But to tell the truth, I was not cold at all."

"But brother, how can that be? You spent the entire night uncovered, except for your cloak, and once the fire burned down, it was bitterly cold."

"Well, little sister, I have asked you this question before, but where does our sense of well-being come from? Do you think it comes from our physical environment?"

"No, Qiang, you have told me it comes from our inner world."

"Indeed, that is right; it comes from our minds. And when the room got cold, I retreated to a warm place in my mind. It is a pleasant place I go sometimes when I need to."

"I must confess your body feels warm enough."

The governor opened his eyes and lifted his shoulders from the floor. In the light of the fire, he could see Qiang sitting with his sister with his arm around her. She still had a blanket around her shoulders. They each had a bowl of tea in their hands.

Ever aware, Qiang said, "I believe the governor has awakened." Turning to face Ruan Xiu, he asked, "Would you like some tea, sir?"

IT WAS NOW several hours since they had left the way station.

The governor had placed Nuan on his horse again. Nuan was beginning to enjoy riding. Qiang and Lan were happy to see that she didn't have to struggle up the steep mountain path. Ruan Xiu walked in front, leading the sturdy little horse. Qiang and Lan walked together in the rear, chatting amicably as Qiang pushed their handcart. The cold of the night had largely dissipated. The sun had warmed them, but the air was still chill enough that the travelers wore coats or cloaks.

As the little party ascended, the forest grew a little sparser, and the trees were shorter and more gnarled, reflecting the higher altitude and the colder clime. At midmorning, they stopped for a short rest near a small spring. After drinking a little, they sat on the grassy bank alongside the spring, while the governor watered his horse. When the horse had its fill, the man withdrew something from the roll strapped to the horse's back. It seemed to be a leather gauntlet. He carefully wrapped it around his wrist and fastened it with a number of buckles affixed along its length.

Ruan Xiu turned to instruct his companions that they should recommence their journey and saw an enquiring look in Qiang's eyes. "Not seen one of these before, boy?"

"No, sir," Qiang responded. "What is it for?"

"You will see soon enough."

So saying, he hoisted Nuan back up on to the little steed, took hold of its halter, and headed off again up the mountain path.

Although the path continued upward, it was now not particularly arduous. The path was more level, and the trees were a little bigger and more verdant, reflecting the better soil. Qiang, being a farmer's son, could imagine that crops could be grown here. He suddenly remembered his father and his unfortunate demise. Because of the distractions of the last day, he had put thoughts of his father aside. He began to feel guilty that perhaps he should have shown more sorrow. But then, he remembered the words of his mentor, Chagsarka Rinpoche: "Of all the afflictive emotions, guilt is the most destructive. Guilt renders us ineffectual. It smites us with anguish, while preventing us from doing useful things."

Qiang was enjoying the walk now. He had no concerns for his mother, as she was astride the horse. Lan was robust and strong and showed no stress from this morning's walk.

The path led them up a rocky ravine which was closed in with high walls of rock dominating both sides. Atop the rocks were surprisingly large trees. The canopy they made almost created a tunnel for the travelers below.

For some reason, Qiang felt uneasy. It seemed incongruous to him that after a mere half hour, his sense of well-being suddenly was replaced with concern. There was nothing obvious here to be concerned about.

They came to a place where the canopy thinned, and before long, they were in a space covered in sunshine. Looking up, Qiang could see an expanse of clear blue sky above them. Ruan Xiu stopped walking, and seemed to be listening to something. Qiang put down his handcart and walked up to him.

"What is it, sir?" Qiang asked.

"Hush, listen," came the reply.

Then he heard it—a high-pitched repetitive shriek, coming from above. He looked up, and at a considerable distance in the sky above, he saw a speck, obviously a bird at height.

To his surprise, Ruan Xiu let out a high-pitched whistle.

In response, the bird plummeted from the sky. Its descent was so rapid and precipitous that Qiang gasped. Surely it could not drop at such speed and brake sufficiently to avoid being dashed on the rocks. But at the last moment, it stretched its wings wide, with its pinions slightly reversed, and alighted gently on the governor's arm.

Qiang had never seen such a remarkable creature. Its head and the upper side of its wings were black. Its chest was chestnut, with black bars running horizontally across it. It presented a very regal and elegant figure.

Ruan Xiu could see the astonished look on Qiang's face. "What is it, boy? Have you never seen a falcon?"

"I don't believe so, sir. It is truly a magnificent bird!"

"Indeed, he is. He is called Xiang, which in our dialect means 'to soar.' And as you can see, he not only can soar but can fly at great speed."

As the governor talked to Qiang, he gently stroked the top of the bird's head. It was difficult to tell whether the bird enjoyed this attention or not because its eyes maintained a fixed, unemotional gaze.

"So then, sir—you were expecting the bird? That is why you laced the gauntlet onto your arm?"

"Indeed. We are now close to my palace. The bird's handlers knew I was returning today, and they would have released the bird to find me. I am very fond of the bird, and I love to see him, but the practice serves another purpose. If he had returned to his keep, they would have had concern about my welfare and sent some out to find me. The bird has such keen eyesight that from his elevated vantage point he will always find me if I am near. Come; let us resume our march."

Off they went again, with Ruan Xiu leading the way, guiding his little horse with Nuan on board and now with the falcon attached to his forearm. Qiang pushed the handcart, and Lan walked alongside.

FOR A HALF hour or so, they made steady progress. The canopy had closed over again, and Qiang got only fleeting glimpses of the sky above.

It was eerie to follow the trail, almost as though they were walking through a tunnel, with rocky ramparts on each side and a leafy roof above.

Then, suddenly, there came a loud sound from just in front of them. The horse, which had been so placid during the journey, suddenly reared up, almost causing Nuan to be unseated. Ruan Xiu held tightly onto the halter, and Nuan, clinging desperately to the reins, managed to stay on the horse.

"Go back!" yelled the governor, quickly turning the horse around and jogging back down the track, leading the horse with Nuan astride.

Qiang turned around between the shafts of the hand cart and pulled, rather than pushed, it back down the track, with Lan in pursuit.

Then followed a mighty roar, which Qiang immediately knew was the sound of a huge tree falling behind them.

"You can stop now," called Ruan Xiu.

They gathered themselves and then looked to see what had necessitated their flight.

Almost at the spot where Ruan Xiu had halted the horse, the detritus of a large tree blocked the way. It was obviously a softwood variety, and the impact had shattered the tree into many pieces completely impeding the path. The gaunt man looked over the predicament.

Qiang looked inquiringly at the governor. "What will we do, sir?"

Ruan Xiu looked at the mountain of debris in front of them. He thought for a moment. "There is nothing else for it, lad. We will have to shift enough of it for us to get by. If we go back, the alternative route to the palace will take many days to traverse. We can, however, send for help."

He rummaged in his pack and pulled out a small piece of parchment and a piece of charcoal. With a few deft strokes, he drew some characters on its surface and then rolled it into a small tube. He inserted the tube into a tiny metal cylinder. He then called the falcon to him. He spoke soothingly to the bird, which sat stationary on his arm as he tied the cylinder to its leg. He then raised his arm and whispered something to the bird, which immediately took flight and, giving a single shriek, circled steeply into the sky and then was off, like an arrow, to the northwest.

The governor turned to the others. "Xiang will bring help, but it might take some time. In the meantime, we should begin clearing the path."

Qiang looked at Lan and Nuan. He turned to the austere man and shook his head. "That is indeed a daunting task."

Ruan Xiu laughed. "Come, boy," he said, and his voice was like cold steel. "It is time to prove yourself."

The limbs of the tree were quite brittle and had shattered into many pieces. As a result, the task was not as daunting as Qiang had first thought. Methodically, they worked their way into the pile of timber, seizing what they could and pulling it back to where the path was a little wider and stacking on the side of the path. Lan and Nuan did what they could to help. After a time, Qiang could see his mother was struggling. Before he could say or do anything, Ruan Xiu went to her.

"Madam, my horse has been startled by these events. I should tend to him and comfort him, but I must continue with this work. Would you be so good as to take his halter and lead him into the shade, back along the track, and comfort him?"

Nuan paused. She was weary and her back hurt, but she was stubborn and resolute. She wished to contribute. If the governor had asked her to rest, she would have resisted, but she could see the horse was trembling. She had grown fond of the animal that had carried her these last few days and was upset to see it in distress.

She paused a moment and then nodded her head. "Yes, sir, I will do that, but as soon as the animal settles, I will return to help you."

"Very well," agreed Ruan Xiu. He took hold of the halter and led the horse to Nuan, murmuring consoling words as he went. The old lady then led the animal back into the shade, stroking his head and making soothing noises.

Qiang smiled as he worked. This austere man seemed to have a heart and displayed an empathy that belied his severe appearance.

After a time, all the small branches and foliage were cleared away. Lan was exhausted from the exertion.

Qiang said, "Lan, a little way down the track there was a streamlet. Would you mind going back and collecting some water for us? This strenuous work has made me thirsty."

Ruan Xiu had overheard Qiang's request.

"Good thinking, lad," he said. "I could do with a drink as well. And Lan, if you could, would you have your mother take the little horse back with you so that he might drink also?"

Lan gratefully nodded her head. And within a minute or two, the young woman, her mother, and the sturdy little horse were walking back down the track.

Qiang and Ruan Xiu watched them go. When they had disappeared around a bend in the track, the austere man turned to Qiang and said, "Now, young man, let us see what you are made of."

WITH THE SMALLER branches and foliage removed, it was apparent that the track was blocked by two sections of the main trunk of the tree. The force of the impact had shattered the trunk. Closest to them was the top part of the trunk, lying directly across the path. It was about four meters long and mostly just above the height of Qiang's knees. Behind that, there was a slightly longer and thicker piece of the trunk, which lay diagonally across the track.

Ruan Xiu clambered over the first log and stood on the other side. "Let's get this piece out of the way first."

Looking at the size of the log, Qiang frowned. He had his doubts that they could shift it. Nevertheless, he climbed over it and joined the governor on the other side.

"This particular tree is a softwood and the timber comprising it is not very dense. We should have little trouble shifting it," the governor explained.

And so it proved. They pushed on one end, thus turning it parallel to the path, and then were able to roll it to the side, allowing sufficient room for the party to pass.

They then went up to observe the bottom part of the trunk, which had lodged itself further up the path when the tree had shattered. It was much thicker; indeed, the thickest end was up to Qiang's waist. The lad was alarmed at its size and shook his head in consternation.

"What ails you?" Ruan Xiu inquired in a rather severe tone.

"Well, sir, it seems that this piece of the trunk is much larger. I would be surprised if we could shift it."

The austere man shook his head in obvious disappointment. "The others told me that you had the makings of a master. It seems they were wrong."

"I do not know what you speak of, sir. I have no pretensions about being a master."

"Do you think that, if you are so destined, you have a choice? When I plant corn, will it turn out to be rice?"

Qiang was no longer listening. His mind went back to a time when he was with his father.

They were tilling a new field that they hadn't worked before. Qiang's hoe struck a large rock. He scraped away the soil but could not move the stone.

When his father saw Qiang struggling with the stone, he laughed. "Hey, son, that stone is a little large for you to shift."

Qiang looked up at his father and asked, "What am I to do?"

His father smiled. "You need a lever."

"What is a lever, Father?"

"Wait a moment, and I will show you."

Chao walked back toward the hut and duly returned with a crowbar. "This will be our lever," he said. Chao took a midsize rock and placed it close to the large rock that Qiang had uncovered. "And this will be our fulcrum."

He dug the sharpened end of the crowbar into the soil alongside the large rock and pulled the implement back until it rested on the smaller stone. He beckoned to Qiang. "Here, now—shift the rock."

Qiang pulled down on the crowbar and found he could unearth the larger rock with little effort.

Chao, pleased with his instruction to his young son, said, "Sometimes we have to use our heads as well as our arms to do our work well!"

Qiang smiled as he remembered this event with his father. Despite his father's undemonstrative ways, Qiang harbored many such memories.

Coming back to the situation at hand, he said to himself, "We need a lever!"

He looked about to see what the immediate environment offered. The branches of the soft-wood tree would be of little use because they were too brittle.

Then he saw that the fall of the tree onto the path had broken off a hardwood sapling. It had been a straight, sturdy little tree. The force of the impact had severed it near the bottom, where it was ten or twelve centimeters thick. He walked back to the handcart.

"What are you doing?" asked Ruan Xiu.

"I am going to fetch the hatchet from the cart."

The austere man laughed. "Come now, boy. You won't be able to chop through a tree this size with a hatchet. It would take you a month!"

"That is not what I had in mind, sir."

Qiang retrieved the hatchet, which was quite sharp. Chao, like most of those who made a living off the land, had maintained his tools well. First, Qiang chopped the top off the sapling, leaving a pole of perhaps two and a half meters in length. He trimmed off the remaining few small branches. Then he applied the hatchet to the bottom of the pole to shape it as a wedge.

Ruan Xiu watched intently, and he soon understood Qiang's intention. "That is good, boy, but it may not be enough."

Qiang finished fashioning his lever and found a stone to act as the fulcrum. He placed his lever on the fulcrum, after having worked the bottom end of the pole under the log. He looked up at the governor. "Will you lend your strength so that we might roll this log out of the way?"

The austere man shook his head. "No, this is your test. I want you to move it by yourself."

Qiang frowned. "Sir, I don't believe I am strong enough to move it by myself."

"Well, if that is true, it can only be because your mind is not prepared."

Qiang shook his head in bewilderment. He had no idea what Ruan Xiu was talking about. Finally, in desperation, he took hold of his lever and heaved mightily on it. The huge log rose an inch or two, but try as he might, he could not support its weight or turn it over. He was forced to let it fall again to the ground. Three or four times he tried but to no avail. Finally, he allowed the log to fall back onto the ground. In despair, he looked up at the austere man and declared, "I am sorry, but I cannot do it."

"But you can do it. You have not used all your resources yet!"

"I do not understand what you mean, sir."

"What did you learn from your previous teachers?"

"They taught me many things. But principally, they taught me the tenets of the Buddhist philosophy and especially how to train my mind."

"I hoped you would undertake this task like someone with a trained mind, but you have disappointed me. Certainly, you have applied your natural strength and have shown some initiative by fashioning a lever. But you have shown little indication of applying the concerted efforts of a trained mind."

Qiang looked perplexed. "Perhaps, sir, you might tell me what you expected of me."

The governor frowned. "Well, boy, I am not a teacher in the manner of those who have come to you previously. But seeing as you seem deficient in your practice, I am compelled, reluctantly, to take up such a mantle. Tell me—how do you believe that you might prepare for such a task?"

The young man scratched his head. It was obvious that he was confused. He shrugged his shoulders. "Perhaps it might have helped if I had limbered up a little—stretched my muscles in preparation for the task."

"It is obvious," snarled Ruan Xiu, "that your teachers' efforts were wasted on you! Your failure to shift the log has little to do with your physical preparation."

Qiang was taken aback by this response. "I don't understand what you mean. I have earnestly tried to follow the strictures of their teaching. What have I missed?"

"Let me tell you, boy. You have missed the essence of this task! What do you think you have to do here?"

"Well, sir, I thought it was obvious. I need to remove the tree as an impediment on the path."

"And how do you propose to go about that?"

"I had hoped, sir, that by using my strength, which would be enhanced by the use of the lever, I could roll the tree away."

"And that is it? You were to rely entirely on your physical strength, albeit enhanced by the lever?"

"I suppose so, yes."

"Then you are an imbecile. You cannot attempt any difficult task without having the mind in order. Come; let me show you."

Ruan Xiu walked along the trunk of the fallen tree. Qiang, with some reluctance, followed. To the side of where the trunk had fallen was a grassy place. The governor sat on the grass and assumed the half-lotus position and beckoned Qiang to emulate him, which the young man duly did.

"You have, I am told by your masters, learned some basic meditation?"

Qiang nodded.

"Then still your mind for a while, using the techniques you were taught."

Qiang was happy to oblige. He was somewhat stressed by the testing required of him. But despite this distraction, once he began to meditate, his mind soon was clear of thoughts and he was only aware of his breath coming and going in a relaxed way. He was infused with a sense of well-being and peace. This endured for perhaps fifteen minutes before he was interrupted.

In a soft voice, his companion said, "Now, young man, pay attention to me awhile, and we will soon see if you might earn the title of Rinpoche one day."

Qiang was a little startled by this. Rinpoche was a title given only to respected teachers in his society. It was said that those who earned this title did so because they were a reincarnation of a celebrated historical teacher. The talents of such people were innate; they did not need to learn their skills but only to be awakened to them.

The lad was about to protest that he was not a Rinpoche, but before he could do so, Ruan Xiu continued, with a steelier tone to his voice.

"Now pay attention," he repeated. "You have learned that we do not see the world as it is; we see the world through our prejudices and conditioning. You believe that this tree trunk is large, and therefore it must be heavy. It does not have to be that way. Go back now and visualize yourself trying to move the tree with your lever."

Without demur, Qiang did as he was told. He remembered approaching the tree trunk, concerned at how heavy it was, and wondering if he had the strength to move it. He relived positioning his lever and straining, to no avail, to roll it off the path.

"I am not sure how you exactly recollected that event, but I am sure that you went about it by giving strength to the tree and visualizing weakness in yourself. Because your mind was ill-prepared, you could not shift the tree."

Qiang nodded. In retrospect, it now seemed that way to him.

"Let us approach this in another way. Concentrate on the tree trunk. It is only a softwood tree. It could be much heavier if it were made of denser material. Visualize it as something inconsequential. Perhaps you might see it as merely a feather. Now you might see yourself as merely blowing it away."

Ruan Xiu paused while Qiang lived this out in his mind. Then he said, "But we know it is not a feather. So let us just again imagine that it is but a little stick. Go back into your mind now, and grasp the stick and throw it away nonchalantly into the brush."

Again, Qiang visualized this happening and managed a smile when he saw the stick hurtling off into bushes at the side of the path.

The Ruan Xiu continued. "But this impediment on our track is not a stick; it is a substantial log. Yet it is not very dense. It is not beyond the power of one man to shift. Imagine now that you have placed your lever under it. It is not heavy and you can roll it away easily. See? You have hardly exerted yourself, and already you have moved it off the path. Such a task is well within the capability of a young man armed with a lever and with a ready mind. Rehearse it now in your imagination."

Qiang, in his mind's eye, watched himself approach the log, position the lever, and, without undue strain, roll the log off the road. It seemed easy enough.

"Practice it again."

And there he was in his mind, rolling the log over again, but because he had done it before, this time it seemed even easier.

"Do it again."

The young man duly rehearsed the shifting of the log. He did it several times more before Ruan Xiu called, "Enough! And now remove the tree."

Without hesitation and without doubt, Qiang arose, replaced his lever under the tree, and—seemingly with only a little effort—rolled the log away."

At this, the usually taciturn Ruan Xiu smiled and, before he could help himself, said, "Good!"

Qiang seemed a little astounded by this turn of events. "I struggled with the task before, but now it seemed quite easy!"

Quickly resuming his usual demeanor, the governor responded, "Don't get too ahead of yourself. You are not a miracle worker. All I wanted to display to you is that many of us are limited in what we can do by the constraints of our minds. Those who can remove those constraints by proper discipline of the mind can achieve much more as a result. But this is not a limitless bucket you can dip into. You may be able to extend your physical capability, for example, as you have, but all you can do is reach your real limitations. There is no more beyond that. However skillful you become, your body will still have finite capability. Do not let this go to your head."

But of course, Qiang had no such inclination. He was grateful that he had learned to do better. It occurred to him that there must be many other ways that his mind might constrain him, and he should be vigilant.

Before they could continue their discussion, Nuan and Lan approached from down the track, leading the governor's horse.

As they came near, Lan suddenly stopped and clapped her hands. "Why, you have cleared the track," she said in a surprised tone. "How on earth did you do that?"

Qiang said nothing, but Ruan Xiu responded matter-of-factly, "Your brother just discovered he was stronger than he thought. Then it was easy."

Lan looked at Qiang, who was blushing, and in recognition of his natural humility, she probed no further.

WITH THE DEBRIS of the fallen tree removed, the little party gathered up their things and set off again down the path. Before long, the track led back into a more open landscape, and they could see the full expanse of the sky, open forest, and grassland.

Ruan Xiu chatted amiably with Nuan. Qiang sensed that this was his way of diverting Nuan's thoughts from the calamity of the day before. Because the man showed compassion and concern for his mother, Qiang felt no resentment for the man's coolness toward him or his seemingly unreasonable demands. Qiang knew instinctively that his mother and sister were safe in his hands.

Qiang could see that Lan had noticed and appreciated the governor's concern for their mother as well. But Lan still needed to do honor to the memory of their father. As they walked, she talked quietly with her brother. They reminisced about Chao. They remembered how stoic he was, working strenuously, day after day, to provide for them without complaint. While he had not been demonstrative, they knew that he had loved them. They remembered how he would sit outside on summer evenings and make little toys for them—not the most sophisticated of playthings, but they were fashioned of love, and that made a difference.

While they were sharing these bittersweet memories, honoring the memory of their father, they suddenly were interrupted by a piercing shriek. In an instant, Qiang knew what this was—the return of the falcon.

Ruan Xiu immediately stopped. He looked up at the heavens. He halted the gait of his little horse. Nuan was perplexed; she did not know what was going on. Her companion let out a shrill whistle and held his arm aloft. Qiang could see he had restored the gauntlet to his arm. Then they saw the bird. Nuan gasped. It was plummeting out of the heavens like a falling star. It seemed to be coming directly at her. She briefly screamed. But then, in an exhilarating maneuver, the bird pulled out of its headlong dive and alighted softly on Ruan Xiu's arm.

Ruan Xiu looked gently at Nuan. "I am sorry he startled you. He doesn't seem to know any other way to alight, but he has come bearing news." Ruan Xiu withdrew a rolled-up piece of parchment from the little tube on the bird's leg, unrolled it, and read from it.

By this time, Lan and Qiang had caught up and were standing curiously alongside.

"What does it say?" Qiang asked.

"It says a party from the palace guard are on their way to escort us home. No doubt they think that we still need rescuing from the fallen tree."

The governor made a great fuss over the bird.

"You seem very fond of the falcon, sir," Qiang said.

"Indeed, I am, lad. The falcon is important in the history of my family. In the characters that comprise our written language, there is one that represents the falcon, which you no doubt, being a calligrapher, would recognize. I use that character to signify my governorship and indeed to mark out my territory. It is dominant on my flag, my coat of arms, and my robes of office. You will see it on my official insignia and seals."

Qiang nodded. "It is indeed a beautiful bird, but I didn't know it had such significance to you."

"Well, be assured that it certainly has. But come; we must be off again now."

With little ado, the small party set off again. They had barely traveled for another hour when the governor halted the black horse bearing Nuan.

"What is it?" inquired Qiang.

Ruan Xiu pointed up the track. "Here they are," he said.

Qiang focused on the path. Several hundred meters ahead, he saw four riders astride large horses, bearing down on them. The one in the rear seemed to lag behind somewhat, but soon Qiang could see that he only lagged because he was leading another three horses.

The three riders in the front trotted their horses up to the governor and dismounted. They knelt before him and, in deferential tones, asked what they could do to serve him. The last rider remained some distance back, holding the three horses that he had led.

Ruan Xiu responded to the riders in a measured tone of voice. "We must escort these three to the palace. The older lady is a matriarch who has just lost her husband in unfortunate circumstances. Please take good care of her. The girl is her daughter and must also be shown due deference and regard."

The men nodded their understanding.

"What of him?" asked one of them, pointing to Qiang.

The governor smiled scornfully. "He is my vassal and needs to be tested."

TURNING NOW TO the little traveling party, the governor proclaimed, "My attendants have brought enough horses that you all can ride, and consequently, we can hasten to my palace and be there in but a couple of hours." He turned to Nuan. "Madam, you seemed to have bonded well with my little horse, Xun."

Nuan nodded her agreement.

"Then you shall have Xun bear you all the way to the palace." He turned then to Lan. "Young lady, my attendants will help you to mount the gray mare over there. She is a gentle and amiable creature. I am sure she will bear you to my palace comfortably and without incident."

Lan, who had seen her mother ride Xun these last couple of days, had been a little envious of her. She looked forward to being elevated to her mother's status but was still a little apprehensive about riding, having had no previous experience.

"Thank you, sir," she responded.

Qiang stood and listened as the governor made these arrangements. He was pleased at how considerate the man was to his mother and sister. Earlier, when Qiang had agreed to be bound to him, the governor had promised, as a condition, to look after them. But they hadn't completed the agreement yet, and, in fact, the man was not morally bound to be so considerate. Nevertheless, he had been kind to Lan and acted courteously and with due deference to Qiang's mother.

Then the governor turned to the nearest attendant. "This young fellow, however"—he nodded toward the lad—"is not to be mollycoddled. He is to be tested. Give him the piebald colt that you have been trying to train."

The attendant raised his eyebrows. "The horse is a little green for that, my lord, particularly for someone who obviously has not ridden before."

Qiang turned to face the governor. "Sir, as much as I would like to, I cannot ride the horse."

Ruan Xiu smirked. "You are afraid to be tested by this horse."

"On the contrary, I would be happy to test myself against the animal." Qiang looked down at the handcart. "My lord, I must stay with the handcart and bring it to your palace."

"What a feeble excuse, boy. There is nothing there that you will need when we get to my palace. I will provide for you."

"I am sure you will, sir. And I will be grateful. But in this handcart is all that we have to remind us that we are a family who once had a father who cared for us. Also, there are some things of value that my sister and I have created, from which I would be loath to be parted."

The austere man's visage softened a little. "That is no problem, lad. I will have someone from the palace come to retrieve it for you."

"I thank you for your offer, sir, but I am reluctant to leave the items that I value to someone else's care."

"Show me what you are talking about, and maybe I can find a solution for you."

Qiang went to the handcart and pulled out the manuscripts, still wrapped in the oilskin and canvas that they used to protect them at the start of their journey.

Ruan Xiu looked intrigued. "Well, what do you have there?"

The young man carefully unwrapped the parcel and unrolled it on the ground, with the precious manuscripts sitting on the canvas.

The governor's eyes lit up. He saw a collection of work similar to the one he had purchased from Qiang.

"You are right, young man. It is fitting that we seek to preserve these. If you roll them up again and secure them, I will strap them securely to my horse, and I will bring them to the palace with no damage. And then, I will send someone to retrieve your handcart."

WITH THE ISSUE of the handcart and the manuscripts settled, there was nothing for it now but for Qiang to test himself with the horse. When the piebald colt was led up to Qiang, the attendants smiled knowingly. This was going to be a severe test.

"Well, then, lad—get up on your steed," urged Ruan Xiu.

Qiang was not afraid, but something inside him told him he was not ready. But with a little trepidation, driven by the governor's insistence and with the aid of the attendant, he mounted the horse. Nuan and Lan looked on with concern—and with due cause. As soon as the attendant let go of the halter, the colt reared up and then proceeded to buck vigorously to rid himself of this unwanted load. Qiang was violently dislodged and fell heavily to the ground. His mother and sister both screamed in dismay. But the ground was soft and grassy, and Qiang soon arose.

Bewilderingly, he had a smile on his face. He turned to Ruan Xiu. "This is a spirited little horse you have, sir. I must confess I wasn't quite ready for him."

"Then you'd better hurry up and get ready," the governor responded. "This is your next test. If you cannot pass it, I won't enter into the agreement we talked about."

"Then what are the conditions of your test, sir?"

Ruan Xiu scowled at the young man; his cold, steely visage had returned. "These are my terms. I will leave an attendant with you for a while to help you. But we will now leave for the palace. My condition is that if you are not with, us astride that horse, when we enter the palace, then our contract is voided."

Nuan and Lan gasped and were about to protest the harshness of the governor's edict, but Qiang silenced them.

"It is all right, Mother. I know now what I must do." He then turned to Ruan Xiu and said, "Very well, Governor. While I suspect your conditions lie outside what we'd previously agreed, I will accept your challenge."

THE ATTENDANT HAD tethered his own horse and stood holding the halter of the piebald colt. Qiang stood alongside him. They watched as the governor led his little retinue down the path toward the palace.

The attendant then turned to Qiang. "What would you have me do, sir? Do you wish to try to mount the horse again?"

Qiang laughed. "Not quite yet, my friend. I know little of horses, so perhaps you might help enlighten me."

"What is it you wish to know?"

"If the governor and his party proceed to the palace at this pace, how long will they take to get there?"

"Perhaps two and a half or maybe three hours."

"And assuming I could master this little beast, how quickly could I get to the palace?"

"If you were to master the colt and ride him well, then you could be at the palace in no more than an hour!"

Qiang smiled. "Then all is not lost if I can contrive to master this young horse?"

"Well, no, not at all. But do not underestimate the task of mastering the horse! If you are to meet the governor's demands, you need to act quickly. Shall we try to mount you on the horse again?"

"No, that won't work until I am properly prepared. Can you hold the horse a little longer for me?"

"Well, yes, if you insist. But I don't understand what good it will do."

Qiang sat on the ground and assumed his meditation posture. After he had stilled his thoughts, he began to picture himself riding the horse. The horse was at full gallop, and Qiang imagined that he had melded with the horse. He felt the exhilaration of the wind in his face and the joy of being one with the animal as he sped over the ground. Finally, he arose and nodded to the attendant. "I believe I am ready now."

The attendant helped him to mount the colt. The animal was fretful and stroppy, clearly disliking having to carry the youth on his back. The animal reared, but this time Qiang was ready. He clung, lightly but firmly, to the young horse. It settled a little, and Qiang stroked his head and uttered soothing words. It reared a second time but with the same results. Then, in desperation, the colt careened off down the track.

The attendant was bewildered and alarmed by this turn of events. He mounted his own horse and took off in the colt's wake. The colt, however, was galloping so quickly that he was soon far ahead on the track.

Qiang remained relatively calm and continued to talk soothingly to the horse. He pulled a little on the reins, which seemed to slow the horse somewhat. Nevertheless, they soon overtook the party led by the governor. As Qiang approached, he called out to warn them. Ruan Xiu, ever alert, turned around and hastily ushered his fellow travelers off the track, allowing the colt free passage.

After the lad had sped past, the governor allowed himself a little chuckle, something the attendants had never before observed. Then he turned to Nuan and said, "I am not sure whether the boy or the horse is in charge, but it seems your son may beat us to the palace."

After a time, the piebald colt began to tire. The frenzied gallop slowed to a canter and then, finally, a walk. Qiang was greatly exhilarated by his ride. He had not clung on desperately but just imagined himself at one with the horse. And all the while, he had spoken calmly and soothingly to the little beast. He became aware that the greatest fear and the greatest fright emanated from the horse's concern for his own well-being, and Qiang wanted to behave in such a way as to assuage the animal's discomfort.

Qiang was at a great disadvantage, not having ridden a horse before and with little knowledge of horses. He, however, had noticed how the governor had used the reins to steer his horse. So he tried pulling on the right-hand rein to see what would happen. Initially, the horse protested. He reared up again in a vain attempt to dislodge this troublesome rider, who seemed to want something from the animal, although the horse could not understand what was being demanded of him.

When the horse reared, Qiang pulled back on the reins, and to his surprise, the horse came to a halt. He stood and snuffled and whinnied and seemed somewhat in dismay. The young man stroked his neck soothingly and spoke quiet, reassuring words. After a time, the little animal seemed to relax. Then, under Qiang's urging, he began to walk sedately along the path.

They came to a place where the path traversed a broad, grassy meadow. Again, Qiang halted the horse. Here was some room to try to come to grips with the horse and his ways. The grass was long and lush, so that if he was again unseated, it probably would do him little damage. He whispered to the colt and cajoled him. He seemed much more placid now. Soon enough, Qiang had learned to direct him left and right with the reins and then, with his urgings, to have him canter. Within forty-five minutes or so, Qiang and the colt seemed to be at one with each other. It pleased the lad that the horse had become more placid and seemingly had lost his fear of him. As they went through the various exercises that Qiang had devised to control the beast, it seemed as though a bond of trust was forming.

Eventually, Qiang dismounted. He stroked the colt and talked quietly and calmly to him. He held the reins lightly, while the horse bent down and cropped the lush grass. He knew he could have remounted and hastened off to the governor's palace, but he preferred to let the animal be at ease.

After a half hour or so, he spied the governor's procession approaching. When they were a hundred meters or so away, he remounted the horse with no difficulty and waited for the others to catch up to him.

Lan turned to Nuan and said, with a note of surprise in her voice, "Look, Mother! There is Qiang. He is waiting for us. He seems to have subdued the horse."

Nuan just smiled knowingly.

The governor affected indifference as the group approached, but Lan could see that he too was surprised by this turn of events. He merely nodded to Qiang as they came abreast of him, and Qiang, on his little piebald colt, fell in behind the little party as they continued on to the palace.

LAN WAS THE first to notice it. "Oh, see there, Mother—that must be the governor's palace." There was more than a little wonderment in her voice.

She pointed to a cluster of buildings, the roofs of which could be seen above a high stone wall. It was still some distance off, perhaps a kilometer, and slightly to the left of the current direction of the track.

Shortly, they were at the palace gates. A sentry was stationed on the palace wall to the right of the gates. On seeing the governor's approach, the sentry called out to someone below, and the gates began to open. The little party filed through the open gates, with the governor in the lead and Qiang bringing up the rear.

Nuan, who remained close to the governor in the procession, gasped in wonderment at what she saw. The extent and the grandeur of the buildings enclosed by the wall was breathtaking. For someone who had never traveled and had lived only in small peasant villages and farmhouses, the magnificence was overwhelming.

Ruan Xiu looked around and saw her astonishment. "Welcome, my lady, to my ancestral home. My family have lived here for generations, and now it is to be your home as well." He called a young lad over to him. "Jian, we have left a handcart with some of my guests' possessions in it some distance down the track. Will you take one of your friends and go back and retrieve it for me?"

The young man nodded. He called out to another lad nearby, and within a minute or two, they were headed back out through the gates in search of the handcart.

The little party made their way to the entrance to the largest building, and there, they dismounted.

The governor spoke to Nuan. "You, good woman, and your daughter are to be my guests. In a little while, I will show you to your quarters." He then turned to Qiang. "You, however, are my vassal. You will, for now, live with these fellows"—he gestured to the other riders—"but I have something that rightfully belongs to you." He handed Qiang the manuscripts with which he had been entrusted. "These are indeed wondrous and valuable things. You must take care of them. But now, there is to be no privilege for you. I will, as I promised, care for your mother and your sister, but you must take your place with the least of my employees and serve me accordingly."

Qiang nodded his head in acceptance. To him, it was enough that Ruan Xiu fulfilled his agreement to care his mother and sister. If that was taken care of, he would have no complaints about his own lodgings.

The austere man beckoned one of the riders to him. "Will you and the others now tend to our horses? Take this fellow with you, and see that he is given accommodation with the other workers. Then, have Lei bring him to me this evening after he has eaten."

Qiang made to go off with the others but Nuan called out.

"Please, wait." She turned and looked at the governor. "Will we be able to see my son after you have put him to work?"

Ruan Xiu had become rather fond of the sturdy old peasant woman. He would not, however, allow his countenance or demeanor to convey such softness. He looked at her sternly. "Perhaps. I expect to put him to hard work. If he has the strength and resilience to deal with what I have in store for him, he might be permitted to visit you some evenings."

The old lady was perceptive. She was learning to trust this strange man. Besides, she also had great faith in Qiang to master whatever was in store for him. She turned to the governor and smiled. In a disarming way, she said, "Thank you. We would be pleased with that." Then, speaking to Qiang, she added, "Take care, son."

Before anyone could stop her, Lan ran to Qiang and hugged him. She whispered in his ear, "I love you, big brother."

He softly replied, "And I love you, little sister."

Then he turned and strode off with the others, hoping that the governor had not noticed the tear in his eye.

IT WAS SOME distance to the workers' accommodation. But soon enough, Qiang was shown a bunk that would be his, and the arrangements for meals and ablutions were explained. In truth, the lad was happy enough with these lodgings. They were warm and dry, and the workers assured him that although the meals were somewhat plain, they were nourishing and tasty enough.

Meanwhile, at the governor's palace, the governor assigned a handmaiden to care for Nuan and Lan. The young woman showed them to their accommodation, and they were overwhelmed. They had never seen such sumptuousness.

Soon after, a young man arrived, bearing their possessions from the handcart. He asked them to sort which items belonged to them and which should go to Qiang. Once this was completed, he hurried off to Qiang with the handcart containing those things that were rightfully his.

QIANG SAT ON a wooden bench with the other workers and had his evening meal. His companions were curious about where he had come from and what he was doing there. He felt comfortable in their company, as many of them had similar rural backgrounds to his.

He enjoyed the food, and he enjoyed the company, but as soon as he had eaten his meal, he went back to his quarters. He went through the items that the lad had brought him from their handcart. They were mostly of little concern to him, but he was concerned for the manuscripts that he and Lan had produced and that the governor had carried for him. He unwrapped them and was pleased to see that they were in good condition, having been protected from the extreme environmental conditions and physical demands they had experienced on their journey.

He unrolled one carefully and was delighted to see the little drawings that Lan had made to illustrate it. When he looked at the text, he found it was a dissertation on the Noble Eightfold Path and, in particular, a commentary on right livelihood. It emphasized that whatever it was that humans did to make their livings should not result in the harm of humans or other living beings. He had barely scanned the text before he became aware of someone approaching. He hastily rerolled the parchment and put it away.

He turned to look at the approaching figure—a big man of moderate height but very broad. He seemed to be a man who had once been quite muscular but had now gained too much weight. Despite his broad, straight shoulders, there was also an ample stomach overhanging his belt. He seemed to be angry.

"Hey, boy," he exclaimed, "are you the one called Qiang?"

"That is indeed my name."

The big man snorted. "For some reason, I am supposed to bring you to see the governor. I had other plans this evening, and this was the last thing I wanted to do. So don't waste my time. Get off your backside, and we will go to his quarters."

They set off to see the governor, with the big fellow mumbling and grumbling as they went. Finally, he said, "How is it that you're so special that you get an audience with the governor?"

"I am not special. I am merely contracted to work for the governor."

"There must be something special. The governor does not usually send for workers to have an audience with him. There are many workers within the confines of the palace's walls, most of whom have barely spoken to the governor, let alone be granted an audience. I wouldn't care, except that he has commanded me to join you!"

Qiang just shrugged his shoulders, knowing that any response from him was not likely to help.

As they approached the main entrance to the palace, Qiang noticed, to his surprise, that it was guarded by two sentries.

Lei strode purposefully up to them ahead of Qiang and announced, "I am Lei, and I have been commanded by the governor to bring this young fellow to him."

One of the sentries nodded. "We have been told to expect you. I will direct you to him. Follow me."

Guided by the sentry, the two set off into what seemed a labyrinth to those unfamiliar with the palace's many rooms and passages. Before long, they arrived at a reception chamber, where they found the governor waiting. The governor was accompanied by a middle-aged man of slight build but with an appearance that seemed to reflect depth and calmness.

Lei seemed to put aside his feelings of having been imposed upon and rushed to kneel before the governor. "Sire," he said, "you have sent for me, and I am eager to know how I can be of assistance."

Qiang was surprised by the change in the man's demeanor, from being surly to being pathetically obsequious.

The governor beckoned him to stand. "Well, Lei, I have a special duty for you."

Lei frowned but answered deferentially. "What would you ask of me, my lord?"

Looking at Qiang, the governor replied, "I want you to take on this young fellow to assist you in the stables. Now, I want you to do two things for me, in particular. First, I want you to work him hard. He has agreed to be contracted as my vassal, and for that, I have granted him considerable favors. Consequently, he must work hard for me in consideration."

Lei nodded and turned to look at Qiang with a smirk on his face. Then he inquired, "And what else would you have me do, my lord?"

"I would have you teach him all you know about horses. You have managed my stables for many years, and, undoubtedly, you have learned much about tending to my animals. I want you to impart such knowledge to the lad, as you can. Do you understand?"

Again, Lei nodded. "I will do my best to meet your requirements."

"Good! You will start tomorrow. And now you may go."

Lei again bowed in deference; then turned on his heel and exited the room.

Qiang moved to go off as well but the governor restrained him. "Well, young man, that is the first role I will give you."

Qiang nodded. "I am happy to fulfil my obligation to you."

"Good, but first there is a formality we must complete. On our journey here, you insisted that our contract be formalized." The governor bent down and took something off the bench in front of him. "Here is a contract that I have prepared, cementing the arrangement." He handed Qiang a small roll of parchment, which the lad duly unrolled and read.

"This is a fair summary of our agreement."

"Very well, then. I will affix my seal to the document to give it authority within the territories that I command. But now, let me introduce you to someone who I have assigned to attend to your spiritual development. This is the venerable Sunfu Rinpoche. Sunfu is my own spiritual adviser. He will be available to mentor you."

Qiang was rather taken aback by this development. "This sounds like a very generous offer, my lord. But can you tell me what his qualifications are?"

This response seemed to rankle Ruan Xiu. "How dare you, boy, question my judgment on this matter? Is it not enough that I should share with you my own spiritual tutor? I will not suffer such an outrage." And thus saying, the governor arose and stormed from the room.

Qiang was nonplussed. He arose, feeling that he had offended the governor, and thought it appropriate that he should also withdraw.

But before he could make such a move, Sunfu Rinpoche called, "Wait. I would speak with you."

Qiang turned to look at his new tutor. He seemed quite detached from Ruan Xiu's dramatic withdrawal. He looked into the man's eyes and saw the same calmness and equanimity that had emanated from his previous teachers.

THE OLDER MAN beckoned Qiang to come sit next to him on the seat that the governor had vacated.

"I am sorry, sir," Qiang ventured. "I did not mean to offend the governor. To tell the truth, he has shown me considerable kindness. I am grateful that he has seen fit to care for my mother and sister."

The sage merely smiled. "Do not let it concern you, young man. Ruan Xiu, as you seem to have sensed, is basically a good man. But every now and then, he breaks into an irksome display of histrionics. Do not concern yourself. That will soon pass. Although you may struggle to see evidence to support it, he is quite fond of you. But that is of no great import for me. Right now, I wish to learn more about you, and you, quite rightly, expressed a desire to know more about me. So let us spend a little time in getting to know each other."

Qiang felt quite comfortable in the company of the sage and conveyed to him his life's history. Sunfu Rinpoche took a great interest in Qiang's story, listened attentively, and asked questions that confirmed his understanding as the young man spoke.

The sage sought clarification on a few issues that Qiang mentioned. Finally, he nodded his head and said, "Thank you, young man. I believe I know your story pretty well, although I must confess that I had the benefit of the testimony of others as well. Now, what is it that you wish to know about me?"

Qiang was a little perplexed at the sage's reference to *the testimony of others*, but he put it aside in his desire to know more about his new teacher.

He asked many questions in the next hour or so.

Sunfu Rinpoche had been the pupil of the legendary Master Xang Quin. Xang Quin had declared that his lot in life was not just to teach but to teach those who would nurture new masters in the Buddhist tradition. Xang Quin was the most famous teacher in the country, and his teachings were revered. As a result of this calling, however, he took on few pupils, but those he had were particularly spiritual and intelligent. They, in turn, swore to take on the cause of nurturing young men to become exemplary Buddhist teachers and role models.

Sunfu Rinpoche described the arduous nature of his instruction. He did this without complaint and expressed his pleasure at having been selected to follow such a noble calling.

Qiang became quite apprehensive as he listened to the sage explain his history.

Finally, he said, "There seems to be some mistake here. I cannot believe that if your calling is to instruct young men to become exemplary masters that you have chosen me as a pupil. I am no one special. I am a farmer's son with no special talents, beyond the fact I have some competence at calligraphy."

The older man softly chuckled. "Humility is one of the qualities I seek in my pupils. I have other evidence that you are an appropriate student. But beware—this is not going to be easy for you. I suspect, however, that you have no choice in the matter."

"Why do you believe that?"

"The governor tells me that he has a contract with you that requires you to do his bidding, in return for his care of your mother and sister. And he has dictated that you should come under my tutelage."

Qiang sighed. "That is true, and I will honor my undertaking. But what is it that you will have me do?"

"I need you to spend a little time with me on most days. I know that the governor has given you over to Lei to work in the stables, and I suspect that Lei will be quite demanding." The old man paused and frowned. "I am not sure that was a good idea."

Qiang raised his eyebrows. "Why do you say that?"

"It is probably none of my business, but I have heard some disconcerting things about Lei. I can't say anymore, but I caution you to keep your wits about you when you are with him. Now that Ruan Xiu has placed you under my tutelage, I have a duty of care for you as well. Now, about our lessons—I would prefer that we meet every morning when that is convenient."

"What about my work in the stables. Would this not interfere?"

"It might, but I am sure, because of my relationship with the governor, that he will agree to such an arrangement. I will take it upon myself to gain his assent that we should meet for an hour or so each morning, before you start work at the stables."

"I suspect Lei might not be happy with this arrangement."

"No, perhaps not, but I suspect that the governor will agree that what I have to teach you is far more important than anything you could learn in the stables. But let us confront one last thing, young man."

"And what would that be, sir?"

"You have a contract with the governor to do his bidding in return for his securing the welfare of your mother and sister?"

"Indeed, I do, sir."

"Despite the governor's desire, I cannot work with someone who comes to me under compulsion. I will only take your mentorship if you desire it. If you don't desire to do so, I will not make things difficult for you with the governor. I will find a way to shield you from his disapproval."

Qiang smiled. "Oh no, sir. I would be most grateful for your instruction. I have had the good fortune to have had a number of masters who have helped me greatly. I suspect you will be the same. Let me assure you that despite any obligation I have to the governor, I look forward to working with you."

"That is good, young man. We will start tomorrow."

And so, the next chapter of Qiang's life began.

True to his word, Sunfu Rinpoche obtained the governor's assent. For an hour or so each morning, he continued Qiang's tuition in meditation, mindfulness, and compassion.

Qiang also began his work in the stables, and although it was often demanding (and perhaps others might have thought it was demeaning), he enjoyed the close association with the animals and developed skills and a real aptitude to relate to the horses. He was, however, never comfortable in the presence of the stable master, Lei, and it seemed obvious to Qiang that, for whatever reason, Lei was resentful of him.

As the governor had promised, Qiang was often able to visit his mother and his sister. Despite his mother's protestations, the governor doted on her. Even though she would have dearly loved to contribute to the work of his household, he insisted that she should be treated as one of his court. The governor, however, was aware of Lan's artistic talents and commissioned her to do a series of paintings that he wished to hang in his palace. By and large, Qiang was elated at how well his mother and sister were treated. He felt no regret in agreeing to bow to the governor's will.

QIANG SAT CROSS-LEGGED on the grass alongside his new master. "What would you have me do, sir?"

"Let us just meditate a while. That would be a good beginning."

They both sat in the lotus position on the ground, and, putting thought aside, just concentrated on the breath.

After a time, his master said, "That will do for now. Now, let us give some thought to altruism." Sunfu Rinpoche looked up at Qiang. "Why do you think that altruism is so important?"

The young man paused and thought a while, and then he said, "The Buddha taught us to practice loving kindness. That is the embodiment of altruism."

"It is true that the Buddha espoused loving kindness, but that is merely avoiding the question. Why do you think it was so important to him?"

"From what I can remember, the Buddha taught that the main cause of misery was selfishness. It probably follows that happiness is enhanced by loving kindness."

"Good, but to whom must we extend loving kindness to achieve this outcome?"

"Well, to everyone."

"Do you think this is achievable?"

"Yes, but it is probably difficult for many."

"Why do you think that it is?"

"Humans seem to have a propensity to want to differentiate themselves from their fellows. They seem to emphasize those things that appear to make us different from one another, like ethnicity, nationality, religion, opinions, and so on, whereas we should be confirming our oneness. Ultimately, when our sense of compassion extends to all, we are intimately touched by their joys and their suffering."

"That is a very perceptive response, young man. When I instruct my pupils in altruism, I usually start with a meditation about helping someone close to you and then gradually extend that sense of belonging to all beings. It seems from your responses that I can accelerate that process with you. But, of course, you have already had some instruction."

"Indeed, Master. But I have always had one reservation."

"What is that?

"Well, surely altruism is good because it provides benefits to others, but when I extend loving kindness to others, I feel good. It concerns me that I might just be practicing altruism for my own selfish benefit."

The master laughed, and then he replied with a parable. "A farmer sets out to grow wheat, but when the wheat is harvested, he gets straw as well. This does not detract from the fact that his purpose was to grow wheat. If we set out to act altruistically, our prime purpose is to help another. Just because we derive some satisfaction from the process does not detract from our altruism; it, fortunately, facilitates it."

Qiang smiled. His master's practical response embarrassed him slightly but relieved him of his irrational guilt.

"Come," said Sunfu Rinpoche. "Let us now begin our meditation practice on altruism. But you must remember that altruism is important because at the most essential level, we are all as one. Once you understand that, compassion and altruism will come naturally."

AFTER HIS SESSION with his teacher, Qiang walked briskly back to the stables. When he arrived, Lei was there, feeding some of the horses. He looked up at Qiang's arrival and sniped, "Oh, the little master has arrived. Can it be that he has deigned to do a little work in the stables? I don't know what it is that keeps him from his duties. Maybe it is the smell. Perhaps it might be useful to get him more used to it. Here, boy, take this shovel and clean out the stalls." Lei pointed toward a large handcart. "When you have filled this with horse manure, take it out to the gardens. Find the head gardener, Shang, and deposit it wherever he desires, and then come back and continue until all the stalls are cleared."

Qiang set about his assigned task. Although he sensed Lei was trying to humiliate him, he was not greatly concerned. He duly filled the barrow with horse manure and trundled it out to the garden, where he found a few young lads, hoeing and weeding. Farther along, there was an old man, pruning some vines. Leaving the barrow, Qiang approached the man and inquired, "Sir, would you be Shang, the head gardener?"

The old man looked at Qiang. He had a very weathered face and a balding head, adorned by a few wisps of sparse white hair. But the feature that seemed to distinguish him most were his twinkling eyes.

"Ah, I am, indeed, Shang. And who might you be?" he asked with a little chuckle.

"Sir, I am Qiang. I am working in the stables with Lei, and he has sent me with a load of manure for your garden. Where would you have me deposit it?"

"Thank you, Qiang. Your master is a hard man with some difficult ideas. He seems to think that the manure from his stables is somehow disgusting. He does not seem to understand that the vegetables he eats each night rely on it for nourishment. But if you look over there to your left, there is a pile of manure fenced in by some stout logs. If you don't mind, you can deposit it there. I like to compost it somewhat before I feed it to my vegetables."

Qiang looked around at the thriving plants in their orderly rows. "My, you have a fine garden, sir!"

"Thank you, Qiang. But what would you know about gardens?"

"Well, sir, I am a farmer's son and gained satisfaction from tilling the soil and growing plants."

"Can I show you around my garden?"

"Oh, that would indeed be a joy, sir, but I dare not. I must hurry back to Lei to continue my work."

Shang nodded. "I understand your predicament. But come by if you ever have any spare time. I would be pleased to show you my plants and"—he winked knowingly at the young man—"tell you my secrets!"

Qiang laughed. He knew that every farmer and every gardener had their "secrets"—the special little tricks and processes that they believed helped in their propagation of productive growth.

"Thank you, Shang. I would enjoy that immensely."

AND SO IT was that day after day, for weeks and then months, Qiang would clear the stalls, load his cart with manure, and take it to Shang's garden. Lei obviously believed he was giving demeaning work to the lad and smirked when he saw him with his full barrow, trundling off to the garden. Although there was another stable hand, who was called Biming, he was never given the task of cleaning the stalls. But Qiang never minded in the least.

Qiang was at peace. He was comforted that his mother and sister were being well looked after, as the governor had promised. He had his regular sessions with his new teacher, Sunfu Rinpoche, which he enjoyed immensely. As he pushed his barrow to the gardens, he would go over his lessons. And far from finding his work demeaning, Qiang, as a farmer's son, felt gratified to contribute to Shang's flourishing garden.

Then one day, after his morning tuition, Qiang arrived at the stables to find most of the horses had gone. Biming was there, and Qiang asked him what had happened to the horses. Biming explained that the governor and his retinue had set off to visit another province and would be away for three or four days.

As well as the horses, Lei was nowhere to be seen. When Qiang inquired about that, Biming seemed unsure.

"When I arrived at the stables this morning, I noticed he wasn't around. I made some inquiries, and it seems that there has been a death in his family, and he has gone to attend a funeral in a village, some considerable distance away. Nobody seemed to know how long he will be gone. I am at a loss to know what to do, Qiang."

Qiang, ever practical, replied, "Well, Biming, we should at least attend to the animals that are left in the stables. Perhaps you could feed them, and I could clean their stalls, and then let us take stock."

Because there were few animals left in the stable, it took little time to complete those tasks. When Qiang returned from the gardens, Biming had fed all the horses, bar one.

"Ah, Qiang, this little beast will have none of me. He won't let me feed him, and he won't let me touch him. It is for this very reason that the horse was left in the stable. None of the governor's men can ride him."

Qiang walked to the stall where Biming was trying to feed the horse. He was surprised to find that the recalcitrant horse was the little piebald colt that he had ridden to the governor's palace. The horse seemed frightened and skittish.

"Biming, go and fetch a bucket of water for the colt. I see the trough in his stall is half empty. While you are gone, I will see what I can do with him."

Although Qiang had no real authority over Biming, his assuredness gave him some personal presence. Besides, the young fellow had tried for some time to attend the little horse with no success. It was with a sense of some relief that he willingly complied with Qiang's suggestion.

When Biming left, Qiang entered the stall with the horse. Biming had been trying to feed the animal from outside the stall. Qiang shut the stall gate behind him. The piebald colt immediately reared up in anxiety. Qiang adeptly dodged his flying hoofs and began to utter consoling words. He spoke quietly to the horse for some time. Then, he slowly raised his hand and stroked the little animal's mane.

When Biming returned with his pail of water, he was surprised to see Qiang hand-feeding the horse inside the stall. He scratched his head and asked, "How did you manage that?"

Qiang smiled and then replied, "We have a little history, this horse and I. Do you mind if I feed him daily now?"

"I'd be delighted! The little terror is always trying to bite me or kick me when I try to tend to him."

Qiang laughed. "Well you can leave him to me now."

The next day, Biming attended all the horses except the colt, while Qiang cleaned out the stalls. Qiang duly loaded his barrow and transported the manure to Shang at the garden. With Lei away and a reduced amount of work to be done, Qiang spent an hour with Shang.

He helped the old man weed a garden bed as they talked. The two had grown quite close. As a result, Shang would often give Qiang some fruit or berries to take to Nuan and Lan, who thought this was a marvelous treat.

When he returned to the stables, Biming was there, waiting for him.

"I have tended to all the horses except the piebald colt. You agreed to attend to him. Is there anything else I should do, Qiang? They are now, with the exception of the colt, all fed, watered, and groomed. There are so few that I can manage that in a couple of hours."

"I do not see much point in your hanging around here, Biming, when all your work is done. Why don't you go off and amuse yourself? I will tend to the colt and then do the same."

As Biming walked out of the stables, Qiang entered the stall of the piebald colt with a bucket half filled with maize, which he had garnered from the wastage from Shang's garden. While at first reluctant, the little horse was soon eagerly eating the bucket's contents.

Qiang quietly stroked the animal as he ate. He remembered, with fondness and some exhilaration, the day that he had come to the governor's palace on board the little horse. He began to wonder whether he could again mount the horse. Then, on a whim, while talking gently to the piebald colt, he hoisted himself up onto the animal's back and sat astride him, all while talking gently and reassuring the little animal.

When he first mounted the horse, the colt gave little whinny to express his dismay but very quickly returned his attention to the contents of the bucket.

Every day thereafter, Qiang followed the same process. Soon, the horse did not protest at all at Qiang's weight on his back. Then, the lad took a step further, and after the horse finished eating, he applied a bridle to the animal. Qiang knew that he'd had a bridle on before; he'd been equipped with one on the day Qiang rode him to the governor's palace. Again, after a little hesitation, the animal seemed to accept the straps on his head and the bit in his mouth. Qiang didn't know whether the horse's acquiescence was because the horse remembered their previous encounter or because Qiang had again earned his trust.

Finally, after all this preparation, the day came when Qiang applied the bridle and led the horse from the stall. After walking him around the stables, talking to him and stroking him, Qiang mounted the horse and rode him out into the palace grounds. On a whim, he walked the little animal to Shang's garden.

Shang was surprised to see Qiang mounted on the little horse.

"Ho, Qiang—what are you doing?"

"I am exercising the little horse."

"Does Lei approve of your riding the horse?"

The lad laughed. "Lei is not here."

Shang frowned. "Be careful, Qiang. Lei can be a vicious man if you cross him. I do not think he would approve of the stable hands riding the horses. You see, in this society, only the nobility are allowed to ride."

Qiang shook his head. "But how can that be, old friend? On the very day I arrived at the palace, the governor commanded me to ride this very horse."

Shang looked surprised. "Then he must have made such a gesture to show his esteem for you."

Qiang laughed. "I doubt it. He ordered that I should ride the horse to test me."

"Well, you seemed to pass his test. But I still think it wise that you don't provoke Lei by riding the horse."

The young man thought for a moment before replying. "No doubt you are wiser than I, Shang. I will heed your counsel."

AFTER A FEW more days, Lei returned to the stable. He was surlier than ever. Qiang and Biming tried to avoid him as much as possible.

Then one evening, Qiang was summoned to the governor's residence. When he arrived, he was surprised to see that the governor had Lan with him, as well as another figure, who seemed familiar to Qiang.

As he approached, Qiang suddenly remembered—it was Fung Tszu. This was the man who had first bought manuscripts from him when he'd sat on the pavement in front of the emperor's court.

"Ah, Qiang," began the governor, "I have a visitor for you—someone I believe you have met before."

"Yes, Excellency. I believe this man is called Fung Tszu. He was a generous benefactor who bought manuscripts from me. That helped save my family from starving during the great drought that ruined our farming livelihood. I will forever be in his debt. But sir, why is my little sister here as well?"

"All in good time, Qiang. I need to tell you a little more about the venerable Fung Tszu before that can be explained."

Qiang murmured. "As you will."

"Fung Tszu is an emissary from the governor of Sun Nang province, Chin Chao. Chin Chao is my closest ally. His province adjoins mine to the west. In days gone by, our provinces were the most lawless of those presided over by the emperor. Many years ago, we made a pact to drive out the bandits who harassed our people in their villages. Eventually, that was achieved but not without some sacrifice. But our territories are now relatively secure and peaceful. For this, we owe Chin Chao a great debt. The governor sacrificed a lot to enable this outcome to be achieved. I will always acknowledge my debt to this great man. Fung

Tszu is also a friend. I have asked him what I might do to express my gratitude for his support in those difficult times. Fung Tszu tells me that Chin Chao is a very devout man. When I asked him what Chin Chao would value most as a gift, he didn't hesitate to suggest that he would be grateful to receive some manuscripts, such that you and your sister produce, illuminating the basic precepts of the Buddhist faith. Accordingly, I would like you and your sister to manufacture some such pieces that I might give to him as a reward for his continuing support."

"I would be pleased to do that, sire. It would be good to practice my calligraphy again and even more so if I can work with my sister."

"Excellent!"

Lan clapped her hands in excitement but said nothing.

"I will fit out one of the anterooms in the palace, which you can use as a workplace."

Qiang nodded his agreement, but after a little thought, he said, "Sir, it has been some time since I have used my calligraphy skills. You might need to be patient with me as I practice. No doubt, you wish for me to do my best work, and it might take a little while to hone my skills again."

"That is understood, Qiang. As you say, I want nothing less than your best work to serve as a gift to my friend."

In the months ahead, Qiang and Lan worked on most evenings to produce a portfolio of manuscripts that covered Chin Chao's favorite passages from the Buddhist oeuvre. Of course, Nuan came to watch and encourage her offspring as well as she could.

The governor provided the best of materials and equipment. Occasionally, he passed by to monitor progress. He was vastly impressed by the quality of the work that Qiang and Lan produced, but in his usual taciturn way, he gave little hint of his approval.

Qiang was ecstatic at this turn of events. After working in the stables, he would hurry off in the early evenings to pursue this joint venture with his sister. Despite the sometimes-difficult circumstances at the stable, knowing he could do creative work with his adored little sister in the evenings more than compensated for any indignities he might have to endure.

His sense of contentment soared, and he felt greatly blessed.

BUT QIANG'S EVENING project had not gone unnoticed at the stables.

Since Lei's return, he seemed to get surlier and surlier with the lad. And sometimes, it seemed to Qiang that Lei was under the influence of drink.

Finally, Qiang seemed compelled to understand the growing disaffection from the stable master.

One morning, drawing up his courage, he confronted Lei. "Sir," he inquired, as respectfully as he could, "you seem to be somehow angry with me. Can you tell me what I have done? I have no desire to aggravate you."

Lei was startled by the question. His lips curled in a snarl as he contemplated his response. "You have eroded my authority, you little cur! Don't you understand that?"

Qiang was taken aback. "Whatever do you mean, sir? I have been obedient to you and have tried to faithfully follow your commands."

"That is all a charade. You seem to do as you are told during the day, but at night, you hurry off to the governor's palace to conspire against me. Before you came along, the governor looked up to me as head of his stables, but now, he consults with you and never takes my counsel."

"Oh, sir, you are wrong. I only go to the palace to work with my sister on a manuscript the governor has commissioned for his friend Chin Chao."

Lei shook his head in disbelief. "How could it be that the governor would commission a simple peasant boy to undertake a project such as this? I do not believe it. You have inveigled yourself into his favor, and now you are plotting against me."

"Sir, I don't believe that I have ever mentioned your name in any of my discussions with the governor."

"Well, there you are, you little wretch. It would be more than appropriate for you to promote my status with the governor, seeing as I am your master. But you no doubt spend your time promoting your own welfare at my expense. Get back to cleaning out the horse stalls, and don't bother me any further." Lei stormed away in a huff.

Qiang, seeing that there was little he could do, merely shrugged and returned to his work.

LAN AND QIANG continued work on their project. It took some time for them to again hone their skills, but after a month or so, they fell back into place, and the two began to produce exquisite, breathtaking work.

Whenever they worked together, Nuan would sit nearby and bask in the joy that her children provided her.

Even the taciturn governor could not help but utter words of praise when he occasionally checked on their progress.

Qiang apologized for the slowness of their output but reminded Ruan Xiu of his desire for excellence.

The austere man nodded his understanding and, standing before their fine work, never once complained.

EVEN THOUGH LEI sought to make Qiang's days in the stables as uncomfortable as he could, the young man gained such satisfaction from his work with his sister that nothing Lei did could upset his equanimity.

But Qiang was not able to avoid Lei's antagonism.

One day, much to everyone's surprise, Ruan Xiu made his way to the stables. He walked up to Lei and, in a good-humored way, inquired after his health. Then, after some small talk with the master of the stables, he inquired after the progress of Qiang.

"I left the lad with you, Lei, so that he might learn how to look after the horses. How has he progressed?"

Lei was nonplussed by this enquiry. He had not required anything of Qiang but to clean the stables. In his vindictive way, he believed that this would demean the lad, but Qiang had accepted the task without demur and had cleaned the stables assiduously without complaint.

"Well, sir, I am still familiarizing him with the basic duties around the stables. To tell the truth, he has not shown much interest in the horses."

"I find that hard to believe, Lei. When I brought him to my palace, he arrived on that little piebald colt that you have not been able to tame. They seemed to have developed an amiable relationship. Now, I want you to mentor him in your skills dealing with horses."

The stable master looked down at his feet, feigning deference. "As you will, Excellency," he murmured.

"Treat him well, Lei. This is an important part of his development, and, in confidence, I must tell you that I have great plans for this lad."

The governor spun on his heel and walked back to the palace, leaving Lei seething.

QIANG KNEW IMMEDIATELY that something was afoot. He was meditating with Sunfu Rinpoche in the palace gardens when Biming came running up, calling his name.

"Qiang, Qiang, come quickly!"

Sunfu Rinpoche and his pupil sat cross-legged on the grass. Sunfu Rinpoche looked up immediately and inquired, "What is it, young man?"

"Sir, Stable Master Lei has demanded that Qiang come to the stable at once. He says he has been commanded by the governor to give Qiang certain instruction, and Qiang must come at once."

"In what state is Lei?"

"Well, sir, he is very angry, and it seems to me that he might be affected by drink."

Sunfu Rinpoche shook his head. "I thought as much."

Qiang looked up at his master. "What should I do, sir?"

The old man contemplated a moment and then said, "Go to the stables, Qiang. But be careful. Lei might threaten you physically, but remember your lessons."

"Very well, sir. I am not afraid of Lei."

Enigmatically, as Qiang rushed off with Biming, the old man said quietly, "It is not you I am worried about, Qiang; it is Lei."

OUTSIDE THE STABLE area, where the horses were housed, there was a circular yard fenced in by a substantial wooden fence. As they approached, Qiang and Biming noticed the Lei was standing by the gate that provided access to the yard with a whip in hand. Qiang frowned but did not falter. He hurried straight up to the stable master.

"You sent for me, sir?"

Lei's face was red, and his knuckles on the hand clutching the handle of the whip were white with tension. He took a step forward and seemed a little unsteady on his feet.

Out came a torrent of expletives as he cursed the boy.

In the face of this violent outburst, Qiang remained passive. Biming scuttled off in fear and hid behind a fence post. Finally, when Lei stopped to draw breath, the lad ventured quietly, "Why did you send for me?"

Lei choked with rage. When he eventually regained his breath, he shouted, "Because your friend, the governor, requires that I should teach you how to manage horses. And today, to honor his request, I am going to teach you a very good lesson! I am going to teach you how to break a horse, how to conquer its will, how to make it obedient."

"But with respect, sir, all the horses are obedient and amenable to handling. It would seem they have no need of this lesson."

The stablemaster sneered. "But there is one unruly horse that has not yet been subjugated to my authority. He needs to be taught a lesson. And just as per the governor's instruction, you do as well!"

Qiang now grew a little afraid. He guessed to which horse Lei referred.

"Biming, where are you?" the stable master slurred. Lei looked around and finally saw the boy, peeking out from behind the fence post. "Go into the stalls and bring out the piebald colt."

Biming was shaking with fear. "Oh, sir, I can't! He won't let me near him! Qiang is the only one who can handle him."

"Yes, so I hear!" Lei exclaimed. And then turning to Qiang, he continued. "In fact, old Lin, the baker, said he saw you astride the horse when I was recently away. Who gave you permission to ride the governor's horse?"

"No one, sir," confessed Qiang. "It just seemed to me that the horse could do with a little exercise. Because no one seems to be able to ride him, he just languishes in the stable. Surely, a young horse needs exercise."

"So you are the horse expert now, are you? But no doubt you are right. If Biming won't fetch the horse—and he will be punished later for disobeying me—then you had better fetch the horse. And put the halter, with the long rope attached, on him so we can run him in the exercise yard."

Qiang nodded resignedly. "As you wish."

The lad went into the stables and was gone about five minutes before returning, leading the horse. There was probably twenty meters of rope attached to the halter, but he walked the horse calmly into the fenced arena, with the rope coiled in his left hand and his right hand on the rope close to the halter.

Biming had opened the gate to the enclosure, and Qiang, Lei, and the horse walked in, at which time he quickly closed the gate behind them. All the while, Qiang talked gently to the horse.

"Now run the horse," commanded Lei.

Qiang let go of the rope where he had held it close to the halter and then transferred the free end of the rope to his right hand. He slapped the horse gently on the rump. He ran out to the length of the rope and then trotted slowly, in a counterclockwise manner, around the enclosed yard.

AFTER QIANG AND Biming had run off to the stable, Sunfu Rinpoche arose from the half-lotus position and walked purposefully off behind them. He was perhaps a hundred meters away when he saw Qiang lead the piebald colt into the yard. Alongside the old man was a wooden trough, where sometimes the horses were watered. He sat on the plank that adjoined the front of the trough, content to just sit and watch what transpired. None of the others had noticed his approach, being focused on the events transpiring in the horse yard.

THE HORSE RAN gently around the circumference of the fenced yard.

Qiang, seeking to appease Lei, said, "See, Stable Master, the colt does as he is bidden."

Lei snorted. "For the time being. Turn him around."

The young man halted the horse. He walked up and grabbed the horse's halter and gently led him in the opposite direction. He gave the horse a little slap on the rump and walked back to take up the full extent of the rope. The colt now set off in a clockwise manner, running easily within the perimeter of the fenced yard.

Qiang looked toward Lei. Although the lad had managed to persuade the horse to follow the directives that Lei had required, he could see the stable master was furious. It became apparent that Lei had no desire to see the horse do as requested. Lei wanted the horse—and consequently, Qiang—to fail.

"Stop!" called Lei. "It is not enough that the horse should obey you alone. If he is to be of any use to the governor, he must obey any who needs to ride him."

Qiang had duly halted the young horse, which stood trembling quietly at the end of the rope.

"Here—pass the rope to me!" demanded Lei.

Reluctantly, Qiang did as he was told. Lei, still holding the whip in his right hand, grabbed the end of the rope in his left. He shook the rope vigorously and exhorted the horse to run.

The horse, clearly afraid, was confused as to how to react. Finally, he reared up on his hind legs and struggled to free himself from the rope.

Lei was now livid and shouted, "Run, damn you, run!"

Again, the horse reared up in fear. He struggled to get away and remained straining at the rope.

Lei, now beside himself with anger, strode closer to the horse and raised the whip.

"No!" shouted Qiang. "Don't strike him!"

But the whip was raised up inexorably, almost of its own accord, and the leather thong snaked out to the horse's flank and struck the horse with a resounding *crack*.

The whip's lash still did not provoke the horse to run but merely caused another paroxysm of rearing and whinnying.

Again, Lei raised the whip. Qiang called out in protest, causing Lei to turn to face him.

"He must be taught a lesson," snarled the stable master, "and maybe so should you."

Lei's arm arched back and then suddenly forward. The leather thong of the whip was propelled straight toward the lad's head. In defense, Qiang turned his back to Lei, allowing himself to be struck across the shoulder blades, with the end of the thong passing over his left shoulder. At the instant it struck, Qiang gritted his teeth and stretched his right arm out and managed to grasp the lash. His agility and quick reflexes surprised Lei.

"Let go, you little cur. You will pay for this!"

But Qiang did not let go; he pulled on the thong with all his strength. Lei was determined not to let go either. Now, however, whether because of his inebriation or because of the undue exertion, the force of Qiang's response caused Lei to fall forward on his face. This undignified outcome caused him to release the whip from his grip. Qiang gathered the whip to him and flung it into the fence. He strode forward and stood over the stable master.

His mind was now in turmoil about what he should do next. But as he stood and pondered over the pathetic figure at his feet, a familiar voice called out, "Enough! Let him be, Qiang. Attend to the horse."

He turned to see the reassuring figure of Sunfu Rinpoche. The old man had left his vantage point and had hurried down to join Qiang. Biming opened the gate for him, and he strode up to Lei, who remained prostrate on the ground.

Qiang turned and walked slowly up to the horse. He spoke quietly and soothingly. He did not attempt to grab the rope hanging from his halter. The little beast backed up against the fence. He made to rear up in defense but finally settled. Qiang was soon standing alongside him, stroking and reassuring him.

"Take him back to his stall, Qiang, and then wait for me in the stable. I will be with you soon."

Qiang took the horse by the halter and untied the rope, all the time talking gently to the colt. He coiled up the rope and put it over his arm and then led the horse quietly out of the enclosure.

When he passed his master, Lei rolled over and sat up.

The young man looked at Sunfu Rinpoche with concern. "Will you be all right, sir?"

"Do not concern yourself, pupil. Just wait for me in the stable." As Qiang walked out of the gate, he heard him say, "Oh, Lei. Has it come to this?"

And then he heard a plaintive voice say, "What will become of me now?"

Qiang fancied those somber words might have been lubricated with tears.

BIMING AND QIANG walked slowly back to the stable. Qiang led the little horse. He continued to talk to him in a soothing voice. The horse had quickly settled and followed quietly alongside Qiang.

After he had stabled the horse, Qiang sat alongside Biming on a couple of bales of hay and waited for Sunfu Rinpoche.

Biming looked across at Qiang. "You were more than a match for old Lei," he said with a chuckle.

"That wasn't hard, in his inebriated state," Qiang responded.

Biming seemed elated by the events, but Qiang seemed strangely subdued.

"You have won a great victory," said Biming, beaming.

"No," responded Qiang. "There is no joy in subjugating an inebriated old man in such a way."

But before Biming could inquire about this surprising statement, they saw Sunfu Rinpoche approaching, and both stood up to greet him.

"How is Lei?" Qiang inquired. Qiang's query surprised Biming.

Sunfu Rinpoche smiled in appreciation of Qiang's concern. "He will be all right, in due course. But he will not be returning. So until the governor makes other arrangements, Qiang, you and Biming must manage the stables by yourselves."

"But where will Lei go?" inquired Biming.

"Do not concern yourself with that. It is enough that you should know he will not bother you again."

"I am pleased. And I am sure that Qiang and I can manage the horses."

Qiang nodded his agreement.

Sunfu Rinpoche could see the concern in his pupil's eyes. "But Qiang, something else seems to be bothering you. What is it?"

The young man looked crestfallen. "Why, Master, I must apologize to you for my behavior."

Biming looked surprised at this assertion.

But the old man spoke reassuringly. "Do not concern yourself, pupil. In the main, you did well, and I congratulate you."

Qiang shook his head. "I could have done better!"

"We can always do better, but you, at least, did well! But enough! You have had sufficient learnings for today. Let us talk about it again at our session tomorrow morning. Now, you and Biming must attend the horses."

And with that, the old man strode off.

THE NEXT MORNING, Qiang and his master sat cross-legged on the grass in the gardens of the governor's palace. They had gone through their normal meditation routine, and now Sunfu Rinpoche had brought Qiang back to normal awareness.

After a time, as each reengaged with the world, Sunfu Rinpoche inquired of his pupil, "You seemed to have some concerns about yesterday's incident with Lei. Can we talk about that?"

"I would be pleased to, Master." Without further encouragement, the lad said, "There are two things that concern me, sir. First, I indulged in some anger yesterday, when I know, from your teachings and those of my previous masters, that my efficacy is enhanced by maintaining my equanimity. I felt, in this way, I had betrayed my masters and denigrated their teaching." Qiang looked crestfallen, seemingly overtaken by his guilt.

Sunfu Rinpoche allowed him to sit quietly for a few moments and then gently prodded him. "And there was something else?"

The young man sighed. "It was Lei. You tell me that I should not be judgmental. But I was so incensed by his cruelty to the little horse that I found it difficult to find any human characteristic that he possessed to which I could relate. And I know that is not right. We are all shaped by our heritage and our circumstances, and I could not begin to understand what might have fashioned him to act in such an abominable way."

"Ah, young man, you have presented me with a double challenge! First, we must look at the nature of you, and then we must look at the nature of him. Despite the dramatic events of yesterday, most of our problems can be defined in this way. We ask ourselves—what should we reasonably expect of ourselves and what might we reasonably expect of others?" The old man paused a while and then continued. "To begin with, I did not detect excessive anger in your demeanor. No doubt, you were considerably provoked by Lei's assault on the horse. Aside from stripping him of the whip, which was probably necessary, your actions did not portray undue anger."

"But, sir, when I stood over Lei after removing the whip, I did feel anger. When it was all done, I wondered if I would have struck him if you hadn't intervened."

"But you didn't strike him, Qiang. You are but a young man. While you have received some instruction in these matters, you are not an adept. I have been involved in such practice for nearly fifty years. And even now, unless I maintain my awareness, I can be momentarily distracted by such destructive emotions. I am satisfied with your progress. So let us put that concern aside for the time being. That is not to say that you have attained the desired end state. You must continue to work at that. But for now, be satisfied that you are progressing well."

Qiang bowed his head in deference to his master.

Then, Sunfu Rinpoche continued. "I suspect, however, that it would be profitable to talk a little while about Lei."

His pupil nodded his agreement.

"Tell me how do you feel about Lei?"

The young man contemplated a moment before replying. "To be honest with you, Master, I am filled with abhorrence at his behavior. Not only was he cruel to the piebald colt, as you saw, but he has been a bully as well. I don't mind so much for my own sake, because I am reasonably robust. But I have felt for Biming, who is hardly more than a boy and has little capacity to defend himself. And I have been greatly disappointed."

"And what has been the source of your disappointment?"

"Well, when the governor first assigned me to the stables, he said Lei was to teach me how to deal with horses. I like animals, and the thought that I might acquire such skills pleased me. But Lei taught me little about horses, except how to clean out their stalls and feed and water them. The negative feelings I have for Lei give me concern that, in some ways, I have failed my teachers."

"Put aside your guilt, Qiang; it is not helpful. It is hard to criticize your assessment of Lei. Superficially, Lei comes across as heartless and cruel. Let me put two questions to you. First, can you imagine why Lei might act this way? And second, do you believe he has any redeeming features?"

"Are you trying to test me, Master?"

"Not particularly, young man. I make no judgment of your concerns about Lei. I only seek to expand your understanding. Now, take your time, and try to answer my questions."

Qiang pondered for a minute or two. "Well, I suppose he must have some redeeming features. Surely the governor would not have placed him in charge of the stables unless he knew of some qualities that warranted giving him the position. The governor seems to be quite shrewd and unlikely to have rewarded Lei with such an appointment without justification."

Qiang thought a little longer before continuing. "Just recently, he was absent from the stable. Some said he went to a funeral. If that was the case, he must have cared for someone enough to go to that trouble. He was away for some time. As for an explanation for Lei's behavior, I have none." Then he frowned and added, "Although it has seemed that since his return, he has been surlier and more demanding. Perhaps something happened to him to cause this. Could you perhaps tell me more about him, Master?"

"But of course, young man! It always has been my intention to do so."

QIANG SAT LISTENING attentively as Sunfu Rinpoche related Lei's story.

"Lei was born into the family of farmer Quong Wai and his wife, Shui Fei. Lei was their third son. The family lived in a village to the northwest, at the far edge of Governor Ruan Xiu's province. They worked the land, and although there were trials—droughts and floods and other natural disasters—by and large, because of Quong Wai's skills, they survived the ordeals and prospered when conditions allowed.

But at this time, the bandits were very active in the nearby countryside.

Quong Wai had grown up with the bandit chief Lang Tun. They had lived on adjoining farms when they were young and often played and, later, hunted together. However, when Lang Tun grew older, much to the consternation of the village elders, he abandoned his family and became a robber. At first, he would assail merchants who sought to ply their trade between the rural villages. He was a big, athletic fellow and fearsome in his demeanor. He was quite a successful robber, and before long, he had drawn to him some other like-minded miscreants. With the growth in his power base, he became more ambitious in his expeditions and would often raid farms, taking away their livestock and plundering their harvests.

Because of his friendship with Lang Tun, Quong Fai's farm was never raided. But just for insurance, when he prospered, the farmer paid some tribute to Lang Tun. And so, Quong Wai entered into an uneasy truce with the bandits.

Eventually, Lang Tun overreached himself. His raids had been so successful that he had begun to think that he was invincible. His spies told him that the emperor was about to pass through the district and that he brought with him considerable bounty that he wished to bestow on the young local governor, Ruan Xiu, in the province to the south, for his dedicated service to the emperor.

The likely booty proved irresistible to the bandit chief. Accordingly, he planned a raid on the emperor's retinue. He and his team of marauders lay in wait at a narrow pass that the emperor's party was compelled to pass through. The locals called the pass Devil's Gate.

When the emperor and his attendants approached, the bandits were dismayed by the fact that he was accompanied, at both the front and the rear, by a strong contingent of armed men.

Despite the overwhelming odds, Lang Tun ordered his followers to charge the emperor's party. Many, however, realizing they were vastly outnumbered, held back. Despite fighting furiously, Lang Tun was soon overcome and killed, as were the foolhardy few who had followed him into the fray.

The bandits regrouped, and a surly fellow from the western mountains, Chang Shun, took over leadership. Unfortunately, without Lang Tun's protection, the bandits soon after raided the farm of Quong Wai, driving off the livestock and killing all the family members, except for Lei, who had been sent to a neighboring village to purchase some farm implements, and his youngest sister, who had managed to hide herself in the barn. Of course, on his return, Lei was devastated and swore to take his revenge on the bandits.

After the bandits dispersed, Lei's sister escaped into the forest. In fear of her life, she subsisted on what nature could provide her. She wandered farther and farther, until one day, she was discovered by a young woman who had ventured out to gather berries and herbs for her household. The young woman overcame her natural fear, and Lei's sister, unbeknownst to any relatives or friends, was adopted into the family of a simple peasant, who was the young woman's husband and who worked a small farm to the north of her home. The couple's names were Chen and Liu.

Lei, on the other hand, could not take his focus off revenge and stayed in the locality to plot his retribution.

Because of his intimate knowledge of the local terrain, Lei often was able to inconvenience the bandits. He stole their horses, thus limiting their mobility. He waylaid the brigands that they sent into the village to bring back supplies. He became a thorn in their sides.

Once the emperor had taken stock of the attack on his party, he resolved to rid the province of the marauders. He sent for Ruan Xiu, exhorted him to overcome the bandits, and promised material support to help him.

Ruan Xiu, in his youth, had been a fierce warrior, and few could best him in combat. In obedience to the emperor, he assembled a troop of competent fighters and led them to disperse the brigands. This was a somewhat unusual approach. Most of the nobility would not deign to fight but would leave the dirty work of war and conflict to trusted underlings.

But the young governor went out in pursuit of the emperor's enemies. When he arrived in the territories that were most affected by the marauders, he heard of Lei's exploits against them and sought him out. Once Lei became aware of the governor's intentions to rid the countryside of the bandits, he readily agreed to join with Ruan Xiu's forces. And Lei proved most helpful in providing intelligence that would help bring them down.

But more than that, Lei himself was a very capable fighter, and in the skirmishes that ensued, driven by his desire to avenge the death of his family, he fought the bandits brutally and without concern for his own safety. Lei earned Ruan Xiu's respect as a warrior.

Finally, Ruan Xiu was joined by Chin Chao from Sun Nang province. He brought with him a large contingent of well-trained fighters. It didn't take long, then, to decimate the bandits and drive the remnants of their band deep into the mountains, where they could do little more damage.

When Ruan Xiu decided to return to his palace, he asked Lei to come back with him. Lei was flattered by this, and now, with his family gone, he felt there was little to keep him in his home district; he agreed to accompany the governor.

Ruan Xiu, impressed by Lei's courage and moved by his personal situation, became his benefactor. He had, over these many years, employed Lei and was generous in his treatment of him. As Lei grew older, the governor found less arduous work for him, which finally culminated in his job as stable master.

Unfortunately, like many men, as Lei grew older, he grew more bitter, resenting those circumstances long ago that took his loved ones from him. But then, he seemed to become rejuvenated. He found that his younger sister had escaped from the brigands. He was delighted to learn that she had been adopted by a peasant couple who had no children.

When Lei discovered this, he was so excited. He went to the hamlet to be reunited with his sister. It was an occasion of great joy for him. In his gratitude, he bestowed on the peasant couple as much benevolence as his circumstances allowed. Now, Lei would go once a month to be with his sister and the couple who had become almost surrogate parents for them both. This was now his family, and he rejoiced in the comfort they provided him.

But then, to his dismay, his sister became ill. Despite their concern and all the ministrations that the family could provide, her health gradually deteriorated. Finally, it became obvious that the woman wouldn't recover. They sent for Lei, and in the last weeks of his sister's life, he sat with her and tried to meet her needs as best he could. In the end, nothing could be done, and the unfortunate woman died. This perverse turn of events made Lei very bitter."

***

Sunfu Rinpoche now said to Qiang, "You remember he left the stable and was gone for some time. That was the reason for his departure. You also were critical of his demeanor when he returned. What I have related to you might give you some understanding of his anguish. I trust that my relating his story to you might help you to find some compassion in your heart."

QIANG SAT WITH his eyes downcast. Finally, he looked up at Sunfu Rinpoche. "I had no idea, Master, of Lei's trials."

"Well, there was no way that you might have learned all of this. But the lesson here is, of course, that we should be slow to judge. Whether we like it or not, how we relate to the world is often shaped by our life's circumstances. I know that you have had your own trials, but you haven't fallen into bitterness and resentment. This is largely due to two factors: you were fortunate enough to have been born with a positive disposition and the personal skills to deal with adversity; and you also were bolstered by a loving environment and the benefit of the counsel and tuition of some wise sages. Very few have those advantages."

Qiang nodded his agreement.

There was silence as the young man contemplated. Finally, he said, "This is an important learning. Thank you Master. And I know I must do something about it."

"What do you propose that we should do?"

"It is self-evident. I must work harder at learning altruism. I must heighten my empathy and practice loving kindness in the manner of the Buddha."

The old man smiled. "That is indeed the appropriate response. In our meditations on altruism, we began by relating to those close to us. That was easy. We must expand our circle of inclusion to all of our fellow beings, no matter how obnoxious they seem. You have learned from your other masters that we are all indeed one. That is only a notion in our heads until we can extend loving kindness to everyone."

Again, Qiang nodded. "That is the obvious outcome to which I must aspire. But Master, there is one thing that is still not clear to me."

"What is that, Qiang?"

"I can see why loving kindness is so important, but is there no situation where it is appropriate to resort to violence?"

"That is a very good question, young man. And yes, there are times when it is appropriate to resort to physical force. It is permissible to physically subdue someone to protect another from assault or in self-defense. Physical force, however, only provides a short-term solution and often exacerbates and inflames hatred and other unhelpful emotions. But sometimes, it cannot be avoided. It is always important to remember that if you must resort to violence, do so in a measured way. Do not allow yourself to be caught up in anger or hatred. Such emotions not only render you less effective, but they will cause you to do greater damage than is necessary and will heighten the resolve of your opponent for revenge. Even your physical response must be rendered in an atmosphere of loving kindness. Your motive must always be human reparation, not punishment, revenge, or vindictiveness. Many masters have not only taught their pupils the wisdom of Buddhism but have also instructed their pupils in physical self-defense. I am not an expert in such matters, but there are some basic precepts I can teach you. But my short answer is yes—there are occasions where even an adept must resort to physical measures of self-defense, but I would counsel you to use such skills sparingly and wisely."

LEI NEVER RETURNED to the stables, and Biming and Qiang were left to their own devices, but they managed quite well at running the stables. Without Lei's presence, they were able to learn from trial and error, without undue criticism or condemnation. And of course, an environment without blame and retribution provides the best learning opportunities.

Poor Biming, who had greatly feared Lei, was a new person. He was happy at his work and grew more confident in his demeanor. He positively idolized Qiang, a situation that considerably embarrassed Qiang.

Qiang had natural talents with the animals, and as the months passed by, he gently instructed Biming, who, after a time, became quite adept at handling the governor's horses.

Having heard Lei's story from his master, Qiang was concerned for Lei's welfare. Sunfu Rinpoche was pleased to see the lad's genuine concern for the former stable master, but his teacher would say very little, except to assure Qiang that Lei was well cared for and that he need not worry about Lei's welfare. Qiang had no doubt that the governor had intervened to protect Lei. He smiled to himself in recognition of his growing respect for the austere man who was Ruan Xiu.

Qiang had only recently learned to ride a horse, but Biming had never been astride one. Qiang took it upon himself to teach Biming how to ride. After a time, they both became proficient riders. Then, they would ride out of the palace enclosure, each leading a small group of horses, which they would exercise along the paths and fields of the nearby neighborhood. In time, because of their devotion to their charges and the extra care and attention the animals were provided, the horses were fitter and healthier than ever. This drew fulsome praise from the governor's men, who had cause to use the horses from time to time. Even the piebald colt came to accept riders other than Qiang.

Qiang and Biming were very happy in their work. Qiang was additionally blessed by having the opportunity to work with his sister in the evenings, preparing the documents that the governor had requested for his friend Chin Chao.

In addition, Qiang's spiritual development was being well guided by Sunfu Rinpoche. They worked well together, and Qiang came to admire him even more than his previous teachers.

It was a time of great satisfaction, not only for Qiang but for his mother and sister as well.

One day, the grand project was complete. Qiang and Lan had finished the manuscripts that Fung Tszu had requested for Chin Chao.

On the evening it was done, Qiang called for Ruan Xiu to come and examine the collective works and to give his approval or request whatever modifications he saw fit.

Qiang and Lan waited expectantly with their mother in the anteroom that the governor had provided them for their work. The brother and sister had worked for a year or more on this project. They had enjoyed toiling together but understood that they might not be the most subjective critics of their own work. When the governor had taken the time to check on their progress, he always had nodded his approval. He was certainly not a demonstrative man, and Qiang and Lan had been encouraged by his positive responses.

They waited impatiently for the governor to arrive. Even Qiang, who from his meditation practice had become assured and robust, felt a little nervous while awaiting Ruan Xiu's judgment.

There was no need for concern. When the governor arrived, he pored through the works and then quietly commented, "This is indeed fine work. You have done well!" Then, he turned to the beaming Nuan and saved his smile for her. "You certainly have talented children, madam."

Nuan's chest swelled with pride. "Indeed, I do, sir."

Addressing Qiang, he said, "Leave your completed works here. I will send for someone to package them securely, such that they might be sent to Chin Chao."

Then Qiang inquired, "Sir, might Lan and I continue to work together in the evenings?"

"Well, of course, young man, but remember that whatever you create will remain my property because you are my vassal."

"Then what would you have us work on, Excellency?"

"Anything you choose, Qiang."

"Thank you, sir. I am sure my little sister will enjoy that just as much as I will."

Lan smiled her agreement.

SOME MONTHS WENT by. Life was good for Qiang. He saw his mother and little sister most evenings. Lan and he were overjoyed that the governor had allowed them to continue to work together. It was exciting to create new works of their own choosing. In the governor's extensive library were not only many traditional Buddhist texts but also Taoist works and fragments from even earlier wisdom traditions. While his work in the stables was menial and sometimes demanding, he was comforted by the ability to extend his intellectual pursuits in the evenings.

In addition, the governor had decided to familiarize Qiang with the skills of falconing. Several times a week, in the late afternoons, they would go out into the fields adjacent to the governor's palace. He would bring his bird, Xiang, and allow Qiang to practice with it. He gave Qiang a leather gauntlet to put on his arm and showed him the different functions that the bird could perform.

First, there were the basic hunting techniques, when the bird would be sent off to hunt a quarry and would return with a grouse or a pheasant.

That was a relatively simple function. Soon after, the governor showed Qiang how the bird might be used for communications. This required not only the bird becoming attuned to the sender (in this case, Qiang) but also the techniques that must be adopted to create a receiver. Thus, Lan was co-opted into the project. After a time, Qiang learned how to attach a message to the bird's leg and instruct it to find Lan in order to deliver it.

It took some time before Qiang could master this, but one day, the governor brought another bird to Qiang.

"To date," Ruan Xiu said, "I have tried to familiarize you with the skills of falconry using my own bird. Soon, I will want you to go back into the world to achieve your destiny. Today, I have brought to you your own bird. Now, we must train it and you, such that when you venture forth into the world, you will have another resource to protect you."

"What is it called?" Qiang asked.

"His name is Kung, which means heaven."

Qiang nodded his head approvingly.

For several months, the lad and the governor worked with the bird until it had acquired all the skills of the governor's own bird, Xiang, including the ability to seek out Lan to exchange messages.

DESPITE ALL THIS extracurricular activity, Qiang still had his duties as stable master to perform.

During the day, he and Biming worked together quite amicably. Through trial and error, they learned how to train the horses and care for them well. They rode the horses often, and those who worked in the confines of the governor's palace and in the fields nearby became used to the sight of the two young men, exercising their horses. Qiang often used the excuse of exercising a horse to visit his friend, the gardener, Shang. Although the two young men worked hand in glove at the stable, Biming always deferred to Qiang. This was a cause of some embarrassment to Qiang, who was keen to see Biming consider himself as an equal and not defer to Qiang. However he tried, Qiang seemed unable to convince Biming that the two should have equal status. Qiang never comprehended that Biming deferred to Qiang because he had stood up to Lei. While Lei had tried to demean Qiang, Qiang had the psychological armor to withstand such assaults. Biming was not so fortunate, and he suffered terribly under Lei's autocratic domination. As a consequence, he would always feel beholden to Qiang. But their circumstances were soon to change irrevocably.

IT WAS NOW quite a number of years since Qiang, Nuan, and Lan had come to live in Ruan Xiu's palace. They had seen the passage of the seasons and the effect it had on palace life. Every year, in the early spring, the governor would set off to rejoin the emperor's court as it reconvened in the place where Qiang had first met him. Then, at the onset of summer, he would return and resume his duties of government and law enforcement.

In the governor's absence, Sunfu Rinpoche would assume the governor's authority. He was greatly respected by the populace for his wisdom and fairness. While Qiang had great admiration for Ruan Xiu, he had come to love his third master, Sunfu Rinpoche. He would always be grateful to Ruan Xiu for caring for his mother and sister and for the marvelous opportunity the governor had provided him. But Ruan Xiu was a difficult man to get close to because of his severe manner and demanding ways. To Qiang's great surprise, however, the only person Ruan Xiu seemed to relate to with genuine warmth was his mother, Nuan. He treated her with great respect, almost reverence.

Sunfu Rinpoche, on the other hand, was a warm and generous man, whose unconditional love seemed to bring out the best in most who came to know him. But it was not only that; he was a great Buddhist master. He was well-versed in Buddhist teachings and adept at the most demanding meditation and other spiritual practices.

Qiang was grateful for Sunfu Rinpoche's generosity in taking time to mentor him. As far as Qiang could determine, he was Sunfu Rinpoche's only pupil, although he still served the governor as a mentor. Qiang was a little baffled by this because Ruan Xiu seemed someone unlikely to be receptive to such mentoring. Nevertheless, the governor was always respectful toward Sunfu Rinpoche, and the master never said a bad word about the governor.

The governor had just returned from his sojourn at the emperor's palace. In the evenings, as they worked on their manuscripts, Qiang could see the governor and Sunfu Rinpoche in earnest conversation. Occasionally, they seemed to look across at the young man as he and Lan were engrossed in their creative work.

Qiang was vaguely aware of this but paid no great attention. It was such a joyous thing to be able to spend time with his sister, doing what they loved.

QIANG WAS PITCHING hay into the stables to feed the horses.

At the same time, Biming was bringing buckets of water to fill up the various watering troughs.

They had settled into an easy routine that they both enjoyed. Feed and water the horses. Groom the horses. Exercise the horses. Since the departure of Lei, they had managed to settle the horses. Qiang and Biming were both gentle carers, and the horses had largely become quieter and more malleable. Things were now so different in the stable.

But then, Sunfu Rinpoche appeared, with a young man of perhaps seventeen or eighteen years of age trailing slightly behind him.

Biming was so engrossed in his tasks that he did not seem to notice the intruders. But Qiang, ever aware, did so immediately. He turned to them and smiled.

"Why, Master, how good it is to see you. And who is this that you have brought with you?"

Sunfu Rinpoche smiled at his pupil. "Qiang, this is Jiao. He comes from a farming community to the north. His parents were pastoralists, and, unfortunately, they perished under the hands of some of the rogue bandits that still thrive there. The governor has decreed that we should find a role for Jiao in the stables because he has skills with animals."

Qiang was moved by the reference to Jiao's history. "Well, then, sir, I am sure he will be a useful addition to the stable's workforce."

The old man looked at Qiang with a wistful look. "It is not the governor's intention that the workforce of the stable should be augmented. He has something else in mind for you. We will talk about that in a little while." He then moved his gaze to Biming. "Young man, the governor has determined that you should be the master of the stables now. And Jiao will be here to help you."

Biming was bewildered by this turn of events. Qiang, seeing his discomfiture, was quick to say, "This is very proper too. Biming is a very competent carer of the horses. The animals will be well tended under his charge."

Biming remained somewhat dismayed. "But what of you, Qiang? What will become of you? You have been so supportive of me that I must confess I will be concerned for you in whatever role the governor might place you."

Qiang was moved by Biming's solicitude. "Do not bother yourself, Biming. The governor has largely been my benefactor. He has often tested me, but I have always felt his intentions were benign."

Sunfu Rinpoche nodded his head. "Although it sometimes may not appear so, the governor seeks only to further Qiang's development."

Biming muttered, "I am glad he does not share the same concern for me!"

The old man still had acute hearing and smiled at Biming's heartfelt remark.

"Now Jiao, I want you to stay with Biming, who will familiarize you with the stables and the duties you will be required to perform. Look after him well, Biming."

"I will, sir. You can depend on that."

Biming was very fond of the old man who was Qiang's mentor and was grateful for his intervention in the affair with Lei. But then, a thought prompted a query. "But sir, what will happen to Qiang? He has been a wonderful companion for me, and I fear he will be taken away, and I won't see him again."

Sunfu Rinpoche was moved by Biming's heartfelt plea. "Do not concern yourself, Biming. The governor has another assignment for Qiang. He has asked me to bring Qiang to him to explain his new project."

"But will I see him again?"

"I suspect that when this project is complete, you might see a lot of him!"

"I would like that!"

"Come," Sunfu Rinpoche said, turning toward Qiang. "We must go now to see the governor."

He then strode off and beckoned Qiang to follow.

Before Qiang did so, he embraced Biming. "Do not worry," he said. "I am sure all will be well." He then hurried off to catch up to his mentor.

IT TOOK ONLY ten minutes for the old man and Qiang to walk to the governor's palace. Sunfu Rinpoche, due to his exalted position, did not have to bother with the palace guards but went straight to an anteroom, where the governor waited, surrounded by documents.

He looked up on Sunfu Rinpoche's entrance, and the old man declared, "Here he is, as you requested, sire."

"Ah, Qiang. I need to talk to you," Ruan Xiu said. He nodded to the older man. "Thank you, my friend, for bringing him here." The governor sat for a while before he spoke again. "You and I have an agreement. You agreed to do whatever I asked of you, and, in return, I agreed to care for your mother and sister."

Qiang nodded. "Indeed, sir, that is our agreement. And might I say, you have maintained your half of the bargain very well. My sister and mother have been well cared for."

For the first time in their relationship, Ruan Xiu seemed to display some humility. "Thank you, Qiang, but it is not hard to care for them. Your mother is a wonderful person, and your sister tries her best to meet my demands. It has been a pleasure to be their benefactor. And I must confess that you also have upheld your side of the bargain well."

"Again, my lord, that has not been hard because the duties you have given me have been quite agreeable."

"Well perhaps, but I did not anticipate that you might have to deal with the difficulties that Lei foisted on you."

"I will concede that was a little difficult, but Sunfu Rinpoche was a great help there."

"I am pleased that my old friend was of assistance. But don't think too badly of Lei. In the past, his courage was of inestimable value to me. That is why I have tried to support him."

Qiang was reminded of how this seemingly austere and sometimes demanding man was also imbued with surprising benevolence. Then he said, "I hold no grudge against Lei, but tell me—what has happened to him?"

"I tried to offer him alternative employment, but his shame compelled him to return to the place of his birth. I can only hope he can restore himself to something like his former character." Then, the governor's visage changed. "But enough of this. Let us attend to the business at hand. I have sent for you because I have a new and difficult assignment for you."

Qiang was immediately intrigued. "What would you have me do?"

"I will get to that in a little while. First, I want to change the conditions of your contract with me."

Qiang frowned. "Have I not fulfilled my end of the bargain? I certainly have tried, and I would wish you to point out in any way that I might have failed you."

For only the second time since he had met Ruan Xiu, Qiang was surprised to see the governor's face soften, and then he smiled.

"No. Do not concern yourself. You have met all my expectations of you. What I am about to do is to absolve you of all further responsibilities to me. If you succeed in the task I give you, you will owe me no further indulgences."

"But then, what will happen to my sister and my mother? I will not agree to any change of terms if their welfare is not preserved."

"It is not my intention to abandon Lan and Nuan. I will give you my word that they shall always be cared for in my household."

"Thank you, my lord. That is a most generous offer."

"Perhaps, but you do not yet understand the last project I have for you. To secure the welfare of your mother and sister, I will happily amend our formal contract."

Qiang thought a moment and then replied, "That won't be necessary, sire. I have known you long enough now to feel comfortable that your word is sufficient guarantee. Now, what would you have me do?"

"You and your sister have laboured long to produce some magnificent manuscripts. It has been my intention to deliver them to my friend Governor Chin Chao as a gift. I want you to take that gift to him."

Qiang was somewhat surprised at this request, but he was happy to try to grant the governor's wish, particularly as he had been assured of Nuan's and Lan's welfare.

"This might not be an easy task," Ruan Xiu said. "I would have gone myself, but I am required to return to the emperor's palace for matters of state. And unfortunately, in recent times, the bandits have had a resurgence in the territories between here and Chin Chao's province, which might provide you with difficulties. What's more, if I were to go, they more than likely would assume that I carried something valuable, which would have focused their attention on my entourage. If you go, alone, while it will be dangerous for you, it is unlikely that they will perceive that you might carry something valuable. As well, we will take great care to disguise your manuscripts so as to avoid their attention. Make no mistake; this is a hazardous undertaking. If you decline to pursue it, I will not think ill of you."

Strangely, Qiang felt, for the first time, that he held an equal hand with the governor. Ruan Xiu had offered him succour for his sister and his mother, for which he was grateful. The governor's desire to reward his friend was obvious, but Qiang had no desire to prosecute such an advantage. This strange but decent man was turning to Qiang to deliver something important to him. Qiang found it was hard to refuse.

"How shall I travel, sire?"

"You will need to take a horse. Choose whichever steed you will from my stables. It shall be yours, not only for the trip but thereafter. As well, I will provide you with a map and some introductions to some friends you may need along the way. As well, I shall give you a letter of introduction to Governor Chin Chao, which you must present to him on your arrival. I will provision you as well as possible for the journey. You will have a long way to go, and because you must travel cautiously, it may be some months before you arrive. If I have not heard from you in six months, I will send someone out to find you."

Qiang nodded, signifying his understanding and acceptance of the plan. He knew already which horse he would take—the little piebald colt.

"Now," the governor said, "because this is such a serious undertaking, I don't want you to accept immediately. Take a few days to think about it. Remember it is entirely possible that you might be captured by the bandits, and if you are, you will be lucky to get away with your life." Ruan Xiu looked at Qiang with concern. "You might want to consult with your mother and sister or perhaps your mentor, Sunfu Rinpoche, but in the end, the decision is yours. Come back to me in three days with your answer."

THE LITTLE HORSE ambled contentedly along the well-worn path that headed north from Ruan Xiu's palace. Its rider was in an ambiguous frame of mind. Qiang was exhilarated by the challenge of his quest and the newfound freedom, but he could not forget the tears his little sister had shed when she knew that he would accept the governor's challenge.

His mother, on the other hand, had been surprisingly pragmatic. There was, she knew, something special about her son. Many mothers might experience such feelings about their offspring, but she remembered how her heart had stirred when his first teacher, Chogpen Rinpoche, had named him Takygulpa. And then, seemingly out of the blue, another teacher appeared, Chagsarka Rinpoche, ostensibly to help him produce Buddhist transcriptions using his calligraphy skills but who, on reflection, had taught him the fundamental tenets of Buddhism. And then, finally, he was tutored by the governor's own mentor, Sunfu Rinpoche.

But more than this, she could see his benevolence, the constancy of his sense of well-being, and his determination to make the world a better place. She remembered how, when they had quit the family farm, Ruan Xiu had set off to find Qiang, believing there was a special, albeit difficult, future for him. She had now come to trust Qiang's intuitions about such things. And indeed, she knew that she had no choice because under the traditions of their people, he was now the head of the household, and both she and Lan, while obviously paid respect by the young man, had no option but to accept his decisions.

Ruan Xiu had provisioned him well for his journey. He had provided clothing and bedding, as befitted a traveler, and a small array of utensils, which would allow him to care adequately for himself.

The manuscripts, the gift of which was the reason for his journey, had been wrapped into a narrow tube and sealed with wax, such that they would be impervious to the weather. In turn, the tube was wrapped in a blanket, such that when it lay strapped to the horse, it seemed to be an item of little significance. As well, there was a leather bag that contained sufficient provisions to sustain the young man for a week or so and two goatskin containers of water to quench his thirst.

Ruan Xiu cautioned Qiang to keep the purpose of his travels secret. If he was questioned, he could say that his task was to deliver a message from Governor Ruan Xiu to Governor Chin Chao. One of the letters Qiang carried was a letter from Ruan Xiu to that effect.

"This letter will provide some protection for you," explained the governor, "while you are in my territories. But beyond that, it will provide little assistance for you."

Qiang reminisced on all this but was glad he had commenced his adventure. Despite the fact that the little horse had these various items attached to it, the load was not particularly heavy, and the colt walked easily down the track.

Qiang was exhilarated. He knew full well that there would be difficulties on this journey, but he felt an overwhelming sense of freedom and excitement that was new to him.

Before departing, however, Qiang made a request of the governor. "Sir, would it be appropriate to take Kung with me?" He referred to the falcon that the governor had gifted him.

"No, lad. You will be too far for away for the bird to be useful as a messenger. And caring for him would be another distraction you don't need on your journey."

"I thought as much. I have asked Lan to care for it while I am gone. Would you be able to make sure she has the skills to do so? Although she loves the bird, I am not sure she is competent enough to care for the bird."

"Never fear, Qiang. I will ensure the bird is cared for. What's more, the bird knows you well now. When on your return we believe you might be close enough, we will send it out to search for you."

THE LITTLE HORSE meandered down the track. Qiang was content not to hurry his little steed, knowing there was plenty of time and that he must look after the horse well to ensure he would sustain the long journey. The weather was such that Qiang was glad for the cloak the governor had provided for him. He pulled the cloak close to him. He was excited by the prospect of his mission, but, understanding the dangers, he wondered how it might all end.

The governor had given him a number of letters of introduction to significant people who might help him in his project, as well as the letter confirming Qiang's status as the messenger of the governor.

Ruan Xiu had also provided him with a map, depicting the route he should take. Because of the dangers along the way, the route recommended by his benefactor was not the most direct route but the one he deemed the safest. As well as marking the route, Ruan Xiu also marked out the location of the way stations that Qiang could take advantage of while he was still in the territory the governor controlled. As he remembered from his original journey to the governor's palace, such places would provide him with warmth, shelter, and some basic provisions.

However, Ruan Xiu pointed out that the first such way station was more than a day's travel, so on the first night, Qiang would be required to sleep rough in a convenient place along the way.

By midafternoon, the winding path took him across a small rivulet. Not knowing when he might have the opportunity again, he paused to quickly bathe in the icy waters and allowed the piebald colt sufficient time to fill his belly with water and graze for a half hour on the lush grass by the side of the stream before resuming his journey.

The day had passed pleasantly enough, but in the late afternoon, because it was now autumn, dark seemed to descend quickly. While the weather was still fine, the air became quite chill. Qiang did not want to be caught on the track in unfamiliar surroundings in the dark, so he cast about to find a suitable place to spend the night.

He selected a spot that was reasonably sheltered from the wind by a thick copse of short trees but where there was considerable grass for the little horse to graze. He unloaded the horse and then tethered him on a long rope to give him good access to his feed. Then he foraged among the trees for a little wood with which to make a campfire. When it was lit, he cooked a simple meal and made some tea. Thus satisfied, he assumed the lotus position and meditated.

His mind was at rest, and he felt enervated by the stillness of the evening and the dwindling smell of his campfire. He could hear the quiet sound of the horse pulling at the grass as he fed. Above, the clear sky was full of twinkling stars. As he made ready to sleep, Qiang was quietly content that his embarking on this new adventure had begun well.

ON THE NEXT day Qiang had hardly time to eat and then repack his essential accoutrements and provisions before it started to rain. The rain was not heavy but just a constant mist that seemed to penetrate his soul. Whilst his cloak shed most of the water and provided some warmth, it was enough to render his progress somewhat uncomfortable.

Sometime about noon, Qiang stopped where there was a little rock pool and allowed the horse to drink his fill. Where the pool overflowed, there fortunately was enough grass to feed the horse a little. Qiang meditated while the horse fed, and then, after perhaps a half an hour, he resumed the journey.

About midafternoon, Qiang began to keep an eye out for the way station that Ruan Xiu had marked on the map. The rain still drizzled down, and because of the slippery conditions, Qiang was loath to hurry the horse as he picked his way carefully over the rugged track.

Because of their careful progress, it was not until late afternoon that Qiang eventually discovered the way house. It was a stone building with a thatched roof. The roof surprised Qiang because there was little to suggest that the material to thatch a roof could have been derived from nearby. The building seemed very sturdy and somewhat larger than the one in which he had stayed with his mother and sister and Ruan Xiu. A squat chimney revealed that he should expect a fireplace inside. In truth, he was looking forward to getting out of the weather.

Somewhat damp and a little cold, he was grateful that he had found a place that might offer warmth and comfort for the night. He tethered the horse and removed the various bundles that had constituted the animal's load. He gathered together the things he might need for the night and approached the way station.

To his surprise, he heard voices inside. He stopped, reluctant to intrude, and listened. It sounded like two voices, quietly chanting. The words that were chanted softly, though not of his dialect, were somehow familiar. They were simple, sonorous tones that stirred something deep within him.

And then he remembered. They were chanting the An Cheng mantra that his first teacher, Chogken Rinpoche, had taught him so many years ago.

He assumed the lotus position and meditated, while silently repeating the mantra himself. Finally, he became aware that the sonorous intonations had ceased. Shortly afterward he heard the sound of two men softly talking.

Not wanting to alarm the men, Qiang called out a greeting, and then politely asked, "Would you permit me to join you in there?"

He heard a deep voice exclaim, "Ha, Jian, it seems we have company."

Then came another lighter but mellifluous voice, with a slight chuckle. "Well, invite him in, Bai. I have had enough of your company for the time being."

Immediately, a large figure appeared in the doorway. He was an elderly man, dressed in what appeared to be rough peasant's attire. He was tall and large-framed but rather gaunt and with a slight stoop.

Then the deep voice boomed from out his chest and a smile lit his face. "Greetings, young man. And who might you be?"

"My name, sir, is Qiang. I was hoping to spend the night at this way station."

"I am Bai. And what brings you this way, Qiang?"

Qiang hesitated before responding, remembering the governor's counsel of cautiousness. "I am a messenger from Governor Ruan Xiu. I am traveling to the court of Governor Chin Chao." Wary of divulging any more about his mission, Qiang hastened to change the subject. "Tell me, sir—I heard you chanting the An Cheng mantra, which I haven't heard since my childhood. How is it that you are familiar with it?"

Bai was somewhat taken aback by this question. "Well, young man, it is a meditation aid I have used all my life. It is spoken in the dialect of my ancestors, who are often given credit for bringing Buddhism to this part of the world. In fact, it surprises me that you know of it, as few seem to use it these days. Could you tell me how you came to know it?"

Qiang hesitated, not wanting to divulge too much about himself. But seeing little harm in the question, he finally responded, "When I was a child, I was fortunate enough to have a teacher who taught me the mantra."

"Then you are very fortunate—perhaps more fortunate than you know. The mantra is normally only divulged to adepts. You say your name is Qiang?"

"Yes, sir."

"And who was your venerable teacher who shared this marvelous secret with you?"

"He was called Chogken Rinpoche."

Bai's face lit up with surprise, and then he smiled.

Qiang was intrigued. "Do you know of this teacher, sir?"

"Indeed, I do! And now I know who you are as well."

"But I have already told you that, sir. I am Qiang."

"Well, no doubt that is your family name, Qiang, but you are known among the masters as Takygulpa Rinpoche. And I know by now that you have had other teachers—Chagsarka Rinpoche and Sunfu Rinpoche, perhaps, as well."

Qiang was absolutely dumbfounded by Bai's words. "But how can you possibly know all this?"

"Relax, young man. You are among friends." Bai turned in the doorway and spoke to the man inside. "Hey, Jian! I have a surprise for you. The wind has blown in a young master who would stay with us and entertain us this evening."

"Who is he, Bai? Did he tell you?"

"Not in so many words, Jian. But you know of him. He is the young master Takygulpa Rinpoche."

"Takygulpa Rinpoche, you say. Ho-ho! It would be entertaining to talk to him instead of listening to you drone on for another night. Don't keep him out there in the weather, Bai. For heaven's sake, invite him in!"

Bai turned to Qiang. "Please do come in, young man."

Qiang had bundled up the things he needed for the night. On Bai's invitation, he walked into the hut.

IT WAS A little dim inside the hut, and it took a while for Qiang's eyes to focus. When they did, he saw a large room with a fireplace and a table with two bench seats. The floor was composed of rough stone pavers. In the corner, to his left, was another old man, sitting cross-legged on some bedding. He was attired in white robes, and his contentment radiated from his face. For some reason, Qiang felt immediately attracted to him.

Bai said quietly, "This is my friend, Jian."

Jian smiled at this remark, but Qiang was surprised that the old man seemed distracted and didn't look directly at him.

"And what does this young master look like, Bai?" Jian inquired.

Then it came to Qiang—the old man squatting on the floor was blind.

"He is a strapping young fellow, a little above average height, with dark hair and square shoulders, and he looks as though he could manage a hard day's work without much difficulty."

Qiang was intrigued that the two men seemed to know of him and was somewhat embarrassed that they insisted on calling him a master.

"Put your bedding close to the fireplace, Qiang," advised Bai. "It seems as though this might be a rather chilly night."

"No, sir, the cold does not bother me much, and you both have older bones than I, which, I am sure, could use a little warmth."

Qiang placed his bedding on the floor, leaving plenty of room for the two old men to take up positions reasonably close to the fireplace. Then he turned to Bai and said, "I am curious to find out how you know me. And I would be more than pleased if you would refrain from calling me a master. I am but a farmer's son. It is true that I have been fortunate to have been tutored by excellent mentors, and any wisdom I might have acquired is due to their efforts and not some innate capacity of my own."

Jian said quietly, "Well, he certainly displays the humility of a master, Bai."

Of course, this response frustrated Qiang, and he bit his tongue, not wanting to offend these old men.

Bai looked intently at Qiang. "Whether you believe it or not, you were destined to be a master. When our ancestors came to this country and sought to spread the teachings of Buddhism, they knew that other masters would arise from the native population to help them in their cause. You, of course, know of the legend of the Buddha and how he became enlightened under the bodhi tree. These priests were led by a great master, who purported to be able to foretell some aspects of the future. He passed through the area where you were born more than a century ago. Just outside your home village, where you went to school, he noticed another bodhi tree. He announced to his followers, 'This tree will nurture another great master. He will come to it as a child, and another master must be ready to begin the tuition of this chosen one.'

"As a result, for many years, we ensured a Buddhist master sat beneath the tree, waiting for that child to arrive. When you were young, that task was given to Chogken Rinpoche. When you approached the tree and found him, he knew you were the designated master he had been chosen to nurture."

"That is incredible! How did he know I was just not another curious child? It seemed that way to me. I passed the tree every day and saw the man sitting there, and so I was curious about it."

"We have ways of gauging the inherent depth of a person, even a child. Chogken Rinpoche was soon able to confirm that you had the required potential to undergo further instruction."

"And when you say 'we,' just who do you mean?"

Bai considered this question a while before answering. "Seeing as you are more than likely to soon be one of us, I think it is appropriate that I answer your question. We are a group of devoted Buddhists. We would like to see Buddhism more widely accepted in these communities. We do not wish to foist it on to anybody but just hope, through the demonstration of how we go about our everyday lives, that our beliefs can help people improve their sense of well-being."

"And tell me, how does Ruan Xiu fit into the picture?"

"Well, the governor was chosen in his youth to be a master in our tradition. Might I say, however, that while he was a disciple, he never quite had the qualities to be a master. In time, he was given the opportunity, because of his lineage and the support of the emperor, to become governor. He decided he could make a greater difference by being in a position of authority and supporting our movement than by attempting to become a master. And indeed, I must confess his patronage has greatly advanced our cause. He has, in turn, nurtured many of our masters and adepts."

This gave Qiang a good deal to think about, and although he might have asked a few more questions, he felt it appropriate to take on these significant revelations before inquiring further.

They chatted about inconsequential things for a while, and then Qiang volunteered to cook some dinner. His companions readily agreed to this plan.

Bai showed Qiang the provisions that the governor had provided for the way station. Qiang decided to contribute a few of his own. He lit a small cooking fire and within half an hour had a pot bubbling slowly over it.

As they sat comfortably in the warmth and anticipating a tasty meal (because the slow-bubbling pot emitted attractive odors), Qiang screwed up his courage to ask another question.

"I hope you do not find it impertinent that I should ask such a question, but it would seem that Jian has no sight. How did that happen?"

Jian laughed. "I do not find that impertinent at all, young master. I have a congenital condition. I have been blind from birth."

Qiang was taken aback. "Oh, I am so sorry. I did not mean to embarrass you."

Jian just smiled and responded in his mellifluous voice. "Why would that embarrass me? That is just the way it is. Some people are born with physical deformities. Others are intellectually handicapped. Some are left-handed. Some are color blind. I have merely lost my sight, and despite this, I have led a very satisfying life. I am grateful for my lot. I am sure there are things in my life that I have missed because of my loss of sight. But this loss has heightened many of my other senses. I have never felt any bitterness as a result."

"Oh, that is an admirable response, and I am humbled by the way you have come to deal with your affliction. But I still have cause to worry. When we move on from here, we will come into some territories where bandits prevail. While that is dangerous for all of us, it must be particularly difficult for a man with no sight."

Bai laughed. "You do not know all the truths about this remarkable man. He won't be bothered by the bandits."

"Why would that be so?" inquired Qiang. "I thought that being sightless would make him very vulnerable."

"One would think so, but it isn't the case. He is a very modest man and is unlikely to tell his story to you—but I will." Bai paused to look at Jian. The old man merely shook his head. But Bai insisted, "Oh no, old friend. It is appropriate that the young master know your story."

Bai looked back at Qiang and said, "The bandits who live in these areas have always been particularly pernicious. Some distance farther to the west of here, they have their headquarters. It has been their practice to abduct citizens who are critical of their abominable behavior and to torture them, as a disincentive for others to express their outrage. My friend was once taken as a result of his criticism and brought back to their headquarters, a place they call Xi Nung. There, he was tortured, but he would not resile from his criticism of their vile practices. Once they knew he would not break, they resolved to starve him to death. It was their practice to put such people in a nearby cave, which is called Gorrum, which they then sealed with a huge boulder, which allowed no prospect of escape from the entrance. Consequently, Jian was ensconced in the cave and the entrance was sealed off.

"But what the bandits hadn't reckoned on with our blind friend is that he had heightened senses, and being shut off in the dark was not nearly as frightening to him as it would have been for normally sighted people. Consequently, Jian was able to make his way around in the darkness of the cave, and it seemed to him that there was a fissure somewhere that allowed fresh air to enter. Scrabbling around after searching for some hours, he discovered that high to the rear of the cave was a small opening. With considerable effort, he squeezed through a tortuous passage back into the outside world.

"The next morning, the bandits found him sitting at the cave entrance, softly chanting his mantra while meditating. They were amazed at his escape and attributed him with magical powers. His fame spread far and wide, and now no one dares touch him! Consequently, he is free to roam the countryside without fear of interference. I, on the other hand, have to take more care, as indeed must you."

THE NEXT MORNING, after a frugal breakfast, the three travelers gathered up their possessions and headed off. Qiang so enjoyed the company of the two old men that he decided to walk with them for a while, leading his little horse.

He learned there was a widespread Buddhist community in the villages that dotted the countryside. The old men went from one to another, nurturing and supporting those communities. Most of the people they visited were simple farming folk who sounded little different from his own family. Qiang and his fellow travelers were able to share some common experiences, and by the time they stopped around noon for a short rest and a little to eat, they had developed an easy relationship. In his usual way, Qiang treated the two men with great respect, not just because of their ages—which, in his culture, would have been sufficient reason to show due deference—but because of their wisdom and obvious benevolence.

Shortly after they resumed their journey, they came to a fork in the road.

Bai gesticulated to the left. "This is the way we must go. As I understand it, you will need to take the other path."

Qiang nodded. "According to the map the governor provided me, that is how I must proceed."

Jian said quietly, "Well, little master, we wish you luck on your mission. But you must take great care now, for you are entering dangerous territory."

Bai nodded his agreement. "I know it goes against your nature, but from here, you must be careful not to trust anyone, other than those the governor has recommended to you. These are dangerous regions, and the bandits are growing again in strength, so be extra vigilant. We may be able to provide some assistance to you, but you cannot rely on that. We will know of your progress, but we won't be able to provide you immediate assistance."

Qiang was surprised by this. "How will you know of my progress? That sounds quite improbable!"

"Perhaps you might think so. But nevertheless, we will be monitoring your passage from afar."

Even though Qiang pressed Bai for more information, he would say no more.

QIANG HAD LOST track of time, but it seemed a week or so since he had said goodbye to Bai and Jian and struck off on his own to fulfil his obligation to the governor.

He had heeded the warning of his friends and had sought to avoid coming in contact with others on his journey. While there seemed to be few travelers on the road, at any indication that someone else was coming, he removed himself from the path and waited until he was sure the traveler had passed before he resumed his journey.

At night, he was careful to make camp well away from the track and extinguished his campfire so that he would not be noticed or disturbed by other travelers.

As he had experienced at the beginning of his journey, he continued to endure persistent drizzle and a biting wind. As a result, all his clothes and even most of his bedding was now damp.

But then, one day, the clouds dissipated, and the sun finally prevailed. While the wind was still a little chill, Qiang resolved to take advantage of the weather to dry his clothes and bedding. Around midmorning, he guided his little horse off the path and found a wide-open rocky area with a few sparse, dead trees. He tethered the horse on a long rope over a grassy patch so that he might feed and then unpacked all his clothing and bedding. He spread the bedding out on some flat rocks under the warm sun and draped his clothing over a few dead branches, leaving the sun to do its work.

To the north and only several hundred meters away, he could see a tree-lined watercourse. He remembered how, in his childhood, his father would take him foraging. They would trap hares and gather berries, mushrooms, and various wild herbs and occasionally catch fish in the nearby streams, before the drought came and dried them up.

These were some of his most favorite memories of his father. In his concern to be a good provider for his family, his father had augmented their larder in any way he could.

Qiang had packed a little braided cotton fishing line and a couple of hooks. He foraged through his chattel until he found them and set off toward the watercourse to see what potential it had. As he walked, he noticed that after the prolonged period of drizzling rain, many mushrooms were pushing up from the sparse soil on the alluvial flats of the watercourse. He smiled and resolved that he would pick some for his supper on his return.

There wasn't a great deal of grass, but as he approached the watercourse, it grew a little thicker and more verdant. And with that, there was an increase in insect life. He spent a little time collecting a few grasshoppers and crickets that he might use for bait, if there was water in the watercourse and there were fish to be had.

As he got closer, it was apparent that there indeed was water, and he could see a few long waterholes connected by a gently flowing stream. His father had instructed him that he must approach the water cautiously, so as not to alarm the fish. Accordingly, he moved slowly toward the bank and stood behind the wide trunk of a tree on the bank of the creek.

From his vantage point, he could see quite a number of fish. He slowly took his line from his pocket, placed a grasshopper on the hook, and flicked it into the water some four or five meters from the tree. The fish seemed to take no notice of his bait, so he retrieved his line. He then remembered another trick his father had used. If you want fish to take a bait on the surface of the water, you can sometimes stimulate their interest by flicking small objects onto the water's surface to gain their attention. He peeled a little bark off the tree and broke it into small pieces. He flicked small pieces of bark onto the water's surface. After five minutes of this activity, a few fish began to congregate on the surface. Then, Qiang flicked his bait out again onto the surface of the water, and immediately, a fish inhaled the small grasshopper and was caught.

Qiang pulled the fish in. It was only of modest size but quite plump. The activity had frightened the other fish so now there were none to be seen. But Qiang remembered how his father had counseled patience.

He waited quietly behind the tree trunk, occasionally flicking a piece of bark onto the surface. After fifteen minutes or so, a few fish had congregated on the surface of the water. Once they had settled, Qiang again flicked out another bait, and sure enough, it was taken by a slightly larger fish, which he pulled in to lie with the other.

This was enough—two nice plump fish! He would need no more. He went from the stream and gathered some mushrooms and herbs and walked back to where his clothing was drying, quite satisfied with his foraging. While he felt grateful for the food, his sense of well-being was more augmented by his memories of his father.

It was midafternoon when Qiang arrived back at the location where his clothes were drying and his horse was feeding. He retethered the horse so the colt could have access to more grass, and then he lit a small fire, dressed the fish, and made a very satisfying meal with these fresh ingredients.

The sun had done its work, and all the items he had spread out in the warmth of the sun were now dry. He decided to repack his clothing and other possessions that had been wet in order to resume his journey in the morning.

IN THE MORNING, after he had eaten, he went back to the creek to wash his cooking pot and utensils and then bathed himself.

Back at his campsite, he reloaded the sturdy little horse and then set off again. He made his way back to the path and resumed his westward journey. As he progressed, he seemed to be gaining altitude, and as he did, so the country became more rugged and wetter. Misty showers engulfed him again, and despite his best efforts, he was soon damp.

The path now regularly traversed small streams, and on one occasion, he came to a more sizable stream, about twenty meters across, which was spanned by a suspension bridge. When the little horse, so sure-footed and confident, steadfastly tripped over it, Qiang could not help but be reminded of his father. Even though the stream was not so wide and the current not so torrential as the place where his father met his death, he could not suppress a tear as he made his short crossing.

He was very aware that he was now in dangerous territory. Whenever he could, he found a vantage point and would stop to look back and forward along the path. Sometimes, the misty rain impeded his ability to see very far at all, but nevertheless, he thought it prudent to make the effort.

On one such occasion, midmorning, he spied a small group of men approaching from the west. There seemed to be six of them, and they were leading laden donkeys. They appeared to be traders, but taking no chances, Qiang led the horse off the track to a thick grove of trees and waited until they passed.

After that, he made reasonable progress and encountered no further travelers that day.

From this point, the path changed direction and headed almost due north.

In the late afternoon, he made his way from the path and again was able to find a reasonably secluded camping spot close to a small stream. He made his camp in the lee of a rocky rampart and under a low, squat tree. The terrain was now quite harsh, and most of the vegetation was quite stunted. The tree, although also stunted, had a surprisingly thick canopy.

Being aware of his horse's need, Qiang had allowed him to graze occasionally along the way when there was sufficient pasture, being unsure when there might be another opportunity. But now, before he established his camp for the evening, he would see if there was any chance for the horse to feed further overnight. He led him along the bank for a little distance before encountering a flat with ample grass, where Qiang tethered him for the night.

The rain still persisted as frequent, misty showers. The canopy of the tree, however, was thick enough that the ground underneath was comparatively dry. Fortunately, because of the shelter of the tree and the rockface, he was able to find enough dry kindling to start his cooking fire. Once he had finished eating, he added more fuel to the fire, removed his wettest garments, and placed them on the adjacent rocks. hoping they might dry out. The night air was quite cold, but he meditated for a while and then recharged the fire before rolling into his bedding and soon was asleep.

In the morning, he was pleased to find his clothing dry again. He at least would be comfortable when he set out this morning. Surprisingly, the clouds seemed to have cleared somewhat overnight, but the wind had picked up a little and was decidedly chill.

Confirming the northward trajectory of the path, the sun had risen on his right.

It took no time to raise a little cooking fire from the embers, and soon he was enjoying a little tea and basking in the contentment that its warmth brought to him.

A HALF HOUR after sunup, Qiang retrieved the horse and loaded him up again to resume the day's ride. Qiang stroked the little animal and spoke to him soothingly. He was grateful for the animal's loyalty and stoicism. They had formed a strong bond, and in the quiet hours of their arduous journey, he appreciated the animal's silent company.

Because the terrain was now more difficult, progress was slower, but the morning was uneventful. They stopped during the middle of the day, and Qiang allowed the horse to graze a little on a verdant patch by the edge of the track. While the horse quietly fed, he fished out the map the governor had provided him to try to make sense of his location. It seemed to Qiang that today he would pass over the highest mountain pass and would soon find himself in terrain more amenable to travel. The pass was marked with the title "Devil's Gate," which seemed somehow familiar and foreboding to Qiang. Then he remembered Sunfu Rinpoche's story of Lei, Ruan Xu, and the bandits. This was the very place where the bandits were defeated.

He also seemed to be close to the next safe house the governor had suggested. It was probably less than two days away, and he had the governor's letter of introduction.

In the early afternoon, he came to the mountain pass that the map indicated. He stopped and dismounted. The path ahead was quite narrow, and what was visible to him was quite steep. He tethered the horse and went off to climb up a knoll to his left. When he achieved the summit, he found that because of the narrowness of the path, he could not see far ahead. When he looked back, he was surprised to see a solitary man on a horse, quite some distance back.

Qiang was eager to conquer the pass and move on to easier going. It seemed to him that there was little likelihood that the figure in the rear would overtake him easily. As he stood, he rationalized that he never could ensure there would be other travelers on his journey forward through the pass. Consequently, it was sensible to go forward and see what the mountain pass held in store.

Accordingly, he descended from his vantage point and untethered the horse. In deference to the steep slope, he chose not to mount the horse but led him carefully up the path. After a half hour, they had crested the pass. Both horse and master were somewhat exhausted by the ascent. Qiang sat momentarily on a rock at the side of the path, holding the horse's bridle. He looked down at the path of their required descent. Again, the track was narrow, and high, rocky cliffs hemmed it in from both sides. He could see no cause for alarm in proceeding farther, and he was mindful of the rider approaching from their rear.

He had progressed only another five hundred meters when he heard a shrill whistle from behind. He turned but could see nothing behind him. When he then looked ahead, he saw two men on horses emerge. They apparently had been hidden by a rocky promontory that jutted into the path about fifty meters ahead. They were armed with swords. He turned his horse and made to go back, but now, on the path behind him, two men on horses appeared; they were also armed. It seemed to Qiang that they must have been in hiding as he passed and then alerted the men in front—by the shrill whistle he had heard—that he was approaching. The path was effectively blocked in both directions now.

Qiang turned the horse again to progress farther down the pass and walked slowly up to the men who were impeding his way.

ALTHOUGH HIS PROGRESS seemed to have been thwarted, Qiang was not particularly afraid. As he approached the armed horsemen who blocked his progress, he inquired, "You seem intent on stopping my journey. Is there something you want from me?"

The larger of the two men replied, "You have come this way without our permission. You cannot expect to continue until you have paid tribute to us."

The two horsemen who had appeared in the rear of the pass had made their way forward and were now quite close. Qiang was surrounded by the armed bandits, two in front and two behind.

The big man continued. "You are now entering our territories, and you cannot do so without our permission. To begin with, you need to tell us what brings you here."

Qiang thought for a moment and then replied, "I am here as an emissary of Governor Ruan Xiu. I have a letter of introduction from him to establish my credentials. Do you want to see it?"

The big man laughed. "A letter from your governor has no authority here! He has, in fact, been a source of some grief for us in the past, and if you come here on his authority, not only would we not recognize such authority, but it serves to prove you are our enemy."

The other man now interjected, "Lim, it is clear that this young fellow is antagonistic to us. Let us just kill him and take his horse and possessions back to our leader. Fan would take comfort from the fact that we slaughtered an emissary of Ruan Xiu."

The big man retorted, "Don't be so hasty, Hong. If we were to take this young fellow back to Fan, we might be able to extract some intelligence from him that would aid our cause."

Lim now turned back to their prisoner. "And what might you be called, young man?"

For a moment, Qiang wondered whether he should divulge his name, but he reasoned that if the bandits took the trouble to read the governor's letter of introduction, they could soon learn his name anyway. He looked calmly back at Lim and replied, "I am called Qiang."

Lim just nodded. He was strangely disconcerted by Qiang's demeanor, as he seemed so calm and showed no sign of fear.

By this time, the two riders from the rear had approached quite close to Qiang.

The big fellow, Lim, seemed to have some dominance over the others, who appeared to accept his pronouncement and made no further debate.

Lim looked at Qiang and said, "You see, young fellow, how generous we are? We have, for the time being, preserved your life. But you must now obey us, and we will take you to our leader, who shall determine your fate."

Qiang quickly assessed that there was, as yet, little chance of escaping these bandits, and it would be sensible to comply.

"First, we need to ensure that your horse follows us so that you don't do anything foolish and attempt to run away from us." Lim motioned to Hong, who took the reins of Qiang's horse. He tied them together and then rummaged through his saddlebag and emerged with two long strips of rawhide. He looped one length through the joined reins so that he could lead the horse from three or four meters in front. Then, using the second, shorter strip, he bound Qiang's wrists together tightly in front of him.

Lim laughed. "Now that should keep you under control."

They then set off in single file to complete their passage through the pass. Lim headed the entourage, closely followed by Hong, then Qiang, while the other two riders brought up the rear. The bandits seemed in no hurry and merely ambled along, engaging in banter and laughter, mostly at the expense of their captive.

Finally, the pass was breached, and they gathered their formation a little closer together. Even though the track was wider and the terrain considerably flatter now, they still did not hurry.

It was late afternoon before one of the riders in the rear chanced to look behind. He quickly called the group to a halt.

"What is it?" queried Lim.

"Someone is approaching from behind."

They all turned to look. Sure enough, although some several hundred meters away, a rider was closing in on them.

Qiang was not surprised. When he had scanned the track before entering the pass, he had observed a rider following him, but at that stage, he was some considerable distance in the rear. It was inevitable that, with their slow rate of progress, he should catch them up.

"He seems to be a big fellow," murmured Hong.

"He continues to approach. He is either not afraid, or he is ignorant of our reputation."

Lim laughed. "Let us hope it is the latter!"

ALL THE RIDERS, including Qiang, turned to observe the new arrival, who seemed unconcerned about the waiting group and approached without hesitation.

As the figure got closer and his features could be more clearly discerned, Qiang gave a little gasp of surprise. He looked right and left to see if his captors had noticed, but they were so intent on the man's approach that they were not aware of his reaction.

Qiang's surprise had been elicited by the fact that he was sure he knew the man who was approaching them. It was Lei!

His big frame was easily identifiable. Yet Qiang could see that Lei was different. He was leaner and more muscular.

Soon after, Hong also seemed to recognize the approaching horseman. "Have no concerns," he said. "This is Lei. We know him. He lives on a small farm nearby. He has paid his tribute."

Lei came up to the group and nodded his acknowledgment. He looked straight at Qiang. Qiang was about to say something, but Lei frowned and shook his head. The lad immediately understood that Lei did not want Qiang to divulge that he knew Lei.

This gesture intrigued Lim. "Why do you shake your head, Lei?"

Lei looked at Lim with steely eyes. "I am just bewildered that this foolish young fellow has dared to enter these territories, alone and unarmed. Don't you know about these ruffians, lad?" he inquired of Qiang.

Before Qiang could answer, Lim responded, "He says he is an emissary from Governor Ruan Xiu. He even claims to have a letter of introduction from the governor."

Lei laughed. "A fat lot of good that would do for him with you scoundrels!"

They all laughed at Lei's rejoinder.

"And where are you off to, Lei?" queried Hong.

Lei turned to him in disdain. "It is none of your business, Hong. I have paid my tribute to your leader, Fan. I understand I owe you no other consideration."

"Settle down, Lei," interjected Lim. "We are just trying to be sociable."

Qiang could detect a sneer in his voice. He suspected that Lim knew that they could overwhelm Lei physically, if they needed to.

Lei was a little more respectful to Lim. "Well, if you must know, I am going to visit the peasant family who cared for my sister before her death. They are wonderful, caring people, unlike you cold-hearted villains."

Lim laughed. "That is almost a compliment, Lei. You are held in some regard around here as a fierce fighter. But you must accept that your fighting days are over. We won't interfere with your passage, but it would ease the pain of our memories of your past if you could give us a little more than the tribute you paid Fan. You see, we are the ones who have to deal with you on a day-to-day basis, and unfortunately, Fan didn't share any of your tribute with us. It would help to convince us to ease your way if you paid a little tribute to us as well. We could then be your benefactors."

Lei responded fiercely, "I have no money with me, and even if I did, I would not hand it over to brigands like you."

"Oh, how uncharitable you are, Lei. We don't necessarily want your money. Just a little donation of any sort would be appreciated."

Lei glared at Lim. He was silent for a while, and then his voice softened. "Oh, very well, then. I brought rice wine with me, which I intended to give my friends on my arrival. Perhaps I could donate that to you." Lei dismounted his horse and, after a moment or two, produced a large container that he handed to Lim.

"I must confess it is a waste, bestowing so much fine rice wine on a group of ruffians like you, with no ability to appreciate its quality."

Lim's eyes lit up. "Well, that is a fine tribute, Lei. I am sure neither I nor my colleagues will harass you further after delivering us such a magnificent gift. You have satisfied all our requirements, so be off with you now."

Lei remounted his horse and then, skirting the bandits, made his way off along the path.

AS LEI, ASTRIDE his horse, made his way along the trail, the bandits resumed their journey. Just as before, they seemed in no great hurry, merely ambling along, chatting and joking. It was late afternoon now.

Hong called out to Lim, who was just in front of him. "Hoi, Lim, where are you planning to camp tonight?"

Without turning back, Lim called over his shoulder, "We will camp by the stream in the same place as we did three nights ago. We should be there in under an hour."

Hong nodded. Having now negotiated the pass, the country became more hospitable. What's more, the weather had improved, and in the lee of the hills they had just traversed, the wind had dropped, and the sky had cleared.

Except for the thongs cutting into Qiang's wrists and despite his perilous situation, he certainly felt physically more comfortable than he had for some time.

Soon after, Hong again queried Lim. "Hey, Lim, how about sharing some of that rice wine with us?"

Lim just shrugged. "Not now, Hong. You don't hold your liquor very well, and I don't want to see you falling off your horse! Perhaps after we've eaten tonight."

Qiang heard the two riders in the rear chuckle at the thought of Hong falling off his horse.

"Very well, then, but what have we got to eat?"

"Just some rice."

"Is that all?"

"Can I help it if you fellows made pigs of yourselves with what we stole from the last traveler? You ate it all last night, with no thought about today."

"Maybe our prisoner has something tasty we could add to the rice," said Hong. He turned to Qiang. "Do you have any provisions with you?"

"A few bits and pieces," replied Qiang.

"Good! We will take a look when we make camp."

Soon, the path began to meander downward into more forested country. It wasn't long before Qiang could see a tree-lined watercourse.

"There's the spot," called out Hong.

Ahead, there was a tree with a very dense canopy of leaves on the bank of a pleasant stream that gurgled its way over a rocky bed.

The riders dismounted and unpacked what they might need for the night.

Hong then approached Qiang. "I am going to untie your wrists so you can dismount as well. Now, don't try to escape. If you make such an attempt, we will surely kill you."

He untied the thong from around Qiang's wrists, and Qiang duly dismounted.

"Now unpack what provisions you have."

Hong was impressed because even though Qiang carried only a small quantity of provisions, there was quite a variety of foods and spices. It seemed well beyond the range of staples on which people normally existed in their travels. He thought for a moment and then said to Qiang, "It seems you must know something about cooking."

"Just a little."

"Maybe we will put you to work to cook for us this evening."

"As you wish."

Hong went to his bundle of possessions that he had unpacked from his horse and unpacked some cooking utensils. "Will these suffice to cook a meal?"

Qiang nodded. "I will need a little water."

Hong nodded. "Go down to the stream, and fill your pot."

The other bandits had been going about their business, unpacking their bedding and tethering their horses. But soon enough, they were back at the campsite.

Hong proudly declared, "I think I have found a chef for us tonight." He beckoned to one of the other bandits. "Take my horse and his, and long-tether them like you have done your own, while I supervise our new cook."

"Shall I unpack any of his things?"

"No, let him sleep rough tonight. It is mild enough, so it won't kill him!"

The bandit took the horses away, watered them, and then tethered them along the grassy bank of the stream so they could feed during the night.

Hong fetched the rice that Lim had, and then he watched as Qiang constructed a small fire and went about the task of cooking the meal. In a half hour or so, some delicious fragrances started to emanate from the cooking pot. It was not long before the hungry men began to gather about the campfire.

Finally, the meal was cooked, and they all ate lustily.

After they had finished, Lim nodded his head in appreciation. "You have provided for us well, young man. I could be tempted to bring you along on our next expedition, just to cook for us."

Hong interjected, "He might be useful as a cook, but he would not be much use for anything else." He turned to Qiang. "Have you ever used a sword?"

Qiang shook his head. "I have been taught to exercise loving kindness. Swords are not helpful in such a pursuit."

The bandits laughed. Lim, who seemed to have some sympathy for Qiang, responded, "When a man comes at you with a sword, loving kindness will hardly act as an adequate shield."

"A sword can only defend your self, which is just a manifestation of your ego. When you know who you really are, you will find that is an inadequate defense."

This seemed to be more than the brigands could take in.

Hong said, "Take our cooking utensils and eating implements down to the creek and clean them. It is time for Lim to break open the rice wine."

Qiang did as he was told and was acutely aware that he was being observed very closely by his captors. When he had finished, he brought the equipment back to the fire, and Hong duly stowed it in his baggage.

By now, each of the bandits had sampled the rice wine a couple of times, and the congregation became quite loud and merry.

But then, Lim said, "Before we indulge ourselves too much, let us ensure we have properly secured our prisoner."

Hong led Qiang away and both secured his wrists behind his back and tied his ankles together.

Lim motioned to one of the other bandits. "Throw some more wood on the campfire so that we might have light a little longer."

The bandit immediately complied, but his legs were somewhat wobbly from the rice wine, and he almost stumbled.

As Hong finished tying him, Qiang laughed and said, "This is a fine way to treat your cook."

Hong was not amused. "You are lucky to be alive." Once Qiang was trussed up, Hong hurried back to the others to be sure he got his fair share of the rice wine.

Qiang noticed that, in his haste to get back to the carousing, Hong had not tied his bonds as tightly as he previously had. He fancied that if he persevered, he might be able to loosen them and eventually be free of them. He began to flex the bonds and test them. It was harder than he thought, and he was in such an awkward position that he soon tired.

After a time, he noticed the singing and laughter had quieted. The flames from the fire had died down considerably, and just a few yellow tongues flickered around the logs.

After resting a while, Qiang again attempted to loosen his bonds. He felt he had made a little headway but then had to rest again. As he lay resting, Qiang was acutely aware of the night sounds. He could hear crickets and the occasional night bird, but the dominant noise was the snoring of the inebriated bandits. But then, quite close by, he heard a twig crack and then the sound of heavy breathing. Before he could make inquiry of the intruder, a low voice whispered, "Hush. Be quiet." He knew immediately it was Lei.

The big man knelt down and soon removed the thongs from Qiang's wrists. Qiang leaned over and untied the strap around his ankles.

Lei whispered, "Go down now, and retrieve your horse. You are more light-footed than I am. Besides, your horse knows you and is unlikely to be startled at your approach. Meet me back here."

Qiang did as Lei suggested, and after three or four minutes, he was back, leading his horse.

"Now follow me," whispered Lei.

Lei strode off purposefully into the night. The sky was clear, but the moon was on the wane, and the night was reasonably dark. After about ten minutes of walking, Lei called over his shoulder, "We should be able to talk now. Those ruffians are pretty well under the weather, but I wanted to take no chances with them because they are dangerous."

"Thank you, Lei. It was brave of you to come to my rescue. But how did you know where we were?"

"Oh, that was easy. After I left you and got a reasonable way ahead, I went off the path and found a vantage point where I could wait for you to pass me. Once your party passed me, I merely followed you at a discreet distance, taking care not to be seen. Once you encamped, I knew those fellows would over-imbibe on the rice wine and approaching your camp would be easy. Ah! Here's my horse. Let's mount up and get out of here."

"Where are we going?" asked Qiang.

"Well, first I need to see the friends who cared for my sister, Chen and Liu. I need to warn them about the bandits. They should be okay because I have paid tribute on their behalf as well. But they are dear to me, and I will do my best to protect them. Then, you need to tell me where your next destination was supposed to be. I know the governor, and I suspect he gave you a number of safe houses to assist you on your way."

"I can easily tell you that, Lei. My next port of call was to be Sinh Hua. I have a letter of introduction to him."

"Excellent! I know the old fellow well, and I will see you safely to him. Now, the bandits are likely to have a slow start in the morning, being somewhat the worse for wear after their carousing. But I suspect once they discover your escape, they might make an effort to catch you. Do they know where you are headed?"

"They only know I have a message for Governor Chin Chao."

"We are in luck, then. If I take you to Sinh Hua, that is a deviation from the most direct track to get to Chin Chao's palace, and I suspect the bandits are unlikely to seek you that way."

Qiang was a little surprised. "Do you think they will continue to pursue me?"

"Undoubtedly. It was the coalition between Ruan Xiu and Chin Chao that originally vanquished the bandits. They will suspect that your visit to Chin Chao will have something to do with a renewed effort to suppress them. If you had been brought to their leader, Fan, then I have no doubt you would have been tortured to extract whatever intelligence they could get from you."

The young man pondered this a while. "Is that why you came back to rescue me?"

"Not entirely. When I left the stables, Ruan Xiu called me to him. He had heard Sunfu Rinpoche's account of our little fracas there. I came to him, embarrassed about my behavior. He has been my benefactor, which I suppose was meant to repay me for my work in helping him quell the bandits."

Lei said nothing more, and Qiang could see he was reliving this experience in his mind.

After a time, Qiang murmured, "And what happened then, Lei?"

Lei was silent, and because of the darkness, Qiang could not see that he was weeping, but he could sense Lei's discomfiture.

Trying to ensure that Qiang did not see his tears, Lei wiped his eyes. He coughed in order to regain his voice, and then he said, ever so softly, "Ruan Xiu came forward, embraced me, and said, 'You are a good man, Lei, and you have served me well. I do not understand what has happened to you to change you so much.' I found that difficult to respond to. When I searched my soul, I realized that what I yearned for most was the governor's approval. My altercation with you was largely because I perceived that the governor was giving you special attention, and, to be frank, I was jealous. No doubt also, aspects of my life had changed, which caused me great sadness. I had taken to drink as an unsatisfactory antidote. But overall, my life had declined into a meaningless, loveless vacuum."

"What has happened since then, Lei? You seem quite different. For one thing, you look much fitter."

"It is hard to explain, Qiang. When I was at the governor's stables, I had little motivation. If the truth be told, I had a sense of entitlement. I had helped him suppress the bandits, and he heaped great praise upon me. But underneath, I was dissatisfied. The work was largely meaningless to me. When I look back, I will admit I was in a rather pathetic state, and the only thing that gave me any joy was the governor's praise. Well, that is an extremely vulnerable place to be. The governor surrounds himself with many able people, and although he is generally taciturn, his occasional praise of others was like a barb in my heart. When I left, I was very bitter. But after a time, it became obvious to me that my sense of self could not depend on the approval of others, if I was to have any satisfaction from my life."

Qiang murmured his approval. "That is a very important lesson, indeed, Lei. I commend you for that realization."

But Lei was barely listening to his companion. A wistful look came over his face. "Finally, I decided to go back to my family's farm, which had been abandoned all those years ago. The farmhouse still stood but was in ill repair. I had a little money saved from my employment by the governor. To tell the truth, when I was living under his protection at the palace, there was little for me to spend money on. I had come to drink too much, but even that cost was but a minor impost on my savings. Finally, I had a purpose—to restore my family home and farm. I largely have been working on that project since I left the stables. I hardly ever drink now, and the hard work and the austere life I now live has somewhat restored my body. I have become physically fitter, but even more important, I feel much more content because I am doing something useful and important to me."

Lei was silent for a moment or two before continuing. "And then I remembered my gratitude for the old couple who adopted my sister after the death of our parents. I owe them a debt that I can never repay. I try to help them in any way I can. I was on my way to see them when I, surprisingly, came across you."

Qiang smiled but said nothing. He remembered his teachers applauding gratitude. They told him that this was one of the more positive emotions that led to benefits for not only those who received it but, more importantly, to those who gave it.

"Despite your dilemma, Qiang, I want to go to them in the morning and check on their welfare. When we get there, I will ask you not to accompany me."

"Whatever you wish, Lei."

"I don't mean to be difficult, but I suspect those ruffians will try to regain you. If they believe I was your rescuer, they will try to follow me. I told them I was on the way to my friends who cared for my sister. More than likely, they will come to question these marvelous old people. If I go alone to see them, they won't have to lie about you and will probably convince the bandits that I came alone to visit you. It is bad enough that they should be harassed by these despicable fellows, but it would be easier for them if they don't have to lie."

"Of course, Lei. I don't want to impose any burden on those who saved your sister."

AFTER SOME HOURS of riding, Lei, riding in front, reined in his horse. He turned back to Qiang. "It might be wise if we had some rest now." He nodded to his left, where a dense thicket of trees stood. "Let us make our way over there and tether the horses under cover, and try to grab a few hours' sleep. We have put sufficient distance between us and those ruffians. I think we can safely rest awhile."

Qiang nodded, and within twenty minutes or so, they had secreted the horses on the far side of a copse of trees and had made themselves comfortable. It seemed to take little time at all before both fell asleep.

There was a dull glow in the east when Qiang awoke. The air was chill, and it had become somewhat overcast again. Nevertheless, there were a few birdsongs, and that always gladdened his heart.

Qiang looked across to Lei, who was beginning to stir. He was bemused by the seeming change in the big man. He was leaner and fitter, and whatever had happened to him seemed to have changed his demeanor. Qiang found it hard to believe that Lei had gone out of his way to rescue him. There seemed no resentment in the man now. He recalled Sunfu Rinpoche's words after his dispute at the stables with Lei. He had counseled Qiang not to judge Lei too harshly and had encouraged Qiang to have compassion for Lei. Qiang understood now that it surely had been sage advice.

"Ah, Qiang, you are already awake," Lei said as he raised himself from the ground.

The young man smiled. "I wish I could offer my rescuer a little breakfast, but those villains deprived me of my small store of food."

Lei chuckled, something Qiang had never heard before. "I have learned recently that I can make do with less food than I once craved.

My waist has shrunk somewhat, and I suppose another missed meal won't do me much harm!"

This was an affable, good-humored Lei that Qiang had never seen before.

"We are only a couple of hours away from my friends' farm. If we set out now, we will be there well before midmorning—that is, if you don't faint on me from lack of nourishment."

Qiang laughed. "Do not concern yourself, Lei. I am a farmer's son who has gone through a drought or two. Many a day, our poor family had little on the table."

Without further ado, the two packed their bedding, mounted their horses, and set off.

The track now entered a well-grassed valley with just the occasional copse of trees. Qiang could see that the countryside they now were traversing was more suitable for farming than any he had seen for some time.

The track was now broader, and the terrain flatter, so that the going was comparatively easy now. The two now rode side by side.

After a time, Lei turned to Qiang.

"I see you ride that piebald colt that gave me such trouble."

Qiang merely nodded.

"You know, young man, I despised you because you could master that horse when I couldn't. If I had been in my right mind, I should have admired you and your ability to deal with the horses in such a masterful way. It is concerning to me that my judgment became so distorted. I should apologize to you." Lei turned away, not wanting Qiang to see the tear in his eye.

Qiang was aware of the older man's emotional distress and looked straight ahead. "There is no need to apologize to me, Lei. It is now apparent to me that I didn't understand what a decent person you are. Most people don't have to deal with the trials that you had to endure. I want no apologies. I would be more than satisfied if you and I could be friends."

Lei shook his head in disbelief. "I would consider that a privilege, Qiang." He paused a while, obviously deep in thought. "It is now clear to me why Ruan Xiu and others referred to you as a 'young master.' I once resented that, but now, I am sure that it is true."

IN ACCORDANCE WITH Lei's forecast, they were soon in view of a farmhouse. It was the kind of dwelling with which Qiang was familiar—a rather sparse, simple building, comprising no more than two or three rooms.

"This is where my friends, Chen and Liu, live," murmured Lei.

Qiang reined in his little horse. "It seems there is a stream over to our right."

Lei nodded. "That is where my friends draw their water."

"I will go over there and wash and water my horse while you visit your friends."

"That sounds a good plan," conceded Lei. "I may be a little while."

"Take your time, my friend."

Lei nodded his gratitude and slowly walked his horse to the homestead.

Qiang watched Lei approach the little house. He then dismounted from his horse and walked the piebald colt toward the stream. He watered the horse and then tethered it with a long rope so that it could feed off the verdant grass along the banks of the watercourse. The young man then stripped off his clothes and plunged into the water. The coldness of the water took his breath away, but soon his body had attuned to the temperature of the water, and he felt quite exhilarated. He then removed himself to the grassy bank, dried himself, and restored his clothes.

The stream ran slowly along its course, punctuated with a rock bar that created some small rapids, which swirled around the remains of a fallen tree. This seemed an admirable place to catch a fish. He fetched his fishing line from his pack and went out to hunt some insects for bait. After an hour or so, he had caught four plump fish. It had taken great patience because the fish were not very active in the cold water, and the water was so clear that it was very easy for the fisherman to spook his prey.

Qiang retrieved a knife from his pack and cleaned and scaled the fish. He then went for a walk along the creek bank and very soon uncovered some field mushrooms and a few wild herbs, which he stored in a little leather bag.

He returned to where he had tethered the horse, packed up his new food supplies, sat under a shady tree, and began his meditation practice.

Sometime later, Qiang heard a horse approaching. Because of his heightened awareness, when he turned to confirm this intrusion into his consciousness, he saw Lei and his horse, some two hundred meters away.

As Lei approached, Qiang inquired, "How were you friends?"

Lei nodded. "As well as could be expected."

Qiang could see the concern in his eyes.

Lei continued, "I have told them to expect a visit from the bandits. I paid tribute on their behalf a little time ago because, heaven knows, they didn't have the means to do so. That should at least hold them in some good stead." He turned to Qiang. "But then, you know, they showed more concern for my fate than their own. They are such wonderful people, and they don't deserve to be harassed by those ruffians. What's more, they insisted I accept a little bag of rice from them to sustain me on my way."

"That was very generous," said Qiang.

"You know, Qiang, they have brought sense back into my life. When I was stable master, I thought how important I was. Such an appointment, conferred by the governor himself, led me to believe that I was somehow special. But, of course, that is not the case."

"Lei, you are no less special now than you were then. My masters have taught me that nobody is particularly special. Or perhaps you might say that everybody is equally special."

"You are lucky to have had such wise teachers. What else did they teach you?"

"So many things, my friend, that I could not begin to tell you, all in just an hour or two. But one thing I have learned, which is pertinent to your situation, is that altruism is a marvelous tonic that distracts us from ourselves, while benefiting others. Having this old couple to care for will, no doubt, also be good for you."

Lei nodded his agreement. "I certainly believe that is true. But come; let us be on our way. We must get you to Sinh Hua's house."

"Thank you for your kindness, Lei."

"Don't thank me, young man. I owe it to the governor to take care of you."

THEY RODE ALL day through largely an unforgiving terrain, with stunted trees and sparse grass. The wind was quite cold, and by late morning, it clouded over and started to drizzle again.

Surprisingly, Qiang enjoyed the ride. It was largely because Lei turned out to be a congenial traveling partner. With their respective rural backgrounds, they had quite a lot in common.

With the sky overcast by late afternoon, it became quite gloomy. The terrain had become much rockier and more difficult now. The path grew narrow again, and because of the hilly nature of much of this countryside, the incline was often steep, causing the horses to labor.

"We will need to find somewhere to spend the night soon," Qiang remarked.

"I have a place in mind," said Lei.

Qiang was intrigued by this response but refrained from questioning Lei.

Not long afterward, Lei pulled his horse to a halt and dismounted. Qiang stopped as well. Lei turned to him and said, "Hold my horse a moment, Qiang." He passed Qiang the reins of his horse. "I won't be too long."

Lei made off to his left. It was not obvious to Qiang where he might be going because, in the gloom, he could see nothing but a seemingly insurmountable rocky outcrop. Lei seemed to move a few dead branches out of the way and then quickly disappeared from view.

The horses stood quietly, obviously enjoying a rest after the recent strenuous efforts in traversing the difficult terrain.

True to his word, Lei reappeared after about twenty minutes. He took the reins of his horse again and beckoned to Qiang to dismount.

"Follow me," he commanded.

Lei led Qiang down an ill-defined path. What had seemed to Qiang to be an impenetrable rampart turned out to have a narrow fissure through it. After they had entered the passage through the rock, Lei turned and restored some dead branches across the entrance, effectively hiding it from view. About fifty meters down the path some ancient rockfall had caused a huge granite slab to bridge the fissure, a mere two meters or so above the ground. It would have been impossible to have stayed mounted on their horses to negotiate it, but once they went under the rock bridge, the path gave them access to a broad meadow. Nestled under the rocks to their right, Qiang could see a little hut, with an old man standing in front.

Lei confidently strode toward the hut, with Qiang in tow.

"Ho, Li, this is my friend Qiang."

Qiang nodded deferentially toward the old man.

"Welcome, Qiang. This old reprobate has begged for some shelter this night. He tells me you are on a mission on behalf of Ruan Xiu. Ruan Xiu is an old friend from previous times, so anyone in his employ is welcome in my hut."

"I thank you for your kindness, Li," responded Qiang.

Lei turned to the young man. "Unpack your bedding and anything you may need for the night, Qiang, and I will do likewise. Then, we must tend to our horses. They have had a pretty arduous day."

"Your horses will be quite safe untethered," said Li. "Over the years, I have had quite a few animals and have let them roam over this little meadow. There is no outlet at the rear and the way you came in is daunting enough that they will not escape that way."

Lei nodded. "That was how I remembered it in the past."

"And beyond the house and to the left is a spring that feeds a rock pool where they can water," said Li. "Indeed, it is where I draw my own water. They will surely find that without your help. So just gather your things and bring them inside, and leave the animals to their own devices."

"What is this place, Lei?" asked Qiang. "How did you know of it?"

Lei chuckled. "In days gone by, it was called the Falcon's Nest. Li showed us this little hideaway when we were fighting with Ruan Xiu to overcome the bandits. We and our little band would retreat here to safety and then mount raids on the bandits' strongholds." He turned to Li, and Qiang could sense both camaraderie and admiration. "This old fellow was a great fighter and was possessed of such cunning that he often devised traps for the bandits that helped weaken their position considerably. He was one of Ruan Xiu's trusted lieutenants."

It was now starting to get quite dark. Li lit a little oil lamp. He then stirred the embers on his hearth. "I don't have much food to share with you both. Times have been tough again, with those marauding ruffians terrorizing the countryside."

"Never mind, old friend. We have a little rice, and combined with your company, that will make a pleasant evening."

"Well, I have something to add to that," said Qiang. He took out his leather bag and displayed its contents of fish, mushrooms, and herbs. The coolness of the day had ensured the fish wasn't spoiled, and Lei could hardly contain his amazement.

"How did you come by this, my friend?"

"When you went to visit the old couple this morning, I did a little fishing and then a little foraging."

Li clapped his hands in approval. "My, you have a resourceful young man with you, Lei."

"It seems that I do," responded the big man.

Qiang volunteered to cook while the older men reminisced. He added a little wood to the embers and soon had a little fire going in the hearth, sufficient to cook with. Li found a bottle of some sort of alcoholic beverage. Li and Lei shared a small tot or two, but Qiang declined.

Before long, he had cooked a meal and made a little tea as well. They ate heartily and complimented Qiang on the meal. The young man cleaned up and prepared his bedding for the night. He then retired, leaving the other two chatting quietly in the faint light of the dying embers of the cooking fire.

As he lay on his makeshift bed, Qiang smiled. It was good to see Lei now engaged and enjoying the company of his old friend. It was something that would have been beyond his belief when Lei was stable master. He silently thanked Sunfu Rinpoche for convincing him to suspend his judgment about Lei.

As he was falling asleep, Qiang could hear the wind blowing strongly through the trees at the top of the hills that surrounded Li's little refuge. But the little hut nestled snugly at the base of the cliff that bounded the western side of the retreat, and indeed, it was amply sheltered from the wind on all sides. Consequently, Qiang knew they would sleep well enough in their simple beds. Lulled by the distant sound of the wind and the muted sound of the other two occupants' quiet conversation, he was soon asleep.

QIANG WOKE FIRST in the morning. He engaged in his usual meditation practice. He then rekindled the fire and left a small pot of water to simmer as he went to fetch the horses. He watered the horses at the rock pool before leading them quietly back to the hut, where he then tethered them.

By the time Qiang entered the little hut again, the other two were stirring. He made tea and served Lei and Li a small cup each as they warmed themselves around the little fire, stretching their limbs back to some mobility after a night's sleep with minimal bedding on the hard stone floor.

Qiang warmed up some rice left over from the previous night, which they all shared. Lei and Li resumed their conversation from the night before. Qiang just sat politely and listened. It became apparent to Qiang that they both had played a significant part in Ruan Xiu's intervention to quell the influence of the bandits. Even allowing for the natural exaggeration that old men who reminisce are wont to do, he knew he was not in the presence of two ordinary men.

But after a time, Lei reluctantly raised himself. "Li, old friend, I am afraid we must go. I have promised to deliver this young fellow into the safe hands of Sinh Hua."

"Hah! Sinh Hua, that old reprobate. Do you dare trust him to look after this fine young man? Do you remember that time I posted him as sentry while we went to steal the bandits' horses, and he went to sleep? We could have all been killed!"

While the old man's words were a little alarming, Qiang could see he spoke with a twinkle in his eye.

Lei laughed. "All I can remember is your hitting his fat rump with a rather large stick to wake him up!"

This caused such mirth that even Qiang could not help smiling.

When they recovered from their mirth, Li admonished Lei. "You must take care of this young man, Lei. He seems a fine fellow to me. If he comes with the recommendation of Ruan Xiu, he must have some good qualities." Then, smiling, he added, "He also seems deferential to his elders, and what's more, he is an adequate cook. He seems worth defending, Lei."

Qiang was understandably embarrassed by this outburst. But then, he was gratified by Lei's response.

"You know, Li, I think I could get to like him myself." Then Lei turned to Qiang. "Qiang, would you mind packing the horses while I have few more minutes with my old friend?"

"Not at all, Lei. Take your time."

Qiang then turned to Li. "Can I thank you, sir, for providing us a secure bed and a night of good company? I appreciate your generosity."

Li smiled fondly at Qiang. "Young man, you are one of us. You pay obeisance to the governor Ruan Xiu, just as we do. You wish to be rid of the bandits, just as we do. Let me tell you that if ever you are in need of succor in my little refuge, you are welcome to join me. Just remember to be discreet, and cover the entrance if you have to avail yourself of my shelter."

"Thank you, sir. That is a kind offer indeed. And I can assure you that I will never knowingly place you in danger."

LEI AND QIANG had ridden for about an hour since leaving Li's refuge. Lei seemed more relaxed after the evening with his friend. Qiang was unable to determine whether this was because of the congenial evening they had spent or because Lei was confident they had outdistanced the bandits. More than likely, it was both these reasons.

They had hardly spoken so far this morning. To begin with, the track was still quite rugged, and it took all their attention just to ensure their horses negotiated the path without injury, and it was still so narrow that they could only ride single file. But then, after a couple of hours, the going became easier. The terrain was less rocky and more wooded, with swaths of grasslands between the pockets of trees. The path became wider, allowing the two travelers to ride comfortably side by side.

Qiang jogged his horse along until it came up alongside his companion. Lei no longer seemed in any great hurry, and their horses now carried them at a brisk walk. Consequently, it was easy enough to converse.

"Lei, I really enjoyed meeting your old friend last night."

The big man turned to Qiang and smiled. "I am pleased, Qiang. Li is a great fellow. He is brave and resourceful, and I admire him greatly. He has qualities I wish I could emulate."

Qiang remained silent for a while. Lei was obviously regretting his misdemeanors of the past, and Qiang did not want to add to his burden.

After a time, Qiang diplomatically changed the subject. "What do you have in store for us today, Lei?"

"Well, I have pledged to deliver you to the safe house of Sinh Hua. Unfortunately, even if we hurried, we couldn't make it there today. I know another place we can stay tonight, where we will be safe. We easily should be there by late afternoon. That will mean we should have but a couple of hours' ride tomorrow."

"I must say I am very grateful to you, Lei. I doubt I could have navigated this journey without your help."

Lei shook his head. "You underestimate your power, young man. You are the supposed Buddhist master, and I am but a servant of the governor. You can obviously recall the teachings of the Eightfold Path?"

Qiang nodded.

"Is not the second element of the path Samma-Sankappa, that we usually colloquially call 'right thinking'?"

This observation rather surprised Qiang, who had never thought of Lei as having any spiritual training. "That is true," he responded.

"It would seem to me, from my flawed experience, that those who have the knowledge and the discipline to indulge in right thinking will always have influence beyond what they might expect. It was always thus with you. Before I understood this, I resented you. Now that I understand your particular talents, I want nothing more than to assist you. But I can assure you, even without my help, you are influential beyond your understanding."

The day passed uneventfully enough.

The bond between the two companions seemed to be growing.

With the improved terrain, the land was more arable, and here and there, off to the side of the track, Qiang could make out little homesteads. Lei occasionally waved to a farmer in the field, tilling the soil or managing his livestock. It was obviously a more prosperous and bountiful landscape than Qiang had seen for some time. There were also children, often helping the farmer in the field or tending to the little flocks of poultry that seemed to surround most households.

Qiang turned to Lei and asked, "These folk seem reasonably prosperous. Are they not plum targets for the bandits?"

Lei shook his head. "These people are protected by Sinh Hua."

"How is it that Sinh Hua can secure the safety of such folk, Lei? He must be a very powerful man."

"That is true, Qiang. He is a very powerful man but largely it's because he is a very wealthy man."

"How did he acquire his wealth?"

"Well, he was very fortunate that he didn't have to acquire it himself but inherited it from his father. His father was a great merchant and trader and forged strong trading links with nearby provinces. His father formed an alliance with Ruan Xiu. After his father died, Sinh Hua took over his father's trading business. Although the governor was principally concerned about the welfare of his citizens, when he resolved to suppress the bandits, Sinh Hua was a great beneficiary because it made it far easier for him to trade with his far-flung customers and suppliers. Consequently, Sinh Hua was an ardent supporter of the governor's efforts to rid the countryside of the bandits."

"What does he do to ensure the safety of the local people?"

"Well, he employs what you might call a private army. His men patrol the main tracks and byways in these areas. They are well-armed and well-trained and have no fear of confronting the bandits. The bandits know if they take advantage of the peasants around here, they will face certain retribution. That is why they concentrate their efforts on waylaying travelers and farmers beyond the area that Sinh Hua polices."

EARLY IN THE afternoon, the two travelers came upon a pleasant little valley with a gently meandering stream running through it.

"Let us stop here a while," said Lei. "We can water the horses. I would also like to wash some of the grime of travel off me before we come to my friends' house. It is quite close by."

They duly watered their horses and tethered them by the stream. They then quickly bathed in the cool, clear water. The water was bracing and, as usual, Qiang felt invigorated when he exited the water.

Soon after, they remounted and continued on their way.

As Lei had suggested, within a half hour, they were approaching a farmhouse. It was a far more substantial homestead than Qiang had been used to. It was a sturdy stone structure, and the roof was tiled with wooden shingles. Beyond the house, there was a sizable barn, which indicated there likely would be considerable livestock. There was a fenced-off area, where vegetables were growing, protected from the livestock. There was also a small orchard with lychees and stone fruit. When Qiang remembered his family's small farm and the struggle his father had to make a meager living off it, this place, in comparison, seemed a verdant, bountiful paradise.

As they got closer, Qiang could see human activity. A tall, young lad was digging in the garden, a younger girl was feeding poultry, and another boy was returning from the nearby creek, the same in which Qiang and Lei had bathed, with two pails of water.

It was the young fellow who spotted them first. He called to the house, "Father, Father! Two horsemen are approaching." He set his pails on the ground and was about to run to the house when he recognized the large man. "Father, Father, it is Lei!" Then, instead of running to the security of the house, he turned to run toward the approaching horsemen. "Lei, Lei, it is you."

The big man stopped his horse. The little fellow ran up to him excitedly. Lei leaned down low, wrapped a strong arm around him, and seated the boy on the horse in front of him. "Of course it is me, little Bao. I told you I would return soon, didn't I?"

The boy laughed excitedly. "But it has been months since you have visited us."

To Qiang's surprise, not only had the commotion roused a man and a woman from the farmhouse, but the older boy and the girl came running to greet them at the door as well. This excitement all pointed to a Lei that Qiang had not known.

The man strode forward with a huge smile on his face. "Welcome, my old friend. How good it is to see you." Then, nodding toward Qiang, he inquired, "And who is this you have brought with you?"

Lei said in a matter-of-fact manner, "Ah, Chao, this is Qiang. He is a young Buddhist master and an emissary of the governor, Ruan Xiu."

"Well, if he is in the employ of Ruan Xiu, then we are duty bound to help him. Welcome, young man."

"Thank you, sir. How is it that you know my traveling companion?"

"Well, that is a long story, and it is getting a little uncomfortable out here in the chill wind. Why don't you come inside, where it is warmer, and I will tell you?" Chao turned to the older boy. "Chun, would you tend to the horses of our guests? Then bring the water inside. You have done enough for today, and I know you will be interested in what has happened to Lei and his young friend."

"Of course, Father," said Chun, and after the two travelers dismounted, he led the horses off to be fed and watered.

Chao ushered them into the house. Turning to Qiang, Chao then introduced his wife, Lijuan.

Qiang was surprised by the spacious cottage. He contrasted it with the sparse hovel that he and his family had lived in when his father was farming. This man, friend of Lei, was a farmer and shared much with Qiang's own father, including his name, but Qiang's father, perhaps, would have been jealous of him. Qiang's father was able to eke out a living for his little family on his little plot, which was much smaller than this farm and seemingly less fertile, largely because of his farming skills. In contrast with his own family, this one seemed rather well-off. Remembering the austerities of his youth, Qiang was grateful that this family was blessed with more.

Chao fussed around and made sure his guests were comfortably seated. He looked toward Lei. "Well, big fellow, it is good to see you again. Might we not celebrate with a little rice wine?"

Lei chuckled. "You should not be leading me astray, Chao. I don't drink so much these days, but let's just have a little one for old times' sake."

Chao offered Qiang some wine as well, but Qiang graciously declined. But soon after, Lijuan, who had disappeared into the kitchen, returned with a teapot on a tray, along with a small china bowl, full to the brim with fragrant, steaming tea, which Qiang gratefully accepted.

CHAO AND LEI exchanged news and inquired after old friends for perhaps a half hour. Qiang sat quietly and listened, slowly sipping his bowl of tea, which Lijuan occasionally topped up.

Once the children had finished their chores, they sat respectfully at the rear of the room, listening to Lei talking with their father. They had an obvious affection for Lei. Lijuan came and went between the sitting room and the kitchen, where it was obvious she had begun preparing the evening meal.

Finally, Chao turned to Qiang. "Earlier, you asked how I came to know this fellow, and I promised you a response. Well, let me tell you my story."

Lei chuckled. Qiang fancied he was a little embarrassed.

"Chao is a bit of windbag," Lei said with a laugh, "so this might take quite a while."

"Then I'd better refresh your drink before I commence."

Despite Lei's protestations, Chao poured more rice wine for them both.

This was Chao's story:

"My father was a farmer, as indeed was Lei's. We lived close by, as did the father of the bandit chief Lang Chun. You have no doubt heard how Lang Chun grew to be a formidable figure, challenging all the local populace to pay him tribute or, if not, to be marauded.

"Lei's father had an uneasy relationship with the bandit chief Lang Tun, which initially afforded him and his family some protection from his predatory raids. But finally, as you may know, Lang Tun was killed in an aborted attempt to ambush the emperor and his retinue at Devil's Gate. With the demise of Lang Tun, Lei's father's farm was no longer afforded any protection, and his family were all slain, except for his little sister, who managed to escape. Lei, for many years, was unaware of his sister's survival.

"Our farm, where indeed we all sit today, was nearby, as I said, and the bandits had long coveted it because of its fertility and productivity. But my family had a close connection to the family of Sinh Hua, whose sanctuary, I understand, you are seeking.

"Sinh Hua's family had always been extraordinarily wealthy. Consequently, they could afford to hire mercenaries who could protect them and their allies from the bandits. My family were fortunate enough to be so protected. Sinh Hua tried to ensure there were enough mercenaries around to dissuade the bandits from attacking our farm. But unfortunately, his protection could not always be afforded to us.

"My mother had come from another farming community, about a half-day journey from here. When the countryside was more peaceful, before Lang Tun had asserted himself, my family would often visit my mother's community. It was always a joyful time for us, as my mother's community embraced us and made us feel welcome.

"And it was how I came to meet my beautiful wife, Lijuan. Lijuan was the daughter of one of my mother's cousins. When we visited my mother's relatives, I always, of course, sought out Lijuan. But she was, in the nature of peasant girls, very demure and very shy, and it was consequently difficult to court her.

"And then, Lang Tun started to assert himself, and our visits to my mother's community were curtailed. By then, I was irrevocably smitten and could not bear to be apart from my sweetheart. I had a very fast horse and thought I knew the countryside well. So I would venture out, often at night, seeking to evade the bandits so that I could be with my true love.

"One night, on such an escapade, I blundered into a trap the bandits had set for me. Their intelligence must have alerted them that I frequently traveled to my mother's community. I was overcome by a group of bandits, and, struggle as I might, they took me to one their camps.

"They obviously knew who I was and understood that my family came under the protection of Sinh Hua. Consequently, they deduced that I might attract a ransom from my family's benefactor. The bandits bound me and then beat me. Then they sent a messenger to Sinh Hua, demanding a ransom. They insisted that if the ransom wasn't paid within three days, I would be killed.

"I was taunted and tortured by the bandits. The leader at the camp told me he would rather that Sinh Hua not pay the bounty because he would rather kill me than receive money to release me.

"After two days, I believed I surely would die. I made my prayers and prepared myself that if I should die, I would do so with dignity, so as not to sully my beloved's opinion of me.

"Then, on the third night, Lei came for me. He disabled the sentry who had been allocated to guard me, rendering him senseless. He threw me, still bound, over the saddle of his horse. He untethered the bandits' horses and scattered them into the night, and then he sprang up alongside me and rode off. I could hear the cries of the bandits as we sped away. Once we had put a safe distance between us and the bandits' camp, he drew up his horse, lifted me to the ground, and untied the thongs that bound my arms and legs. And that was how Lei rescued me and saved my life. In gratitude, I asked if I could join him in his resistance to the bandits. We mounted a guerrilla campaign, along with some other like-minded fellows. Eventually, Governor Ruan Xiu sought us out and urged us to join with him in routing the bandits, which we duly did.

"Lei tells me he brought you to meet one of our old comrades, Li. Li was a fiercely brave member of our band as well. But you see, I owe my life to Lei and will forever be in his debt."

CHAO'S CHILDREN OBVIOUSLY had heard this story many times. They just sat at the back of the room and beamed, lapping up the marvelous account of their father's rescue yet again.

And Lijuan could not contain herself. "If it was not for the courage of this man," she said, nodding toward Lei with a tear or two in her eye, "I never would have had the chance to marry my wonderful husband and raise this family that means so much to me."

Qiang smiled. "Do you know he also rescued me from the bandits' camp?"

Chao chuckled. "Rescuing the innocent from the clutches of the bandits seems to be something at which he is well practiced!"

Qiang then related his story. The children sat open-mouthed in wonder, listening to another of Lei's exploits. Lijuan clapped her hands in excitement. Chao merely smiled.

Lei, on the other hand, shuffled uneasily. The adulation was making him uncomfortable.

At the end of Qiang's story, Chao praised his friend's courage. He offered Lei a little more rice wine, which was duly accepted. But Lei remained taciturn.

All went quiet for a time. Finally, Chao said, "Something seems to ail you my friend. We all sit here celebrating your courage, yet you look sad. What can it be?"

"Well, Chao, I find it hard to articulate. It is only because you and Lijuan are very dear to me that I will try to explain." He turned briefly to look at Qiang. "I suspect this young man could put this better than I can."

Chao raised his eyebrows in surprise but said nothing.

"Since I have come to know Qiang," Lei said, "I have had to reconsider some of my fundamental beliefs. You all know my basic story. My family was unjustly killed by bandits, except for my little sister, who, unbeknownst to me, had escaped. The only tool I had in my armory to deal with this disaster was revenge. What's more, I was big and strong, and I found it easy to overpower others, physically. My effectiveness at fighting the bandits was subsequently rewarded by the governor Ruan Xiu, who took me back to his palace with him and gave me a sinecure of a job as stable master.

"But, in fact, I could not give up fighting. My sense of self was somehow related to my effectiveness as a fighter. Once we had overcome the bandits, much of my reason for existence was taken from me. In the absence of bandits, I had to conjure up other things to fight. Without a constant opportunity to have people affirm my worth, I felt worthless. As a result, I became sullen and vulnerable and would take offense at the smallest perceived slight, no matter how trivial. The only consolation I had was the continuing regard of Ruan Xiu. But when Qiang came along, even that was threatened. Even though the governor had placed Qiang under my charge as a stable hand, I thought he seemed to show Qiang more favors than me. I bridled at this perceived injustice. I, who had risked my life in support of Ruan Xiu, now had to play second-fiddle to a peasant boy, who, to my knowledge, had no particular traits to warrant such treatment. In my irrational jealousy, I became enraged and determined to put the young man in his place. All I succeeded in doing was to make a fool of myself, which only resulted in my plunging into greater depths of depression.

"Despite my despicable behavior, Qiang never lost his composure, and neither did he seek retribution. I fled the governor's palace and made my way back to the place of my childhood. For a time, because I was so humiliated, I was tempted to take my own life. But after a while, I began to gradually reconnect with my past.

"First, it was the little family that had adopted my sister. They are such generous people that it opened my heart to see what I might do for them. It certainly then occurred to me that taking my own life would be a futile thing to do, while I could still help such people.

"Then I reconnected with as many of the fighters as I had been comrades with. Many of them are now old and in need of support. What sort of a man would I be if I had forsaken them in their time of need?

"And, of course, I reconnected with you and your lovely wife. I know there is little that you want for, but spending time with you and your children reminds me that there are havens in this world where a man's soul can be refreshed.

"So I have come to understand that there are still meaningful contributions I can make. I have now put my anger behind me and believe I still have some purpose in my life. But is has been a hard lesson to learn. What's more, on reflection, I suspect I owe a lot to Qiang's example. When I felt I had to compete with him for the governor's approval, I treated him poorly. But through all that, he displayed no rancor and continued to display equanimity. He provides a fine example of how a man should live a life."

BECAUSE LEI HAD assured Qiang there was little distance farther to travel to Sinh Hua's safe house, they tarried a while in the morning. Lei sat a while and talked with Chao and Lijuan, catching up on local gossip.

Qiang went outside with the children, and after ensuring that his and Lei's horses were well fed and watered, he assisted the children with their chores. They fed the chickens and collected the eggs. It brought back fond memories of his own childhood, when he and Lan would search for eggs in a playful competition. Chao's children were surprised at how good Qiang was in locating those elusive eggs, even though he was unfamiliar with the chicken run. He then helped the older boy hoe the rows of cabbages to keep the weeds in check. Midmorning, the children went back inside the house to have a cool drink of water and say their farewells to Lei.

Lei could see from the good-natured banter between Qiang and the children that they had enjoyed their morning together. When they saw that Lei was still engaged with their mother and father, they went back outside to the front porch. Qiang found a nice piece of wood and began whittling. As he did so, he told the children the fabulous stories that his own mother had related to him when he was small. They listened intently to the folk myths that Qiang had grown up with, loving every minute. By the time he had related his last story, Qiang had sculpted an exquisite little doll from the piece of wood. He handed it to the little girl, who clasped it to her breast, wide-eyed in excitement.

"Oh, thank you, Qiang," she exclaimed and ran off, animatedly, to show her mother.

Qiang bowed his head a moment and thought of his father and how he had habitually manufactured such toys for Lan and him.

Finally, it was time to leave. Qiang could see the love that existed between Lei, Chao, and Lijuan, but he could see that, somehow, he also was included. The children obviously adored him, but more than that, because Lei had demonstrated his approval of Qiang, the little family seemed automatically to embrace him as well. Qiang found this all very gratifying, but more than anything else, it was a confirmation of Lei's stature. It reinforced his belief that Lei was basically a good man, whose circumstances had embittered him but who now seemed to have had his equanimity restored.

After the loving farewells were bestowed on them both, Qiang and Lei rode two abreast along the road, which inevitably would lead them to Sinh Hua's house. Lei said very little, but Qiang could see from his smile that his visit to his friends had restored his spirits and reaffirmed his worth.

IN NO TIME at all, the two companions were riding through a much more closely settled countryside.

Soon, the dirt road became a broader thoroughfare, paved with cobblestones. The noise of the horses' hooves striking the surface echoed back from the walls of the nearby dwellings. They passed men pushing barrows full of manufactured produce and others with baskets full of vegetables, tied to the ends of poles, which they carried across their shoulders. Even though they had left the rural farms behind, most of the houses still had gardens, where the peasants grew a few vegetables to eke out their meager existences. Children played by the road, and a few flew kites.

This was a city larger than Qiang had ever experienced. Even in his youth, when he had gone down to the emperor's court to try to sell his calligraphy, he had not encountered such dense settlement. And the farther they rode, the more densely populated the city seemed to be.

Finally, Lei reined back his horse and said, "There it is."

Just ahead, on the left of the road, was a magnificent building, although little of the building could be seen because it stood in the center of a walled enclosure. The walls were perhaps three meters high, and they had been meticulously constructed of dressed stone blocks, cemented together with mortar. Yet over the top of these imposing walls, Qiang could see an extended edifice of gilded parapets and spires.

Qiang took a little while to take it all in, and then he turned to Lei and asked, "Is this really the safe house of Sinh Hua that I was advised to seek?"

"Indeed, it is, Qiang. While I have some misgivings about Sinh Hua, I have no doubt you will be safe here."

They dismounted from their horses and led them up to the gates of the enclosure. As they walked, Qiang was surprised to see Lei draw out a short staff that had been strapped to his horse. Lei seemed to use it as a walking aid, even though Qiang had seen no signs that his walking was in any way impaired. Before Qiang could ask the purpose of this staff, they were already at the gates.

The gates were guarded by two large men, each carrying a sword. As they approached, one of them stepped forward and, drawing out his weapon, called out, "Halt! You can't enter here without our master's permission." The other guard seemed to hang back with a smirk on his face.

Lei moved steadfastly forward.

"I can't see why you would want to prevent me from seeing my old friend Sinh Hua," he responded.

"You are not permitted to enter without his permission," said the guard, going red in the face.

But Lei continued to advance.

The guard rushed forward with his weapon raised. "I warned you," he cried.

And then, to the guard's dismay and Qiang's surprise, Lei deftly sidestepped the man, struck him across the back with the staff, which caused him to stumble and fall, and, in an instant, disarmed him.

The other guard let out a belly laugh. "Well, Lei," he exclaimed between chuckles, "it seems you still have some fighting prowess."

"Just a little, Dong. Now, tell your friend to be a good lad and run off to tell Sinh Hua I am coming in to see him."

The first guard struggled up off the pavement. "Dong, why didn't you come to my aid?"

"There was no need. I know this fellow, and I knew he would do you no serious harm. I also know that Sinh Hua holds him in high regard. Now, do as he says, and tell the master that Lei has arrived and is bringing him a visitor."

The man shook his head. "He will berate me for not properly guarding the entrance."

"Don't be silly! Just tell him that you are responding to my behest, knowing that he would not deny Lei access to him."

Reluctantly, he went off into the interior of the enclosure.

Lei and Dong exchanged pleasantries and reminisced for a while. But then Lei said, "I'd better go and introduce Sinh Hua to Qiang. We could chat a little more when I have carried out my duty."

"I look forward to it."

"Does Sinh Hua still regale himself in that same ridiculous throne room that he set up."

Dong laughed. "Yes, that's where you will find him."

"Will you tend to our horses?"

"Of course. When Shang returns, I will see that they are properly stabled."

"Thank you, Dong." Lei then turned and put his hand on Qiang's shoulder. "Well, young man, I'd best take you in to introduce you to your next benefactor."

They marched together through the gates and toward the entrance of Sinh Hua's palatial residence. Before they reached it, a portly man came scurrying out, followed reluctantly by the shame-faced Shang. Qiang correctly deduced that this rotund man, holding his robes high so that they would not trip him as he rushed forward, must be Sinh Hua.

"Why, Lei, you old scoundrel. It is you who would assault my guards, leaving me at the mercy of the bandits. And you are supposed to be my friend."

Lei just smiled in an amiable way. "If you want to feel safe, you had better find some guards who can handle themselves better than that fellow." He nodded toward Shang.

The other guard, Dong, could scarcely contain his mirth.

Sinh Hua now closed on Lei, embraced him, and then vigorously slapped him on the back. Qiang could see that Lei was a little repulsed by this but gritted his teeth and endured Sinh Hua's ostentatious display of affection.

Sinh Hua finally stepped back and looked up at Lei. "But what brings you here? The last I heard, you were working for Ruan Xiu. Did you tire of the governor's patronage?"

"The governor is a noble, gracious man. I will forever be grateful to him." Lei then turned to Qiang. "This young man, Qiang, is a trusted emissary of the governor. He comes to deliver a tribute from Ruan Xiu to the governor of the western province, Chin Chao. Ruan Xiu advised him to seek you out to gain refuge from the bandits and to seek your help in navigating the next stage of his journey, in order to deliver his tribute to Chin Chao."

"Anyone in the service of Ruan Xiu can count on my support," said Sinh Hua. And so saying, he waddled over and embraced Qiang. When he withdrew, he beckoned the two travelers and said, "But come inside, and let me make you comfortable."

Once inside Sinh Hua's residence, Qiang was dismayed to see it exceeded the grandeur and splendor of Governor Ruan Xiu's palace. They sat and chatted for a while in a sumptuous anteroom. Sinh Hua and Lei reminisced about their shared past in putting down the bandits. Again, Qiang was surprised to see in what high regard Lei was held by Sinh Hua for his bravery in protecting the peasants from the bandits.

Lei also related their recent adventures, emphasizing that the bandits had regrouped and were profiting from the peasants, stealing their produce and livestock and attacking them in their homesteads.

Sinh Hua nodded his head. "I am aware that the bandits are resurgent. It is perhaps time that we convinced Ruan Xiu and Chin Chao to again put them down."

Lei nodded his agreement.

Sinh Hua offered accommodation to Lei, but Lei said, "I will only stay one night. I have obligations with the peasant families that I must fulfil. Tomorrow, I will begin the return journey home. But that is unimportant, my friend. What is important is that you see this young man safely to the palace of Chin Chao."

"I will do my best, Lei. But it might take a little while. Some of the farmers to whom I offer protection will soon be taking off their crops. I must wait until we have safely brought their crops to market before I can put together a stout band of men to accompany him to the governor's palace."

Again, Lei nodded. "That is fair enough. I am pleased that you still support such folk. As you know, I have many friends among them."

"Lei, are you able to get a message back to Ruan Xiu, confirming that Qiang is now safely with me? I am sure he would want to know."

"Of course! I will ensure he is thus informed."

THE NEXT MORNING, Lei took his leave.

Qiang now faced a period of inaction, waiting for Sinh Hua to have his men available to escort him to Chin Chao's palace. As usual, Qiang endured all this with equanimity. He had ample time to progress his meditation practice, which gave him satisfaction. But he still wished to be useful.

He approached Sinh Hua and asked whether he might have leave to help some of the peasants with their work in the fields.

"No, Qiang. We can't afford to put you at risk until you have been delivered to Chin Chao."

"Be that as it may, I would feel better if I could be of some use."

"Well, I have been thinking of putting you to work myself."

"What would you have me do?"

"Two tasks—one for my benefit and one for yours."

Qiang was intrigued.

"First, I have heard that you are an accomplished calligrapher. I wish to record my family's history for posterity. I know most of it, but we could do a little research to augment my knowledge, and you could record it for me."

Qiang thought a while before assenting. "I can do that, but you would have to provide me with parchment, brushes, and ink."

"Of course, that can easily be done. But I also want you to do something for your own benefit."

"What would that be?"

"I want you to learn how to fight."

Qiang was taken aback by this suggestion. "But Sinh Hua, I have no desire to hurt anybody. My masters have all taught me that I should practice loving kindness. How might I reconcile fighting with that objective?"

"Well, my desire to have you learn to fight is not so much that you should be aggressive but that at least you can protect yourself. If, for example, on your journey to Chin Chao's palace, you were set upon by bandits, would you not want to defend yourself so that you could deliver your tribute to Chin Chao? Or if you were confronted by those of ill-intent, might you want to be able to thwart their evil desires so that you could return to your mother and sister? From what my friend Lei tells me, you have some special attributes that, even if they are unimportant to you, should be preserved for the greater good of us all."

"No, no. I don't want you or anyone else to believe that I am someone special. I am merely a farmer's son who, through good fortune, has been exposed to enlightened sages, who were able to instruct me in the philosophy of Buddhism."

"Well, I hear your protestations clearly. Yet some have told me that you were chosen for your vocation, even before you were born. Remember your first teacher who waited for you in your childhood, under a tree. It seems likely to me that your fortunate history is not a random act of fate. That first sage knew you were special. He taught you to meditate. But let us put that aside. Let me be brutally frank. As I understand it, your father is no longer with you. You are the titular head of your family now. Do you want the bandits to capture you, injure you, or perhaps even kill you? Then what good would you be to your mother and sister?"

"My mother and my sister remain under the protection Ruan Xiu. I would not be here if I had not been assured of their safety."

"Be that as it may, surely you must want to play some further part in the lives of your mother and sister. Ruan Xiu may be a noble man, but families are built on kinship and mutual love. I am sure you have much more to contribute. And besides, surely you derive pleasure from being with the members of your little family?"

Qiang thought a while before finally responding. "I must concede you are right. Nothing gives me greater pleasure than being with my mother and my little sister. And while I believe I must display loving kindness to all, my greatest ambition is to ensure the continuing well-being of my mother and little sister. So perhaps there is some justification in my learning to protect myself. But if you are to school me thus, I have no interest in learning how to harm others. I would accept your offer of instruction, only as long as the objective is for my self-protection and not to inflict hurt on others. I have no desire to use offensive weapons."

Sinh Hua nodded his understanding and agreement. "I have an excellent instructor for you, if you want to pursue this enterprise. And I can assure you that he will concentrate on the development of your skills to defend yourself."

"If that indeed is the objective, I will agree to such instruction."

Sinh Hua smiled. "But he has other skills as well that might prove useful to you."

SINH HUA SOON introduced Qiang to his mentor, who would instruct him in self-defense. They met in a great barnlike structure at the rear of Sinh Hua's palatial residence. Mounted on the wall was a fearsome array of weapons.

"This is my military academy," announced Sinh Hua. "And here is your mentor. His name is Cheng."

To Qiang's surprise, he was an older man, well into middle age. Sinh Hua was effusive in his praise of Cheng and explained how well he had trained the members of his private army. Consequently, his men had little fear of the bandits, as they were confident of their ability to best them in combat.

Sinh Hua left Qiang alone with Cheng. As Qiang had previously experienced with the masters who had come to instruct him, he felt straightaway at ease with this man. This caused him more than a little wonderment because a fighting instructor seemed the least likely source for further wisdom insights. Yet here again, he could tell from Cheng's eyes that this was a man at peace with himself.

Cheng waited until Sinh Hua had left before turning to Qiang. "So you are Takygulpa Rinpoche, whom I have been hearing about for some time. Welcome!"

"Why do you call me by that title? My name is Qiang."

"That is merely the name your family bestowed on you. My brothers had, from an early stage, agreed that *Takygulpa Rinpoche* would be your title. But I am happy to call you Qiang, if it puts you at ease, particularly when we are in company."

"And who are these 'brothers' to whom you refer?"

"Come, now; you should have some inkling about who they are. Among them are Chogpen Rinpoche, Chagsarka Rinpoche, Sunfu

Rinpoche, and the sages Bai and Jian. It was not just a matter of fate that they have guided you on your way."

"Are you a Buddhist sage as well?"

"That is not for me to say, nor is it a matter of any importance to me. I am just here to instruct you, as well as I can."

"Well, I thank you for that. I am looking forward to your instruction."

"Young man, I count it as a privilege to be able to help you!"

And thus commenced one of the most fulfilling relationships of Qiang's young life.

For two hours each morning, Qiang worked with Cheng. Initially, they did little physical work. They would sit and meditate to begin.

Cheng said, "You are an accomplished meditator, and compared to most, you have cultivated mindfulness well. But if a warrior is to survive, he must have exceptional awareness. We will now begin to work on this."

Cheng asked Qiang to continue sitting in the lotus position after their meditation session. "Now I am going to position myself behind you. With your eyes closed, please count to ten. When you have finished, I want you to tell me where I am. To begin with, we will keep it simple. You need only respond that I am to your left, to your right, or directly behind you."

This seemed a strange exercise to Qiang, but in due deference to his mentor, he cooperated.

Cheng moved silently into position, and to begin with, Qiang had little success in guessing where he stood.

After three or four failed attempts, Cheng called the process to a halt. "You are trying too hard, Qiang! Let us meditate again."

They resumed their meditation practice for some time. Finally, Cheng called it to a halt. He then said to Qiang, "If you are to succeed in this exercise, you must bring all your attention to bear on my presence. You seem to be trying to sense my presence with your hearing alone. I make little noise, so quite often, that will not be enough. You have sensory capacities you are not even aware of. Let your intuition guide you."

And so began another instructional period in awareness. After a month or so of practice, Qiang found he was able to detect his master's presence on almost all occasions.

Finally, Cheng said, "I feel you have mastered awareness well enough now. It is time we moved on to how to master a weapon."

Qiang recoiled in horror at this suggestion. "Oh no, Cheng. I have no desire to hurt anybody, as I have told you."

"It is not my desire to have you hurt others but only to prevent others from hurting you. The brigands that abound in this region will have weapons, like swords, knives, and sometimes bows and arrows. If you are to defend yourself, you will have to learn to contend with these. You don't need a sword to defend yourself from a sword or a knife to defend yourself from a knife. My strategy for you is to teach you how to wield a staff."

Qiang thought back to the day the Lei had brought him to Sinh Hua's palace. Lei had quickly disarmed one of the guards using a short staff. Maybe Cheng's strategy was sound enough.

"All right, Cheng. I would be happy to have you teach me how to use a staff."

"Good! And remember that the true warrior only uses his weapon, whatever it is, as a measure of last resort. Many of the best fighters I have tutored are just as reluctant to use their weapons as you are. In the end, it will provide another option for you to use at your discretion."

Thus began Qiang's instruction on how to use the staff. But surprisingly, they had many lessons when he never even picked up a staff. Cheng skilled him on how to sharpen his reflexes, how to dodge and weave, how to anticipate a thrust, how to use the momentum of his attacker to bring him down, and so on.

Qiang enjoyed being with Cheng. The older man was still very dexterous and supple, with amazing reflexes. But even more than that, he exuded practical wisdom.

In the evenings, Qiang worked with Sinh Hua, developing the manuscript to record his family's history. Every evening, Qiang would ask how the harvest was going and when it would be possible to set off to the palace of Chin Chao. But Sinh Hua always had another excuse for delay. There were still crops to harvest out to the northwest; a wagon that was necessary to transport produce had been stolen by the bandits; his soldiers had been temporarily diverted to help rebuild a barn that had burned down; and so on. All the excuses seemed plausible enough, but Qiang was beginning to suspect Sinh Hua was taking advantage of him.

Finally, one evening in late autumn, Qiang said to Sinh Hua, "I appreciate the support you have given me, but I feel I must continue my journey. If you don't have the men available to protect me, I will just do the best I can on my own."

Sinh Hua raised his eyebrows in surprise. "But Qiang, you can't go yet. You haven't finished my manuscript, and besides, you have not completed your course in self-defense."

"I am sorry, sir, but my first obligation is to Ruan Xiu. I have given him an undertaking to take material to Chin Chao and that must take precedence over all else. As much as I would like to complete your manuscript, I cannot give that the same consideration as fulfilling my undertaking to Chin Chao. As for my ability to defend myself, Cheng has aided me considerably. I am happy to take my chances. I will stay two more days. In that time, I can complete the main part of your family's history. Surely you have access to other calligraphers who could complete the work. In that time, I will make my preparations to set off again on my journey."

Sinh Hua, as Lei had implied, was a bit of a scoundrel, and he had been selfishly delaying Qiang for his own benefit. Incongruously, he was still a generous soul who had worked tirelessly to secure the safety of the local community. He also knew that he would incur the wrath of Ruan Xiu if the governor came to know that he had deliberately thwarted Qiang's attempt to deliver his tribute to Chin Chao.

"Well, young man, there are other calligraphers to whom I could turn, if necessity forced me, but their work does not have the quality of yours. But if you are determined to go, I will make do with lesser artisans. And certainly, if you are determined to go, I will help however I can. I will provide you with a company of four armed men to take you beyond the mountain pass to the north, after which, you should be safe to proceed on your own. I will provision you as well as I can."

Qiang was well pleased with the notion that he might now progress his journey further. It was not that he begrudged laying out the history of Sinh Hua on a manuscript. In fact, the family history had begun to intrigue him. But in his heart, he knew he had a more pressing obligation to Ruan Xiu.

So it was with mixed feelings that he made his preparations to depart. But he was filled with exhilaration at the thought that he was about to continue his adventure.

This, however, was all to no avail.

He was sitting in the library with Sinh Hua, diligently recording his family history on the next evening, when an attendant burst in. Sinh Hua glared his disapproval, but the attendant would not be put off.

"Sire," he burst out, "Raibin has returned from the north and has news for you."

Sinh Hua looked at Qiang and said, "I am sorry, but this might be important. I need to hear from Raibin. He is a trusted leader of my men."

Qiang merely nodded his understanding.

Turning to the attendant, Sinh Hua said, "Bring him here so that I might hear his news."

Shortly afterward, a big, strong fellow came striding in and stood before Sinh Hua.

Qiang could see the respect in Sinh Hua's eyes as he quietly inquired, "What news, Raibin?"

"Sire, unfortunately, I haven't been able to carry out your command. I set forth to the north to reconnoiter the road to Chin Chao's domain, but I was halted by some early blizzards, which have closed the mountain pass to the north. We pushed our way past the first avalanche that had blocked the pass but then encountered a mountain of snow and ice on the road that was impossible to surmount. It seems to me that we will be blocked from traveling that way until after the spring melt."

"Did you all return safely, Raibin? Were there any casualties among my men?"

"No, sire. Perhaps a little frostbite, but nothing too serious."

Sinh Hua uttered a sigh of relief. "I am pleased about that. Thank you, Raibin; as usual, you have done your best. I could ask no more than that. Did you encounter any of the bandits?"

"No, sire. We did not directly encounter any of them. But on quite a few occasions, we saw those whom we took to be bandits on the ridge lines and various vantage points. They would not have attacked us because we had the advantage of numbers and arms, but, no doubt, those traveling alone or in small parties would have been easy pickings for them."

Sinh Hua nodded his agreement. "I thank you, Raibin, and your men. There was nothing more that you could do. We will have to think carefully about taking the northern road."

"Sire, I suppose it is impertinent of me, but can I ask you why it was necessary to reconnoiter the northern pass so late in the year. We would seldom try to go that way in these months."

"Raibin, I have a distinguished guest here who was keen to make his way to Chin Cao's palace. Before he left, I wanted to check how safe the passage might be. It is important to me that he not be put at risk."

"Anyone who traveled that way now would be in mortal danger."

Qiang was bemused by this conversation, but then he interjected, "Sire, might I ask Raibin a question?"

"Certainly," agreed Sinh Hua.

"Raibin, when did you set off on your task?"

"Well, young man, it was almost a month ago."

"Thank you, Raibin," said Qiang.

Raibin chatted with Sinh Hua a little while longer and then withdrew.

Qiang did not know what to think. Sinh Hua had sent Raibin off well before he had announced his intentions of setting out for Chin Chao's palace. He had harbored concerns that Sinh Hua was taking advantage of him, but now, it seemed that perhaps Sinh Hua was really concerned for his welfare.

Sinh Hua escorted his trusted lieutenant to the door and then returned to the library. He found Qiang sitting somberly in his chair, deep in thought.

"What is the matter, Qiang?"

"I am disappointed that my journey has been delayed. I had given my undertaking to Ruan Xiu to go as expeditiously as I could to Chin Chao. Now, I find myself stranded and unable to progress further until after the winter. My benefactor will be disappointed by my idleness."

Sinh Hua smiled. "You are very hard on yourself, young man. Ruan Xiu will understand the difficulties of progressing further at this time. In fact, I will ensure that he is informed of your plight. This should also provide some comfort to your family."

Qiang's eyes brightened. "Are you able to do that?"

"Of course! Winter will not prevent my men from bringing a message to the palace of Ruan Xiu. As you know, they have the bandit's measure and should not be impeded, and the way south is much easier in the colder months than the way to the north."

"I would be most grateful if you could do that. It would not only give Ruan Xiu assurance that I am still determined to fulfil my obligation to him, but it would also give some solace to my mother and sister, who no doubt are concerned about my welfare."

Sinh Hua, in a surprising display of warmth, put his hands on Qiang's tense shoulders and said, "Have no fear, Qiang. It shall be done."

"Might it be possible, my lord, that if you send an emissary to Ruan Xiu, I might give him a letter to deliver to my mother?"

Sinh Hua smiled. "Of course, of course."

QIANG HAD BEEN concerned that being confined with Sinh Hua for the winter would be a tedious time.

But it turned out not to be so.

Every day, Qiang worked with Cheng on his self-defense skills. Cheng was not only an adept instructor in the art of self-defense, but he was also very learned in Buddhism. So again, Qiang had found a teacher who not only tutored him in physical skills but deepened his spiritual understanding.

Of an evening, he continued to work on the manuscript, recording Sinh Hua's family history, but that was soon done.

Sinh Hua gave Qiang access to his extensive library. This proved a great boon to him. There were many ancient manuscripts that either recorded the history of the region or outlined the spiritual beliefs of the Buddhists, who had founded the local community.

Qiang began to understand that his work with Sinh Hua was to provide his own addition to these tomes. Sinh Hua seemed to believe that was required to legitimately assume an exalted place in the local history.

As winter neared its end, Qiang frequently inquired whether there was any news of the pass to the north and if it had reopened.

Sinh Hua merely shook his head.

After many such inquiries, Sinh Hua said, with some exasperation, "Qiang, you don't have to ask every day about the northern pass. I have men stationed up to the north who have explicit instructions to notify me as soon as the pass is opened. Be patient. A good Buddhist like you should have learned by now that we must let nature take its course, and there is nothing we can do to hurry her."

Qiang hung his head, a little shamefacedly. "Of course, you are right, sir. I will not bother you further."

IN GOOD TIME, the snows began to melt, and the roadways cleared. After their morning exercises, Cheng took to riding out into the countryside with Qiang. At Cheng's insistence, Qiang took his short staff with him. Cheng showed Qiang how to tie it to his horse, such that it prevented no obstruction but was easily accessible if it should be needed. Qiang had protested that he did not need it, and he only carried it in deference to Cheng.

Cheng told Qiang that one of his duties was to check on the welfare of the local farmers. Qiang was gratified that Sinh Hua showed such concern for those under his protection.

At first, because the snow was still abundant, they were able to access only the nearby farms. Cheng was a welcome guest in all the farmsteads they visited. He spent a good deal of time checking on the welfare of the farming families and catching up on their news. Cheng had a fabulous memory and could largely remember the names of all the family members, down to the youngest child. Most of the families had fared well. There had been a couple of births during the long winter months and, unfortunately, also a death, with one family losing an elderly grandmother who was well revered and loved. But by and large, most of the livestock had been preserved, and the families were now venturing out a little, supplementing their stores of firewood and eager to begin planting their crops. These were robust, stoic people, accustomed to dealing with the vagaries of the land and the variabilities of the seasons. Cheng was well loved by these simple folk, and once they learned of Qiang's background, he was readily accepted as well.

Not unexpectedly, these visits brought back memories of Qiang's own childhood, and he became nostalgic, thinking of his own little family and the triumphs and difficulties they had faced. On the return journey from one such sojourn, Qiang was lost in thought, internally reminiscing about his childhood.

Cheng interrupted his reverie. "You seem somewhat distracted, Qiang. You know, in these parts, it is wise to keep your wits about you. If there were bandits about, they would look at you and I as easy game."

"I am sorry, sir, but when we visit these people, I am overwhelmed with memories of my own childhood. I can feel their lives coursing through the very marrow of my own bones. I can't help but admire them and love them. At the same time, they remind me that I lost a father, a devoted father who tried his best but blamed himself for not being able to provide for his family as he wished. It also reminds me that the two people who I love most in all the world, my venerable mother and my beautiful sister, are residing with Ruan Xiu, and I must fulfil my obligation to him to ensure their continued welfare."

"There is no doubt that our life experiences, particularly our early life experiences, have a great influence on our personal development. You have had many experiences since you left your family home, and they will shape you as well. It is time to acknowledge that you are more than a farmer's son. You have been earmarked by the most venerable masters to become a Buddhist sage—indeed, a master in your own right. You will always be a farmer's son, and there is nothing wrong with that, but you will become much more as well. I know a little of your background. It is no accident that you have had to face various trials, and it is no accident that you have been fortunate enough to have received instruction from many adepts along the way."

Qiang thought deeply for a while before responding. "No doubt, you are right, Cheng. I am not ungrateful for the opportunities I have been given. I indeed have been very fortunate. But what concerns me most is that I don't seem to have been given any choice in the matter. It seems as if this mantle I have assumed of a master-in-training—or whatever you might like to call it—was something I never sought. What choice did I have?"

"How much choice do any of us have? Our lives are mostly determined by things beyond our control. But you do have some choice."

"And what choice is that? It is not obvious to me."

"That is not surprising because it is not obvious to most. The choice you have is how you choose to view the world. And that statement is, in itself, a little misleading because once you understand the world properly, there really is no choice because the decision to be made is self-evident."

"That is a strange statement, Cheng. Surely the world is just as it is, and we all see it the same."

"That might seem true of the physical manifestation of the world, but the world has more significant dimensions than that. Even the way we perceive the physical world is colored by our worldview."

Qiang thought for a while before responding. "You have told me, Cheng, that we each have different worldviews, and because we see the world differently, we respond to the world differently."

"Yes, that is so."

"But how can these viewpoints be so different?"

"Some of us are inwardly focused and fearful, and as a result, we can't see very far. We are always looking for those things that we believe are threatening us. We can't see beyond the next slight or insult. We see the world as a threatening place. This is the worldview of fear. Others, who are more at ease with themselves, are able to see the world more benignly. To them, the world is hardly threatening at all, and they are more likely to be at one with their world. Of course, they understand that sometimes bad things happen, which they must accommodate, but, in general, they don't believe that the world is inimical to them."

Qiang looked a little puzzled.

Taking this cue, Cheng continued. "Let me relate to you a Buddhist parable regarding the matter. There once was a green ant, living with its colony in a mangrove tree. The ant was gnawing at the edge of a leaf. All of a sudden, a gust of wind arose and broke the leaf from its branch. The leaf, with the ant clinging grimly to it, tumbled down into the water. The tide was running out, and the leaf was whirled around by the eddies formed where the mangrove roots meet the water. The ant was thrust violently about and hung on for a grim death. Eventually, the leaf emerged into the main stream and was washed farther down the estuary.

"Soon, the leaf came to a sandbar. This impediment to the flow of the tide created small waves in the water, but to the ant, these seemed like huge cataracts. Once over the bar, the water became calm, and another gust of wind arose and pushed the leaf, with the hapless ant aboard, to an overhanging branch. The ant quickly grasped the branch and hauled itself out of the water. It sat, exhausted, for a while on the branch, its little heart beating furiously. "Whew", it thought," I'll never go near the sea again. What a treacherous place it is, with whirlpools and cataracts and mountainous waves."

"The poor thing," exclaimed Qiang. "What a traumatic experience!"

"All the while the ant was enduring its journey down the estuary, a sea eagle was soaring high overhead. The warm sun created a strong thermal that enabled it to hover effortlessly above the estuary. "What a lovely day", thought the bird. "The estuary is so calm and beautiful. I feel at one with the world". What the ant saw as frightful and traumatic, the sea eagle saw as tranquil and beautiful. We are like the green ant and the sea eagle. Those who are self-obsessed and driven by fear see the world as a frightening place. They are compelled, through no fault of their own, to be defensive and pessimistic. They see traps and dangers all about them. They look at others as competitors who are trying to succeed and progress at their own expense. That is the worldview of fear.

"On the other hand, the sea eagle was at peace with the world. He knew he was at one with the land, the sea, and the sky. In general, for him, the world was a bountiful and inviting place. Certainly, on occasion, he would need to endure some hardship, but that was not because the world was inimical to him; it was just the random cycles of nature with which we all have to contend."

Qiang considered this for a while. With a smile on his face, he said, "Then the question for me is, do I choose to be like the green ant or the sea eagle?"

"That is true in metaphorical terms, but there is no decision, no choice to be made at all, once you realize who you really are. When you meditate and allow your thoughts to fall away so that your egoic self disappears and only the witness remains, it becomes obvious that the witness is all there is, and it is shared by us all. Whether you are male or female, a prince or a farmer's son, your essential essence is the same as everybody else's. When there is a realization that there is no separation between one and another, that is the basis of the worldview of love. It is not something you choose or something you can find; it is just the true nature of the world. It was always there, just waiting for you to realize it."

THE WEATHER CONTINUED to warm, enabling Qiang and Cheng to venture farther afield. On this particular day, they ventured out to ascertain the welfare of a number of farmers toward the extremities of the territory under Sinh Hua's protection. Cheng sought after the wellbeing of three farming families with whom he was familiar and was gratified that they had survived the winter and were now making plans to sow new crops, as the weather allowed.

Cheng and Qiang rode contentedly back home after this sojourn. The sun was low in the sky, as it had been a long day. Now that the snow had retreated, grass had begun to grow alongside the well-traveled track. The evening coolness evoked birdsong, and Qiang felt very contented. While he had not yet been able to resume his journey north to Chin Chao, he felt great satisfaction from going out with Cheng and confirming the welfare of these peasant farmers.

The track meandered down a long grassy slope toward a small creek. As they approached the creek, there were small clumps of trees, now sprouting leaves, heralding the passing of winter.

Suddenly, Cheng shouted, "Watch out, Qiang! Take out your staff, and gallop toward the creek."

Qiang turned his head and saw a swarthy fellow, astride a horse, emerging from a copse of trees, with a sword drawn. His horse was in full flight. Just as it appeared they might outdistance the man, another appeared on the track in front of them. He also had emerged from a copse of trees near the creek bank. Cheng and Qiang had been effectively ambushed. The one in front was a big fellow, and he too held an unsheathed sword in his right hand.

As they slowed to confront the new threat, Cheng said, "I will deal with this fellow in front. Turn your horse, and engage the one coming from behind."

"But what should I do, Cheng?"

"Just use your staff as I have taught you. Be not afraid."

Cheng charged on. As he approached the big man, he feinted with his staff, causing the man to take a wild swing with his sword. Cheng was now level with him, and with a deft jab of his staff, he unseated the man. Startled by the melee, the man's horse galloped off down the track, leaving the big man on the ground, moaning.

Cheng turned to see how Qiang was faring. The pursuer in the rear had slowed his horse and was approaching Qiang.

Qiang's assailant laughed. "You mean to defend yourself with a stick? My sword will render it to kindling, and then I will take pleasure in piercing your chest with it."

Surprisingly, Qiang felt no fear. Maybe he was about to die, but his awareness was heightened, and his demeanor was calm. "Put down your sword," Qiang said, calmly but firmly. "We mean you no harm."

The man charged forth on his horse, drew the sword back, and swung it heftily at Qiang. Qiang nimbly avoided the blow, and as the rider passed, Qiang struck him a heavy blow on his back, which unseated him from the horse.

Cheng called to Qiang, "Well done, lad! But let's be gone now before these two can regather themselves."

"But I think I hurt that man, Cheng. Shouldn't we stop and render aid?"

"No. The worst he'll have is a bruise or two or maybe a cracked rib. Just remember—those two would have readily murdered us. No doubt, they had plans to maraud some of the homesteads we visited as well. It is noble that you should want to do no harm, but it is more than acceptable to render some consequences for outrageous behavior, in the hope that it will prevent a greater hurt."

IT WAS ONLY a day or two after the incident with the bandits that Sinh Hua came to Qiang. "The time has finally come for you to continue your journey to the north."

"Ah, I am pleased. When can I begin?"

"I intend to accompany you on the first part of the journey, where some danger may still present itself, but I have made appropriate preparations. I propose we leave tomorrow morning."

Qiang smiled. "That sounds an excellent plan to me."

"Go now and make ready. We will leave at first light. I will have a half dozen of my best men accompany us—but from what I hear from Cheng, you seem to be more than competent in protecting yourself."

Qiang blushed. He had made no mention of their run-in with the bandits, but apparently, Cheng had related the story to Sinh Hua. In deference to Sinh Hua, Qiang returned to his quarters and gathered up his things, ready to strap them to his horse on the morrow.

He extracted the prized manuscript from its careful packing. Once assured it was still in good order, he carefully repacked it. He smiled a wry smile as he recollected how he had come to craft this precious gift from Ruan Xiu to his friend Chin Chao. While its creation had been a labor of love for him, he had to concede that delivering the gift had been more problematic than he originally had believed.

After he had completed his preparations, he sought out Cheng. "I am finally off, Cheng. We head to the north in the morning."

Cheng smiled. "I know. Sinh Hua has told me. I am pleased for you."

"I will miss our rides into the country, Cheng. I will miss your instruction and counsel as well. You have been very generous to me."

"Not so, young man. You are part of my destiny, just as I am part of yours. Like your other teachers, I knew, someday, you would come, and it is my appointed duty to assist you. But I must say, it has been a pleasure for me."

"Thank you, teacher. Do you have any last words for me before I go?"

"Well, of course," Cheng said with a chuckle. "Keep that short staff close!" Then his face grew more serious. "I suspect there will be many more trials for you, Qiang. You will prevail, as long as you remember who you really are." He smiled again. "Be off with you now, and be sure to come to me again when you are able."

Impulsively, Qiang stepped forward and hugged the older man, who seemed to be a little taken aback.

"Thank you," said Qiang, releasing him. He then turned and strode briskly away.

THE FROST HAD laid white carpets alongside the road. Even so, the impending spring was obvious, with the verdant shoots of the tougher grasses and the previously dormant trees now pushing their new life through the dwindling cold.

Six staunch warriors in the employ of Sinh Hua led the little entourage northward.

In their wake came Sinh Hua himself, atop a magnificent bay horse, and alongside him, Qiang, on his little piebald colt.

Their progress was particularly leisurely, not because Sinh Hua wished it so but because his escort was determined to secure their safe passage. Consequently, the men leading the entourage stopped frequently to reconnoiter the way ahead to ensure they didn't expose Sinh Hua and Qiang to undue danger.

Despite his impatience with delivering his manuscript to Chin Chao, Qiang remained calm and did not complain about the slow rate of progress. He and Sinh Hua were content to converse as the little group slowly wended its way forward toward the northern pass.

Sinh Hua recounted stories of how he and Ruan Xiu and Lei had combined to see off the bandits in the past and then, with his concern for the local peasant population, managed to secure some degree of safety for those within the areas he felt he could protect.

Qiang had had his misgivings about Sinh Hua in the past, but listening to these stories (if they were to be believed), he slowly understood that this man might have his flaws, but his concern for and his benevolence toward the local population was admirable.

Sinh Hua lapsed into silence, which came as a little surprise to Qiang because his benefactor seemed to enjoy telling his stories and elaborating on the detail. As they rode quietly forward, Qiang contrasted Ruan Xiu and Sinh Hua in his mind.

Ruan Xiu was an austere and seemingly unemotional man. It would be easy to assume from his external appearance that he lacked compassion and empathy. But Qiang had learned that he was undoubtedly a good man who cared for people. His treatment of Qiang's mother and sister attested to that. And Qiang could see that Ruan Xiu loved the big man Lei, despite his flaws. What's more, the governor worked tirelessly to further the well-being of those common people who lived within his sphere of influence.

Sinh Hua, on the other hand, was a garrulous, ebullient person. On the surface, he seemed shallow and self-serving, but Qiang had seen the efforts he had made to secure the welfare of the nearby small farming communities.

Qiang concluded that it was indeed folly to judge people from their external appearances.

It took three days of riding to eventually top the northern pass. Overall, it had been uneventful. Sinh Hua had offered the thought that the bandits had been deterred by the presence of his elite fighters.

"You must be careful," he advised Qiang. "On your return journey, you will more than likely encounter these villains, and you must keep your wits about you."

Qiang nodded.

The little party camped off the side of the track, having ascended the pass, on the third night.

When they awoke in the morning, Sinh Hua bid his farewells. "It is time for me to leave you, little master. There should be no impediments now to prevent you from proceeding to the court of Chin Chao. He knows you are on your way, and I am sure he will welcome you with open arms. I want to thank you for the work you have done for me in recording the history of my family. But I must warn you of my concerns for your return journey. We have protected you in coming thus far. You may not have such support on your return journey. These bandits are ruthless and pitiless. If you can get word to us when you start your return journey, I will do what I can to protect you. But I suspect your return journey will be a hazardous undertaking."

Qiang was moved by Sinh Hua's concerns. "I thank you, Sinh Hua. I am pleased to have been of some use to you. I thank you also for allowing me to be instructed by Cheng. His counsel and development of my skills has been of immense benefit to me. But might I ask one favor of you?"

"Certainly. I will try to do anything within my power to assist you."

"I know I have asked for this previously, but are you able to get word to Ruan Xiu regarding my progress? I am particularly anxious that my mother and sister should know I am well."

"Of course, of course, Qiang! It had been my intention to relate to the governor your passage to the western province. Go safely now!"

So saying, Sinh Hua wheeled his horse around and waving a last goodbye. He set off ahead of his little band of men, leaving Qiang alone, astride his piebald colt.

AS SINH HUA had predicted, Qiang's progress now was unimpeded. It took the best part of a day to descend the mountain pass. As he did so, the weather grew a little more temperate, and the countryside grew more verdant, with spring already having begun to show its green face.

He made camp for the night on a grassy bank alongside a little stream. After watering his horse, he tethered him, as usual, with a long rope so that he could feed relatively unimpeded. Qiang bathed in the little stream but soon withdrew to his little campsite because the water was very cold, having originated from the melted snow from the mountains behind him.

Sinh Hua had provided him with ample provisions, so he manufactured a simple meal and sat contentedly in the glow of his campfire and ate. It was now some time since he had been in the countryside alone, and he enjoyed the quiet solitude. The evening was cool but not uncomfortably so. He reveled in the clear, starry sky and wondered what adventures were in store for him.

He arose early on the morn and was on his way, astride the piebald colt, before the sun had bestowed much warmth on the earth. His cloak kept out the morning chill, and he was in good spirits. Finally, he was close to fulfilling the objective of his journey.

Having traversed the mountain pass, the path before him was reasonably flat and easygoing. Before long, he began to see evidence of human habitation. The track sometimes now wandered between cultivated fields. To the left and the right, he would see the occasional peasant dwelling. Around midday, he passed through a small village. The people seemed very friendly. Women, hanging out their washing, waved to him as he passed. A few cheeky children ran alongside his horse, making boisterous noises and seeking some attention. A peasant, hoeing a plot in preparation for planting, called out a cheery greeting. Qiang smiled. He recollected the coming of spring from his childhood. In the peasant society in which he had been brought up, once winter had passed and the family had survived, everyone was happy, in anticipation of a bountiful season.

For two more days, he traveled in like fashion. In the early afternoon of the second day, he crested a small hill and was amazed to see, not far away, a rather large city. No doubt, this was the city that had grown up around the palace of Governor Chin Chao.

Qiang wended his way down the gentle slope and soon enough found himself among the houses of the citizens. The outlying houses seemed largely to be the quarters of peasants who worked in the city, providing various services to the population.

He now approached the palace and could see its high boundary walls.

The closer he came to the palace, the more opulent were the houses. These, he surmised, would be the residences of the court officials and the aristocracy, who were closest to the governor.

And now, at last, he had reached his destination. At the palace gates, he dismounted his horse and rummaged through his possessions until he found the letter of introduction to Chin Chao that Ruan Xiu had provided him at the start of his journey. As he approached the palace gate, a guard, with a drawn sword, surlily shouted at him.

"Stop! You can't enter here without the governor's permission. Who are you, and what is your business?"

"My name is Qiang. I have been sent by Governor Ruan Xiu to bring a message to your governor, Chin Chao." Qiang thrust his hand forward, displaying the document Ruan Xiu had provided for him. "This is a letter of introduction from my master."

The guard laughed. He looked askance at Qiang, who was rather disheveled as a result of his travels. "Why should I believe you, you impudent young ruffian? You are more than likely a spy, sent by the bandits."

Qiang had not bothered to make himself presentable. Glancing down, he saw that he indeed was a little unkempt. He merely smiled and replied amiably, "I have come a long way, sir, to do my master's bidding. If you examine the document I am proffering you, you will see that it is embossed with the seal of Governor Ruan Xiu. Please have someone take it to Governor Chin Chao. I will wait patiently until he has been able to verify my credentials."

The guard, who was more than likely illiterate, examined the document and the elaborate wax seal of Ruan Xiu. It was impressive enough to suggest he should check out the document. He knew he would be punished if he inadvertently turned away an emissary from Ruan Xiu. Most knew of the friendship between the two governors and that, when they were younger, they had driven away the bandits.

The guard turned around and called loudly to someone behind him. In no time at all, another armed man stood beside him. "Watch this fellow, will you? He claims to have a letter for the governor. I need to check the veracity of his claim."

With that, the guard strode into the palace.

The replacement guard looked suspiciously at Qiang, but Qiang merely smiled at him.

"Do you mind, sir, if I tether my horse here for a while."

He received no response, so Qiang tied the reins on his piebald colt to a protrusion from the palace wall. He then sat cross-legged on the ground in the shade of the palace wall and began to meditate.

Sometime later, Qiang was roused from his meditation by a commotion in the courtyard beyond the palace gate. He stood up to see a tall man in splendid robes approaching, followed by three others, struggling to keep up.

The guard's jaw dropped as the man swept by. "Your Excellency," was all he could say in dismay.

But the man, who was obviously the governor, brushed past the guard, asking, "Where is my young visitor?" Then he spied Qiang, standing alongside his horse. "Ah!" he exclaimed. "Is this the young master, Takygulpa Rinpoche?"

The guard, confused, sputtered, "He says his name is Qiang, sire."

"Ah, so. Yes, that is him." He turned to Qiang and put his arm on the young man's shoulder, "I have been eagerly awaiting your arrival for some time. I am so pleased you are now here."

Qiang smiled. "You must be Chin Chao."

"Ah, yes. Yes, indeed. I am Ruan Xiu's friend. I believe he is the one who sent you here. It is a long and dangerous journey. I am so grateful you made it here safely."

"Fortunately, because of the influence of your friend, I have had a little help along the way."

"That is no doubt true, but even so, it would not have been easy for you. But come now, into the palace, so I can make you comfortable." Chin Chao turned to the guard. "Have someone stable the horse and unload Qiang's things and bring them into the palace. He will be allocated the guest room I keep for visiting dignitaries. You may deposit his possessions there."

Before the guard could do anything, Qiang called out, "Wait! There is something I must retrieve first."

The young man strode to the horse, unbuckled some leather straps, and retrieved the tube with the manuscript in it. He then looked up at the guard and announced, "There! You may tend to my horse now, as the governor has requested."

He walked back to Chin Chao with the tube under his arm.

QIANG SAT ON a divan in a sumptuously appointed room in the palace. The governor sat opposite. Attendants had brought food and drink and placed them on a low table.

"Ruan Xiu sent me a message that you were on your way, but he gave me no indication of the purpose of your visit, save that you had a special place in his heart and that I should take good care of you."

"That was generous of Ruan Xiu." Qiang held out the tube. "This is the purpose of my visit. It is a gift to you from him."

Chin Chao's eyes lit up. "How wonderful. But Ruan Xiu must know I don't want for much. It must be something very special. May I see it?"

"Of course. Perhaps you might allow me to open it for you."

"I would be delighted, Qiang. Please go ahead."

Qiang carefully unwrapped the tube and drew the manuscripts out. Together, they laid them flat on the carpet in front of the governor.

Chin Chao gasped in wonderment.

Qiang, on the other hand, had to look away momentarily, for when he saw the exquisite drawings of his little sister, he realized how much he missed her, and an unbidden tear came to his eye.

"This is beautiful work, Qiang. And it includes some of my favorite passages. Can you tell me who manufactured these little masterpieces?"

The young man blushed. "Well, sir, I performed the calligraphy, and my little sister, Lan, painted the illustrations."

"You are both very talented. How did Ruan Xiu know what might appeal to me?"

"I believe, Excellency, that Ruan Xiu may have had some guidance from a benefactor of mine, Fung Tszu."

Chin Chao clapped his hands in delight. "Of course, my old friend would have known well what might please me. And indeed, it has pleased me. It is unlike anything I have ever been given. I can't tell you how grateful I am. I will treasure these delightful works all my life."

AT CHIN CHAO'S insistence, Qiang stayed some weeks in the palace. Qiang enjoyed the company of the governor, who was both well-read and deeply spiritual. Despite the joy Qiang found in communing with Chin Chao, it was not long before Qiang began to yearn to return to his mother and sister. Even though Chin Chao protested, Qiang took his leave and began his return journey, satisfied he had met his obligations to Ruan Xiu.

Before leaving, Chin Chao gave Qiang two letters. The first, he said, was to Ruan Xiu, thanking him profusely for the wonderful gift. The second, Chin Chao said, was a letter that confirmed that in the governor's territory, Qiang could rely on Chin Chao's protection. Chin Chao conceded that the letter would have little import the farther Qiang traveled, but it would certainly provide him with some protection for the first few days of his return journey.

Finally, he pressed into Qiang's hand a small leather bag. On inspection, Qiang was surprised to find it contained a handful of gold coins. Qiang protested that he did not need such benevolence because he was reasonably self-sufficient, but Chin Chao would have none of it and insisted Qiang take the purse. He warned Qiang, however, to hide the purse well, so it did not fall into the hands of the bandits. Qiang was rather naïve about such matters and had no idea how he might hide the small bag. Chin Chao quickly came to his aid. He called to an aide and whispered something in his ear, and the man strode purposefully away. In ten minutes or so, he was back, carrying a set of leather bags with straps.

Chin Chao took the bags and handed them to Qiang. "Take these," Chin Chao said.

"What are these?" inquired Qiang.

"They are saddlebags. They can be strapped to your horse to carry your essential equipment."

"But surely, if I put the bag of gold in one of these, that is the first place a thief would look."

"Of course. But this is a rather special set of bags. You see, one of the bags has a secret compartment that a thief will usually overlook."

Qiang was astounded when Chin Chao showed him the secret compartment, which was not at all obvious. The skills of the artisan who had made it were very considerable. Chin Chao showed Qiang how to open the compartment that would allow him to secrete the bag of gold. They then placed the bag inside the secret compartment and closed it off. Qiang was impressed that there were no signs of his treasure from the outside and no indication from the inside that there was a hidden treasure.

"Thank you, sir, for this gift. I would have had little notion of how such a thing might be hidden."

ON THE NEXT morning, Qiang set off on his return journey. He had been well provisioned by Chin Chao and knew he would not have any concerns for his subsistence for a week or so. The saddlebags had been duly installed and carried most of Qiang's essentials, including the little bag of gold coins, which was safely stowed in the secret hiding place. And readily at hand was the short staff that Cheng had given him.

In the short time of their acquaintance, Qiang had come to admire Chin Chao. The governor appeared to be not only a devout man but a compassionate one as well. In some respects, Qiang would have enjoyed spending more time with this splendid man. But once he had fulfilled his obligations to Ruan Xiu, he was compelled to return as quickly as possible to his mother and sister. It had been so long now since he had left them, and his heart was fully focused on his reunion with them; nothing could divert him from that objective.

For four days, he traveled southward. Although he was keen to return to Ruan Xiu's palace, he did not hurry unduly, knowing he must care for his horse if he was safely to negotiate the long journey back. The going was easy, the people were friendly, and his heart was full of joy in anticipation of being reunited with his mother and sister.

On the evening of the fourth day, he camped by the small stream on the northern side of the mountain pass, where he had spent a night on his outward journey. Maybe the water had warmed, or perhaps his heart was warmer, but he enjoyed the clear water on his body as he bathed. Last time, he could barely manage a minute or two in the water; it had seemed so cold. After his bracing bath, he made a simple meal, which, in his current state of well-being, seemed to surpass the delights of the lavish banquets that Chin Chao had provided for him to demonstrate his gratitude to Qiang. Then, he slept easily under a clear sky and a brilliant canopy of stars.

Little did he know it then, but it would be some time before he again slept so peacefully.

QIANG BROKE CAMP quite early. By midmorning, he and his little horse were wending their way carefully up the northern side of the mountain pass that had delayed him for so long with Sinh Hua. The trail was now quite rough, with rocky rubble underfoot that troubled the usually sure-footed piebald colt. Qiang dismounted and murmured words of encouragement to the stout little horse, before resuming their progress, with Qiang leading the horse. Although the weather had warmed somewhat since Qiang had last made the crossing, a cold northerly wind blew up the pass, and the young man was glad he had the protection of his cloak.

As he trudged up the slope, he practiced his walking meditation. In his heightened state of awareness, he sensed the presence of others. Somewhere a little behind him, a rock was dislodged. He didn't look back. He increased his pace, but they were now at the steepest part of the ascent, and even with his best efforts, he knew he couldn't travel much faster until he could again remount his horse.

And then, suddenly, he was at the top of the pass, and he quickly remounted. Just as he did, from just behind him came a piercing whistle, and in response, three men emerged from the boulders just in front of him. He turned to see who was behind him and saw, some fifty meters behind, another three rough-looking scoundrels, all with swords drawn. The track both in front and behind was blocked, and the terrain was so rough that he knew he could not expect his horse to gain enough speed to assault these brigands. He briefly thought of extracting his short staff to try to fight his way out, but he was significantly outnumbered and knew such resistance would be futile.

As he approached the men in front, he called out, "What do you want of me?"

"Well, glory be, Hong! It is the elusive Qiang. We had him once, but he escaped. There is no likelihood we will let that happen again."

Qiang sighed. He recognized that two of the bandits in front of him were Lim and Hong, who had previously captured him as he went to traverse the pass known as Devil's Gate.

"Ah, the gods have smiled favorably on us, Lim. We have unfinished business with this one!" Hong turned to Qiang. "What brings you here, young man?"

"Well, as I told you at our previous encounter, I am an emissary of Governor Ruan Xiu. He had sent me to Governor Chin Chao with a message and a gift, which I have duly delivered. I am now returning to Ruan Xiu." Qiang turned and rummaged through his saddlebags. "Here—I have a letter of safe passage from Chin Chao, if you wish to see it." He held the letter out in front of him.

Hong merely laughed. He tore the letter from Qiang's grasp and cast it onto the ground. "Spare yourself. Chin Chao has no authority over us. We care nothing for your letter."

Lim snarled, "Let us not waste our time on this young wretch. Let us just slay him, and be done with it. We must put him to the sword. He escaped us once before. He won't do so again, once he is lifeless."

Lim pushed his horse forward with his sword raised, but Hong raised his arm to stay Lim's progress.

"Not so fast, Lim! You are a rather impatient fellow. Whenever we are faced with a problem, the only response you know seems to be with your sword."

Sullenly, Lim put his sword back in its scabbard. "Well, what now, Hong? Are you going to let this little snake escape again?"

"No. That is not my intention, Lim. Let me put two propositions to you. First, this young man has been consorting with two regional governors. Consequently, it is likely that he might have intelligence that might be of use to us. Second, if we are to truly punish him for escaping, the sword would be too easy."

Lim now had a sardonic smile on his face. "And how do you suggest he should be punished?"

"I thought he might profit by a long stay in the cave at Xi Nung."

Lim laughed. "I can't fault your thinking in that regard. Fan might enjoy a little interrogation of this fellow, particularly if it were to be followed by incarceration in the cave."

As on their last encounter, the bandits bound Qiang's wrists and applied a long thong to the horse's halter so it could be easily led. The bandits seemed to be mightily pleased with their catch and were determined to return with him immediately to their hideout at Xi Nung. Once they had descended the mountain pass, and the woodland was sparser and the terrain more level, they left the beaten path and headed generally westward.

For three days, they progressed at a steady pace. Qiang was kept tied so that his wrists began to chafe and bleed. The bandits tended reasonably well to the needs of Qiang's little horse because he was an asset of some value to them. But Qiang was continually jostled and demeaned. They occasionally flung some food his way and offered water a couple of times a day because, as Hong said, there was little value in interrogating a dead body so he must at least be kept alive.

Qiang endured the privations as stoically as he could. He spent many of the uncomfortable hours meditating, often repeating his favorite mantras. As well as he could, he shut out the world from his mind. After a time, because of his lack of response, the bandits gave up taunting him.

Cheng's parting words came back into his consciousness. "I suspect there will be many more trials for you, Qiang. You will prevail, as long as you remember who you really are."

A look of steely resolve came to his face. He knew who he really was.

Late on the third day, despite his staunch efforts to control his mind, he fainted—probably because of lack of food and water—and fell off his horse.

Fortunately, he slipped slowly off his mount, and there was a carpet of soft grass underneath, which prevented any serious injury. The bandits merely laughed at Qiang's predicament. When a few prods could not arouse him, they threw some water on his face. Qiang slowly came back to consciousness.

The bandits jeered at him.

"Have you been drinking too much, Qiang?"

"Ho, that frisky little horse has shed you from its back."

"What sort of a governor's emissary are you? You can't even stay on your horse."

Qiang struggled to stand. The bandits roughly threw him back on the horse's back. But in his stupefied state, he could not sit upright; he lay forward on the horse's back, feebly grasping its mane to prevent his falling off again.

And it was, with Qiang in this undignified state, an hour or so later that they reached the stronghold of Xi Nung.

HONG UNCEREMONIOUSLY THREW Qiang off his horse and onto the ground. Qiang stirred and struggled to sit upright.

"Lim, go get Fan so he can see our prize."

Hong turned to one of the other bandits and said, "Fetch this fellow a little water. It might help him talk more lucidly with Fan."

It took some time for Fan to appear. In the meantime, Qiang had a couple of sips of water and seemed to recover somewhat.

Fan was a tall, gaunt man. As he approached, Qiang could see a sardonic smile on his face.

"So this is the one that Ruan Xiu sent out as an emissary. You would have thought he would have sent someone more capable. What is your name, young man?"

Qiang now sat upright in a more dignified position. In a steady voice, showing no sign of fear, he replied, "I am Qiang."

"Ho! In the local dialect, that name means 'strong and good.' You may be good, but your strength is not particularly obvious."

"Perhaps not, but it is unwise to judge a man's strength by the capacity of his muscles, when it is the strength of his mind that is most important."

Fan was a little taken aback by this answer. "Where might you have learned such rubbish?"

"My masters have taught me this. But in truth, there was no need because it is self-evident to those who understand the human condition. The masters have taught me some of the immutable laws of the universe. This is surely one."

"Who are these masters you speak of?"

"There have been quite a number. It is unlikely that you would be interested in their teachings. They preach loving kindness, whereas you and your men engage in murder and pillage."

Fan laughed. "You are a rather insolent young fellow. I doubt if you will be able to maintain your insolence after what I have in store for you."

Qiang merely shrugged his shoulders. "You might be able to render all sorts of indignities on my body, but my mind is my own."

"We shall see. We shall see." Fan turned to the assembled bandits. "Throw this fellow in the dungeon. Provide him with some sustenance so that he doesn't die. I would be disappointed if he expired before I have my way with him. I am going to enjoy silencing his insolence."

In response, two of the men raised Qiang off the ground. Each grabbing an arm, they dragged him fifty or so meters to a stone dungeon. They removed the thongs from his arms, threw him inside, and locked the door. They debated whether they should throw in a blanket for the young man. Finally, one said, "It will probably be cold tonight, but I doubt that would kill him."

So saying, they left Qiang alone, splayed on the hard, cold stone floor.

QIANG WAS RESILIENT. After a time, he raised himself and struggled into the lotus position and began to meditate.

Once he was in a meditative state, his sense of well-being was restored. He meditated for some hours. The sun had long set, and his cell became dark. Outside were a few oil lamps, the illumination of which made faint flickering on the walls of his cell.

Sometime later, two figures appeared at the cell door and cautiously opened it.

A mocking voice broke the silence. "Well, young man, the generous Fan has decreed you should be given something to eat and drink. Here is a veritable feast for you."

So saying, he laid a small tray on the floor and immediately locked the door behind him.

Qiang looked up, and in the gloom, he could barely make out a few meager crusts of bread and a small jar of water.

He sipped a little water and then slowly ate the bread. He practiced mindfulness as he ate, taking small bites, savoring the flavor, and chewing well before swallowing. The bread was obviously stale, but to Qiang, it proved satisfying enough. He sipped a little more water before putting away the now half-empty jar. He knew his jailers were unlikely to bring him more in a hurry, so he deemed it wise to keep a little aside to guard against later thirst.

He then resumed his meditation.

IN THE MORNING, his meditation was rudely interrupted by a big, strong fellow throwing open the gate to his cell.

"Get to your feet," he commanded Qiang in a steely voice.

Qiang knew he had no option but to obey. As he struggled to rise, he asked, "What will you have of me now?"

The man hastily bound Qiang's wrists. The response was a snarl. "It is time for Fan to have his little chat with you."

They approached an imposing building, where guards protected the entrance. They obviously knew the man who led Qiang. As they entered the building, one of the guards called out, "Ah, Shu Ming, it looks like you are in for some fun today!"

Qiang's companion did not reply but merely smirked.

The guard chuckled. "Call me if you need some help." He laughed callously.

Fan sat on a high chair that was adorned with ornate carvings. In front of him on the floor was a rough mat.

Shu Ming pushed the young man to the floor and grunted, "Kneel there."

Qiang did as directed. He looked up at Fan and saw the cruelty in his eyes. He knew there would be no mercy from this vile man. He gathered his composure and began focusing on his breath, awaiting what Fan might have in store for him.

Fan, sensing Qiang's resoluteness, frowned and did not speak for some minutes. Shu Ming stood behind Qiang, menacingly, awaiting his master's orders.

Finally, Fan addressed Qiang. "Now, you young cur, this is the second time my men have apprehended you in our territory, where you have trespassed without our permission. You need to tell me what has brought you surreptitiously into our lands."

Qiang sighed, sensing that his answer, whatever it was, would be to no avail.

"I have told you before that I was sent by Governor Ruan Xiu to deliver a gift to Governor Chin Chao of the western province. I have completed my task and am now returning to be restored to my family."

Anger welled up in Fan's face. "Ruan Xiu and Chin Chao are the most reviled of all people. In the past, they have assailed and harassed my men. Let me assure you that nobody associated with these vile governors will ever be welcome here! What's more, the greatest thing they have in common is a desire to destroy us. And no doubt, your little journey has been associated with another attempt to subdue us. I demand that you provide us with any intelligence you have regarding their plans to harass us."

"You pose an impossible task for me, Fan. I have no such intelligence. But to tell the truth, if I did, I would not divulge it anyway. No matter how you might assault and defile me, there is nothing I know that could assist you. I kneel now before you, defenseless, but with no knowledge that might be useful to you. I suspect your intentions to punish me and degrade me are not related to what I might tell you but mainly to your gratuitous desire to inflict your sadistic impulses on me. I have told you before that you might injure my body, but you will not shake my mind."

"Those are brave words, young man, but you do not understand the nature of Shu Ming's unique talents." Fan turned to the other man. "I will leave him with you to do as you will, Shu Ming. Get what you can out of him, but do not kill him. I might have other plans for him."

Fan walked out, leaving Qiang and Shu Ming alone. Once Fan had removed himself, Shu Ming dragged Qiang into a nearby cell and began his evil interrogation.

"You must tell me what you know of the plans of Ruan Xiu and Chin Chao to disrupt us," said Shu Ming.

"Because I know nothing, I intend to say nothing," responded Qiang.

Shu Ming then began beating Qiang. Every little while, he would pause and say, "Have you had enough now? What can you tell me?"

Qiang, true to his word, didn't utter a sound. This seemed to infuriate Shu Ming, and he would resume his beatings with even more violence. Finally, after some hours of this torture, Qiang fainted. He could prevent his mind from being assailed by such violence, but his body finally succumbed to the torture.

WHEN QIANG REGAINED consciousness, he found himself back in the cell where he had started his day. His body was sore and bruised, but his limbs were all intact, and nothing was broken. He had to concede that this outcome seemed to be due to Shu Ming's talent for inflicting pain without threatening life.

Despite the soreness of his body, Qiang laboriously assumed the lotus position and began his meditation. He had no idea what time it was, only that it was dark. Over the years, he had found it easier to meditate without the use of mantras by merely concentrating on his breath. Even though he had begun his meditation, his mind was still somehow fuzzy from the beatings that had been inflicted on him.

Bring love,
And peace,
And hope,
And joy.

The An Cheng mantra he had learned in his childhood instruction kept invading his thoughts. Somehow, it brought him serenity. No matter that his back ached, no matter that his limbs were sore, no matter that his head hurt, he was soon enough in a state of bliss. Neither Fan nor Shu Ming nor anyone else would be allowed to assail his mind. He knew he could endure anything that might be imposed upon him. He knew who he really was.

But as his mindfulness grew, it suddenly seemed to him that the mantra was not a product of his own meditation. Then, it came to him that the mantra was being chanted in a quiet voice by someone outside the window of his cell. The gentle sound was vaguely familiar to him. Finally, he recognized it as the voice of the blind sage, Jian.

He concentrated on the sound for a moment. The chanting of the mantra continued in a soft, mellifluous voice. Painfully, he stood up and made his way to the barred window. Peering through the gloom, he could vaguely make out a figure squatting on the ground, adjacent to the wall of his cell.

Finally, he whispered, "Jian, is that you?" He was mindful not to draw attention to the old man.

The reply was a subdued chuckle. "Yes, it is indeed me, Jian."

"What are you doing here, Jian?"

"I have come to help you, Takygulpa."

"How did you know I was here?"

"My ear receives whispers from many sources. How are you? Did Shu Ming injure you?"

"Well, he beat me rather severely, and I am bruised and sore, but nothing seems to be broken."

"I might have guessed. Fan is very sadistic. He will seek to prolong your suffering, and Shu Ming is very adept at that."

"I do not understand why he should do this to me. I can tell him nothing that would be of advantage to him."

"He can't be sure, can he? You have had the ear of two governors, both of whom would like to see the end of him. But despite that, because of his sadism, he will delight in making you suffer."

"Then I suppose I should just resign myself to the ongoing torture. If I should die, would you be able to bring a message back to Ruan Xiu? I would like the governor to know I tried to fulfill his wishes. I would like to express my gratitude to him for caring for my mother and sister. And I want my mother and sister to know of my undying love for them."

"Of course I would do that, but we don't intend to let you die."

"When you say 'we,' whom do you mean?"

"Bai and me, of course. We promised we would try to look out for you, and we shall do our best. We have already secured your horse in anticipation of your escape."

"My horse, you say! How did you manage that?"

"It is a trivial thing, and you should not bother yourself with that. By the way, we also have your saddlebags, and they contained a little treasure."

Qiang was astounded and amused. "How did you find that?" he asked, laughing.

"Secret hiding places only work for the sighted. The blind can often 'see' things that the sighted can't."

"But I ask you, if you don't intend to let me die, what are you to do?"

"The bad news is that I don't think we can manufacture your escape for a while yet. That means you must be prepared to endure Shu Ming's torture for some time as well."

"If there is a chance you might save me to be able to rejoin my mother and sister, I will endure any torture."

"That is easy to say now, and I am glad that you seem willing to display such stoicism. But I warn you—it won't be easy."

"Did not the Buddha teach us that life is suffering?"

"He did, indeed, but the suffering you are about to endure will test even a master like you. But enough now. I don't want to alert the guards to my presence, so I must scuttle away. I will come as often as I can to check on your welfare."

"Thank you, Jian. You are indeed a saint."

QIANG'S TORTURE CONTINUED on a daily basis. His tormenter took perverse pleasure in inflicting exquisite pain on the young Buddhist. How long this lasted, Qiang could not tell. Each day, he would be dragged from his cell and given over to Shu Ming to work his evil. Qiang hardly spoke through his ordeal. He focused his mind on being in a pleasant place with his mother and sister. His strength of purpose was such that the pain began to feel more distant and less intrusive,

Back in his cell each evening, he ate his meager meal and sipped a little water. He could not escape his bodily soreness, and sleeping became difficult.

He mused over the fact that Fan was trying to extract information he did not possess. Maybe he might have felt a little more noble if he indeed was withholding information in the face of such torture. When he could not provide information, it all seemed rather pointless. He had no doubt that he would not have betrayed Ruan Xiu in any case, but with his ongoing beatings and meager diet, he seemed more and more to be in a dreamlike state. Physically, he was no doubt getting weaker, but his resolve remained strong, and he began to sense Shu Ming's growing frustration.

He felt like he was a mouse that had been captured by a cat—Shu Ming. The cat was toying with him. The cat could kill him whenever he chose, but he wanted a reaction, perhaps a struggle or some protest or expression of hurt.

But the mouse did not oblige. He accepted every indignity without flinching, without complaining, without protesting.

Shu Ming's frustration became increasingly apparent.

Finally, he snapped. "Damn you, Qiang. Why don't you fight against your torture? Why don't you scream to have me stop? I can kill you, you know."

In the midst of his pain, Qiang smiled. He knew he had won the battle of wills.

"Damn you, you little cur. What are you smiling at? If you dare provoke me like that, I will smash your face."

"It is of little import, Shu Ming. My face is not that important. But you have misunderstood this entire endeavor. I never had anything of any import to relate to you, but you have never believed me. Let me be as clear as I can: I have nothing to relate to you that might be of the slightest interest to you or your master."

"You seem to forget that I know that you are a close confidant of both Ruan Xiu and Chin Chao. You must have information that is useful to us. Your horse and your accoutrements were somehow stolen some days ago, but before they were, we found in your saddlebags a letter addressed to Ruan Xiu. In it, Chin Chao requested Ruan Xiu send an expedition to join him in exterminating me and my comrades. And yet you pretend to know nothing."

"I know I had in my possession a letter from Chin Chao to Ruan Xiu, but I had no knowledge of its contents. Do you think that I would have opened the private correspondence between the two governors? That would have betrayed my position of trust. I only know that both those men would like to put an end to the terror and injustice you bring to their people. I have no knowledge of what plans or tactics they might have to do that. When I left Ruan Xiu, I had been managing his stables. What likelihood would there be that he might confide in me about such matters? As for Chin Chao, I merely acted as an emissary of Ruan Xiu, charged with delivering a gift to him."

"Why do you persist with these lies? You know I have absolute control over you and can kill you in an instant, if I so desire."

"There is no doubt, Shu Ming, that you have control over my physical well-being. You have amply demonstrated that by the torture you have inflicted on me. But I tell you now—you do not have control of the one thing that is of importance to me."

"And what would that be, you little snake? Tell me what it is, and I will demonstrate to you that you have nothing I cannot control."

Qiang smiled and looked at his torturer in a benign way. "I think I might have already demonstrated to you that you are not in control of my mind. There is nothing now that you can do to me that will take away my equanimity."

"Do you not fear me? Do you not know I hold the key to whether you live or die? How you must hate me. I have inflicted great physical pain on you. I have taken away your freedom and inflicted all sorts of indignities on you."

Qiang was silent a while. His head was buzzing and his body aching. Then, he said quietly, "I do not fear you, Shu Ming. And I do not hate you."

This seemed to stun Shu Ming. He got to his feet and called for the guards outside. "Take this fellow back to his cell." As Qiang was being dragged off, Shu Ming shouted at him, "You will certainly regret this! Tomorrow, I will bring you back before Fan. And I can assure you there will be no mercy!"

QIANG WAS CONFUSED. His head swam. He lay on the cold stone floor of his cell, and for some time, it was more than he could do to raise his prone body off the floor.

He seemed only half conscious, and he was grateful for that because it provided him some relief from his physical discomfiture. He tried to meditate. Comforting words came into his mind.

Bring love,
And peace,
And hope,
And joy.

He tried to say the words of the mantra, but they wouldn't come. How he wished he might express these words of comfort, such expression was beyond him. He gave up trying. Yet in his swirling mind, they continued to be repeated. Oh, love—back with his mother and sister; and peace—away from the torment of his torturer; and hope—that somehow the people might prosper again devoid of the bandits; and joy—when he could fulfill his duties and be content.

The mantra, of course, was meant to be a prelude to meditation. But as he settled his mind and tried to begin his meditation practice, the words kept ringing in his ears. Finally, it dawned on him that the words were not coming from his own mind; they were external to him. The reality suddenly occurred to him—he had again been deceived.

"Jian," he called out rather weakly, "is that you?"

Then he heard a familiar chuckle. "Yes, little master, it is I, Jian. I am so glad to hear your voice. I was beginning to think that they might have rendered you unconscious."

It had raised Qiang's spirits tremendously, realizing that it was Jian's sonorous voice and that he was lodged just outside the window of his cell.

"No, Jian, I am still with you, even though somewhat battered and my mind somewhat woolly."

"That is good, young master. You have been courageous enough to outlast your tormentor. Few have achieved such an outcome. You indeed have a strong mind."

Qiang laughed ruefully. "I am pleased I have a strong mind, Jian, but I wish I had a more durable body. My physical comfort seems a little wanting."

"Well, one way or another, I suspect you might not have to endure much more."

"Why do you say that?"

"I have heard that Fan has lost patience with you."

"And what does that mean?"

"It means he will try to kill you."

"But he could have killed me any time since my capture."

"That is true, but because he believed you had useful intelligence that might be helpful to him, he chose to torture you instead."

"So now, he will have me executed?"

"No doubt he will try."

"Why do you say that? Surely if he has made up his mind to kill me, that is easy enough to achieve."

"You would think so, but you need to consider Fan's sadism. It is not enough that he should kill you; he will more than likely want you to suffer. This will be an example to those who defy him that their defiance will be punished mercilessly. Most of those who have steadfastly resisted him have been sealed in the cave of Gorrum and left to slowly starve to death, just as I was."

"Well, that seems a daunting prospect, but if I have to, I will face my death with equanimity. I have done my best to serve Ruan Xiu, as I promised. I will sorely miss my mother and sister, but at least I am satisfied that they will be well cared for."

"But don't despair yet, Takygulpa Rinpoche. There is still hope."

"Oh, Jian, I will be optimistic till my last breath. But realistically, in the scenario you paint, I think I would be foolish to expect too much."

"That would generally be true, young master, but you forget something important."

Qiang paused a moment to think. Although his mind was somewhat addled as a result of his physical torture, he remembered his first meeting with Bai and Jian. He recalled Bai's story of how Jian was revered because his impossible escape from a cave.

"Jian, could it be that Gorrum is the cave you escaped from?"

Qiang heard the familiar chuckle and then a merry response.

"That is indeed true, Qiang. I know the way out of Gorrum. Let us hope that Fan chooses this fate for you, and then it might be possible that our friends and I could rescue you."

SHU MING DRAGGED Qiang into the room and then flung him onto the floor. Qiang looked up to see he was in front of Fan, who was sitting on an ornate couch with embroidered cushions. The big man looked at Fan. "Here is the little cur. What will you have me do with him? Shall I cut his throat, or would you have me throttle him?"

"Don't be so hasty, Shu Ming. We don't have to dispose of him that quickly." Fan turned to Qiang. "Young man, you have continued to defy me. You will regret that, you know."

Qiang struggled to rise, but Shu Ming struck him down again. "Stay on the floor where you belong," he hissed.

Qiang struggled resolutely to stand.

Shu Ming was about to strike him again, but Fan stayed him.

"Let him be for a moment."

Qiang was so unsteady on his feet that he had to hang on to the end of Fan's couch to prevent himself from falling again. He waited a while to regain his breath.

"Well?" demanded Fan. "Do you have something to say?"

"It seems," Qiang said in a wavering voice, "that you are determined to kill me."

Fan smiled. "Indeed, that is my intention."

"Then I shall be absolutely truthful with you."

"That would be good. It is a pity that you weren't more forthright before. It probably would have saved you some pain."

"I doubt it," Qiang said. "No matter that you might have thought otherwise, I had no intelligence of any use to you.

Fan sighed. "So you have repeatedly said."

"I have continued to tell you that because it is true. But let me tell you something else."

"And what would that be?"

"Even if I had known anything, I wouldn't have divulged it to you, because you and your men are evil predators who prey on the simple, good folk who struggle to make a living off their small plots. I am the son of a farmer. I know how they struggle, and there is nothing I would do to aid your predatory activities. I am pledged to support Ruan Xiu, who has sought to protect these people. I am not motivated by revenge, but I suspect Ruan Xiu might be, and you may well regret taking my life."

Fan laughed uproariously. "We have no fear of Ruan Xiu, but I must say, I admire your impertinence."

"Shall I dispatch him now, my lord?" inquired Shu Ming.

"No, no. After such a performance, I think he has earned the comfort of the cave. Take him to Gorrum."

QIANG WAS TRUSSED and bound by his tormentors and then roughly thrown into a cart. He did not have the strength to rise and therefore had little idea of the path they took. The only thing he knew was that the track was rough, causing the cart to bounce, which pained his battered body. He seemed to pass in and out of consciousness. Finally, he became aware that the cart had stopped. Hands grabbed at his person, and he was deposited roughly on the ground.

Lying on his side, he could see that Shu Ming was accompanied by three others. They seemed to have arrived at the mouth of the cave. The cave was sealed by a large circular stone. It appeared to have been so formed by both the work of stone masons and a long history of having been rolled back and forth across the cave mouth. A race had been cut in the stone at ground level to the right of the stone disc, which would guide its path when rolled away. A steel peg had been set in the stone's center. The men unpacked ropes, levers, and pulleys, which they proceeded to deploy in an organized way, which convinced Qiang that they had moved the stone many times before. But even with the mechanical aids, it still required considerable physical effort to roll the stone away from the mouth of the cave along its manufactured track.

Eventually, the task was done.

They then returned to Qiang and unbound him.

Shu Ming laughed. "There will be no need for such constraints once you are behind the rock. There is no escape from this place. It may take some days, and I hope it is prolonged, but you surely will die an excruciating death. And that is all because you failed to cooperate with us." Shu Ming paused and thought a while. Then he said, "Perhaps it is not too late for you to give us the information we desire."

Qiang merely shook his head and said in a weak voice, “I have nothing to tell you. As I have repeatedly told you, I would not do anything to progress your evil ends. I have no interest, Shu Ming, in revenge, but I am sure you will come to regret your evil ways.”

Shu Ming kicked Qiang’s prone form. “Impertinent to the last. You deserve to die. Take him inside.”

Qiang knew that in his decrepit state, it was futile to resist. They threw him roughly on the floor of the cave, and moments later, he heard the sound of the stone rolling back into place to seal the entrance.

QIANG WAS SOMEWHAT dazed and lay face down on the floor of the cave. It took him a little while to roll over and to try to ascertain his surroundings. The rock sealed the mouth of the cave well so that only a diffuse light was apparent surrounding the very edges of the entrance. The light was feeble and only penetrated a meter or two into the cave. After a time, his eyes became accustomed to the gloom, and he could make out the vague outline of some shapes, which were apparently large stones. The floor of the cave seemed uneven, but in his immediate vicinity, it was covered in loose dirt. He reached out around him to try to better familiarize himself with his horrid environment. He became aware that there were objects lying on the dusty floor. He felt one or two of them before he realized that they were bones—human bones! Qiang initially was repelled by the thought of being surrounded by human remains. But then he smiled, as he remembered the teachings of one of his masters.

"How should I view my life, Master?" he had asked. "It seems so precious on the one hand and yet so inconsequential on the other."

The master had replied, "Imagine it is night, and you are a bat. You fly through the darkness. Eventually, you approach a small hut. In the hut, there is a candle. The candle lights up the room with its brightness. By good fortune, the window is open. You fly through the window and out the open door on the other side. That short passage through the lightened room is like a life!"

"Is that all there is?" Qiang had said in surprise. "What about reincarnation?"

"Perhaps there are other huts with open doors or windows up ahead," the sage had replied, "but can you rely on that?"

Qiang was impressed with the analogy, and in later years, he used it himself.

But then his master had continued. "Many of us are so afraid of going out into the dark that we don't make best use of our time in the light. We should not be so afraid. In order to prepare ourselves, it is useful to meditate on death."

He'd then taught Qiang to meditate on death, to visualize his body in the ground with its flesh decomposed into the soil, leaving only his bones.

"Imagine," he had said, "that your body is in a graveyard alongside many others. Turn your attention to the bones of those nearby. How can you distinguish them from your bones? You may have had a deposit from some arthritis you suffered, or perhaps you lost different teeth. Maybe your bones are smaller or larger. Notice, though, how they are similar. The differences are really few. What evidence now of the smooth skin or the toned muscles you admired?"

Qiang reached out and felt a large bone close by. It was smooth and slightly cool in the dank environment of the cave. It was a marvelous thought that this had been part of a live human being. But it was tragic that the poor fellow would have perished through thirst and starvation at the whim of the callous Fan.

He was reminded of the first of the Four Noble Truths of the Buddha: we must all encounter suffering, but it is an injustice that we should impose it on another.

Surprisingly, the cave seemed well ventilated. No doubt, there were gaps around the rock that sealed the cave to allow the ingress of air. That alone would not allow the air to circulate, but remembering that Jian had found a way out of the cave, there must be another aperture, and that would account for the throughput of air.

Qiang became aware of how uncomfortable his bruised body was, lying on the rough floor of the cave. He did not have the strength to stand or to take his customary lotus position to meditate, so he wiggled his body into the most comfortable position he could and began to focus on his breath.

He did not know whether he fell into a trance or merely fell asleep, for it seemed, somehow, that before long, he was no longer aware of his body. Visions of his childhood flooded his mind. He remembered the humble farmhouse of his childhood, the comfort of his mother, the joy of his little sister, and the gallant efforts of his father to sustain a livelihood for them. He experienced a great sense of contentment and then lost consciousness.

HOW LONG QIANG stayed unconscious, he could not tell. As awareness returned, he still felt a sense of well-being. Perhaps he might die, but he was prepared for that.

Bring love,
And peace,
And hope,
And joy.

This was the mantra he loved so much. It inspired him. If there was any more life to live, this would be his guiding ambition.

"Bring love and peace and hope and joy."

His body was protesting the indignities it had suffered under Shu Ming's sadistic ministrations. Qiang wondered what the mind of such a man might be suffering to compel him to do such evil. He would rather die, with his mind in order, than live with such a dysfunctional mind.

"Bring love and peace and hope and joy."

The words were a salve to his mind, and when his mind was in order, the state of his body became of little concern.

"Bring love and peace and hope and joy."

How beautiful were the words and how sonorous was the voice. Then he realized, again, that it was not his voice; it was Jian's voice.

Qiang opened his eyes. "Jian, is that you?"

He heard a deep-throated familiar chuckle. "Of course, little master. I have been here meditating over you for some time. I knew if I could join your mind with mine, I could raise you into consciousness so that I can get you out of here. There is a way out, as I have related to you. But the aperture is high in the cave's roof, and I will need some assistance from you to gain your escape."

"What would you have me do?"

"To begin with, slip this over you."

So saying, Jian passed a noose of rope over Qiang's shoulders, lodging it under his armpits.

"What is this for?"

"Well, I have a big, strong fellow standing above the aperture in the cave's roof at the other end of the rope. He is going to assist with your escape. But on the way up, there is a lot of loose rock, and it would help if you could take your weight occasionally by placing your feet on firm standing, so as not to make the job of the man at the top too demanding."

"I will do my best," said Qiang, "but I must confess that I have little strength in my legs."

"Do as well as you can, and leave the rest to us." Jian then called out, "Take up the tension on the rope."

Almost immediately, Qiang felt the rope tighten around his chest.

Even though the rope was quite thick, it seemed to cut into Qiang and restrict his breathing. After a time, whoever was doing the hauling got into a rhythm. He would tug hard on the rope, lifting Qiang up a meter or so, and then relax a little. These short intermissions allowed Qiang to take a deep breath and steel himself for the next lifting event. Qiang's feet scrabbled around on the loose rock, searching for a foothold.

Jian struggled up the slope behind Qiang. When the tension on the rope eased, Jian would take Qiang's weight by wedging his shoulders under Qiang's buttocks.

Often, when Qiang tried to gain purchase on the loose rocks, they tumbled away from him. When that occurred, he was concerned that he might somehow be injuring Jian.

"Jian, are you all right?" he asked.

"I am getting better every minute as you approach your escape," the blind man said, chuckling.

Soon, Qiang could see some light above him.

Whoever was hauling on the rope seemed to be a man of considerable strength, but it seemed he might be tiring. He was now taking longer breaks.

Sensing this, Jian called out, "Not long now. We are nearing the top."

After a few more hearty tugs, it became much firmer underfoot for Qiang and Jian. Their feet now met with solid rock, and even Qiang, as sore and exhausted as he was, was able to take a bit of weight off the rope, making it easier for the one at the top who was doing the hauling.

Qiang could feel the breeze stronger on his face now. The cavern, being largely vertical, acted as a chimney, funneling the air that leaked in at the mouth of the cave up to the aperture at the top. As the cavern narrowed, the wind velocity increased.

They surged up perhaps another ten meters.

Jian called out, "Stop!"

The tension went off the rope. Jian turned to Qiang. "The passage gets quite narrow here, and I will need you to progress alone. The way forward is almost vertical, so you must try to gain purchase from your feet on the rock to your side."

Qiang shook his head in disbelief. "But Jian, this must be the way you made your escape from Gorrum all by yourself. However did you do it?"

Jian merely laughed. "I was younger then. Are you ready to continue?"

"Yes, but I hope it is not much farther, as I have little strength left."

"You have done your best to use your legs so far. Now it is time to use your mind."

JIAN CALLED UP to the man above. "Rest a while now. Qiang will have to manage this last part of the climb by himself. The aperture is too small for us both to go up together. He needs to gather his strength for a moment before we proceed."

Turning to Qiang, Jian said, "As the aperture reduces, the biggest assistance you can give the one above who is hauling you up is to relieve him of your weight by trying to seek a foothold on the rocks at the side. Keep your legs spread a little and when you detect an irregularity in the rocks, try to push your toes into any crevice or on to any protuberance that you can. That will help reduce the load somewhat. But rest a little now, and put your mind to affecting your escape. We will take a break for five minutes or so."

The tension on the rope relaxed.

Jian had said that Qiang must prepare his mind; he wondered how he might do that.

Then his mind went back to the time when he and Ruan Xiu had cleared the tree from the path, when he and his mother and sister made their trek from their modest farm to live with the governor.

Qiang considered those things that might aid his escape, and two immediately came to mind: it would help if he were lighter and if his legs were stronger.

His exhausted body felt like a dead weight to him.

He started his breathing meditation routine. He noticed and counted his breaths and soon had little perception of his body.

He knew he was not his body. Whatever was the essential Qiang did not comprise flesh and blood. In his mind, he began to dissociate from his body. Whatever was required to survive this experience had no weight at all. What might the metaphor be? Was he like a cloud, essentially weightless but being blown across the vastness of the sky? Was he like a sunray that illuminated the space around him, touching all but weighing down on none? Was he like the sound of the bamboo flute bringing sweet music to the world but casting a load on none?

Perhaps he was light-headed from his injuries and his efforts to escape with Jian, but after a time, his body did not weigh down on him at all.

He returned his mind to his body. He knew he was not his body, but right here and now, his body was the host for his essential essence—what his masters had called "the witness." Therefore, he must give further attention to how his body might escape. Even if his body no longer seemed to weigh much, he must still use the power of his legs to clamber up this narrow rock chimney.

He concentrated on his legs. They initially seemed weary from all the exertion in trying to affect his escape. He remembered the times when he had relied on his legs. They were surely powerful legs. He had used them to leap across chasms, to walk long distances, to carry heavy loads, to climb rockfaces, to mount and control his little horse, to run, and to do all manner of things that enhanced his physical impact on the world. He imagined his legs as being the roots of a large tree—they effortlessly gained purchase in the earth and held the massive tree upright.

A voice came down from above. It was quite loud, which encouraged Qiang that he must be nearly at the end of his climb.

"Are you ready to commence again, Jian?" the voice inquired.

"What say you, Qiang?" Jian asked quietly.

"I am ready, Jian."

Jian called up in a loud voice, "We are ready."

The thick rope went taut around Qiang's midriff. His preparations were such that he now looked forward to progressing farther up the rock chimney. The rope no longer seemed so tight. His legs easily anchored themselves in the rock niches, taking the weight off the rope and enabling the lifter above to expedite Qiang's passage up the rock chimney. It seemed as if this last stage of his escape took only ten minutes or so, and before he knew it, he lay gasping on the grassy ground in the cool night air, under a canopy of stars.

A large figure loomed over him.

"Well, Qiang, you seem to have survived your privations. It is good to see you again."

It was dark enough that Qiang could not plainly see the figure, but he knew at once from his voice that it was Lei.

Qiang struggled to his feet. He was a little wobbly, not only from his recent exertions but also still suffering the effects of Shu Ming's ministrations. He put his arms around the stout body in front of him.

"Oh, Lei, how good it is to see you again. Why have you gone to such trouble and exposed yourself to such danger on my account? I am nobody special."

Qiang never heard Lei's response; he fainted. The big man quickly caught him and lowered him gently to the ground. The sage Bai quickly ran to Lei's aid.

He reassured Lei that Qiang was not in any present danger. "I will tend to him, Lei. Go now, and help Jian extract himself."

Lei made his way back to the aperture at the chimney's top and called down. "The little master is now up with us, Jian. I will throw the rope down again to draw you up as well."

Within a few minutes, Jian had scrambled to the surface as well.

"How is Qiang? Is he all right?"

Bai said, "He appears to have fainted. He most probably over-exerted himself."

"Well, I don't know what he did," responded Lei, "but as I hauled him up that last stage, he seemed as light as a feather."

"He is truly a master, Lei. Even though he was wounded by Shu Ming and is suffering physically, he still is in control of his mind. A man who can put aside his physical discomfiture and prevail over the material aspects of his life is someone to be admired, indeed."

QIANG LAY ON the grass. Bai had rolled up his coat to serve as a pillow for Qiang. The young man slowly regained consciousness. He felt a great tiredness. His limbs felt like lead. A wry smile came to his face. The last he could remember was scaling the final section of the rock chimney, when his limbs felt powerful and his body as light as a feather. He could hear nearby voices murmuring. He surmised it was Bai, Jian, and Lei. Nothing would have given him more joy at that moment than to join them. He went to rise, but it was more than his body would now allow. As he sank back despondently, he remembered the words of Ruan Xiu. His mind went back to the time on the way to the governor's palace, when the way had been blocked by the fallen tree.

The governor had urged Qiang to use his mind to help remove the obstacle. But when he had done so, Ruan Xiu counseled, "All I wanted to display to you is that many of us are limited in what we can do by the constraints of our minds. Those who can remove those constraints by proper discipline of the mind can achieve much more as a result. But this is not a limitless bucket you can dip into. You may be able to extend your physical capability, for example, as you have, but all you can do is reach your real limitations. There is no more beyond that. However skillful you become, your body will still have finite capability. Do not let this go to your head."

Now was not the time for his mind to be called into play to handle issues of strength. It was time to give attention to pain and lassitude. He commenced his meditation practice. When he retreated into the quietness of his mind, there was no pain because there was no perception of body to distract it. He knew that he was not his body, even though his body accompanied him everywhere he went.

Similarly, after meditating, despite the indignities that his body had suffered, he was overwhelmed with contentment. When his mind was in order, he could deal with whatever the world threw up at him. The Buddha taught that life inevitably involved suffering but that a trained mind was able to put suffering aside. The external world impacted on a person's sense of well-being, only to the degree that the mind allowed it to do.

When he roused himself into worldly consciousness a second time, he was able to raise his upper body off the ground. There, gathered around a little fire they had kindled, he saw the familiar faces of Lei, Bai, and Jian, lit gently by the light of the small, stuttering flames. They were drinking tea and talking quietly.

Bai looked around and saw Qiang stirring.

"Well, look. Someone seems about to rejoin us." He hurried over to Qiang. "How are you, young master?"

"I am somewhat better, Bai. But I think I might benefit from some of that tea you have." He made to stand up but staggered a little.

Bai was quick to hold him. "Make your way over here so you can join us. I will help you." The old man took Qiang's arm and put it over his own shoulder so he might help bear some of Qiang's weight. It was only a few steps, and he soon had Qiang settled on the grass, a meter or so from the fire. Qiang was comforted by the warmth of the fire. Bai went back and retrieved his jacket that he had folded into a pillow for Qiang's head. He draped the jacket over Qiang's shoulders.

"Thank you, Bai," Qiang said. "That feels better. I have never felt the cold much, but I suspect my recent ordeals have depleted my mental resources to deal with it."

"Undoubtedly, that's true, Qiang. Come; we need to plan what to do with you, now that you are free of the cave."

Qiang nodded. "But first," he said, "I want to thank you all for organizing my escape. And I am intrigued, Lei, how you came to be part of the enterprise."

Jian had filled a bowl with tea and delivered it to Qiang. Qiang sipped the tea with obvious satisfaction.

"These exemplary men, Qiang, have, from time to time, provided succor to the couple who cared for my sister before she died. When I recently visited the couple, they recounted that Bai and Jian had been there just before me. They gathered from the conversations between Bai and Jian that you had been captured again by the bandits. That's a bad habit we should teach you to avoid, Qiang." The big man chuckled at his little joke.

Qiang, smiling, responded, "I think that would be a good idea, Lei."

"I hurried off to catch up with them to see what I might do to help."

"That was noble of you, Lei. There is little that I have done that would deserve such consideration."

"No, that is not true, Qiang. That I have become a better man is largely due to your influence."

"Enough!" interjected Bai. "Cease this self-congratulatory back-slapping," he continued with a laugh. "Time enough for such pleasantries when we are in safety. We should lose no time in putting some distance between us and this profane place." He looked earnestly at Qiang. "Are you able to ride, little master?"

"I think so, Bai. At least, I will try. I share your concerns in removing ourselves from this place, but I suspect I might need to rest occasionally until my body recovers from the indignities that Shu Ming inflicted on it."

Bai smiled. He was impressed by the way Qiang was able to differentiate between his essential self and his body. "Very well, Qiang. We need to be off as quickly as we can, but we will try to ensure we do no further damage to your body. We will take frequent rest breaks, but it is urgent that we get you away from here."

LEI HELPED QIANG mount his little horse. His discomfiture was obvious, but he took the reins and turned to smile at the others.

"Let us be off, but please, not too quickly!"

They moved off quietly in single file. Lei, who knew the territory best, led the little party. Jian came next. His horse seemed old and placid. It seemed to know that its duty was just to follow the horse in front. Then came Qiang. While he attempted to stay upright in the saddle, he soon exhausted himself and lay forward on the back of his little piebald colt. In the rear rode Bai. His attention was almost entirely on the young master. It was vital that they should bring him to safety.

They pressed on into the night. Just before dawn, Lei led them to a well-wooded area next to a little stream. They set up camp and made themselves comfortable to wait out the day.

"If we travel by night and hide ourselves during the day, the bandits are less likely to find us," Lei explained to the others.

They settled Qiang onto his bedding, gave him a little food and water, and waited out the day.

This was to be the practice for many days, but eventually, the little party arrived at the house of Sinh Hua, all intact and without further adventure. Qiang had been gradually recovering and, for the last two days, had been able to negotiate the journey by sitting upright in his saddle.

They received a warm welcome from Sinh Hua, who was dismayed by the reported activity of the bandits.

He offered hospitality to all, but Bai and Jian gracefully declined his offer and begged their leave. Lei, on the other hand, said he would stay with Qiang and accompany him back to Ruan Xiu's palace when he was well enough to travel. Sinh Hua vowed to care for Qiang and restore him to his normal state of health before he would allow him to journey back to Ruan Xiu. But after hearing Qiang's story, he sent a messenger off to Ruan Xiu to warn him of the resurgence of the bandits.

QIANG WAS RESILIENT, and within a few weeks, he had overcome the physical damage that the bandits had inflicted on him during his captivity. During that time, Lei rode out and visited his friends, Chao and Lijuan, and their children. On his return, Qiang could see that Lei looked troubled.

"What is the matter, Lei? Are your friends and their family well?"

Lei sighed. "They are well enough, Qiang, but after my previous visit, the bandits came and burned down their barn. The bandits said that they learned that I was friends with the family, and they wished to teach them a lesson. They will need to rebuild the barn to house some of their animals and to stock food through the winter. They could usually rely on their neighbors to help in such an enterprise, but we are now in the middle of harvest, and such help is not available. And of course, they don't have money to hire labor to do such a task. I will enlist Sinh Hua's support in ensuring that the family is guarded against further harassment by the bandits, but I am concerned that the barn should be reconstructed before winter."

Qiang shook his head. "That is terrible, Lei. They are such nice people. We must try to do something to help them in their dilemma."

"But what can we do, Qiang? I doubt whether you and I could build a barn, and I don't have money to give them to hire someone to do it."

Qiang frowned. He would love to solve this little family's dilemma. Maybe he and Lei could build a barn, but to be realistic, he had little experience in building anything. He had helped his father build a rough shelter for their hens when he was young, but that was about the extent of his building experience. There must be another way.

Then he smiled. He remembered that he had some money. There were the gold pieces that Chin Chao had secreted in his saddlebags for him. He said to Lei, "My friend, I might have a solution to your problem. Wait here, and I'll be back in a moment."

Lei, with a puzzled look on his face, merely nodded.

Within minutes, Qiang was back, clutching a little leather bag.

"Whatever have you there, Qiang?" inquired Lei.

"Let me show you, my friend." And so saying, Qiang opened the leather bag and poured its contents into his hand. There were a dozen or so gold coins. "Would this be enough to pay for the construction of a barn?"

Lei was astonished. "That is more than enough for three or four barns."

"Good. Give this to your friends, and tell them it is a gift from Governor Chin Chao."

"That is very generous, Qiang, but might it not be prudent for you to keep a little of this for yourself?"

"Oh no, Lei. I have no use for money. If it is more than your friends require, give some to other needy folk, or keep a little for yourself, if you wish."

Lei just shook his head in bewilderment. The big man took a few gold coins and said, "This more than enough to build a barn Put the rest away to use on another day".

WHILE HE WAS recovering, Qiang was delighted to reconnect with Cheng.

At first, while Qiang was basically immobile, Cheng would come and sit near Qiang's bed and recount fabulous fables from the Buddhist tradition. And then, they would meditate together.

Soon, Qiang was up and walking. They would then make their way to the palace gardens. Qiang was pleased to be out in the open air again. They would have philosophical discussions and meditate.

Although Qiang was now keen to return to Ruan Xiu, Cheng cautioned him about being too hasty.

"Let us go out and ride together a little while each day. In this way, you can prepare yourself for the long ride back to Ruan Xiu's palace. Besides, Lei is to accompany you, and he is still busy supervising the construction of his friends' new barn, which I understand has been made possible by a generous donation from you."

Qiang blushed. "They don't have me to thank but the generosity of Governor Chin Chao. But putting that aside I would be delighted to ride out with you into the countryside in preparation for the completion of my long journey."

For a couple of weeks, Qiang and Cheng visited the various farming homesteads and hamlets in the immediate vicinity. As before, he took great joy in communing with the peasant farmers, sharing their pain and their joys, as they eked out their living from the land. It reminded him again of his childhood and the pleasant times that he and his little family had spent together before the great drought.

One evening, Lei came to see him. "I understand you and Cheng are riding together into the countryside these days. Tomorrow, when you ride, perhaps you might like to ride out to Chao's farm and inspect his new barn."

"I would be happy to do that, Lei. And I would be delighted to be reacquainted with your friend and his family. I will talk to Cheng in the morning."

THE DEW WAS still on the grass, and the sun had just crested the low range of hills on their left as the three rode out the next morning.

Qiang was surprised that Lei and Cheng were well acquainted. They chatted amiably as they rode. Lei told Cheng a few stories about Shin Hua from their shared past, which caused Cheng to chuckle.

It was almost midmorning when they approached Chao's farm. Even from a distance, they could see the impressive new barn. Soon, they saw Chao, toiling in a field close to the homestead.

Lei called out to Chao. "Look who I have brought to visit."

"Why, it is the little master!" Chao said.

Qiang turned to Lei. "Who taught him to call me that?"

"I did, of course."

"Oh, you shouldn't, Lei. It is very presumptuous."

Cheng smiled at the young man's humility.

Lei said, "When I first met you, I didn't think you were a little master. I thought you were a little brat! But the more I've come to know you, the more I believe you have earned that title. What say you, Cheng?"

"I say it is of little import what you call him. What is most important is that he truly knows who he is."

Lei seemed somewhat nonplussed by this response. "Whatever you say, Cheng, but he is a master in my eyes."

"That is generous of you, Lei. Whatever you call him, I am sure he won't let you down."

By now they had drawn close to Chao.

"Ah, Qiang," said Chao. "No doubt you have come to admire my new barn."

Qiang smiled. "It looks impressive, Chao."

"Indeed, it is. It is far better than the barn the bandits burned down. It will easily accommodate my livestock with sufficient fodder for winter. I cannot thank you enough for your generosity."

Qiang was embarrassed by such praise. "You don't need to thank me, Chao. It is the generosity of Governor Chin Chao that should earn your gratitude."

"No, Qiang. I think it is you who should be grateful to Chin Chao for bestowing his beneficence on you. But I know for sure that I should be grateful to you for providing my little family and me with such a boon."

"No matter," said Qiang. "It is enough that you and your family will be secure for the winter."

"Indeed, that is true."

"Now, where are those children of yours? We should go and hunt for some eggs."

Chao laughed. He called the children. They came running. "Chun," he said to the elder boy, "would you take our guests' horses and water them and tether them? And then, I gather that Qiang would like to search for eggs with you."

The younger ones squealed with delight. Chao led Cheng and Lei into the house. Chao knew Cheng well from his sorties out into the countryside to check on the welfare of the peasants. They chatted amicably while Qiang amused the children.

After their pleasant visit, Qiang, Cheng, and Lei wended their way home. Cheng and Lei spoke quietly of their pleasant morning, but Qiang was lost in his own thoughts. The time at the homestead reminded him again of his past.

Finally, Cheng asked, "What are you thinking, Qiang? You have been so quiet."

Qiang smiled. "I am thinking I should be on my way back to Ruan Xiu, Cheng. But more particularly, that I should be reunited with my mother and sister."

Lei nodded his head. "Good! We will take a day to make our preparations. And then let us head off to the governor's palace."

"That sounds like a plan to me!" replied Qiang.

WHEN THEY RETURNED from the visit to the peasants' homestead, Qiang went immediately with Lei to see Sinh Hua.

They were ushered into Sinh Hua's chamber by the guards.

Sinh Hua looked up from parchment he was reading and, with a concerned look on his face, inquired, "Ah, Qiang. What can be the matter?"

Qiang smiled. "There is nothing the matter, sire. I just came to tell you that Lei and I intend to head back to Ruan Xiu's palace, the day after tomorrow. I just wanted to thank you for your hospitality as I recuperated. Cheng and I, as you know, have been riding out into the countryside for some time now, and I feel quite restored."

Sinh Hua nodded. "I suspected that time was nearing, Qiang. I couldn't convince you to stay a little longer?" The portly man chuckled. "I could always find you another project, you know!"

"No, Sinh Hua. I can impose on your hospitality no longer. Besides, I have exhausted all the history of you and your lineage. It's time I spent a little time on my own family instead."

"I'll be sorry to see you go. And you too, Lei. You bring back fond memories. But let me ensure that you both are well-equipped and provided for as you start this leg of your return journey."

Lei spoke up. "We appreciate your generosity, Sinh Hua. What you lacked as a fighter you have made up for in your munificence. We would gratefully accept a few provisions to take with us. But might I beg another favor of you?"

Sinh Hua laughed. He seemed unconcerned regarding Lei's disparagement of him as a fighter. "What would you have me do for you, Lei?"

"You are aware the bandits burned down the barn of my friends, Chao and Lijuan. They are very dear to me. Can you have your men ensure the bandits don't harass them again?"

"Of course. Of course. Cheng has already spoken to me of your friends and their confrontation with the bandits. I will take special care to ensure they are safe."

"Thank you, Sinh Hua. That means a great deal to me."

Qiang could tell that despite Lei's misgivings about Sinh Hua, he was touched and gratified by this response.

IT WAS EARLY morning. Lei and Qiang were at the stables, loading their horses with the essentials they needed for Qiang's final stage of his odyssey. They were in good spirits and looking forward to the journey, but they could not put aside the possibility of a confrontation with the bandits. Qiang felt confident that Lei would provide some protection. He was wise to the ways of the bandits, and even if he was now older, he was still surely a formidable opponent and skilled in the arts of fighting.

Qiang was gratified that he had now developed an easy relationship with Lei and knew he would value his companionship as they journeyed together.

Lei finished strapping the last bag of supplies to his patient horse. He turned to Qiang. "Well, little master, I am ready. Shall we begin?"

Qiang nodded. "Let's be off."

But before they could stir their horses to set off, they heard a call.

"Wait! Wait!"

They both turned to see the source of this plea.

It was Cheng. He was on his horse, which seemed also to be well-laden. He quickly approached them. "You weren't planning on leaving without me, were you?"

Lei looked at Qiang before responding. "We had no idea you were planning to ride with us."

Qiang frowned before asking, "What about Sinh Hua? Does he approve of your leaving him to join us on our journey?"

Cheng merely laughed. "I have worked with Sinh Hua for some years. But I owe no obeisance to him. He does not determine whether I come or go or, indeed, what I should devote my time to. I am a Buddhist monk, as you know. And right now, I believe that what I can contribute best to the world is to see you return home and fulfill your destiny as a Buddhist master."

Qiang seemed a little nonplussed by this response.

"You seem somewhat surprised by this," Cheng said. "But just as you were destined to be a master, there are many who came before you who have been given a role to ensure that outcome. Many of them, you already have met; they have played a significant part in your life. I feel privileged to be one of them."

"I am not sure I know what you are talking about, Cheng, but I should be honored if you would join us."

Lei, who had listened to this little exchange, merely chuckled.

"Why do you laugh, Lei?" Qiang asked.

"Well," responded Lei, "I know little of the mysterious matters Cheng speaks of. But I know his reputation as a strong arm and as a doughty fighter. I am very pleased he has sought to join us. So come—let us be off now."

Qiang smiled at the practical assessment of his companion.

INITIALLY, AS QIANG recalled from his outward journey, the road leading from Sinh Hua's palace was of an even grade and, as a result, was easygoing. They passed by many farms and farmhouses and the occasional hamlet. Both Lei and Cheng seemed to be known by many of the peasant farmers, and greetings and some banter were exchanged.

Qiang felt very easy in the company of the two older men. It was probably due to his steely resolve to return to his family that his friends didn't loiter with those they met along the path.

On the first two evenings, Qiang, as usual, took the role of cook, and the little company enjoyed the meals he was able to concoct from the generous provisions that Sinh Hua had provided. As they lay beside the remnants of the cooking fire in the evenings, Qiang enjoyed learning more insights from Buddhism that Cheng provided. Lei, on the other hand, merely rolled over and went to sleep.

On the third day out, Lei turned to Qiang and said, "I know you are eager to be back with your family, but we are approaching old Li's little hideout, The Falcon's Nest. He is a dear friend, I feel obliged to check on his welfare. Would you mind if we took a small diversion, just to see how he fares? I promise I won't keep you long."

Qiang could see the concern on Lei's face. Without hesitating, he replied, "Of course, Lei. That would be the proper thing to do. Besides, I found Li to be a wonderful fellow, and I would enjoy seeing him again."

As they approached the entrance to The Falcon's Nest, Qiang knew immediately that something must be wrong. The dead branches that had been so carefully arranged to hide the entrance into Li's hideaway were strewn all over the place.

Lei immediately roused his horse to increased speed, although the tortuous, narrow path prevented him from a full-on gallop. The other two followed as best they could.

Qiang and Cheng had barely made the open space where the little hut was situated when they saw that Lei was already dismounting at the open doorway.

"Li! Li!" he shouted.

There seemed, at first, to be no response.

Lei rushed into the hut. "Li! Li! It is Lei."

The big man heard a groan. There, at the back of the hut, lay the prostrate form of the old man.

Lei hurried to his side and kneeled down alongside his friend. Lei's face was ashen. "Oh, Li, whatever has happened to you?"

Li was in obvious distress. There was blood soaked into his clothing. He looked emaciated. He looked up into Lei's face. "Oh, Lei," he said with a weak smile and in a voice that was barely a whisper. "I am so pleased to see you."

"Well, old friend, I am not so pleased to see you in such a condition. What happened?"

The old man looked up and replied in a barely audible voice, "It was the bandits. They came one evening and—"

The struggle was too much, and the old man lapsed into unconsciousness.

Cheng bent over him and placed his hand on the old man's forehead. "He is very ill, Lei. We must do what we can to help him."

Lei was very distraught. "What should we do, Cheng?"

"I suspect all we can do is dress his wounds, keep him warm, and, if he regains consciousness, provide him with a little water and perhaps some broth to aid his sustenance. But I should warn you—he is very ill, and despite any ministrations of ours, he will likely die."

Lei, the renowned warrior whose bravery seemed legendary in these parts, began to weep.

Cheng put his arm on Lei's shoulder. "None of that now, Lei. We must try to save him, however impossible that might seem. Strip his clothes off as gently as you can. I have packed some ointments that might help heal his wounds. And Qiang, go fetch some water so we might wet his lips when he is ready. Perhaps then, you might unload and tend to our horses while Lei and I try to dress his wounds."

Qiang nodded. "Certainly, Cheng. And then I will cook a little broth and some rice for our dinner. If Li regains consciousness, then there will be some broth for him as well."

"That would be useful. Thank you, Qiang."

THE THREE TRAVELERS sat quietly talking by the remains of the cooking fire. Li had been attended to, with his wounds dressed and bandaged. He now lay in clean clothing on his bedding at the rear of the room, with a blanket covering him. He had not stirred since they had first arrived.

They had eaten a little meal, but their hunger had been abated by their concern for Li. Their attention turned to the old man.

Cheng said, "It is obvious the bandits beat him—perhaps tortured him—and left him to die."

"What should we do now?" Qiang inquired.

After a moment or two, Lei spoke. "Well, little master, I know how much you want to get back to your family, and you must resume your journey without delay. But I must stay and attend to Li as best I can. He was one of the noblest men I have known, and I cannot abandon him."

"Nor would I want you to, Lei. But I am reluctant to leave you by yourself in case the bandits return. With Cheng's agreement, I think we should wait with you. If Li improves sufficiently, we could take him back to your friend Chao's place. I am sure he would care for Li."

"No doubt he would, Qiang. But you must go. I can't keep you from your family any longer. Also, there is a part of me, I must confess, that would welcome an opportunity to smite a few bandit heads."

"I have been gone for so long now, Lei, that I am sure a few days more won't hurt too much. And as much as you might like to smite some bandits' heads, I would not forgive myself if it was your head that was cracked. Besides, Li went out of his way to provide succor to me as well. The least I can do is stay with him now."

Lei was about to respond but Cheng interjected. "Qiang is right, Lei. Let us stay a while with Li and see how he progresses. That is the least we can do."

As they talked, they heard a moan from Li. He seemed to be partly conscious. Cheng immediately went to him and raised a cup of water to his lips. The old man took a couple of sips and then fell back, unconscious, onto his bed again. Cheng felt his forehead and then checked his pulse before returning to the others.

"He is very weak," was all that he said.

Lei shook his head in despair. "I thank you both for your kind consideration. You are indeed good friends. I think I might go outside for a while."

Again, he averted his gaze because his eyes were moist. He stood up and walked slowly outside into the cool night air.

Qiang sat silently contemplating. His mind went back to his time at Ruan Xiu's palace. This certainly wasn't the man he had known as stable master!

QIANG AND CHENG left Lei to his personal meditations. There was still a little broth in the cooking pot, and Qiang added some wood to the cooking fire, lest Li wake and take some nourishment. But the old man's breathing was labored, and he seemed to be completely unconscious.

Qiang and Cheng arranged their bedding on the floor of the hut and retired for the night.

During the night, Qiang awoke. The remaining embers of the cooking fire provided little light, but it was enough to see Lei, sitting alongside his old friend, gently stroking his head.

In the morning, Qiang arose before the others were awake. He noted that Lei was now lying on his own bedding, a yard or two away from Li. He walked outside and down to the rockpool that Li had pointed out to him on their first visit. He carried with him a bucket to bring back some water for drinking and cooking. The spring that fed the rockpool was bubbling gently, and the clear, fresh water was inviting. It seemed that the season had been good, and there was substantial water overflowing the rockpool and into the little creek behind it.

Qiang stripped off his clothes and immersed himself in the cool, pristine stream. He felt exhilarated by the refreshing water.

After about twenty minutes, he removed himself from the pool, dressed, and took up his meditation position. After meditating, he filled the bucket with clear spring water and headed back.

When he returned to the hut, both Cheng and Lei were up and about. Cheng was in the lotus position on the front porch, attending to his own meditation practice. Lei was stirring life into the cooking fire. Qiang filled a small pot with water. In good time, the pot was bubbling, and Qiang made some tea. They each had a little tea and shared the leftover rice from the previous evening's meal.

While they were finishing eating, Li stirred a little and moaned slightly. Lei quickly went to him and pressed a cup of water to his lips. The old man sipped a little water and then slumped back onto his bed.

The three travelers sat together and discussed how they might spend the day.

Lei said, "I am just going to stay here with Li. I want to be here in case he regains consciousness and wants anything. What about you, Cheng?"

"Well," replied Cheng, "I need to get a little exercise. I will tidy the hut, and then I think I will go forage for a little more firewood, on the assumption we might have to be here a few days. There is barely any left by the hearth. Li has lived here a long time, so I presume there won't be anything suitable close by, and I might have to forage to find some. And you, Qiang?"

"It is my intention to go back to the entrance to Li's hideout and drag the branches back across the path. Although it is obvious that some of the bandits know their way in, we don't want to encourage others to impinge on Li's solitude. And then I thought I might forage for a little fresh food so that we don't unnecessarily draw down on our supplies."

Cheng responded, "That sounds useful, but what on earth might you find that is edible?"

Lei quietly chuckled. "I'll wager he is going fishing."

Qiang just smiled.

IT WAS LATE afternoon now.

Lei still sat beside Li.

Cheng had gathered his firewood, chopped it into useful pieces, and restored the woodpile beside the hearth.

Qiang had caught a few small fish and gathered some wild herbs and mushrooms. He had dressed the fish and was now concocting a meal for the travelers. As usual, above the small cooking fire was a cooking pot, starting to simmer, and a pot of water, dedicated to making tea.

The light was quickly fading outside.

It was not long before the meal was ready. They ate hungrily and then sat quietly, talking and sipping on their tea.

But then, they were taken aback.

Li raised his head off his bed and called feebly, "Lei! Lei! Is that you?"

Lei hastened to the old man's side. "Yes, Li. It is I, Lei."

Li slumped back on the bed. "I am so glad you came," he said.

Lei placed his hand on the old man's forehead. "Here, Li. Let me get you a little water."

"No, Lei. It is past all that. Can you find me something a little stronger? I want to have one last drink with my old friend."

He spoke so softly that neither Qiang nor Cheng could hear his words. But they sensed this was an intimate time and were reluctant to impose themselves into this personal discourse.

"I am sorry, Li. I don't have any liquor with me."

"No matter, Lei. I was hoping you would come again. In anticipation, I put aside some fine rice wine to share with you. Look inside the large cooking pot beside the hearth."

Lei went to the cooking pot and, as the old man had said, he found inside a little ceramic container sealed with a cork stopper.

Li could see Lei's success. "Pour us each a parting drink. It is how I want to farewell you."

Lei protested. "You shouldn't sound so fatalistic, Li. We have gotten out of plenty of scrapes in the past. Bear up, and we will have you up and about in no time."

Lei poured them each a drink. He helped Li raise the cup to his mouth. Li took a little sip.

"I toast you, Lei. I have never met a finer fellow."

Lei raised his own drink to his mouth. His eyes moistened. "You are a true friend, Li. When things were tough, there was no one I would have rather had by me. But no more pessimism. I want to share many more toasts with you."

"It would be nice to have that to look forward to Lei, but this old body has had enough. I do not have the vigor I once had—nor, indeed, do I have the will. My passing should not be something to mourn. I am satisfied with the life I've led. It is indeed a bonus to be with you one more time."

Lei turned his head away, but Qiang could see he was weeping. In a little while, he regained his composure.

"This is indeed a fine drop, old friend, worthy of a reunion of old warriors. Can I help you have another sip?"

"Of course, please, Lei." Li chuckled. "This does not seem to be the time for undue temperance on my part! And please, when you depart, take what is left with you as a little memento from me."

"Tell me Li," asked Lei, "how did the bandits find you?"

"Unfortunately, Lei, I was careless. I had spent a day visiting some of my friends. When I returned, the bandits must have followed. I was pulling the branches across the entrance when they arrived and overpowered me. They beat me and took me back to the hut. But it was obvious they were not interested in me. They wanted information about you and the young master. I had nothing to tell them, although I would have told them nothing, even if I did. They brutalized me and left me for dead. And I remember nothing more until I regained consciousness a moment ago and was gratified to see you here. By the way, is the young master with you?"

"Yes, he is here."

"I understand that he has had a hard time of it lately."

"That is true. He was captured by the bandits and was very fortunate in being able to escape."

"Was that your doing, Lei?"

"I had a hand in it, but it was largely due to the efforts of Bai and Jian that he was able to make good his escape."

"You know, many years ago they told me that a new master would come to help bring compassion and Buddhism back into many of our lives. I have no idea how they knew, but they seemed quite confident that they would one day meet him. I am most grateful that you brought him to me, Lei. He seems such a wonderful young man. Protect him as best you can."

"I will do my best, Li. Now, another sip of wine?"

"Yes, please. But that will do. I feel so weary now. I am so glad I was able to see you one last time. You have been a brave and wonderful comrade."

Lei held the cup up to Li's mouth. Li sipped a little of the wine. He reached out weakly and clasped Lei's hand. He sighed and then slumped back, unconscious, on to his bed. Lei pulled the blanket up over the old man. He sat quietly, still holding the old man's hand.

After a time, Cheng went up to Lei and placed his arm on Lei's shoulder.

"Come and rest, Lei. There is nothing more you can do now."

Lei disengaged from Li and slowly rose. He then looked at Cheng and replied quietly, with a faltering voice, "You are no doubt right, Cheng. But if you don't mind, I might just sit outside a little while and finish my wine."

QIANG OPENED HIS eyes. It seemed close to dawn. He could hear birds singing, and the blackness of the night was starting to ameliorate. As usual, he would arise and go outside to start his meditation practice.

But something did not seem right. As he stood, he saw in the half-light that Lei was kneeling alongside Li, holding the old fellow's arm. Lei's torso was rocking back and forth.

Qiang quietly approached and put his arm on Lei's shoulder. "What is wrong, Lei?"

The big man looked up, and there were tears running down his cheeks. "He is gone, Qiang. He died during the night."

"Do not despair, Lei. He knew that he was dying. That was why he was so gratified that he had one last night with you. We should be grateful that he went peacefully. I saw a smile on his face after he had a drink or two with you. Is not that a good death?"

"That might be so, Qiang, but he didn't need to die. If the bandits hadn't beaten him so severely, he would still be alive."

"But Lei, everybody needs to die. It is our fate. Certainly, the bandits hastened his death but by how much, we will never know. He was an old man who led an exemplary life. We should be grateful for his life, not saddened by his death."

"I am sorry, but I cannot dismiss his death so easily. He is the best man I have ever known. There will be a hole in my heart as a result of his passing."

"I am sure that is true, and it is appropriate. It is obvious that you loved him and that he loved you. That is a very special thing and not to be discounted in any way. But Lei, it is you who is suffering, not Li."

"It is true that he is not suffering, but it is also true that he is no more. And that is the problem. I will never see him again, and he was my best friend."

"Again, Lei, you misunderstand. It is only Li's body that is no more. And it was an old body that probably wasn't very comfortable for him to inhabit any longer. But Li was not his body. How could it be so? When he was born, he had a baby's body. And throughout his life, that body continually changed. He inhabited a body that was then an adolescent, then a mature man, and, most recently, an old man. Although his body changed, the essential essence of the person who inhabited it remained the same."

"What am I to make of all this? Do you imply the essence of Li still exists somehow?"

"That is what I believe."

"Then where can I find it?"

"I cannot tell you, Lei. Many Buddhists believe in the cycle of life—*samsara*, as it is known. This purports that we all face a cycle of birth, life, death, and rebirth. After each cycle, the essence is maintained by its attachment to another body. But such rebirth just ensures the spirit must endure another cycle of suffering, as we learn in the Four Noble Truths. However, it is said that those who strive to meet the requirements laid down in the Eightfold Path will be reborn into a better life. Doing good is thus rewarded. But just as the Buddha taught us that life entails suffering, he also taught that nothing is eternal. When finally the spirit is perfected, it escapes to Nirvana and is no more. Yet that is not to be feared because all such spirits are then as one, in pure bliss."

"I know you mean well, Qiang, but that is not so comforting to me. Li is gone forever, and a big part of my life has been erased."

"That is a natural reaction, of course, Lei. But, you see, the Buddha pointed out to us that most of our suffering comes from attachment. You believe that your well-being—or at least a significant part of it—is dependent on Li. As much as it seems unlikely to you now, your sense of well-being is not determined by anything outside yourself."

"You are cruel to me, Qiang. Just let me mourn my lost friend in peace."

"I do not wish to hurt you in any way, Lei. I have come to admire you greatly. You have done remarkable things of which I was not previously aware. But let me put this to you: you thought your life was devastated once before, when you lost your sister. And then, to your great credit, you rebuilt your life. I am sure you would have said, back then, that you could never be happy again after your sister died. But you have been happy, and, on occasions, I have shared that happiness with you. But by all means, mourn your friend. That is the proper thing to do. He was indeed a wonderful man. When you love somebody, it often hurts you because it makes you vulnerable. But that is the human condition and not something to be decried. You may not believe it now, but that hurt will pass in time."

Unbeknownst to Qiang and Lei, Cheng had awakened and overheard most of this discussion. He walked up to the pair and placed a hand on the opposite shoulder of Lei to the one Qiang had embraced.

"I am sorry, Lei, for the old man's passing, but we must now help his spirit to successfully exit and take whatever step his karma has allowed. Qiang, go and make us a little tea. Lei, step away now. You must unhand his body."

Qiang and Lei did as they were told, but Lei was compelled to ask, "What are you going to do?"

"I am going to perform some rituals to help ease the spirit of your friend on its journey."

Cheng knelt alongside Li's body and began to chant. The chant was both sonorous and repetitive, but it was also consoling. Qiang could not understand the words, although they sounded similar to the words of the ancient An Cheng mantra that his first teacher had taught him. It then became obvious to him that Cheng must be part of that ancient tradition.

Qiang and Lei sipped their tea and listened to the hypnotic chant. They said nothing because there was nothing to say. Cheng was now in charge and they knew his efforts were aimed at assisting the passing of Li.

The sun was now up, and looking through the door, Qiang could see that it seemed sunny outside and still.

Qiang and Lei sat still while Cheng continued to intone the ancient verses.

He went for some hours with his ministrations. The other two could only watch and listen. Finally, by midmorning, Cheng paused. He sat motionless, with his eyes closed.

All of a sudden, a great wind arose. It blew for some minutes. Looking out the window, Qiang could see leaves and dust being tossed around. But then, as suddenly as it had begun, the wind was gone. The air became still. Cheng maintained his kneeling position on the floor for another five minutes. And then he rose and looked at his traveling companions.

"It is done," he said wearily. "His spirit has departed. You need have no further concern for him, Lei."

THE THREE TRAVELERS meandered their way along the track. They had traveled over the fertile farming country and now entered more difficult terrain. The friends progressed somberly. It wasn't so long since they had buried the body of Li. Lei seemed particularly despondent. He hardly talked, except to reminisce about Li. He told of Li's bravery in their efforts, led by Ruan Xiu, to put down the insurgence of the bandits.

Qiang led the way on his piebald horse. He was far enough in front that he could not hear the discussions between Cheng and Lei.

Cheng, who was riding alongside Lei, remarked, "You were indeed fortunate to have such a friend, Lei. But he is gone now. It is time to put aside your grief, and be grateful that fate brought you together."

"Perhaps, Cheng, but my memory of him is too dear to let it go easily."

"I am not suggesting that you should put aside your memory of him. You will carry that for the rest of your days. But you must take joy in your memory of Li, not let it bear you down into despair."

"But I can't put aside the injustice of it all, Cheng. There was no reason that those ruffians should have beaten him. If they hadn't followed him into his little lair, he would still be alive."

"Perhaps, Lei. But he was an old man and maybe his end was near, whatever transpired. Buddhism teaches us to be reconciled with the impermanence of the world."

"What irks me most is that those who perpetrated this outrage will go unpunished."

"That should not concern you, Lei. The universe is essentially just. You know about the law of karma, don't you? Sooner or later, we all must pay for our misdemeanors."

"Perhaps, but I suspect I would gain more satisfaction if I could crack some of those fellows' heads right now and help the universe do its work!"

"You must be careful, Lei. Anger and hatred are some of the afflictive emotions the Buddha warned us about. No one who harbors such emotions can be truly happy."

"Right now, I must confess, Cheng, I would rather have revenge than be happy. Maybe if I could enact my vengeance, then I could be happy."

"You are mistaken Lei. A sage has said that seeking vengeance is like taking poison and hoping it will kill your enemy! These afflictive emotions poison our hearts. Qiang has been greatly wronged by these fellows as well. Do you think that he hates them or desires revenge?"

Lei thought a while and then shook his head. "No, I don't, but I also think it is unfair that you should compare me with someone who not only seems to have innate goodness but has been trained by sages in how to deal with the world. I mistreated him when he worked in the stables with me, but he has never shown any resentment. I have come to admire him."

"And he admires you as well, Lei. What helped him most to come to this realization was when he came to know your history and circumstances. Does that not have a large bearing on how people behave?"

"Yes, of course it does."

Lei thought for a while without speaking. Cheng did not interrupt his cogitation.

Finally, Lei said, "You know, Qiang has suffered too, but he is not bitter. Why is that?"

"Lei, it would not have escaped you that Qiang is not your average person. He not only has particular innate qualities that caused him to be selected to be trained as a master, but his mentors are fine men who have taught him much. Qiang's great strength is that he knows himself well. Consequently, he feels secure in his identity and is relatively impervious to how others might view him. He knows, with certainty, that his personal well-being is determined by how he views the world and not by the assessment of others. He is destined to be a great master, but he already has passed the first test in mastering himself. That is certainly the prelude to greatness. And I don't speak of the ephemeral greatness of status or wealth or power but the greatness of a fine mind that is a positive influence on others."

THE DAYS PASSED without incident. There had been no sign of the bandits. They passed a few travelers, but they seemed not to talk about the brigands. Lei told the others they almost certainly would have paid their dues to enable them to travel.

But the journeying was quite pleasant. They enjoyed each other's company. In the evenings, before retiring, Qiang would receive further instruction from Cheng, and the two would meditate together.

Qiang had now completely recovered from the injuries Shu Ming had inflicted on him. The three made good progress on their journey, and although Qiang maintained an outwardly passive demeanor, inwardly, he could not help but feel a little excited as each day brought him inexorably closer to his family.

One night, after they had made camp and eaten, the travelers sat around the remnants of the little cooking fire and drank a little tea.

Qiang quietly inquired of Lei, "My big friend, if my memory serves me right, tomorrow we must traverse Devil's Gate."

Lei nodded. "That is the last real hurdle for us. Once we are over the pass, we are back into territory over which Ruan Xiu maintains strict control. We will also be able to avail ourselves of the way stations that he provisions and won't need to sleep in the open so often. Do you remember the last time we were here, young master?"

"How could I forget it, Lei? You rescued me from the bandits' clutches by getting the villains drunk on rice wine!"

They both had a little chuckle.

"What is this story, Qiang?" Cheng asked. "It is not one I have heard."

"Lei's humility would prevent him from telling you, Cheng, but I will tell because he saved my life."

Qiang proceeded to tell Cheng the story. When he was done, Cheng shook his head.

"Does this surprise you, Cheng?" Qiang asked.

"Not in the least, Qiang. It is just the sort of thing he used to do when Ruan Xiu was subduing the bandits. It pleases me that the big fellow still has it in him."

Cheng and Qiang spent a little more time together, discussing some Buddhist teachings. Then they meditated a while before retiring.

As he lay on his bedding, Qiang thought about having to negotiate the pass the next day. While he had a sense of foreboding, he also felt a strange sense that he must confront his fate. He was comforted by the fact that he was joined by two stalwart friends, who were both skilled warriors. Certainly, they were no longer young, but they were both very capable.

He had no desire to harm anybody, but he accepted the rationalization of his masters that sometimes, it is justifiable to injure another to prevent even greater harm. He had grown to love Lei, knowing now his circumstances and also because the big man had taken considerable risks to protect him. Cheng had also proved to be a helpful mentor and a devoted friend. Qiang felt compelled to help secure their welfare.

THE THREE COMPANIONS broke camp early the next morning. Lei took it upon himself to lead the little party. Qiang and Cheng lagged a little in the rear.

At first, the going was pretty easy, and Qiang and Cheng chatted amicably.

"Cheng, have you traveled this way very often?" Qiang asked.

"Oh, many times, Qiang."

"Why would that be so?"

"Well, I have been fortunate enough to be part of a group of Buddhist monks that Ruan Xiu has sponsored over the years. We have tried to be a constructive part of the governor's efforts to bring peace and goodwill to these parts."

"And who was in this group?"

Cheng laughed. "Most of them you already know Qiang."

"Really! And who would these monks be?"

"Chogken Rinpoche, Chagsarka Rinpoche, Sunfu Rinpoche, and, of course, Bai and Jian."

"And of course you?"

"Yes indeed, Qiang. So I have traveled this way many times but not recently."

"Have you had any confrontations with the bandits?"

"No. You see, in the early days, when the bandits were active, Ruan Xiu would insist that a group of his fighters should always accompany us when we traveled. But once he and Chin Chao suppressed the bandits, it was safe to travel anywhere without protection. It has only been in relatively recent times that travel has again become problematic."

"Then tell me—how did you become such a formidable fighter that now you instruct others?"

"To begin with, my father was a renowned warrior, and when I was young, he tutored me in the principal techniques of fighting. But after I studied Buddhism, I, like you, was drawn to the precept of loving kindness. My father, who was a man of great character, accepted that but insisted that I continue my tuition so that I should be able to defend myself, if attacked. He advised also that it was useful to have such skills so that I might defend others against unjust aggression."

Qiang smiled. Cheng looked at him quizzically.

"Forgive me, Cheng, but I was just remembering that you used the same justification for teaching me such skills."

Cheng laughed. "Indeed, I did, Qiang. Is it not surprising that our fathers should have such influence on us?"

Qiang reminisced wistfully about his own father and was quick to concede that his father, Chao, had greatly influenced his own behavior as well but probably in different ways.

"But you must have demonstrated your fighting prowess well," Qiang said, "to have someone like Shin Hua engage you to train his men."

"Well, Qiang, I spent a long period in the more remote provinces, helping the peasants try to thwart the predations of the bandits. Unfortunately, that meant I was often compelled to fight to protect them. In this regard, my father was right. Sometimes, you have to fight to prevent injustice."

"That now seems to be the case again, Cheng."

Up ahead, Lei had turned his horse around and was waiting for the other two to catch up.

They nudged their horses forward to join Lei.

"This is it," said Lei. "This is the beginning of the pass we know as Devil's Gate. Although we have seen no sign of the bandits, this is the most likely place they would seek to ambush us. We need to stick close together now. If they can isolate one of us, it would make their foul enterprise much easier. If they are going to attack us, it is most probable they will seek the little master. Consequently, I suggest that I should go forward in the lead, Qiang should follow next, and Cheng should bring up the rear."

Qiang protested that he should not be given special treatment, but Lei and Cheng insisted. Thus, so arranged in single file, they ventured into the pass.

AS THE LITTLE group progressed, the terrain got steeper. Eventually, they were forced to dismount from their horses and lead them up the pass, which was now narrow and rough. Every now and then, there were fissures in the rock to the left and right of the path. Qiang remembered how he had been ambushed by the bandits. They must have hidden in one of these side apertures, he thought, waiting for travelers to pass. Another group would have been in hiding up ahead, so that when he passed, they signaled to the group ahead to come out and confront him, with the group in the rear emerging, preventing his retreat.

For some time, the group struggled on. Finally, they crested the top of the pass. Qiang could see open grassland now in the far distance, and it seemed that within an hour or two, they would be beyond the dangers of the pass and emerge into the lands under Ruan Xiu's control, where they would be safe. Perhaps it would not be long before he was reunited with Nuan and Lan.

With the going easier now, the three remounted their horses.

Qiang had been surveying the track in front and how it wound its way down to the pastures below.

Cheng had not been so distracted. "Lei," he said in a hushed voice, "there were a half dozen men on our left back there, hiding in a side dead-end branch of the pass. There is another aperture just up ahead on our left. Let us pull in there and see what happens. More than likely, there is another group lying in wait up ahead. If we pull to the side in the next narrow aperture, we will only have to deal with the bandits on one front. If we continue on, we more than likely will have to deal with them from front and rear."

Lei said nothing but nodded his agreement.

Sure enough, only another thirty meters farther on, there was a narrow fissure in the rock. Lei dismounted and led his horse into the narrow channel in the rock. It was something of a squeeze for their horses to pass through. Once they had pushed the animals forward some forty meters, the fissure opened into a much wider expanse—a circular meadow, like an oasis in the towering rocks, perhaps two hundred meters across, surrounded by precipitous rocky cliffs about fifty meters high.

"Leave the horses," said Cheng quietly, "and let's go back to see what happens. But just in case things get out of hand, bring your staffs with you."

They hurried back and stopped only when the main artery of the pass was again in sight. They pressed their bodies back against the rocks so as not to be readily seen.

Soon, they could hear the sounds of horses' hooves striking the rocky floor of the pass, progressing toward them on their right. Then, they heard the sound of a loud, shrill whistle.

"They are summoning the party up ahead," said Qiang softly, "just as they did on the day they ambushed me."

The clattering of the hooves had now ceased. It appeared as though they were now waiting for the gang of bandits who were in front of them to move into the pass and confront the travelers.

And sure enough, within five minutes, they heard the sound of hooves approaching from their left. Judging by the sounds they made, it seemed as though there were probably another five or six mounted horsemen.

Soon after, they could hear a rancorous discussion between the two groups. A loud voice asked why they had been summoned when it was apparent there were no travelers to ambush. But an authoritative voice from the other group asserted that a group of three had passed by them shortly before.

"Then, where are they? They can't have disappeared into thin air!"

"Well, you dolt, it is obvious that they must have found a niche to hide in off the main pass, just as we did while we were lying in wait."

"Then let us search for another such aperture in the walls of the pass."

The leader of the group on the right was the bandit Hong, whom Qiang had encountered twice before. He exclaimed, "We have passed no such aperture, so if it exists, it must lie ahead of us."

The men split up to progressively explore each side of the pass. Inevitably, before long, they came upon the fissure into which Qiang, Cheng, and Lei had retreated.

"This must be where they are hiding," shouted Hong.

The group milled around a while in front of the entrance to the aperture.

"How many did you say there were?"

"We saw three."

"Did they have weapons?"

"None that we could see."

"Good. Now you, you, and you"—he gesticulated toward the group—"take your swords and go in and see what you can find."

One of those so nominated said, "The aperture isn't very wide. I'm reluctant to take my horse in there. It might get stuck. Or if the travelers assail us, I won't be able to turn the horse around."

"Very well, then, go on foot."

Accordingly, the three brigands dismounted and made their way warily into the fissure.

Qiang and his companions had heard this discourse. Although they were some distance from the bandits, the high rock walls reflected the sounds so that they were clearly audible. Lei pushed his way to the front.

"Let me deal with this," he said.

Qiang looked at Cheng, who merely shrugged.

"Follow close behind me," continued Lei, "but make sure you give me room to move."

Lei moved slowly out toward the main pass. Just ahead, there was a turning of the fissure to the right. He moved up to the bend, pushed himself closely back against the rock wall, and gestured to the others to do the same.

Soon, they heard the sound of faltering footsteps—the three bandits were approaching cautiously. Each wielded a sword. The leader held his sword upright in his right hand. It was an evil-looking curved blade. Although its edge was well-honed, there were notches in the cutting edge, which attested to previous rough usage.

The big man pounced surprisingly swiftly. His staff struck the forearm of the man holding the sword, which almost certainly broke the man's arm, causing him to drop the sword to the ground. The bandit fell over backward in dismay.

"That was for Li!" called out Lei, as he jumped forward over the fallen body. As he did so, he thrust his staff into the stomach of the bandit who was following, winding him. The force of Lei's blow knocked this fellow over backward as well. Lei immediately stomped on the wrist of the hand that carried the sword, which was duly released to fall to the ground.

The third bandit turned and fled in terror.

Cheng sprang forward and picked up the sword of the first man and held it to his throat. "Don't move," he said quietly.

Meanwhile, the second bandit had staggered from the ground and turned to run. Lei struck him another resounding blow on his buttocks, which caused him to stumble. As he regained his feet again, Lei called after him, "And don't come back."

He then turned to the fallen man whom Cheng stood over.

"Move back, Cheng," said Lei.

Cheng did as suggested. Lei stepped over the body of the man on the ground, not taking too much care to avoid standing on him. He turned then and, grabbing the man by the shirt, drew him upright. The man groaned in pain as his arm brushed over the rocks at the side of the fissure.

"What is your name?" demanded Lei.

"Gang," came the feeble reply.

"Well, Gang," Lei said, "I want you to go back to Hong with a message. You tell Hong that we have been very benevolent on this occasion and that we have killed no one. It is unlikely that we will be so generous next time. We know you were responsible for the death of Li. And if you give me the chance again, I will more than likely take my opportunity for vengeance. Make no mistake; you have no chance of defeating us, and if you persist, you will only bring harm upon yourselves."

THE THREE SAT at the base of the rock wall. Qiang was intrigued.

"Lei, why were you so assertive with the bandits? To hear you speak, one would think that you are confident of overcoming them."

"Well, I am, Qiang. They can only approach us through the fissure, one at a time. And I believe any one of us is a match for any one of them. But even if I wasn't confident, the last thing I would want is for those brigands to believe we fear them. That is their chief stock in trade—fear. And the thing that heightens my confidence most is that I know that neither you nor Cheng are afraid either."

"Our biggest danger," Qiang said, "is that they may outlast us. If we eke out our supplies carefully, we probably have enough food for a week. But I suspect we will run out of water well before then."

"But they face the same dilemma."

"Well, not quite. They can continue to besiege us but still send out riders to restore their supplies."

"Um, I suppose that is true. What do you think, Cheng?"

"Well," replied Cheng, "I am confident that we can prevail, if we are careful and brave."

Qiang mused a little before responding. "Perhaps you know something that I don't, master, but I trust your judgment."

"I am confident that if we can repulse those who are sent to assail us," Cheng said, "we will prevail. But we must be prepared."

"What do you mean, Cheng?" inquired Lei.

"Well, big fellow, you were very imposing today, but we cannot leave it all to you. If the bandits send a large number of fighters to engage us, sooner or later, you will tire. And if you tire, and they strike you down, we will be doomed. If they assault us again, we must each take a turn at confronting these villains. You need to have faith that we can step in behind you and do our part as well."

Lei, somewhat embarrassed, coughed. "Of course I have faith, Cheng. What do you have in mind?"

"If we are attacked again, it is appropriate that you should lead our defense. It is obvious that they fear you, and we would be unwise not to take advantage of that fact. But I will stand behind you, and Qiang, behind me. You should retire when you are ready and allow us to take up the fight."

Lei nodded his agreement. "Yes, that makes sense. We also now have a couple of more formidable weapons. We have the two swords that the bandits abandoned. I am quite practiced with the use of a sword. What about you, Cheng?"

Cheng nodded. "I have tutored Sinh Hua's warriors in swordsmanship. I am reasonably adept with the weapon."

Qiang commented, "I have never held a sword, nor have I any desire to do so. You will just have to rely on my skills with the staff to get by when I take my turn."

"I am sure you will be able to hold your own," said Cheng.

"Now," said Lei, "we need to get organized. One of us needs to be stationed here at all times to ensure the bandits can't sneak up on us unexpectedly. My suggestion is that Cheng should take the first watch. Qiang might prepare some food for us, and I will tend the horses. There is a good deal of pasture in the meadow at the rear of the passage, so I suspect the horses will have sufficient feed for a week or so. There seems to be some sort of a spring or soak under the rear rock face. I will try to open it up enough for the animals to drink a little so that we can eke out our water for as long as possible."

Cheng nodded. "That sounds a reasonable plan, Lei. I am happy to take first watch."

Qiang said, "There are a few shrubs and brambles in the meadow. I am sure I can find enough fuel for a small cooking fire. When I have prepared the food, Cheng, I will bring a serving to you. And then when you are ready, I will take over the watch."

Cheng picked up one of the swords that the bandits had dropped and handed the other to Lei.

The night passed uneventfully. The bandits seemed to have been taken aback by Lei's ferocity and were uncertain about what to do.

IT WAS DAWN. Lei was standing watch at the bend, where he had fought off the bandits the previous day.

Qiang had made tea. He brought a bowl up to the big man. Cheng accompanied him, ready to take over the watch.

"No sign of any movement?" asked Cheng in a whisper.

"None at all," replied Lei.

"Perhaps they've gone."

"No. I know these fellows too well. They won't leave us."

"While we are all together," Qiang said, "I have an idea to share with you."

"What is that?" inquired Cheng.

"When I went to tend to the horses yesterday, I noticed that the cliff at the rear of the meadow is sheer but definitely scalable. I propose that when there is a lull in the proceedings, I should climb up and survey what the bandits are doing."

"That could be useful, Qiang," said Cheng. "What do you think, Lei?"

"I agree. It would be useful to know what these villains are doing."

"But not now," whispered Cheng, alerted by his heightened awareness. "Listen—I can hear the muted sounds of footsteps approaching. Remember not to try to do it all yourself this time, Lei."

"Okay, Cheng. I will leave some for you. Get in behind me now, both of you."

It took some minutes for the bandits to arrive.

First, an arm wielding a sword appeared around the corner. Lei needed no further invitation. He struck the upper arm forcefully, grievously injuring the bandit, who screamed and let the sword fall to the ground. Lei then punched the man in the face with his free hand, knocking him unconscious, so that he dropped lifeless to the ground.

The second bandit rushed forward, with his sword in front of him. Lei parried his thrust but then, in seeking to go forward to attack the man, tripped over the body of the first assailant. The bandit drew back his sword and raised it strike Lei. But he was no match for Cheng, who nimbly vaulted over Lei's prostrate form and pierced the bandit's right shoulder with his sword, causing him too to drop his weapon.

While Qiang was impressed by Lei's brute strength, he was astonished by the grace and agility of Cheng's attack.

The three other bandits, following in the rear, now beat a hasty retreat back to the pass.

Cheng still had his bandit pinned back to the rock wall, with his blade lodged in his shoulder.

As before, Lei went up to him. "What is your name?" he demanded.

"Wang Long," the unfortunate man stammered.

"Well, Wang Long," continued Lei, "I want you to go back to Hong with a message. You tell Hong that, again, we have been very benevolent today, and again, we have killed no one. It is unlikely that we will be so generous next time. Our patience is running thin. Make no mistake; you have no chance of defeating us, and if you persist, you will only bring harm upon yourselves."

Cheng withdrew his sword. The man was bleeding profusely but his bones seemed intact.

"We don't want our camp littered with ruffians like you lot. We are going to let you go, and we want you to take this other villain with you," said Lei, pointing to the body on the ground.

"I am not sure I can."

"I will help you a little way, and then I must leave you to your own devices. But if you call for help and your companions return, be sure that I'll lop your head off."

Lei stooped down and threw the fallen bandit over his shoulder. He carried him some thirty meters out toward the pass and then dropped him unceremoniously on the ground. Cheng had accompanied him in case the others returned.

Lei slapped the bandit on his buttocks with the flat of his blade. "Be off now. Get your friends to tend to this fellow, lest he bleed to death. And don't forget to relay my message to Hong."

Lei and Cheng strode vigorously back to the bend, where Qiang was waiting.

Lei turned and thanked Cheng. "I owe you some gratitude, indeed, in coming to my aid when I stumbled. You surprised me with your agility and speed."

"No gratitude needed, Lei. We are now brothers in arms."

"Indeed, we are, Cheng. And I am pleased my brother is so adept. But I want you both to think back to when we first encountered these brigands. How many do you think there are?"

Qiang mused for a moment before answering. "I suspect, Lei, there were twelve or thirteen of them. The two bands seemed of relatively similar numbers, perhaps six or seven in each group."

"Good! We have now made a little dent in their numbers. We have disabled four. Our odds are steadily improving. Do you think you could manage to scale the cliff at the rear in the dark?"

"Yes, I suspect so, Lei."

"Then why don't you do that this evening and see what is going on out there? They have shown little inclination to attack us at night. It might be safer if you made your move then. What do you think, Cheng?"

"I agree, Lei. But be careful, Qiang. We can't afford to squander our increasing advantage by having you injure yourself."

Qiang smiled. "Don't worry. I will take no undue risks."

IT WAS DUSK now. Qiang had started to scale the cliff, knowing that by the time he arrived at the top, it would be dark enough for him not to be detected by the bandits below. He experienced little difficulty in gaining the top of the escarpment. Surprisingly, at the top of the cliff, the rock was reasonably flat, enabling him to make good progress until he came to the main fissure, which opened onto the pass.

He crawled gingerly to the edge of the cliff that overlooked the camp of the bandits. The main camp seemed to be slightly to his right and was pitched in front of the access to the fissure where he and his companions had sought shelter. A large fire was burning there, and he could count seven bandits sitting around the fire and seemingly drinking. They were rowdy and seemed somewhat inebriated. At the rear lay a number of figures that Qiang assumed were the bandits who had been wounded in their attempts to overpower him and his companions.

Farther up to his left, barely illuminated by the campfire, he could make out a temporary impoundment enclosing a dozen or so horses. One man was posted there, guarding the horses.

Qiang scrambled back over the rocks, descended the cliff face, and walked back to the little campfire, where Lei and Cheng sat waiting.

"What did you find, Qiang?" asked Lei immediately.

"It was largely as you suspected, Lei. There seem to be eight able-bodied men left. And they seemed somewhat inebriated."

"You know," said Lei, looking at Cheng, "we could overcome this lot if we had to."

"Well, perhaps you're right, Lei. But let's wait a day or two before doing anything desperate. We still have plenty of food and water. I suspect that we are in the ascendency here and don't need to chance our arm. There is more to happen in this saga that will advance our cause."

"You seem to know something that I don't, Cheng, but I will be patient, if that is your counsel."

"It is, Lei. Just bear with me. These scoundrels will not best us."

THE DAYS PASSED slowly.

The bandits showed little sign of attacking them again.

Some would come to the mouth of the fissure and shout taunts at the three besieged, daring them to come out and fight.

As the days passed, however, Lei got more and more agitated. Finally, he proclaimed, "Cheng, we have to do something. Our horses have just about eaten all the grass in our little pasture, and soon they will be starving."

Cheng remained calm. "Be patient, Lei. We are not desperate yet."

Late in the afternoon, Cheng said to Qiang, "Young master, Lei is starting to fret. Why don't you scale the cliffs again while it is still light, and see what you can see? Try to ensure that you are not seen. If you can find a good vantage point, see if there is anyone approaching from the south."

Qiang raised his eyebrows at this request but made no comment. Soon, he had mounted the rocky bulwark and found a spot where he, unseen to the bandits below, could clearly see the southern approach. In the clear air, he could see quite clearly a few kilometers of the track, but there was no sign of any activity on it.

Another day passed, and Lei was beside himself. He paced up and down impatiently, muttering under his breath. Cheng merely smiled.

Again, in the late afternoon, he bade Qiang climb the rocky ramparts to see what he could see. Qiang struggled up to the vantage point he had found the previous day. He stood up to survey the southern approach again. He strained his eyes, but as far as he could see, there was no sign of anyone approaching. He wondered what Cheng was expecting him to see. No doubt, Cheng would be disappointed again, but of course, Cheng would reveal no such emotion.

The sun was almost on the horizon now, and the light was beginning to fade. No matter what transpired, Qiang was at peace with himself. He sat down on the rock and allowed himself the luxury of watching the sun set. He turned to the right and watched the golden globe slowly merge with the earth on the horizon.

Then came a piercing sound. The source of the sound seemed high above him. But it came closer and closer, which caused him to look up. Then he saw an avian thunderbolt closing in on him. In an instinctive response, he thrust his arm out. And then, within a few seconds, the falcon alighted on his arm.

He gently caressed the bird's head. "Ah, Kung," he said, "you have found me. Where have you come from?" He looked down at the bird's leg, and sure enough, it had a message tube affixed to it. "And look, you have brought me news as well."

He extracted the little roll of manuscript from the tube and perused the message. It read cryptically: "On our way north. Where are you?"

He smiled, knowing only too well this had been written by Ruan Xiu.

He transferred the bird to his shoulder to enable his two arms to be free for climbing down the rock face. He spoke soothingly to the bird, but it clung steadfastly to the shoulder of his tunic until he was at the bottom. Still with the bird attached, he hurried up to Lei and Cheng.

Cheng looked bemused. "What have you there, Qiang?"

"It is my falcon, Kung."

"Whatever is he doing here?"

"He brought me a message. Here, let me show you." He passed the little roll of manuscript to Cheng, who quickly read it.

"What does it say, Cheng?" asked Lei.

"In short, Lei, it says Ruan Xiu is on his way."

"How far away is he?"

Qiang responded, "We don't know, but if he sent my falcon out to find me, he can't be too far away."

"That seems a strange thing to do."

"No, not at all. When I first came to Ruan Xiu's palace with my mother and sister, and we were about a half-day ride away, the governor's people sent out his falcon to find him. We had been cut off by the fall of a large tree across the track, and he was able to summon help for us."

"What are you going to do now?"

"I will send a message back to Ruan Xiu, telling him of our plight and urging him to hurry."

Lei nodded.

Qiang rummaged through his things and found some manuscript to write on and a slender stick of charcoal. He trimmed off a small piece of manuscript and wrote:

"Besieged by bandits at Devil's Gate. Hurry!"

He rolled up the scrap of manuscript and placed it in the message tube attached to the falcon's foot. He caressed the bird gently and murmured softly into its ear. Then he raised his arm with the bird attached and said, "Be off now, Kung. Good speed to you. Bring us assistance to thwart these bandits."

The bird took off, a little confused initially by the close confines of the cliffs. But soon, he found his way free of those restrictions, and he rose and soared before flying off like an arrow to the south.

DESPITE THE NEWS that their rescue might be imminent, Lei was still impatient. He strode agitatedly around in their confinement, muttering to himself.

"Whatever is the matter, Lei?" inquired Cheng.

The big man stopped. He stood in front of Cheng. "Ah, Cheng, I have dishonored Li."

"I don't see how that could be the case, Lei."

"Well, these thugs effectively killed my friend. I should have avenged him and meted out a fit punishment in his honor."

"Well, pray tell me what good that would have done?"

"It would have satisfied my need for vengeance."

"Vengeance is a problematic motivation, Lei. You should put it aside."

"And why is that, Cheng? Surely it would be just that those villains be made to suffer because of what they did to Li."

"There is no doubt that they will suffer for their misdeeds, Lei, but if you resort to vengeance, you will surely suffer as well."

"Then what would you have me do?"

"It is not my place to tell you to do anything. The only advice I might give you is to be careful in indulging such conflictive emotions—anger, jealousy, greed, vengeance, and so on—because you will invariably hurt yourself."

"What, then, is the antidote to the passion I inevitably feel when these emotions arise?"

"It is easy to say but hard to enact. We not only save ourselves from anguish but help those who we might feel have wronged us when we exhibit empathy, tolerance, and unconditional love."

"But then, should these villains be let off without punishment?"

"I suggest to you that those who behave badly suffer many natural consequences. Seeking vengeance is another transgression of right living and brings its own suffering. You are inherently a good man, Lei, but unfortunately, because of your social history, you have learned some ways of behaving that are not helpful."

"Do you mean I should just let these scoundrels do as they will?"

"No, of course not. It is entirely appropriate that you should intervene to prevent their hurting others. The counsel I am trying to impart to you is to try and help you from hurting yourself."

Before Lei could respond, Qiang was suddenly there.

"I climbed the cliff again," he said. "In the distance, I could see Ruan Xiu's party not too far off. And then Kung came like an arrowshot out of the sky. He alighted on my arm, and, again, there was a message."

"What did it say, Qiang?" asked Lei.

"Well, Lei, it said, 'We shall come tonight.'"

WITHIN THE CONFINES of the cliffs, evening came early. The three friends sat at the entrance way to their hideaway, listening and waiting. The flickering light of the bandits' campfire cast flickering shadows on the cliffs around them. The bandits already sounded boisterous; no doubt, they were consuming the rice wine with gusto.

Cheng said to Lei, "What do you think we should do to help when Ruan Xiu arrives?"

"It occurs to me, Cheng, that Ruan Xiu and his men will approach from the south. If they are discreet enough, they should overcome the fellows tending their horses, who, Qiang has told us, are on the southern side of their camp. Hence, when the governor arrives at their camp, their only escape will be on foot to the north. I propose we block that escape. What say you, Cheng?"

Cheng mused for a moment or two and then responded, "Yes, Lei, I think that would be useful. But I do not want to risk injury—or worse—to Qiang. He has come all this way and carried out his duties so thoroughly that I would be loath to see him not complete his undertaking to the governor."

Lei smiled. "Then it is decided. You and I will block the access to the north, once Ruan Xiu attacks the bandits' camp."

They looked inquiringly at Qiang.

Qiang shook his head. "No, that will not do! How can my life be viewed as any more important than either of yours? Cheng is a fine teacher and a Buddhist sage. Lei is a noted warrior and has demonstrated courage in the face of great adversity. I will not allow you to unduly shield me from my own responsibilities in this matter. The subjugation of these bandits is important for the welfare of the ordinary people who inhabit these lands. I must do what I can to advance that cause as well."

Lei looked at Cheng and laughed. "See, Cheng? I told you that would be his response. Good for you, Qiang—a very fitting response."

"Indeed, indeed. Well said, young man. We will be happy to have you join us in thwarting the bandits. But let me advise you not to indulge in too much bravado, for you have yet much to do as a Buddhist master yourself."

"I will take care, Cheng, not because of any sense of duty I might have as a Buddhist sage but because of the duty I have to my mother and sister. If we are successful, I will soon be with them."

"That should prove incentive enough, Qiang. Let us now prepare ourselves for one last confrontation with these ruffians."

Soon, the three ventured out a little farther toward the main pass to make it easier for them to attempt to thwart the escape of the bandits. They sat silently, each tending his own thoughts, but comfortable in the company of each other and assured of their combined competence to deal with any issues that might arise in the melee that most likely would ensue when Ruan Xiu arrived with his men.

It was some three hours after sundown when their reverie was disturbed by shouts and sounds of fighting.

"Let's go!" Lei called out.

The three sprang out into the opening of the main pass. To their left, they could see, in the glow of the campfire, that the bandits were attempting to defend themselves against the greatly superior numbers of Ruan Xiu's band.

It was soon apparent that the bandits could not escape from the governor's fighters. Some threw down their weapons and pleaded for mercy, but four turned and ran from the fray, only to encounter Lei, Cheng, and Qiang, blocking their way. This was too much for one, who stopped in his tracks, dropped his sword, and slunk back to the main group with his arms up in the air. The remaining three slowed as they approached Qiang and his friends. As they came nearer, it became clear that the figure in the lead was the bandit chieftain, Hung. He stopped some ten meters away from his adversaries.

"Why, it is Ruan Xiu's little cur and his pathetic protectors! They've finally found the courage to come out of their rabbit hole and fight." Hung glanced at his companions. "I have a score to settle with the big fellow, Lei. He was once an able fighter, but I doubt he has retained his former prowess. Nevertheless, he is probably the most formidable of the three, so leave him to me. Come on—let's settle this."

So saying, Hung rushed forward and lunged at Lei with his sword; the other two came at Cheng and Qiang.

Cheng made the first conquest. His subtle, lithe movements completely confounded his assailant, who soon found himself disarmed, with his face on the ground, with Cheng's foot on his back, and the point of Cheng's sword on the back of his neck.

Cheng watched the other two battle their opponents.

Qiang's style was much like Cheng's, which wasn't surprising, as Cheng had been Qiang's self-defense tutor. Qiang danced around lightly, easily avoiding his opponent's sword. Finally, an opportunity arose, and Qiang thrust his staff, striking the man heavily in his diaphragm, winding him. The man reeled back, breathless. Qiang observed him passively. The man was furious. He inhaled deep breaths and then ran forward at Qiang, shouting, "I will fix you, you little cur!"

Qiang, of course, had planned to provoke such an attack. He easily sidestepped the man's assault and struck him heavily on the back of the head. The blow rendered his opponent senseless, and the man dropped his sword and fell on his face. Qiang quickly rolled him over onto his side so that the man might breathe easier. Qiang felt the man's pulse, which, while rapid, was still strong.

Cheng nodded. "Well done, Qiang. I suspect he will recover okay."

They then turned to watch the ferocious battle between Hung and Lei.

Hung and Lei were formidable warriors. They flung their swords at each other ferociously. The sound of the clash of metal upon metal echoed loudly within the confines of the pass.

Finally, to Cheng and Qiang's horror, Hung aimed a terrific blow at Lei. Lei parried, but the force of the blow was such that Hung's sword glanced off Lei's weapon and struck Lei on his side, cutting through his tunic. Lei reeled back and instinctively placed his hand on the bleeding wound.

Hung laughed. "You seem to be getting a little slow, Lei. Maybe you should just put down your sword and let me pass."

"Never!" Lei shouted.

Cheng moved to go to his friend's assistance.

"No, Cheng! Let me finish this!" Lei called with a steely resolve.

Hung laughed again. "The only way you will finish this is on the point of my sword."

"We will see about that!" Lei muttered.

Hung assailed Lei with a ferocious battery of blows.

Cheng and Qiang watched, grim-faced.

Lei seemingly was being forced backward under Hung's furious assault. Emboldened by this, Hung thrust his sword at Lei's chest, hoping to deliver a fatal blow. But Lei, although inconvenienced by his wound, had been merely feigning weakness to deceive Hung. Lei easily avoided Hung's thrust. He then brought his sword down on Hung's own sword, just above the sword's pommel. The force of the blow severed two of Hung's fingers and sent his sword flying across the ground.

Lei, with his right hand still on his sword, struck Hung with a heavy blow to his jaw, which caused Hung to fall to the ground.

"That was for Li," said Lei.

Hung cowered on the ground, convinced that he was about to be dispatched. Lei raised his sword high above his head, looking menacingly at Hung.

But then, he sighed, flung his sword to the ground, and walked away. His mind was in turmoil, and there were tears in his eyes.

"Well done, Lei," said a familiar voice. "You know, I never doubted you." Lei looked up in surprise; it was Ruan Xiu. "But you have found mercy. Wherever did that come from?"

"I have had a new teacher, my lord."

"And who might that be?"

Lei's tears were replaced by a smile. "I don't have to tell you. You already know."

"Ah, perhaps I do. But what did he teach you?"

"He taught me not to pursue vengeance."

"And why would that be?"

"Because vengeance would be more hurtful to me than to whom I wished it."

Then, surprisingly, Ruan Xiu hugged Lei. Nobody had ever seen such a display of affection from this taciturn man. After Ruan Xiu withdrew from Lei, Ruan Xiu saw there was blood on his hands.

"You are wounded, old friend. Let us get someone to tend to your wound."

The governor called to some in his entourage, and before long, Lei's wound was bandaged. After they had ministered to him, Ruan Xiu asked, "How are you now?"

"I am fine, Governor. But there is another who is wounded." He nodded in the direction of Hung, who was still prostrate on the ground. "Would you have your people tend to him as well?"

"Of course, Lei. Who am I to thwart your newfound sense of mercy?"

All this time, Qiang and Lei stood watching. Now, Ruan Xiu walked over to them. First, he spoke to Qiang. "Young man, it would seem that you have fulfilled your obligations to me."

"I have done my best, sire."

"You have done well, Qiang. I know it has not been easy for you."

Qiang looked down at the ground, somewhat embarrassed. "Well, I must confess there have been trials, but fortunately, my lord, I have had the aid of many fabulous people. But tell me, sire, what news do you have of my mother and sister?"

"They are both well and have been anxious for your welfare. It was all I could do to restrain Lan from coming with us. She is very headstrong, your sister. But she has a strength of character I can only admire. As for your mother, Nuan, she has a privileged place in my household, and I will care for her as long as she lives."

"I appreciate your concern for my mother, but surely it will be my responsibility to care for her from now on."

"That might not be possible, Qiang. Your role in the world as a Buddhist master might preclude you from establishing a permanent household where you might care for her. But don't concern yourself with that yet. I promise to care for her for the rest of her days, if that should be your fate, and I do that willingly and lovingly. But your sister, Lan, has a surprise for you when you get back. She has made me promise not to divulge what it is so that she can tell you herself. Your reunion with your family is only a day or two away now, and I look forward to it almost as much as you do. But now I must thank Cheng for his role in supporting you."

He walked over to Cheng, who had sat himself on a rock while Ruan Xiu's men tended to the bandits they had overcome. He had heard the governor's conversation with Qiang and was pleased that Ruan Xiu had approved of Qiang's efforts.

"Well, Cheng, the little master now seems well able to defend himself. I suspect you might have had a hand in that."

"Just a little, Governor. We can't have somebody as important as he is wandering the countryside, defenseless. But I must confess he is a reluctant warrior! He takes no pleasure in harming others, no matter how evil they seem to be."

"That is not surprising, Cheng. You are the ablest fighter I have ever known. You might not have the brute strength of someone like Lei, but your subtlety and agility more than make up for that. I remember how hard it was to convince you to stand with us against the bandits. But you always did, when I could convince you that your efforts contributed to a greater good."

The governor gathered all three of the friends together. "I want to thank you all for your courage. I will be forever grateful for your efforts. I know there need be no urging for Qiang to return with me to my palace to be reunited with his family, but I would appreciate it, Lei and Cheng, if you would come with us as well."

Cheng smiled. "I had always intended to accompany Qiang back to your palace. I see no reason not to continue with that plan."

"And you, Lei?"

"Well, Governor, the last time you were well pleased with me, you made me stable master, which I am afraid did not work out well for any of us."

Ruan Xiu laughed. "Rest assured, I have no plans to make you stable master again, Lei."

"That's a relief. On that condition—and that condition only—I will journey back with you."

THE SIGHT OF the governor's palace in the distance gave Qiang a strange feeling of joy and anticipation.

A half dozen strong, armed men led the retinue. They were followed by Ruan Xiu, Lei, Cheng, and Qiang, who talked amiably among themselves—except for Qiang. The governor finally turned to Qiang and remarked, "Does something ail you, Qiang? You have hardly said a word."

Qiang shook his head. "No, sir, nothing ails me. In fact, I don't think I have felt better in my life."

Ruan Xiu smiled knowingly and then continued his conversation with Cheng.

A half hour later, they were at the palace gates.

It was obvious that the population was aware of the approach of the governor's party. Once the gatekeeper had opened the gates, the governor's entourage was faced with a sea of smiling faces. The crowd rushed forward. They were eager to congratulate Qiang on his achievement, which most had heard about.

But the governor raised his arm imperiously. "Stop," he called. He gestured toward Qiang. "I know you all want to join in the celebration of the return of the young master, and, in due course, we shall do that. But first, we must ensure that Qiang is reunited with his mother, Nuan, and his sister, Lan. Please let them through."

Nuan and Lan, who had been at the rear of the crowd, made their way forward. Qiang quickly dismounted and ran to embrace them. The crowd shouted their approval.

Qiang hugged his mother first and, with tears in his eyes, said, "Oh, Mother, how happy I am to be with you again. I trust you are well."

"Never better," said the old woman, her voice filled with obvious admiration for her son.

Then, turning quickly to Lan, Qiang embraced her as well. Then he stepped back. "My, you have grown, Lan. You look so lovely—still our little orchid!"

Lan blushed. "You have been gone so long, brother, that it is inevitable that I should have grown and changed in many ways. My heart rejoices in seeing you again. I have always loved you so much, and I feared so much for you while you were gone. Yet our mother had such faith in you that she never seemed to worry so much."

"I told you," interrupted Nuan. "You have never appreciated how special your brother is."

"That is unfair, Mother. He has always been special to me and always will be."

"I don't doubt that is true, daughter, but he is special in many more ways than you might appreciate. I knew it was so when the sages sought him out when he was quite young. I must confess that their interest in him intrigued me then. But now, I have realized that the qualities they were seeking were there from the very beginning. But do not fret, Lan. I love you dearly as well. Now don't beat about the bush. Ask him the question that you so dearly want to put to him."

Qiang looked quizzically at his sister. "Lan, what is this question you so desperately need to put to me?"

Lan blushed again and hung her head.

Qiang reached forward and took her hands. "Don't be concerned, Lan. I love you so much that there is nothing you should be afraid to ask me."

"Well," the young woman said, "I want to ask your permission to marry."

"Oh," said Qiang, looking somewhat stunned. "Why do you think that I should give permission for you to marry?"

"Mother said that since Father died, you are the head of the household, and I must seek permission from you to marry."

"And who do you wish to marry, Lan?"

"It is someone you know." She dropped her head again.

"But who?" Qiang gently coaxed.

She sighed and looked up at him. "Well, it is Biming."

"Ah!" exclaimed Qiang. "He is a fine young fellow. You have made a good choice. And do you love him?"

"Of course! Do you think I would seek to marry someone I didn't care for?"

Qiang embraced his sister but then he drew apart from her. "You do not need my permission to marry. I don't care what the tradition might be. My only concern is that you will be happy. And I am happy that you are mature enough to come to that decision yourself. Whatever partner you choose, you do so with my blessing. But I am delighted you have chosen Biming. I am happy to bestow my blessings on both of you."

WHEN THE ENTOURAGE finally made its way into the palace enclosure, Qiang said to Nuan and Lan, "I will deposit my belongings back in the barracks, and then, if the governor allows, I will come to visit you later this evening."

Ruan Xiu overheard this exchange, "No, you won't, Qiang. There is no longer room for you in the barracks."

Qiang was somewhat taken aback by the governor's response. "Oh. Am I not welcome in the barracks?"

"You misunderstand me, Qiang. You are welcome anywhere you wish within the palace confines. But I had thought that because you have served me so well that you might prefer, for the time being, to live in the palace with your mother and sister."

"Thank you, Governor. I would appreciate that very much. But what do you mean 'for the time being'?"

"You are probably not consciously aware yet that you have become a master. You were always destined to be a master. And now, with the help of some significant mentors and on the basis of your own exemplary conduct in the face of many difficulties, it seems you have attained that status. Unfortunately, it is the fate of masters to spend their lives in improving the lot of others. You will learn soon enough that you cannot do that from the confines of my palace. You will always be welcome here. You have repaid your debt to me tenfold. But sooner or later, your desire to be of service to others will drive you to go elsewhere."

THE CROWD HAD gathered in the Great Council Hall. This was the biggest room in the palace and comfortably sat a hundred or more people.

Ruan Xiu sat in an ornate gilded chair that was almost thronelike. The chair was on an elevated platform, a meter or so above the gathered audience.

Qiang had been summoned by an attendant of the governor to be present. He sat in the front row of the audience, alongside his mother and sister. He was intrigued to know what was going to transpire.

The hall was full. As far as Qiang could determine, most were court officials and dignitaries. Some faces, he recognized, had come from nearby districts.

But to Qiang's great surprise, seated alongside Ruan Xiu were a number of people he knew. There were some he had not seen for a very long time, such as his first mentors, Chogken Rinpoche and Chagsarka Rinpoche, but there were also Sunfu Rinpoche, Bai, Jian, and Cheng.

When the audience settled, Ruan Xiu rose to speak.

"I welcome you all to this very special occasion. I am fortunate enough to have alongside me the masters who have tended to the spiritual and other needs of those who abide in the province over which I am humbled to be governor. The great sage and spiritual leader of this esteemed group is Bai. I call upon Bai to make an important announcement."

Bai moved to the front of the stage. He turned to Ruan Xiu. "I thank you, Excellency." He gestured to his audience. "Most of you would be unaware of the governor's generosity in sponsoring and supporting the work we do in his province. He has been quite magnanimous in ensuring that we have the wherewithal to minister to his subjects. But you can see that we are not a particularly youthful group."

Those on stage and the audience tittered because this was self-evident.

"There is a great need to augment our group with younger sages. But we must be very careful that anyone who is admitted to be a master must be tested to ensure that he has the desired qualities. It is not a vocation to be taken lightly.

"Many years ago, the venerable Chogken Rinpoche pointed out to us that in the annals of our tradition, the old sages had foretold that a new master would arrive. It was written that he would be found under a particular large tree outside a little village. Chogken Rinpoche dutifully positioned himself at the base of the tree for some months, just sitting and meditating, and sure enough, in time, the boy found him. That boy is the one known as Qiang.

"We tried our best to nurture Qiang's spiritual development. Many of my colleagues sitting here contributed to that endeavor. Consequently, Qiang, while still in his youth, came to know the basic tenets of Buddhist philosophy. He had also learned how to practice meditation and act out the main element of Buddhist philosophy, loving kindness.

"But it is not easy to become a master. And neither should it be. With the help of Ruan Xiu, we had to test him. He was given an extraordinarily difficult task to complete. And though some of us, from time to time, contrived to help him, he nevertheless succeeded on his own merits.

"Our assessment of someone who might be elevated to the status of master is not only based on his understanding of Buddhist precepts but also on his character. Our observation of Qiang, through all his trials, confirmed that he was courageous, altruistic, and steadfast. We, therefore, had no hesitation in committing to elevate his status to one of a master.

"We are pleased to admit him as one of us and look forward to his contribution to progressing the welfare of our fellow citizens and, in particular, the neediest in our society. I call on our young master, Qiang, to come and join us to celebrate his elevation to the status of a Buddhist master. Please come forward, Qiang."

Qiang was overwhelmed by this address and did not know how to respond. His beaming mother forced his hand and bustled him up to join the others on the stage.

He joined Bai at the front of the podium. Bai embraced him and then turned to the audience.

"Now, in recognition of the holiness of this young man, I urge you to address him by his spiritual name. In our tradition, he must be addressed as Takygulpa Rinpoche. This is the name our predecessors gave him as we awaited his awakening. This is a holy name, reserved for a special adept, who will now join us as an equal, charged with bringing consolation and truth to those who need it."

TAKYGULPA RINPOCHE, AS he now must be known, spent a contented few months with his mother and sister in Ruan Xiu's palace. The young master was pleased when his sister asked him if they could work together in the evening on transcribing and illustrating some Buddhist texts. He subsequently went to Ruan Xiu.

"Governor," he said, "you have been so generous to my family and me that I would like, in some way, to repay you."

"You have no need to repay me, Takygulpa Rinpoche. I only did what was necessary to ensure that you might become another master to help my people."

"Be that as it may, sire, Lan and I have begun to work again in preparing some manuscripts based on Buddhist teachings, and I would like you to have them. And in doing so, I would like to work on material that you might like. Can you give me some indication of what might please you in that regard?"

Ruan Xiu smiled. "That is very kind of you and your sister, and I would value such a gift very much. Here—let me write down some of my favorite passages for you to work on."

Takygulpa Rinpoche and his sister worked joyfully together on this project.

And then, of course, came the wedding. Ruan Xiu, who truly loved Nuan and Lan, provided a sumptuous feast after the simple ceremony was completed.

After the feast, the young master took Biming and Lan aside.

"First of all," he said, "I want to tell you how happy I am that you, my friend Biming, have married my beloved sister, Lan. But I want to give you something to help you start your journey into married life." With that, he handed Biming a little bag.

"Thank you, Qiang!" Biming thought a moment and then apologized. "I am sorry that I have not got used to your new exalted title."

Takygulpa Rinpoche merely laughed. "I have no concerns about what you call me, Biming."

"And you always will be Qiang to me also, brother," Lan said.

The young master laughed again. "Ah, my lovely Lan, you may also call me whatever you will."

While Takygulpa spoke, Biming opened the little bag and gasped. "Why, Qiang, this is a bag of gold!"

"Indeed, it is, Biming."

"But where would you get gold, my brother?" asked Lan, bewildered.

"It was given to me by Governor Chin Chao. He thought it might be useful to me on my return journey from Sun Nang province, but I did not need it, and I have no use for gold. I used some of it to build a barn for some peasants, but they did not need it all. Now, you two might need a little help in establishing your household and perhaps starting a family and so it is only fitting that you should have the residue."

Lan blushed, but then she ran forward and embraced her brother. "You know, old Bai was right. You are a special person—but I always knew that."

WHILE QIANG ENJOYED reuniting with his sister and mother, he was strangely discontented. He spoke to Lei, who also seemed at loose ends. Cheng also joined them.

"I feel useless, Lei," said Qiang. "There seems so much to do out there to help people, but I don't know where to start."

"I know how you feel," said Lei. "Despite enjoying the governor's hospitality, I feel the need to return to those who need my help."

Cheng smiled at his friends. "Lei, Ruan Xiu asked me to have you both come to him."

"What does he want," asked Lei.

"It is not for me to say," said Cheng. "But let us go to him now, and you will soon find out."

Within ten minutes, they were all in the presence of the governor.

"Thank you, Cheng, for bringing Lei and Takygulpa to me. It is time that we talked about some plans for the future. Are you happy to have this discussion?"

Both Qiang and Lei nodded their assent.

"First, Lei, I want to talk about an assignment I have in mind for you." He paused and smiled. "No, I don't want you to go back to the stables! But it occurs to me that we should be taking steps to ensure that the bandits can't get a foothold into our territory again. It seems to me that we are most vulnerable at Devil's Gate. I would like you to take twenty of my men and establish a garrison at the foot of the pass. You will be in charge of the garrison, and the men will report to you. You could escort travelers through the pass and periodically scour it for bandits. I will ensure that you are well provisioned and remunerated. Now, I am sure that this role might be more suited to you than stable master!"

Lei positively beamed. "That is a task I would willingly do, Excellency!"

"Good!" responded the governor. "When I have finished with Takygulpa Rinpoche, I will go with you to the captain of my guard and help you select some stout fellows to accompany you. But you must promise me not to confront each brigand yourself, as you are wont to do. Part of your command will be to develop the fighting prowess of my guards."

Lei nodded his agreement.

Qiang smiled. No doubt, Ruan Xiu knew the big fellow well!

Ruan Xiu then turned to Qiang.

"Well, young man, I do not command you any longer, so what I offer as a mission for you, you are quite entitled to refuse. But I would be most grateful if you saw fit to help me out. Down to the southeast of my province, there is some reasonably fertile country. It is largely inhabited by poor peasants who eke out their existence from the land. They are families rather like your own. There are no brigands in that part of the country, as far as we know, but they need spiritual guidance and mentorship. Cheng is familiar with the area, and if you choose to take on this assignment, he will accompany you and get you settled into the community. Would this be something you might like to do?"

Qiang smiled. "Indeed, sir, I can think of nothing better. But what would you expect of me?"

"I would expect you to minister to the people as best you can. I know that would be beneficial to them. Perhaps once a year, you might return to advise me on the state of those communities and to visit your mother, sister, and new brother-in-law. But you are your own man now, and if you wish to visit more frequently, you can. But rest assured, as I have pledged, your mother and your sister will be well cared for."

"You are more than generous, Governor. I would be delighted to go with Cheng and see what assistance I could provide."

"Good! It is settled, then."

SEVERAL DAYS LATER, Cheng and Qiang readied themselves to travel. Qiang had loaded up his little horse with his traveling equipment, and Cheng had made similar preparations.

They walked their horses to the gates of the governor's palace. Ruan Xiu, Nuan, Lan, and Biming were there to bid farewell.

The farewells were exchanged.

Qiang hugged Lan and Biming. "I wish you both the greatest happiness. And you, Lan, have been a wonderful companion, confidante, and loving sister."

Then he turned to Nuan. "Ah, Mother, I do not know how to begin to thank you. You have been my inspiration." He gave her a hug and a kiss on her cheek. "But now, we must be off. Take care. I shall visit you soon enough."

And so saying, he mounted his horse, as did Cheng, and they trotted off quietly, looking forward to another adventure.

Nuan smiled indulgently. She remembered her son as a young boy, running over the grass exuberantly, with her chasing. She also remembered her conjecturing what her boy would become. How could she have known then that he would become a Buddhist master? Her heart swelled with pride, and, in her joy, a few tears appeared in her eyes.

Ruan Xiu noticed the tears and said protectively, "Are you all right, Nuan?"

Nuan turned to her benefactor. "Oh yes, indeed, Your Excellency. I am indeed all right. How could a mother ask for more?"

She watched the figures receding into the distance and sighed contentedly.

"What a fine young man he is", she thought.

About the Author

TED SCOTT HAS an extensive background in management in the Electricity Industry. His career culminated with his appointment as the CEO of Stanwell Corporation. He received an Order of Australia in the General Division for his contribution to industry and was nominated as one of Australia's top thirty business leaders. Since resigning his post in the electricity industry he pursued a career as an executive coach helping more than eighty executives improve their skills.

But his principal interest is people and human behaviour. As a result he has a strong interest in psychology and spirituality.

Ted has previously written four books. He co-authored with his friend and psychologist, Dr Phil Harker, The Myth of Nine to Five which is a book on management and leadership. Since then he has authored Augustus Finds Serenity, Yu the Dragon Tamer and Froth and Goblets.

Whilst Ted is not a Buddhist, he found some elements of Buddhist philosophy useful in engaging with his coaching clients on various aspects of spirituality. Consequently he wrote the latter three books as extended parables illustrating some of the fundamental aspects of Buddhism. The Making of a Master follows in that tradition.

His ambition is to write books that are not only entertaining but which will give his readers philosophical and psychological insights.

Printed in the United States
By Bookmasters